a love and laughs novel

JACKIE WALKER

The following book is a work of fiction. Names, characters, places, and events included are either the product of the author's imagination or are used fictitiously for entertainment purposes only. Any resemblance to actual people or entities is purely coincidental.

Edited by: Fatima Sibyl Ramos

Cover design by: KiWi Cover Design

Copyright ©2020 Jackie Walker

All rights reserved.

ISBN-13: 9798574924730 (Paperback)

No portion of this book may be reproduced in any form without written permission from the publisher or author, except as permitted by U.S. copyright law.

CONTENT WARNINGS

There may be some topics mentioned this book that some readers may wish to know about ahead of time. I'd like to keep this page as spoiler-free as possible but realize that it's not always possible.

I'm providing a high-level explanation below regarding common reader triggers. Readers may also contact me via email (authorjackiewalker@gmail.com) if they have specific concerns.

This book ***does contain*** profanity, consensual sexually explicit scenes, and alcohol use (by adults only). In addition, one main character experiences sexual harassment in the workplace, including an attempted assault. As far as assaults go, it's a relatively tame attempt - not very violent. Since this is a RomCom, I tried to keep it light and not too upsetting.

As always, I've done my best to present these items as sensitively and respectfully as possible for my readers.

Dedication

For all the single parents who, at one time or another, thought their chance at a Happily Ever After had passed them by.

Prologue

Brody

Three years ago

My muscles are twitching, stomach is rolling, and I'm sweating like I ate the ghost pepper wings at lunch, which I did not. I'm not an idiot. I only do stuff like that on the weekends.

I always get this way before the first Open House Night of the school year. No matter how many years I have taught elementary school, a new school year always gives me more nerves than I know what to do with. Apparently, my fifteenth year as a teacher will not be any different in this regard. Just great. Maybe I should have taken another trip to the gym today to burn off these nerves. Nothing says, "Hey parents, you can trust me with your children's education" like sweaty palms and attempting to hide my belches under my breath.

Why has my stomach acid joined in on my freak-out fest anyway? Who the hell invited it to the collapse of my mental faculties?

Ha! Faculties. That's teacher humor for you.

I know, it's not funny, but what do you expect when I spend more time with nine and ten-year-olds than I do with people my age?

Maybe I'll try some of that self-talk crap that Hudson is always blabbering about. Damn hippie that he is.

Breathe in.

Breathe out.
You got this, Brody.
You are a bad-ass teacher.
Kids love you, dammit.
You are the master of your stomach.
Your stomach doesn't control you.
Breathe in.
Breathe out.

Well, that didn't work. Figures. I guess I can look on the bright side, which is that none of the single moms will hit on me since I look like I am hoping they won't find out where I hid the body.

Once the kids and their parents arrive, I'll be good to go — just like always. It's just like riding a bike.

"What is that smell?" a small voice calls out from the doorway. Looks like my first victim — I mean student — has arrived. Let the fun and games begin.

The nasally sounding blond boy looks around led by his nose and tries to find the offending odor. Is he serious? I cleaned this place impeccably and have three varieties of freshly baked cookies in here, along with fruit and veggies. No nuts, no gluten, and no fun. But they smell good to me. I can't help it that this place has that "old school" smell. You know that smell — it's a mixture of industrial-strength cleaner, urine, and crushed hopes and dreams. Maybe I've just become nose-blind to it over the years. He will get used to it soon enough.

"That smell is the smell of fun and new friends," I say to the young mind, ripe for my molding.

He doesn't look impressed. Apparently, he doesn't yet know he is lucky enough to be in the best fourth-grade class in the county.

"It doesn't smell like that. That's not something you can smell," replies the little wise guy.

I love the resistant ones since they make it a challenge for me. I'll have him high-fiving me and laughing at my lame jokes in no time.

Challenge accepted, kiddo.

"Hush, Bobby. That's no way to introduce yourself to your new teacher," admonishes a thirty-something brunette who is clutching his hand so tight it will be a miracle if he has any feeling left in it to be able to hold a pencil.

Ease up, lady. No need to be nervous. I don't bite.

She looks up at me and takes me in for the first time, gawking slightly as her eyes sweep me from head to toe. Her eyes go wide, and her mouth drops open to make a perfect O shape, right before she realizes what she is doing and closes her mouth suddenly like a guppy at feeding time.

Yep, there is the typical reaction and probably the reason why I am so nervous. As much as this happens nowadays, I don't think I'll ever quite get used to the feeling of being desired strictly on sight alone. It's not as great as you would think to be ogled like a piece of meat.

Excuse me, ladies, but my eyes are up here.

I was always chubby growing up and struggled to get any attention from the female persuasion besides eye rolls and pitying glances. Now, the tables have turned, it would seem, and the ladies are always trying to get my attention. Unfortunately, I cannot even think of encouraging that behavior here, no matter how long it has been since I've had someone in my bed. After all, it is a well-known rule that you cannot date your student's parents, no matter how hot they are. In this case, though, that won't be an issue since this brunette is not really my type. Honestly, I've always been partial to redheads. Something about their feisty nature tends to get my blood boiling.

I internally sigh, forcing myself to not roll my eyes at the shocked and lustful expression on the face of Bobby's mom. Instead, I flash her and her son a welcoming smile, introduce myself, instruct them to sign-in, help themselves to the refreshments, and take a seat.

And so it goes for the next fifteen minutes or so. The room gets louder and louder as more bodies file in to awkwardly introduce themselves and look around in the most scrutinizing way possible, like the little Judge Judys and Judge Wapners they are. I will just tell you now... there is nothing like a bunch of ten-year-olds to keep your ego in check. Since their little filters don't work yet, their brutal honesty tends to come flowing out like lava once they get going. That's okay, though. I like to encourage honesty in my classroom. But that will come later. Tonight is about setting expectations and getting them comfortable. I'm known to be the fun teacher, but I also have to lay down the ground rules so things don't go off the rails.

I glance at the clock on the pale blue brick wall and note that it's seven o'clock sharp, and I'm nothing if not punctual. Time to get this dog and pony show on the road. Walking to the front of the room, I take a breath and start my little "Welcome to the Fourth Grade" spiel. Lots of head nods and expectant faces peer up at me while I go on about how great it is to have them here and how excited I am to be their teacher. All of a sudden, I feel a disturbance in the Force.

Something has shifted.

Addressing the students, I continue, "Each day, you can expect to get my best as your teacher, and in return, I expect to get your best effort. Now, let's talk about..."

Slam!

Startled, my eyes glare towards the right where the door has just been abruptly opened. I'm vaguely aware that the heads of all the parents and students turn in the same direction.

I freeze.

I think I've been struck deaf, dumb, and mute all at once.

Who am I?

Where am I?

What's happening?

My heart is suddenly pounding, and I am now doing my best guppy impression of Bobby's mom from earlier. Now, I understand what it feels like to be on the other end of those lustful shocked looks I've been getting from the mom-squad for years.

Audibly gulping and trying to remind myself how to breathe, I take in the frazzled ginger goddess who has entered my classroom. I stare at her, open-mouthed. She just looks around sheepishly, clearly embarrassed by her tardiness.

Is that music I hear? Are the angels singing the "Hallelujah Chorus" from the rafters? I didn't realize that we had heavenly choirs on standby for the Open House this year. That seems a bit excessive. I'm almost certain choirs aren't in the school's budget.

After a few awkward seconds, which felt more like ten minutes, I finally gather my composure and speak.

"Hi."

Nice, genius. Are you always this articulate? No wonder they call me the *ladies' man*. If this teaching gig doesn't pan out, I could always have a career as a poet laureate.

Words start spewing at an alarming rate from her cute little mouth. "I'm soooo sorry we are late. There was an issue at work, and no matter how hard I tried, I couldn't escape, and then Miles wasn't ready when I got home, and my Grammy needed help with…"

She realizes she is oversharing and stops talking abruptly, looks around, and awkwardly says, "You know, we will just sit down over here. Carry on." She flips her hand at me and moves toward the back of the classroom.

Who is this "we" she is talking about? Is she asking me to sit down with her? Well, I guess if I must. After all, who am I to deny a beautiful lady's request… no, wait a minute. What's wrong with me? She isn't even talking about me. She is referring to her and the kid hiding behind her. That reminds me… kid, kids, students, school, open house.

I try to recover from my dumbstruckness (and yes, it's a word if I say it is. I am an educator, after all).

"That's okay. It's no problem, after all, delays happen to all of us from time to time. Welcome to the class. I'm Brody. Or Mr. Hale as it were. Nice to see you… I mean, meet you. It's nice to meet you."

A hand shoots up from the middle of the class, getting my attention back to where it should be.

"Yes?"

"Didn't you just tell us that rule number three in your classroom is that there is no excuse for tardiness?"

"Yes, Bobby, you know what, I did say that. And thank you for pointing that out to me. That was a test to make sure you were paying attention. Good job."

I make a metaphorical right turn to get this school bus back on the road by continuing with my little speech. I try not to embarrass myself further, all the while sneaking glances at the interloper, who, just moments ago, burst into the room like a blaze of fire. A *late* blaze of fire, but given her bangin' body and gorgeous red locks, I think I can forgive her lateness just this once.

Later, after my speech is done, handouts have been dispersed, all the kids have been introduced to one another, and all the bad jokes have been told, courtesy of yours truly, I invite everyone to stick around to ask questions, mingle, and enjoy the refreshments.

The room starts to clear out, and I slowly but surely wade my way through the line of parents who either want to tell me how wonderful their child is or warn me about their kid's mischievous side. Like I need this little bit of intel? Please, give me a break. When you've been doing this as long as I have, it's easy to spot the troublemakers from the kiss-ups. Case in point, Bobby with the amazing olfactory organ and a keen sense of observation. He's gonna be trouble for sure.

I do my best to feign attention to the parents as they drone on and on. Meanwhile, my eye tracks a blur of red as the ginger goddess moves around the room, and I send up a prayer to the gods of my loins that she doesn't leave without introducing herself. I have an uncontrollable urge to know more about her.

Don't get me wrong, it's not that I don't care about what the other parents are saying, it's just that I prefer to make my own impressions of the kids without the rose-colored glasses that parenthood provides. Most kids are very different at school than they are at home, and I want them all to have a fair chance to make their own impressions with me and their peers.

Finally, she is in front of me, and we are the last two adults in the room. Again, I'm speechless while I peer at her, noticing her tight-fitting skinny jeans and a T-shirt featuring a rather inappropriate slogan: *Save water. Drink margaritas!*

Although, probably not the best shirt to wear when going to an elementary school, it *is* funny. I love a good sense of humor. Two points to House Gryffindor in honor of the redhead with the guts to go against the flow.

She saves me from my inability to produce sounds from my mouth and introduces herself. "Hi. I'm Carina Amos, and this is Miles," she gestures to the brown-haired boy beside her.

"Hey Miles, I'm Mr. Hale. It's great to meet you. Are you excited about the new school year and all the fun we are going to have?" I put on my best *cool teacher* smile as I bend down and give him two big thumbs up. *Who am I, the Fonz?*

Miles looks up at me silently, his lips firmly sealed, and his face giving nothing away. Does he ever talk? Come to think of it, he hasn't said a word all evening except when I called on him and asked him to introduce himself to the class. He stood up swiftly and said, "My name is Miles Nicholas Amos," and then sat back down without making a bit of eye contact with anyone aside from the back of the chair in front of him. Interesting.

Carina blushes, *damn that's cute*, and says, "Miles isn't much of a talker until you get to know him. I'm sure he'll be talking your ear off about Minecraft or trains before you know it."

She seems nervous. Her beautiful pale skin is getting blotchy with red patches the more she stares at me. *I like it.*

"I stuck around to talk to you because I really am sorry about earlier when we barged in and disturbed your speech. It's been a really crazy day for us, but that's no excuse. We should have been here on time. I promise not to make it a habit. We take Miles's education very seriously."

As I stare into her big brown eyes, she nods up and down like a bobblehead doll on a dashboard, and I am once again struck mute. What is it about this gorgeous creature that removes my ability to formulate sentences and then project them out of my mouth via my vocal cords? And how does a redhead have such gorgeous brown eyes? Is that even possible? A mystery to unfold for sure.

"Thank you, but you already apologized. It's really not a problem."

She giggles as she raises her eyebrows and lowers her chin, then points to the "Rule List" hanging on the wall behind me. The same list that the ever-so-astute Bobby pointed out earlier. That little cock blocker in training. I mean, that wonderful young lad. Yeah, that's better.

I just shrug my shoulders in response, so I don't look like a hypocrite any more than I already do. I also shift my notebook in front of my crotch, so she and Miles don't see how much she is affecting me with her constant blushing and sweetheart smiles.

"Well, it was very nice of you not to make us feel bad for our tardiness. I mean, I get enough guilt at home, so anyone that doesn't pile on to that is greatly appreciated."

Outwardly I chuckle at her attempt at a joke, but inwardly I'm wondering who the hell is at home making her feel guilty? Is that something her husband does regularly? And now I'm picturing myself busting in her door and kicking his ass. *Here I come to save the day...*

You know... strike that last part. Let's just pretend I didn't say that. I'm a professional educator and not a vigilante out to save the damsel in distress.

Plus, I can't even let my thoughts go to "defending her honor" until I find out if she is truly off-limits or not. If I'm lucky, maybe she is just a friendly neighbor or aunt who is helping out Miles's busy mom by taking him to *meet the teacher* night. Technically, if she isn't the parent or guardian of my student, I might be able to see if this insta-lust is reciprocated. She had the same last name as the boy, so probably not a neighbor, though.

"So, Miles is your son, I assume?" Fingers and toes crossed as I look at her expectantly.

"Yes. I'm his very responsible and usually punctual parental figure. Oh, and we also live with his great-grandparents, so you might hear him talk about them quite a bit. Once he decides to speak, that is."

"And I guess he'll probably talk about his father..." I trail off and wait for her to finish my sentence.

Well, that was subtle. I'm so smooth, just like crunchy peanut butter.

Her smile fades a little as she leans in closer and whispers conspiratorially, "He probably won't talk about his father much since he is not in the picture anymore."

I feel bad for bringing it up, but at least I know she isn't married to or with Miles's dad. I can take that as a small victory. But unfortunately, she also just confirmed that she is, in fact, his mother. Thus, she is firmly in the no-go zone.

Another swing and a miss.

The first woman I'm attracted to in what feels like eons, and she is off-limits. I'm not sure whether to hope she will be a really involved parent who I'll have millions of reasons to interact with throughout the year, or if she just never shows her beautiful, tempting face here until June.

Not sure which would be better.

After some pleasant chit-chat, she takes her son by the hand and walks out the door with an adorable little smile and a half-armed wave.

I turn around to the now empty classroom and exhale dramatically. I predict this school year will be a bit more interesting and a whole lot more tempting than past years.

For a brief moment, I contemplate how hard it would be to get Miles assigned to a different class without giving the administration a valid reason, but then shake my head in disgust. I need to stop thinking with my lower brain because the year has just begun, and I have twenty-two precious minds to mold.

Cara

What just happened? Wow. Oh my God. Just wow.

When I learned Miles was going to have his first-ever male teacher, I did *not* see this coming. I was expecting a little more *Mr. Rogers* instead of *Mr. Universe*. I mean, when did teachers start looking like *that*?

I can't recall feeling quite so much instant attraction to anyone ever before. I mean, it's not like Jason Mamoa or Alexander Skarsgard will be his new teacher this year. But honestly... it's not that far off the mark.

Mr. Hale is officially to be known as 'Mr. Hottie' from here on out. I can't wait to talk to my friend Helen about him. And I especially can't wait to get her reaction to the pic of him I snapped on the sly — cause yeah I'm that girl. I just couldn't resist. It's not every day you come across this level of fine male specimen. I was documenting it for posterity on behalf of the entire female species.

You're welcome, ladies.

It's just slightly depressing because I could never *go there* with someone so important to my son's education. Otherwise, I might have to break my current *man-fast* rule. It's like a carb-fast or sugar-fast, but with men.

Dammit all to hell! That man is fine as the line between North and South Korea. Why do I have to be cursed with morals and an undying love for my son?

I guess it is good that I'm used to taking a *lookie-no-touchy* approach to the opposite gender, because that man is a very big temptation with all his bulging muscles, dimples, and those sexy, smoldering eyes. And wasn't it adorable how he sort of stumbled through his introduction to me? My cheeks flush simply thinking about that.

Yeah... this year is gonna be interesting, to say the least.

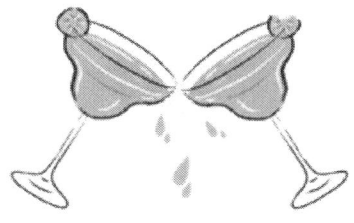

Chapter One

Alesandra, where's the milk?

Cara

Present Day

"I'll be right there, keep your pants on!"

What is it with kids and the elderly? They always want something immediately and have no concept of other people's priorities. I mean, how hard is it to acknowledge that while yes, you do need help with something, it certainly doesn't need to happen immediately with no delays whatsoever? Come on! I can only be in so many places at once.

"Sorry, Cara baby. I just wanted to catch you before you left," calls Grammy Ellie from downstairs.

If she wasn't so dang sweet, she would be a real pill to take most days.

Grammy Ellie is the epitome of a sweet old lady. She is the quintessential matriarch of the family, with a heart of gold. She is the glue that holds this crazy Amos family together. I wouldn't be alive and sane if it weren't for her. And I love her wholeheartedly.

I also want to throttle her at times, just a little bit.

That might seem harsh but come on. First of all, I haven't had my coffee yet today. And second of all, how many times can you tell someone the same thing over and over without wanting to commit homicide — just a small, tiny act of homicide?

That's where I am now.

At this point in my life, as a thirty-eight-year-old single mom to a preteen special needs boy and a caregiver to my aging grandparents, I am one nail short of nailing this coffin so permanently shut that archaeologists in the year 3040 will be wondering what the hell is going on in there when they uncover my tomb. Suffice to say, I'm hanging on by a thin thread, and everyone should proceed with caution.

Let's not even discuss Grandpa Dickie yet. I cannot discuss my grandfather until at least three cups of coffee or a pitcher of margaritas have been consumed — it's your choice.

"I'm coming down in two minutes. And I kindly thank you for your patience!" I yell sarcastically in retort to the old sweet broad. She might need something important after all, so I should try to be nice.

If Grammy knows anything about me, it's when I get sarcastic, I'm handling shit, and she should just step back for a moment, or else I'll likely storm off in a cloud of dust. Then later come back crying and apologizing for my freak out. She doesn't want that kind of drama, and neither do I. But since my astrological sign is Cancer, I really can't help it. My emotions are not something I can exactly control, and outbursts with whiplash level grief are gonna happen from time to time. It's best if you just accept it as part of me and move on. Love me or hate me — you'll never have to guess how I'm feeling at any given time.

I have like three speeds, aka: personalities or moods.

Speed One: Understanding, pleasant, helpful, and open to all possibilities. The world is my oyster. If you can dream it, you can do it!

Speed Two: Frustrated with life's shit… but hey, at least I'm still making forward progress and am generally optimistic about the future at the big picture level. At this speed, I can be frustrated and also channeling my inner Rosie the Riveter at the same time. We can do it! Yes, we can!

And Speed Three: Stand back before I blow, people! This is not a drill! We are at DEFCON 1.

Most weekday mornings around here, I teeter somewhere between speed Two and Three. Today is a firm two point two.

I try to not blame myself too much, though. I'm doing the best I can. And blaming yourself is pointless. It's much easier to blame your parents or childhood, right? This is basic stuff, people. Only self-actualized a-holes look inwardly to solve their troubles, and I am *not* that far down in the evolutionary chain. I'm more of the *hanging by the skin of my teeth* level of cavewoman. Where is that in Darwin's theory? The mystery continues, I suppose...

Let's put it this way. Each evening, when I hit the sheets and I look back at the day, I like to consider it a complete success if my son is home and in bed and my grandparents haven't burned down the house or created an uprising in the neighborhood. Bonus points if my son was fed appropriately. Super bonus points if he actually showered. And epic-mega-super-duper bonus points if he also did his homework. But let's not get ahead of ourselves here. I'm only one woman after all, beggars can't be choosers, Rome wasn't built in a day, and all that jazz.

Today, there are multiple reasons I'm rapidly approaching my third-speed. For starters, we are ten minutes late to leave for school which shall make me late for work again. I can feel my boss's side-eye already brewing.

I also dropped my coffee and broke my favorite coffee mug; the one that says: *I like cats and margaritas. You, not so much.*

Oh, and my son's socks are apparently *fitting funny* this morning, and now Grammy Ellie has something very important she needs to tell me right flipping now. Meanwhile, I'm pretty sure a cat peed on my last clean work polo shirt, and I forgot to bake cookies for Miles to take to class for some stupid reason today. It must be Hippopotamus Appreciation Day or some shit that requires baked goods. Sorry, it isn't in the cards today — the stay-at-home perfect moms will have to pick up my slack this time and come bringing the sweets. I'll PayPal a few bucks to the Parent Partners In Action committee later today to assuage my guilt. All I know is that if he doesn't put his socks on, heads are gonna roll. Well, more likely eyes are gonna roll — namely my eyes. I'm all bark and no bite when it comes down to it.

After doing my best to clean my shirt, I stroll down the stairs. Wait, who are we kidding? I run down the stairs like my hair is on fire and run smack into Grandpa Dickie.

Breathe, Cara. Just breathe. He can only annoy you if you let him.

"Cara, today I need you to get me some more milk. I told Alesandra to put it on the shopping list like three days ago, but we still don't have any milk. I have to have milk at bedtime or else my tummy gets upset, and I'm up all night."

I tell myself not to scream as I nod my head in the most non-condescending way possible given the time of day and my current state of mind.

"Grandpa, I'm so sorry for the delay. I haven't had a chance to go to the store, but I promise I will do it today on my way home from work. I know you need your milk since you are a baby cow and all, but I've had a lot going on. Miles has had auditions for the school play and extra Tae Kwon Do lessons this week after school, and we have a new trainee at work who I'm responsible for. Doing my best here!"

I tilt my head to the right and try to put on a fake smile as I deliver the last line, hoping he will just kindly let me pass.

"Oh, and for the last time — it's called Alexa, not Alesandra. I don't even know where you got that name. Please just stop with that already."

I shift my focus towards the stairs as I move swiftly around Grandpa in his button-down collared shirt and dress slacks. Why does he dress up to sit around the house all day? I make a mental note to get him some yoga pants, so he can be a proper homebody and show some respect for himself.

"Miles, let's go buddy! We are late. Please get moving!"

More than likely, he is still crying over his socks and will be doing so for ten more minutes. One of these days, I'm going to go all *Mommy Dearest* on him and cut the toes out of all his socks, so the stupid lines don't bother him so much. What will he worry about then? Huh?

Okay, we all know that won't happen, but it's nice to dream. I've tried about seventy-two brands of socks so far, and the lines at the toes all seem to annoy him to a point that he simply cannot deal and inevitably has a breakdown of epic proportions. With every brand, style, size, fabric, and color, it's always the same thing. *"The lines, Mommy. The lines!!"* Does he have freak-feet or something? Why are socks so annoying to him? Can't he just suck it up like the rest of us? Son, here is your first lesson in life: *Life sucks*. That's it. The whole lesson.

Okay, that's enough for one lifetime about socks. Allow me to find my center before I proceed. *Inhale. Exhale. Inhale. Exhale.*

All right, that's better.

"Miles, you can skip socks today if it helps," I yell helpfully.

Look at me, being an innovative yet flexible parent and shit. Now, on to the remaining grandparent and other reasons why I drink and swear.

"Okay Grammy, what's going on?"

"Dear, I was trying to tell you that we have a doctor's appointment on the twenty-fifth at eleven in the morning. It's an annual physical for both your grandfather and myself at Dr. Harris' office."

My left eye starts twitching involuntarily.

I glance at my Apple Watch, and it appears today is only the second of the month, so *clearly* it was very important for her to tell me about something happening on the twenty-fifth. Despite the fact she also texted me, using her voice text of course because she can't see worth a damn. I bet when I get to work, I'll also have an e-mail from her about the same topic. Why did I teach her about technology again? Doing crap like that is basically self-sabotaging behavior. But what can I say? I couldn't take the sticky notes anymore — that shit had to stop.

"Grammy Ellie, I will make sure my boss knows that I need the twenty-fifth of this month off so that I can take you both to the doctor's office. Thanks so much for telling me. This was surely important for me to hear this morning."

I am starting to wonder if she even hears my sarcasm anymore or if she is completely numb to it.

"Oh, no dear. It's not this month. It's the twenty-fifth of next month."

Well, that settles it. I'm living in a funny farm.

I start laughing in her face. Like honest to goodness deep belly laughter. She cocks an eye at me, and I can tell she is wondering what is so funny. She legit has no idea how absurd this is, does she?

"Next month? Wow. That's even better. Thanks, Gram. You are the *best*. There is absolutely no chance I'll forget about that happening *next* month. Nope. No chance at all."

I'm totally going to forget about that by next month. I am not even sure what tomorrow's schedule looks like, let alone the end of next flipping month.

She smiles back at me lovingly while palming my cheek gently, and my heart melts at how sweet she really is. Ugh, *great*. Now, I feel guilty for thinking about how crazy she is.

"Thanks, darling. I appreciate all you do for us. And to help out, I'm going to be making dinner tonight. Would you like homemade pizza or spaghetti and meatballs?"

Hmm. Let me think. The last time she made us homemade pizza, she used hot and spicy picante sauce in lieu of tomato sauce because she thought it was close enough. Did I mention her vision isn't what it used to be?

For an eighty-year-old, she is really doing well — but aside from her famous baking, she should steer clear of the kitchen. You never know if it's going to be delicious or warrant a trip to the emergency room. But knowing today is going to be another busy day for me, I gratefully accept the offer of spaghetti and meatballs while sending up a prayer to the food gods that it is edible and doesn't end with any of us in gastric distress.

Let us pray. Amen.

Miles finally comes down the stairs, dragging his backpack with a forlorn look on his face. He looks so excited for another fun-filled day at school that he... you know what. Forget it. I can't even be sarcastic about it at this point. He looks depressed as hell. No jokes to be said. Inside, my heart breaks a little, and I wonder what else I should be doing to make him happier.

"Why so excited today, buddy?" I ask, trying to make him smile.

He sighs, like the sigh to end all other sighs, and gives me an extremely literal answer to my question — as if I really wanted an answer. "Mom! I'm not excited. I'm sad because I don't like my teachers, and I'd rather stay home and play with the cats today."

Here we go again.

"Miles, honey," I start with a kind and only slightly pandering smile. "I know you love your cats, and that's super awesome. I love the cats too. But school is so important because it is going to help you become the best Miles that you can be. Plus, you'll see your friends, learn neat stuff, and it's gonna be so fun. Maybe you will even learn more about sea life today in science, I know you love that. I wish I could go with you, but I have to go to work, darn it all. Grab your breakfast and your lunch from the counter, and let's go."

Sometimes I am so glad that his autism makes it hard for him to tell when I'm being sarcastic or not. Because that was full-on sarcasm right there. Like Emmy winning stuff, if I do say so myself.

I glance over at Grammy Ellie, and she is giving me a side-eye that just won't quit. Although she didn't notice when I was sarcastic with her, she sure as hell notices it in my reply to Miles and clearly doesn't approve. Well, that's too bad. She can go back to planning months and months of doctor appointments in advance and leave me to deal with my twelve-year-old ray of sunshine.

"I don't have any friends in the seventh grade, Mom. You know that. There are too many kids and too many class changes during the day."

Well, that makes me feel like crap. Why can't he make friends? I had lots of friends when I was in school, and he has half my DNA. So, by the laws of science, he should have at least twenty-five percent of the amount of friends that I did. I'm pretty sure that math checks out.

"I'll have Mr. Hale swing by to check on you during lunch and see how you are doing, okay?"

That perks him up enough to get his butt moving. Okay, meltdown averted for now. Bless Brody Hale and his fine ass.

We are headed to the door when I hear my phone ping a new text message at the same time I hear Grandpa Dickie telling Alexa, aka Alesandra, to have a nice day as he thanks her for adding milk to the shopping list, yet again. At this point, I'm not sure if he thinks Alexa is a real person hiding in the little device on our counter or if he is just messing with me and trying to make me think he is insane.

Out the door we go. Once I'm seated in the car, I look across the hood and see Miles trudging ahead. There is really no other way to describe that walk. He is trudging. *Is he going off to war or to school?*

He hates school. I get it. Believe me, I do. He's twelve years old, and what boy his age truly likes school? After all, seventh grade can be brutal even for neurotypical kids. That's what they call "normal" kids these days, neurotypical. And Miles is certainly the opposite of neurotypical.

Miles has high-functioning autism, ADHD, and trouble with his fine motor skills. Really, he struggles with all social situations and has some extra anxiety here and there. But he is so dang smart, I never wanted to see him put in special classes. So, I've fought against that, perhaps in vain. It's been very important for me to keep him in regular public school, and I think he just needs a little push now and then plus some confidence. If only he could make some friends, I know it could turn around for him. I'm sure this year is going to be better than last year. It has to be. Right? At least he is better than he was a few years ago.

He gets in the back seat, drops his backpack, and sighs loudly.

"That's a good sigh, buddy. I rank it eight out of ten points."

He is used to my bad jokes and knows I am trying to make him laugh. This one makes him smile a little. I'll take it. I wonder how many years I have before he starts telling me to shut it?

I notice he didn't grab his lunch box... because why would he? I mean, it's hard to remember to do the same task each morning when you are a kid and have basically no responsibilities whatsoever.

"I see you forgot your lunch box. Wait here and get buckled up while I go in and get it for you."

I run in to grab the lunch box because it is way quicker to do it myself than to send him back, and at this point, we are going to be late for about the third time this month. Yeah, I know it's only the second of the month. That should give you an idea of how high punctuality ranks with me these days.

As I'm walking back to my car, my phone chimes again, reminding me about the text message I got a few minutes ago. I glance over at my Apple Watch, thanks to my sister Millie for that cool gadget, and I see that it is from Brody — the illustrious Mr. Hottie Hale.

My heart flutters a bit as I try to see what bit of wisdom he texted me this morning. It's an image, so I have to look at it later when I can pull out my phone. I bet it's something funny. He always seems to know when I need a laugh. He's good like that. It's like he has a spidey-sense and just knows when I'm going from Speed Two to Speed Three and in need of a good laugh. One text from him, and I am downshifting immediately.

I'll take a look at whatever joke he sent after I drop off my little guy at the Academy — it's a public charter school for kindergarten through eighth grade. I still need to ask Brody to check on Miles during lunch, and I don't have time to reply now. It's nice that he is still in the same school as my son. I'm so comforted by knowing he has a familiar, loving face to see if he has a meltdown.

Brody was his fourth-grade teacher and has since become a dear friend. He adores Miles and the feeling is mutual. With Miles in seventh grade, I have another year before I have to worry that my little guy will be on his own every school day.

As we make the ten-minute drive to school through scenic Clearwater, Miles and I sing along with Twenty-One Pilots, Panic! At the Disco, and Fall Out Boy. Say what you want about my kid, but he has kick-ass music taste. I totally take credit for that — it's all me. Not his sperm donor. If he took after *his* music taste, he'd be listening to Tenacious D and Spinal Tap. But I digress.

We pull up to the Academy's drop off loop, and well, lookie here, there is no long line to wait in. *Ahh, the perks of dropping him off five minutes past the late bell.* I roll my eyes at my internal monologue as I turn to him and give my best smile.

"Have a great day, buddy. Remember, Uncle Cort will be here to pick you up today after school, and he's watching you until I get home from work. I'll pick you up at his place on the way home. And Grammy is cooking your favorite — spaghetti and meatballs."

"Awesome! I love when Uncle Cort picks me up. I'm going to destroy him in Star Wars Battlefront on his Xbox today."

"That's my boy. Just keep that positive outlook all day, buddy. Knock em' dead!"

After he gets out, I glance in the rearview mirror to see how many people are behind me so I'll know if I have a minute to check my phone and text Brody before I head on to work.

Gasp! Really? I'm the *only* one dropping off her kid late this morning? Don't I feel special? Or like a failure actually? Yeah. More like a failure.

Ahh, there she is. My old friend, Guilt.

Haven't heard from you all morning, Guilt, where've you been? It's just not the same around here without you.

Well, you know me, Cara. I was just waiting for you to start to feel good about yourself, and here I am to remind you that you suck. Hard.

I check the text that Brody sent earlier this morning and loudly guffaw before I look around sheepishly as if I was afraid someone heard me laugh. The text is a meme pic of a 1950s housewife, and the caption says: *Sometimes you might feel like no one's there for you, but you know who's always there for you? Laundry. Laundry will always be there for you.*

Brody always knows what to send at the right time to make me smile. We have had whole conversations for weeks at a time simply using memes and gifs. It's the best kind of relationship, really. Always lighthearted and no drama. Just how I like it, and pretty much all I have room for in my life right now.

I reply with the good ol' *LOL* and then ask him to check on Miles today and maybe have lunch with him since he was down in spirits again. By the time I arrive at work, he has replied with a thumbs-up icon, and I know he will make sure my little boy is okay. I can always count on Brody. At least one man in my life is reliable.

There was a time that I wanted so much more from him, though, but that ship has sailed. I was instantly attracted to him a few years ago when we met at the fourth-grade Open House. But since he was my son's teacher, I had to keep him in the friend zone where he has been ever since and shall remain forever and ever. No matter how amazing his shoulders are or how much he makes my liver quiver when he flashes those dimples.

Lookie, but no touchy. That's been the story of my life for a while now, and it's become second nature to me. I don't even think about how hot he is anymore or how soft his lips look or how cute he looks when he forgets to shave and has that little bit of scruff. Seriously, you could be all, "Wow — Brody is hot stuff!" and I'd reply, "Oh? Brody? Oh yeah, he is okay looking I guess." Not even a blip on my radar.

Convincing, huh? Did you believe that?

I didn't either.

Another day in paradise

Walking into work on this perfect fall day, I feel a sense of calm and happiness coursing through my body, sufficiently putting me back into *Speed One* territory, where I hope to remain for the rest of the day. Don't laugh — it's totally possible. I can feel the Zen washing over me.

I love it here at the University of Tampa. The campus is beautiful, and I find my job to be wholly fulfilling. Nothing is more relaxing for me than strolling across these historic grounds. My head swivels back and forth as I survey the breathtaking sights around me and inhale the fresh coastal air. This campus sits up against the Hillsborough River, which leads out to Tampa Bay and then ultimately connects to the Gulf of Mexico. It is also just a hop, skip and a jump from the popular Tampa Riverwalk area too. Nothing beats the Florida lifestyle.

This campus is old, but it has character in spades. No cookie-cutter architecture around here, that's for sure. Most of the residences and lecture halls around campus have dark red brick exteriors, ornate domes, minarets, and steeples designed in mid-19th Century Moorish Revival style. It's a breathtaking mash-up of Classical, Victorian, Gothic, Islamic, and Asian designs.

Iconic buildings aside, there are also grand oak trees, green grassy fields galore, meditation gardens, peaceful ponds, and winding sidewalks to die for.

When life gets me down, an evening walk around campus is a soothing balm to my soul.

As I approach the Athletic Department Building, I see a group of students playing soft music under the shade of a big oak, and I stop for a moment to listen to the strings of the acoustic guitar and enjoy the relaxing melody. After a while, I start to feel like a creepy pervert gawking at kids half my age and decide it's best to move on. Plus, I'm already late, and my boss is gonna throw me some shade, so I might as well get on with it.

While my boss, Peter Peters, is the current bane of my existence, I still adore being a Sports Physical Therapist.

Before I gush about my job — let's take a moment to internally laugh at how stupid his name is. Clearly his parents did not like him even at the time of his birth. The more I get to know him, the more sense that makes. He's only been here for about a year, and ever since then, my happy-place at UT has been rapidly becoming a place to grind my teeth. Maybe I should send him my dental bills.

Before Peter came to lead our team, going to work each day was my escape, and it still is for the most part. No job is perfect, but I really was born to help people heal, and I've always thought athletes were really hot, so this job is perfect for me. Plus, I get to work alongside my baby brother Cort every day. He followed me to college on a whim, and it turns out he actually likes working in this field too.

After I got hired by the UT Athletic Department, Cort kept applying until they decided they couldn't live without his skills, and then all was well in my work-world. Fortunately, he works an earlier shift than me, so he helps me with Miles most afternoons, like today. Miles loves him too, and without a dad in the picture, it's nice he has a male he can look up to.

My thirty-five-year-old little bro, Cortland Amos, whom we lovingly call Cort — or shithead if you're nasty — is three years younger than me. He and I have always been close since we are the youngest of five siblings. Apparently, our parents liked to get frisky quite often. Either that or they hated birth control. I don't really know which it was because they both were killed in a car accident when I was seven, and Cort was just four years old.

We don't always see eye to eye, but a deep bond was forged when we clung to each other at such a young age for comfort as our whole world turned upside down, and we were too young to really understand it all.

My older three sisters are almost a clique at times, although I love them dearly. They just matured differently than me and Cort. We like to laugh, have fun, and do completely inappropriate things like read trashy romance novels, drink margaritas, and plan to take over the world. You know? The fun stuff. My sisters, on the other hand, like to go to Church, read biographies, and have tea and cakes.

Just kidding. They really don't have tea and cakes that I know of, but it wouldn't surprise me if they did. Especially my oldest sister, Chloe. She is forty-four and absolutely zero fun. She is wound up so tight she squeaks when she walks.

My other two sisters, CJ and Millie, are a little less squeaky. My parents had the great idea to give us all names that start with the letter C. They were super original like that. So, some of my sisters tried to give themselves nicknames to differentiate themselves. Apparently, the older you get, the more individuality matters. Not to me, but to them. I'm happy being Carina Skyler Amos and go by Cara most of the time.

Chloe, the unfun eldest Amos, tries to get us to call her "Lo," but we just refuse because it sounds super weird. I once told her to "Quit trying to make Lo happen, it's not going to happen" in my best Mean Girls impression. Cort and I laughed like it was an Eddie Murphy stand-up special, while CJ, which is just short for Cassandra Jane, almost smiled. Meanwhile, Millie, aka Camilla — her nickname was less annoying and thus it stuck — just put her head down and sighed.

But it doesn't matter what they think of my jokes, as long as Cort laughs. I'll feel like a success since he is the other Amos with a sense of humor. When I was a teen, I once heard my older siblings griping behind my back and referred to me as *the loud Amos*, and it hurt a little, not gonna lie. But then I thought about it, and they were totally right. I am seriously loud. I love to sing, and so my voice just naturally propels.

I think they are just jealous. Yeah, let's go with that.

"Ah, there you are Cara. Nice of you to join us this morning," a grating voice greets me as I set down my purse and take out my laptop.

I look over and see my boss giving me a condescending smile. "Sorry Peter, Miles had a pretty epic meltdown this morning, and I did my best. I really apologize, but I'm pretty sure my first appointment isn't until later, so no harm, no foul."

I have no idea if that is true, but he doesn't need to know that. I try to walk around him, and he steps in my path ever so slightly and gives me a leering look that creeps me out as he lowers his voice and says, "That's okay, I guess. We all have crosses to bear, and we can make up for our shortcomings in other ways."

That wasn't creepy at all.

I put my head down because I can't stand the tone of his voice, and if he winks at me, I'm going to puke. I nod quietly out of respect but seal my lips so I don't let it slip that he can take his shortcomings and shove them where the sun doesn't shine.

Get it? Up his ass. He can shove them up his ass.

After I move past him, I see Cort standing nearby, and he gives me a questioning look of concern. Apparently, he can see that Peter said something troubling because I can't hide my reactions from Cort. I make eyes at him that imply, 'Not now' and instead of stopping to discuss *Peter Peters Pumpkin Eater*, I simply hustle to the reception area to see when my first patient will be arriving.

Looks like I'm in luck today. Mandy, our receptionist and all-around bad bitch, gives me a big smile as she tells me my first patient is running behind and hands me his file — a soccer player with legs of steel. Nice.

I fist pump at the good news and quietly whisper, "Yesssss," to my girl.

Mandy is a student intern who has been with us for a few weeks now. She fits in well and is certainly the best receptionist we've had in a while. She's taking classes in a variety of fields, but she's working here because she's starting to lean toward working in Sports Medicine.

Good for her. I hope she makes it.

She reminds me of a younger version of myself, so I instantly felt a kinship with her. Her only downside is that I'm pretty sure she drools over Cort most days, which makes perfect sense because he is good-looking. Although he is my brother, I do have eyes and can see what others see. But it is not cool when my friends or people I know are lusting after my baby brother. It just gives me a sick feeling. Plus, I wouldn't want to see her hurt, and Cort would break her like a twig.

A few minutes later, my soccer player, Pedro, arrives for me to work on his ankle.

"You sure are lookin' good today, Ms. Amos. You ready for me to take you out on that date, yet?"

Pedro is such a cutie pie and always flirts with me. His soccer legs are legendary, and I love that I get to put my hands on them. And I say that in the least perverted way possible. Honest.

The closer I get to forty years old, the more I notice two main themes to my reactions when my patients flirt with me.

One, it makes me feel like a cougar, which creeps me out and revs my engines at the same time.

And two, it makes me feel damn good about myself, like I'm still alive and a female with at least a smidgen of sex appeal. Perhaps this old girl has a few miles left on her engine after all. If these hot young athletes can spare me more than a few glances, I guess I still have something going for me.

It goes without saying that I would *never* attempt anything inappropriate with my patients or any college kid in general, but it is nice to have the attention. Because I'm not dating anymore and currently on yet another *man-fast*, the positive attention from these guys is all I have to look forward to in terms of my love life. So, I'll take what I can get.

"Sorry Pedro. You know me, I'm happily in a committed relationship with Netflix, and I won't stray. Plus, it would be heartless of me to ruin you for all other women." I wink as I walk him back to the table so we can get started on his stretching and strengthening exercises. The fun banter continues, and I find myself smiling happily through the first part of my day, as more student athletes file in and out of the facility.

Around lunchtime, I'm cleaning up in the ice room when I get a text from Mr. Hottie. It's another pic with no caption. Just him and my little guy smiling for a selfie in the lunchroom. I'm grinning like a loon at the phone as

I stare at the pic of two of my favorite people when Cort strolls up and pulls on my red ponytail from behind.

"Waahhh!" I scream like the composed lady I am.

Cort just laughs and shakes his head, used to my overreactions. He knows how easily I startle. *Why must he torture me?*

"Hey, kiddo. How are you doing today?" I ask him with a genuine interest because we've both been pretty busy today, and aside from a few funny faces across the room, we haven't talked much.

"Just had a string of beautiful fit volleyball players of the opposite gender in need of my TLC and magic touch, so I'd say it's been a great day thus far."

He often jokes about the college girls, but sometimes I wonder if he would cross that line and do something stupid to jeopardize his standing here. But then I shake off the thought because as much as he likes to flirt, Cort is a relationship guy deep-down, and he knows there is no future with young college girls, despite their attempts to throw themselves at him.

"Keep your hands off the merchandise, young man. You can look, but if I find out you are touching, I'll have your ass. Or, better yet, maybe I'll let Grammy Ellie take care of you. Yeah, that's a better plan."

"Cara, don't even joke about that. That woman can be lethal."

"Whatever it takes to keep you on the straight and narrow, bro. Perhaps I'll ask her to cook you up a special surprise and make you eat it in front of her."

"You wouldn't!" he gasps dramatically before continuing, "Enough about me. What was up with the pumpkin-eater this morning? I noticed he was all up in your grill. Did he bust you for your lack of punctuality again?"

"Oh, please. As if!" I retort in my best Clueless Alicia Silverstone voice. "Actually, yeah, he kind of did. And like the slime ball that he is, he made it weird by telling me I could make it up in other ways. Gag."

Cort's face gets uncharacteristically serious, and he starts gritting his teeth before saying, "Want me to talk to him for you, Cara? This shit has to stop. It's not the first time he has said something like that. It seems like he is escalating a bit. I swear, if he messes with you again, I can't be held responsible for how I may respond or what I'll do to his ugly face. He might be my boss, but you know where my loyalties are."

"Settle down there, He-Man," I say as I pat his chest in an effort to calm him down. "You know what would happen if you did that, and I won't let you. He's just not worth it, and you don't need to jeopardize your future here because of his dumb-ass. He didn't explicitly say anything that truly crosses a line, and it would be his word against mine. Since I applied for the managerial position last year and he beat me out, they would think I just had an ax to grind. I might be pissed that he came in out of nowhere and got the job that was rightfully mine, but I'm not petty. I'm a classy gal, you know this, Cort."

By the end of my rant, Cort is smiling and nodding. He knows I'm right, and no matter how protective he wants to be of me, Cort realizes that Peter Peters hasn't officially crossed any lines, and he's smart enough to never say anything when witnesses are present. So, my hands are tied. It's really in my best interest to let it go and hope he gets bored here and moves on to ruin another department's morale.

Mandy sticks her head in the ice room where we are chatting and says that Cort's next patient is here early. I can't help but notice the look she gives him, like he is the sun, moon, and stars. Part of me thinks it cute that she is crushing on this big lug, but the other part wants to vomit.

Cort flashes her a flirty smile and winks as he says, "Thanks Mandy. You're the best. Tell him I'll be right there. Just finishing up with this killer over here," as he nods in my direction.

Mandy skips off to the front with sparkles and hearts flying out of her eyes.

"Please spare that girl from your charms. She is young and impressionable," I admonish him. "Now, get out of here, shithead. It's time for my lunch, and you have to leave soon to get Miles, so you can't be running late. Oh, that reminds me, he said something like he is gonna kick your sorry ass in some Star Wars battle and will bring the black rain of death upon you and all of your descendants if you try to get out of it. I don't know what that means, but it sounds serious. So, you should get your game face on and sharpen your light saber or whatever. Stretch out your joystick fingers or something."

"It's not a joystick, it's a game controller, and you know this. You aren't as out of touch as you pretend to be, Cara. I'm onto you and your clueless routine."

"Oh no, Cort!" With my hand on my chest and eyes wide I continue, "Whatever will I do now that I know you've unraveled the secret I've been keeping all my life? If people find out I can think and have brains, no one will want to be my friend anymore." We both chuckle as we leave the room to move on with our day.

My stomach won't stop growling since it's time for my lunch, and I want to eat my salad out in the meditation garden today. After that, I think I will take a nice power walk around campus. Although my job is quite physical, I haven't had time for a full workout this week, and my muscles are stiff from lack of use.

Plus, I love this time of the year, with the cooler temps and lack of the typical Florida humidity blanket that normally makes going outside in the middle of the day, like walking into a sauna — minus the fat, old, and naked men in towels. I've been peeping out the windows all morning lusting over the wind blowing through the trees and those killer blue skies.

Making my way to the meditation garden, I see a coworker, Jane, taking a stroll and stop to greet her for a brief chat. I can never pass her by without asking how she and her daughter are doing. They are two of the kindest people I know.

Jane is the right-hand woman, aka secretary, to the President of the College. I've known Jane for a few years now, but we weren't all that close until about a year ago when her daughter got injured while training in preparation to try out for the crew team. She came to me for physical therapy and was too injured to try out with the rest of the students. But I was so impressed with this young lady, that I asked the crew team coach, whom I have also helped many times through the years, to give her a second chance to try out after she was strong enough. Of course, she killed it and made the team since I had fixed her shoulder up, like a boss.

A few days later, Jane came over to the athletic training building and took me out for coffee to say thanks. She then told me if I ever needed anything, to let her know, and she'd take care of me. And we've been keeping in touch ever since. I'm sure I won't ever take her up on that offer, but you never know.

After leaving Jane, I continue to the garden, and when I arrive, I pull out my phone. One new text from my best friend, Helen. Apparently, she is coming back to Tampa next week and can't wait to corrupt me and save me from my 'mom-dom' as she calls it; which is not to be confused with the BDSM version of Mom-Dom which is most definitely not something that I take part in. Do yourself a favor and don't Google that term unless you want to be a little bit scared. Trust me.

I cringe, not certain that I'll be able to get away from the elderly and the offspring for an evening of debauchery, but honestly, it sounds really tempting. I haven't spent time with her in months since she has been out seeing the world, and I do need some girl time to let my hair down before I snap like Carole Baskin and feed someone to the tigers. Helen and I always get up to some good-time shenanigans when she graces me with her presence. I wonder where the night will take us this time around.

I make a promise to myself to find a sitter and reply, agreeing to hit up the local cantina for margaritas when she returns.

After sending that text, I notice the other conversation I had going with Brody and sigh inwardly and my lip automatically assumes a pouty-face position.

I promised myself I would stop obsessing about him, but I haven't been able to accomplish that task yet. Maybe I should take this time in the meditation garden to remind myself not to screw up a great friendship with romantic complications. Plus, he probably doesn't even think of me like that. The way he pats me on the head sometimes gives me the impression that he thinks of me as a little sister.

He is always helping me with Miles, and I honestly don't know what I'd do with him without Brody's help. Sometimes it seems like Mr. Hottie is the only one who understands Miles and can reach him. And all I bring to the table of our friendship are inappropriate memes and impure thoughts. Oh, great, my old friend Guilt has joined me in the Zen garden. That bitch!

Hey Cara, it's me, Guilt. I heard you were happy in the meditation garden and thought this would be a good time to remind you that you are a terrible friend. Can't you even give the man a proper thank you for all he does for your son? Memes are not appropriate thank yous. You are the worst.

I really hate that voice in my head and wish she would piss off for good. Guilt is a nasty witch. Who does she think she is anyway? But maybe she does have a point. Brody deserves a proper thank you. I pull out my phone and decide to send my super-hot friend something genuine and not sarcastic for a change.

Chapter Two

From the texts of Cara and Mr. Hottie

Cara: Hey Brody, thanks again for helping with Miles today. I'm sure he will be gushing when he gets home telling me he got to sit with you at lunch and how much he loves you and other hero worship. As you know, he isn't like most seventh graders, and he still thinks sitting with a grown-up, a teacher no less, is pretty cool. He is really struggling with friends, and I don't know what I'd do without you having my back at school. You are the best, and I don't deserve your friendship. Luckily, Miles does deserve it though. :) Jokes aside, I hope you know how much I appreciate you.

Mr. Hottie: Who is this? Did you steal Cara's phone? I don't know who you are, but I'll uncover this mystery and get to the bottom of this.

Mr. Hottie: <gif of a monkey dressed like a detective holding a magnifying glass>

Cara: Right back at you. Who stole Brody's phone and gave him an actual sense of humor?

Mr. Hottie: <gif of crying baby>

Cara: <eye roll emoji> Can't a girl give a proper thanks to her friend without a smart-ass reply? Why can't you just say you're welcome? I'm trying to be serious and express my gratitude here.

Mr. Hottie: In that case, I'll come over tonight, and you can express your gratitude more appropriately.

Cara: You mean like you having dinner with me, Miles, and the gray hairs? Grammy Ellie is making her famous (and probably not poisonous) spaghetti and meatballs tonight. Come on by, if you dare...

Mr. Hottie: Oh, would you look at that? Turns out, I have plans with Hudson tonight. We'll have to reschedule.

Cara: Yeah, that's what I thought. You aren't man enough to handle Grammy's balls!

Cara: Wait. That sounds bad. I don't want to have a visual of Grammy having balls or you handling them.

Cara: I'm sorry for that. Boy, this is awkward.

Mr. Hottie: <gif of SNL's Kristin Wiig making the disgust face>

Cara: Well, on that note... I think I'll be going to jump into the reflection pond here on campus to drown myself in my shame and embarrassment.

Mr. Hottie: Don't do that. I'd miss you.

Cara: But not enough to eat possibly toxic meatballs, huh? I am beginning to question your sincerity.

Mr. Hottie: <Winking emoji>

Cara: Don't you have kids to corrupt? Why are you texting me in the middle of the school day?

Mr. Hottie: Don't worry your pretty little head, sweetheart. They are taking a test right now. Speaking of which, I have to go because it looks like I have a cheater I need to bust. Best part of my day. Aside from talking to you that is.

Mr. Hottie: Oh, before I go, you are more than welcome, Carina. You are sweet to thank me, but it's not necessary. I like hanging with Miles. He is a way cooler lunch partner than Mr. Snell and his body odor. Ick!

Cara: Nothing cooler than a guy who says, "ick!" <winking emoji>

Chapter Three

That is so not stoked

Brody

"Three more reps. Two. One. Nice one, dawg."

Grunting, I set the bar up into the resting position after completing the reps. I suck in a big gulp of air as I sit up, shake out my arms, and then we switch positions so I can spot Hudson, as he does his next bench press set. I'm stoked that I am finally able to do the same weight as him. For being as lean as he is, the dude is ridiculously strong. Strength training seems to come easy for him. Lucky bastard.

"So, my dude. Are you finally going to come with me this weekend? Or are you gonna continue to be a little punk bitch?" Hudson jokingly asks in an odd drawl that makes him sound like a Southern Californian surfer, instead of a Western Florida native. We don't have too many people out here that sound like him — thank God. Despite being an out-of-place Jeff Spicoli, at least we are within a few minutes from the beach, although there are no waves for him to surf on this side of the state.

"Huds, this little punk ass bitch has shit to take care of, okay? Not all of us can float on the breeze without a care in the world."

After powering through the rest of his set without breaking a sweat, he finally continues. "Whatever, man. I know you think I'm raging all the time, but I just happen to have a more developed sense of work-life balance. I'm super evolved and shit. I work hard, but I party hard too. You should try it sometime. It's been ages since you've been out there."

"Get off the bench. It's my turn, Mr. Work-Life Balance." We switch places, and I try to change the subject — desperate to get him to get off my back. I know he means well, but I'm just not into the party scene anymore — not that I ever really was. I'm forty-two damn years old, so taking a motorcycle ride across the state to Daytona Beach to get shit-faced on the beach and crash at a cheap hotel curled up to a random piece of ass is not even a little appealing.

He likes to do wild shit all the time, but he is much more of a free spirit than I am. He always seems to have something crazy planned for every weekend and a few nights each week too. Rock climbing, theme park hopping, kayaking, rope courses that take you climbing from tree to tree, and sunrise beach yoga. Sometimes, if it is close to home, I might join him on his tamer adventures, but no matter how much he asks, I don't see myself pretending to be a spring-breaker on the east coast.

"Listen, Brah, here is the sitch. This is the last beach weekend of the season, more than likely. Fall is here, and although this is Florida, I don't like freezing my nads, and the water starts to get too chill after November. My nads are sensitive." He cups himself protectively to drive home his point. I shake my head at him, holding back a smile, as he continues, "So, take this weekend off from your boring life and come with. It's gonna be mad dope. I'm already frothing over the beach bunnies and waves."

"I've got stacks of papers to grade, and I also need to spend some time reading some new textbooks that they want us to use next year. I'm supposed to provide feedback to the school board later this month about their understandability and if they are practical enough to be used in the classroom. I committed to this work, and I keep my commitments."

There, man. That should shut him up.

"I'm not sure what you just said, 'cause it was so painful that my brain saved itself and started thinking about bungee jumping as a defense mechanism instead of listening to your commitment bullshit. I've never heard something that is more opposite of *stoked* in my life. It was anti-stoke, and that is definitely not the type of negativity I need in my aura."

Hudson has a flare for the dramatic, if you didn't catch that yet. "Do you hear yourself? Where has my best dude gone? That was so ball-shriveling, I might not be able to ever get laid again. Thanks a lot, asshole."

Okay, that was a little funny. He got a chuckle out of me and a sarcastic apology.

I admit that my life is less than thrilling to my beach-loving hippy friend. But that is why I have him around — he is my polar opposite and helps me find balance. The amount of balance that won't tip the scales in the wrong direction. I'm very concerned about the scales. By-product of being a former fattie.

"Alright, I can't go to the beach, but I will join you Friday night in Ybor next weekend, okay?"

"Sweet, dawg. I knew you wanted to rage. I'll miss you at the beach, but I guess I have no choice but to accept your pathetic offer so I can get a little bit of time with my bro." He punches me in the shoulder, and I stumble back a second. Fucker is strong. Then, he continues, "I love working out with you, but it would be nice not to have to see you in a tank top once in a while. I'm getting jelly of your shoulders, dude. Looking buff as shit. And your back is shredded."

Well, that's probably because lifting weights has become my only non-work-related activity I've ever been able to stick with. Ever since I lost weight and got myself in better shape, which was totally thanks to meeting Hudson, I've become more and more obsessed with hitting the gym. I never miss a day. Ever. There are no excuses for not getting in a workout. Hudson thinks I work out too much, and he might be right. And I even hide some of my workouts from him — to stave off the nagging. If he knew I worked out every single day, he would be even worse to deal with than he is now, thinking I just do weekday workouts.

But he is different than I am. Hudson just doesn't take anything to the extreme — other than partying and living the high-life. He can't even stick with a career path.

Hudson was a journalist when I met him a decade or so ago when he interviewed me for a fluff piece he was writing for the Tampa Tribune. I was the County's Teacher of the Year, and he was writing a gripping piece about male teachers — thinking there was some kind of new angle. Needless to say, journalism didn't fit him well, and he wound up stopping that profession a few months later. It was a decent article, though.

He has had quite a few career changes since then. Let's see, since I've known him, he has been: a reporter, internet blogger, horticulturist, personal trainer, novelist, motivational speaker (that was a funny one to witness — he said he wanted to bring "stokeness" to the masses), bartender, hot-dog cart owner (he called it being a weinerpreneur), and I think he tried to get ice cream vending machines off the ground for a while. But why would anyone do that when there are ice cream shops on every corner? Personally, I think he was high and just had the serious ice cream munchies.

He swears he doesn't smoke pot anymore, but some of his decisions really make me wonder. However, he is pretty dedicated to health now and still works out regularly. In fact, he was very inspirational about working out when he interviewed me back then. While we were chatting, I confessed that I didn't really know my way around a gym, and my man-pride wouldn't let me ask for help. Back then, my workouts consisted of just a little walking and jogging when I felt like I had some free time — which was pretty much never. I didn't become teacher of the year by fluke. My dedication to my career and those kids has always been front and center, and my nonworking hours have always been filled with researching, planning, and testing out new approaches to create magic in the classroom. I love my job. And when I'm not there, I'm usually here at the gym. A few times a week, Hudson joins me. It's like a flashback to when he got me started and was my personal trainer, helping me lose weight and get swole. I owe him total respect.

"Man, I'm getting fired up with this song. It's got that deep house vibe. Nice!" He starts yapping about the music that is currently blasting from the speakers in here, and at least he has moved on from the topic of my social life, thankfully.

We continue our workout in companionable silence for the most part. Hudson is always counting reps for me and keeping my spirit up with his positive vibes. He is a great workout partner. I always seem to get a better workout when he is here by my side. Some of my personal bests have been when he was cheering me on.

After a while, we finish up with some light stretching. We gather up our water bottles, towels, and gym bags and head out the door. I guess he has had enough silence and starts in on me again. "Bro, look — serious talk for a minute. You know I care about you, right? You are part of my squad, and I've got mad respect for you, but lately I've been getting worried about you."

I'm not gonna lie, Hudson doesn't get serious like this very often, and so as much as it pains me, I give him a chance to get it off his chest. So, I hear him out.

"Oh, why is that? I don't think anything is wrong with me. Nothing has really changed, so what's the big problem?"

"That's just it, man. Nothing has changed for you. Ever since I've known you, you've always been working hard — both at the school and at the gym. When I bug you enough, you eventually cave in and come out with me. Then, after that, you go back to being Mr. Boring. I know you always wanted to have a family, and although that's not the life for me, it has always been important to you. So, why aren't you dating anymore? I just hope you haven't given up on finding your future Mrs. Hale. I hate seeing you alone so much."

"Wow, Hudson. That's touching, really." I try to shrug him off with some sarcasm, but he is relentless and continues, "Answer me this, buddy. How long since you've been out on a date? Or with a woman at all? One-night stand? A fling? Anything? Are you trying to be a monk?"

I pause and really think back and... dammit, I really have to think back quite a bit. How long has it been?

"How long do you need to think about this, man? Judging by that look on your mug and those sad puppy-dog eyes, I know the answer is way too damn long."

"Well, hang on now, just give me a second."

"Tick-tock, man."

"Got it!" I shout victoriously. "I went on a date with that barista from the coffee shop on First Avenue about four or five months ago. It was in the spring, I think, because it was near the beginning of the fourth grading period."

"Wow. That sounds so exciting. So, how did that date go again?" he prods.

"It wasn't great, honestly. So, it was just a few drinks, and then we said our goodbyes. She wasn't the right gal for me. She was so focused on herself and couldn't stop taking selfies the entire night. It was annoying. And now I can't go to that coffee shop anymore because I don't want to run into her."

"But she was hot, if I recall, right? You didn't need to marry her, but you could've at least had a good time... if you know what I mean. In the sheets, that's what I mean."

"I know what you mean, asshole. But I wasn't built that way, you know that. One-night stands are not my thing. I've tried it, and I felt crappy afterward. I need to have some feelings or an actual connection in order to get physical, and there was no connection at all."

"Fine. Okay, so coffee hottie aside, what about before that?"

"Umm, it was a long while before her."

"How long, because I can't even remember hearing about anyone from you for a really long time."

"Well, I think it was about a year and half or so before that when I was with Cindy, and you know how that ended."

"Badly. It ended badly, I do remember. I just never understood why it ended badly. She seemed nice and was totally into you. Why did you dump her again? I thought she wanted marriage and kids and the whole nine yards, just like you."

"Yeah, she was great, and we had a lot in common. But she just wasn't the right one for me, and I didn't love her. I didn't want to lead her on any longer, so I tried to let her down gently, but she kind of went crazy for a time. That sort of scared me off women for a while, I guess. I didn't want to hurt anyone else." I cringe just remembering how bad she took it, and it was like a month-long break-up from hell.

I hate to see a woman cry; seriously, I can't stand it.

As a child of a single mom, I have always been protective of women. I saw how hard she worked and how crappy she felt after Dad left — that piece of horseshit. I hated it when she cried at night before bed; that's when it was always the worst for her. She probably thought I couldn't hear her, but I could, and it gutted me. So, I made it my mission in life to make sure she never cried again. It was something only a dumb kid would think they could control.

And so those behaviors carried over to the other women in my life, I guess. And Cindy cried and cried when I gave her the news that it wasn't working out. She had convinced herself that I was acting differently because I was thinking of proposing. She couldn't have been more wrong. Her tears and wailing made the breakup so much harder. I kept feeling guilty for making her cry, and I would do anything to make her stop with the tears, which led to me agreeing to try again. But I was just delaying the inevitable. After the second or third attempt, I just walked away and had to cut off all contact whatsoever. It was hard, but in the end, it was the right thing to do.

"So, one hard break-up and you just give up? Why do you assume you are gonna hurt someone else if you try again?"

Because no matter who I date, she won't be her. The one I can't seem to get over.

"I just don't see it happening for me, and that's all. I think I'm not meant to have that family and perfect life. I haven't found her yet, and I was looking everywhere for the first forty years of my life, practically. I'd have found her by now," I lie through gritted teeth, hoping he doesn't push or see the truth I'm hiding.

"Is that why you work out so much? 'Cause you are just trying to take your mind off dating? You've just given up?"

"Maybe. I don't know. It also probably has something to do with the fact that I never want to be the chubby guy I was when we first met. And if working out every day makes it possible, then that's what I'll do."

"Dude, you can take more than weekends off and still be fine. You keep working this hard, and you are gonna hurt yourself. Your body needs rest to recover. Didn't you learn anything from me when I trained you?"

"My body is better than ever, Huds. No worries about me injuring myself. I did learn a lot from you, and that includes the proper form and technique. I'm not gonna get hurt, so just drop it. Please."

"I don't know, man. I don't like this. You need to take a break, and let your body heal. Maybe take some time to meditate, and you can find some peace in your head and heart. Perhaps then the world will send you that perfect woman you've been looking for. If you get your head right, the universe will send her to you." He starts to smile at the end as if he is trying to tempt me by dangling that carrot in front of me. Idiot.

"There is no perfect woman out there for me. I'm fine with how things are."

And I'm a giant liar. There is a perfect woman out there for me, and I've already found her. She has beautiful red hair with big brown eyes and a passion for margaritas and loves memes. I just can't have her. It's never been the right time for us, and I still don't think it is. Plus, she is such a good friend I wouldn't want to risk losing that. I'd rather keep her in my life in any way I can have her, rather than risk losing her. And Miles. Such a great kid. He needs me in his life. I can't risk screwing that up because I'm hung up on his mom. She probably doesn't think of me like that anyway.

I remember when I was sitting across from the flaky barista that night, and she was droning on about how many followers she had on Instagram, I decided that if I couldn't have Cara, I didn't want anyone. It's as simple as that. And since that is not in the cards, I'll just have to hit the gym extra hard to burn off my frustration and try to avoid the guilt trips from Hudson.

"If you say so, dude. I just worry about you. You aren't built to be alone. You are good to the women when you are with them, and I feel like it is a waste for you to be single. After all, you bring balance to the dating world. Us players need the good guys like you out there so that women don't give up on the male gender as a whole. Dudes like you basically keep sending women to my bed. So thanks, I guess. Respect."

I chuckle at his stupidity. We say our goodbyes and part for the night. I'll see him in a few days, and by then, he will be on to another topic, and this difficult conversation will be a distant memory.

• ♥ • ♥ • ♥ • ♥ • ♥ •

Home Sweet Home Alone

I park my safe and sensible Camry in front of my apartment a few minutes later. I gather my things and head inside. Home sweet home. Alone. Again.

Maybe I should get a pet? That would probably help. I could get a cat and become the male version of a crazy cat lady. Wonder what the male version of that is? A cat man? No, that sounds like a weird play on Batman. Cat dude? Ha. Hudson would like that one. Maybe I can get a dog and be the dog guy? No, that just sounds like something women call men who are players — they're all dogs. I'm not. Maybe I should be. Nah, that's not how my mom raised me.

Dammit, Hudson. He got me thinking about the family I've always wanted and don't think I'll ever have. And that always leads me to thinking about Cara and how bad I want to hold her, kiss her, and maybe do other things with her, or to her more accurately. X-rated things. Shit… this sucks. Looks like it's gonna be another long, lonely night with my hand.

I shake that thought off and make my way to the shower to wash the day off. As the water heats up and I toss my gym clothes in the laundry basket, my thoughts wander back to where I really don't want them to go.

Realistically, I know I'm not too old, and it's possible that I might find someone and could still build the life I always wanted. I just don't see how it's possible when no one seems to hold a candle to that damn amazing woman. She is the standard by which I judge everyone else. And they all pale in comparison — no one has even come close. The fact that I thought I could make Cindy into another version of Cara is pathetic and laughable. Cindy was nothing like her, except maybe she resembled her slightly.

Cara is funny — strike that, she's hilarious. She is also sweet, caring, a damn joy to be around, and a light in this dull, bleak world. Her smile is like ten thousand megawatts. She is so strong too. Man, nothing can hold her down. She reminds me of my mom in that respect. *Not that I want to bang my mom, that's just gross.* It's just I see that same strong fire in her that my mom had and still has, to some extent.

Thanks to my profession, I'm around kids and parents enough to know it's not easy to be a single mom — or a mom at all, in fact. And to have a kid with special needs, like Miles, that just makes it so much harder on her. Throw in her grandparents — who lean on her way too much — and I don't know how she does it all. But Cara doesn't complain. That's not who she is. She just picks herself up by the bootstraps and gets shit done. It's fucking inspiring, and it's a damn turn on too. She doesn't need a man to come in and save her. But that doesn't mean I can't dream about being that guy.

And now my cock is getting hard just thinking about being her hero. There is something wrong with me. I can't keep thinking about my friend like that. So, I adjust the water to a much cooler temperature and will my cock to stand down. That does the trick, and now that the edge is gone, my thoughts wander back again.

I always thought love at first sight was a dumb fantasy. Something that Hollywood fabricated to sell movie tickets. But then she came tripping into my classroom a few years ago. Late, loud, and absolutely adorable, and ever since then, I haven't been the same.

I wanted her so bad. I remember thinking that maybe, just maybe, she would be single when the school year ended, and I could make my move then. But... nope. Of course, a girl like her won't stay single for long. She is too perfect, and anyone who doesn't see it is blind as a bat. So, I did the dumbest thing imaginable to help myself cope with it and started dating Cindy. That had been a colossal mistake. By the time Cara's stupid boyfriend broke up with her, the idiot, Cindy was all wrapped around me, and I couldn't see my way free fast enough.

Even if I had been single when she and that asshole broke up, Cara would have seen me as a rebound. I didn't want that. I don't want to settle for anything less than a hundred percent of her, romantically speaking.

After she broke up with the douche nozzle, she started talking to me about how much it hurt and how she would never trust anyone again. I met her at the beach one evening, and we went for a walk while she poured her heart out to me. Her best friend, Helen, was out of town on one of her trips, and she didn't want to burden her sisters or brother with it. She just needed someone, and I was there. It was like fate. Miles was in fifth grade at that point, and she had come to school to pick him up. I happened to be chaperoning the parent pick-up loop, and I could tell she'd been crying when I helped Miles into her car. I told her to meet me that evening so we could talk, and she took me up on it. I had to make her stop crying. I was so desperate to cheer her up.

I still can't believe the reason why that asshole broke up with her. What an absolute piece of shit. Honestly, she is lucky to be rid of him. She had told me, "Jimmy said he can't stand to be around Miles anymore. He said he can't stand his meltdowns and how needy he is all the time." She sniffled more, patted her eyes with a tissue, and continued, "He said it's like I'm not even there for him because I'm always with my son. Who says that, Brody? How did I not know he could be so cruel? It's not like I hid the fact that I was a single mom. And he knew Miles just got diagnosed with Autism. Why did I trust someone like that? He said he would be there for me through it all, but he lied. He fucking lied."

We had sat down on the beach, and I held her while she cried. I think I almost broke a crown that night as I was gritting my teeth so hard. I just wanted to kiss her and make her smile. To take away her pain and tell her I'd take care of her and Miles and never let her hurt again. But that's not what she needed. She's way too independent, and she might have thought I was taking advantage of her when she was vulnerable. So, I did what I could. I was her friend.

Although I couldn't save her or fix anything, I was able to be there for her and gave her someone to talk to. I never tried to give solutions or minimize her feelings by telling her that she shouldn't be upset or to calm down. Fuck that. That's where men go wrong. They always think they need to fix a woman's problems. Nope. My mom taught me something very important about women. They just want you to listen to them and love them. That's the secret to supporting a woman through a challenge. Just listen and be there.

Cindy fucking hated how much time Cara spent with me back then, but I didn't care. I knew at that time that Cindy and I were on the decline, and the fact that she wouldn't let me comfort a friend was further proof that she wasn't the girl for me. I thought Cindy knew that I was a natural-born caregiver. And Cindy didn't need care and comfort at that time — Cara did. Cara always came first.

Cindy should have seen the writing on the wall at that point. By the time she and I were through for the last time, Cara and I had become really good friends. Cara had told me multiple times how she was done with men and wouldn't ever let herself be hurt like that again. She started what she called a *man-fast*, where she just gave up on men completely. The only man that would be in her heart was Miles. So, that pretty much told me what kind of shot I had with her.

So, now we are friends, and I have her in my life. I get to see her sometimes, and we text back and forth. I see Miles at school and help him out when I can. It's the best that I can do, and it will have to be enough. I'd rather have this than nothing at all. Even a little bit of Cara is better than a whole lot of another woman.

Fuck.

That woman.

I wish things were different, and we met under different circumstances.

She drives me insane with need. Some days I feel like if I can't have her, I might as well move to the frozen Himalayan Mountains of Tibet and become a Sherpa or some shit. Live somewhere where it's so freezing cold that I no longer have any feeling in my body.

Damn. I can't stand to even listen to myself anymore. Waxing poetically about Cara like she isn't ten minutes down the road. I could see her right now if I ever decided to man up and make a move. She is single now. I'm single now. I'm so close to her, I could probably make her break her man-fast rule... but I don't think she sees me like that anymore. I've just been too damn long in the cursed friend zone.

I check my phone for the thirteenth time since coming home and see she hasn't texted me since our chat today at lunch time.

So, I drift off to sleep in my king-size bed all alone, snuggle up to a pillow, and try not to cry like a ten-year-old girl over her unrequited love. I really need to stop this shit, or I'm gonna lose my man card.

If Hudson knew how lonely I got at night and where my thoughts took me, he'd never let me live it down, and he'd be sending beach bunnies to my door every night. *Ugh. That thought makes me queasy.* Maybe Huds is right, and I am a little punk bitch.

Like he says, this is definitely not stoked.
Not stoked at all.

Chapter Four

BINGO!

Cara

"Unsubscribe," I say as I start typing.

"No, Cara. It doesn't work that way," Cort tells me.

"Okay, then, how about this? Unfollow."

Cort sighs heavily. "Cara, listen, you can't do that. That is an invite to a staff meeting. You have to go so get off your ass and suffer like the rest of us."

"You're mean. When did you get to be so mean?" I click out of my e-mail and grab my water bottle before following him to the meeting. The stupid, pointless staff meeting that probably could just be an e-mail.

"I will sit near you, so Peter doesn't try anything, okay?"

"Thank you. You are really too good to me, little brother. I'm supposed to be the one looking out for you, ya know."

He throws his head back and laughs mockingly. "That's hilarious, Cara. You haven't looked out for me since we were kids. You know I'm more like your big brother, who just happens to be younger."

"And louder," I counter in an attempt to shut him up.

We leave the building and make our way over to the Riseman Fitness and Recreation Center. It's a beautiful new facility on campus that houses the fitness center, cycling room, and a classroom often used for meetings. That's our destination.

As we head through the lobby, I have to slap Cort in the arm about sixty-two times because he keeps staring at the young college girls in their teeny tiny workout clothes.

Slap. That makes sixty-three times.

"Hey, knock it off. We just talked about this the other day. You said I could look as long as I don't touch."

"Yeah, well just don't do it when you are near me."

"I'm almost always near you. If I followed that decree, I'd never be able to look at all these fine asses. Ouch! Hey, stop it." I slapped him firmly on the chest this time.

"Don't objectify women like that! Didn't Grammy Ellie teach you anything?"

"Well, when it comes to women, I guess I follow Grandpa's advice more."

"No!" I protest. "That is the absolute worst idea I've ever heard. Don't ever treat women the way he treats them. Don't you remember when he pulled down Grammy's skirt at their 50th anniversary party?"

"Yeah, that was hilarious, but it still scarred me just the same."

"It was not funny. She was humiliated even though she played it off like it was just another of his pranks. He is such an ass."

Secretly, I found it really funny too. But I can't let Cort think that it's all right to treat women like that. It's not. Even for the sake of good comedy.

We make our way into the conference room, and I look around and cringe. Ugh. Why does he always have to look so creepy at me? Peter Peters gives me chills and not the good kind.

Cort leads me to a seat on the far side of the room, where we can hopefully stay out of Peter's line of vision. As soon as we sit, the damn pumpkin-eater gets up and moves closer to us. Great. Talk about not being able to take a hint. At least he isn't right next to me. I told him I was saving that seat for Mandy.

I wasn't, but I sure as hell am now.

Mandy comes in to save the day. I wave her over and remind her that I was saving her a seat, just like she asked me to. She nods unconvincingly, but since I'm near Cort, she sits down immediately and flashes us both a huge grin. Cort winks at her. Fucking flirt.

She notices that Peter is on the other side of her and turns to me so he is behind her and can't see her face and rolls her eyes in his direction and then makes a gagging motion by pointing her finger in her mouth. Cort and I both bust out laughing, and Peter doesn't like that one bit. Although he couldn't see what she was doing, I have a feeling he knows. Surely he must know how much everyone despises him.

Of course, he knows. And don't call me Shirley. Ha ha. My inner voices crack me up sometimes.

"Okay, if I can have everyone's attention," our department head calls out from the front of the room where he is holding a clicker thing in his hand and standing in front of a PowerPoint. *Boy, this is groundbreaking stuff right here.* "Thanks for taking time out of your busy schedule to join us today. We have a very busy agenda and will get started right away."

He continues lecturing, but I'm suddenly distracted when Mandy opens up her folder and slyly hands me and Cort a piece of paper. I look down, and it takes all of my strength to not laugh. *Fuck, this is why I love this girl!* She fits in perfectly with Cort and I. I bite the inside of my cheek to keep from embarrassing myself with one of my very loud laughs. I close my eyes to take three deep breaths before I attempt to look back up where Mr. Marsh is starting to talk about our mission statement — the same way he starts every meeting. It's so annoying.

After I compose myself, I look back down to the paper Mandy gave me, and I shake my head again. I grab my pencil and make a mark through the square that says, "mission statement" on the *Meeting Buzzwords Bingo Game* that she printed out for us. I swear, when her internship ends, I'm going to make sure they hire her permanently. If she goes, so do I.

A few agenda items into the meeting, and so far, I've marked off: synergy, teamwork, paradigm shift, and ducks in a row. Hell yes, I'll have bingo in no time. Suddenly, I tense up when I hear my name called.

Oh, shit. Am I busted playing buzzword bingo?

Thank Heavens to Murgatroyd. It seems they are calling my name for a different purpose.

I'm asked to stand and approach the front. Mr. Marsh has a big smile on his face, so I'm clearly not in trouble. But Peter Peters, douche extraordinaire, is standing by Mr. Marsh. I don't know why, but I have a bad feeling about this. As I get up there, Peter directs me to stand near him. Gag.

I do as I'm told. He moves behind me and puts both hands on my shoulders as he begins talking. Gross. This is so gross. I need to clean my shoulders with borax and peroxide as soon as I get home.

"As many of you know, Ms. Amos here has been working in the Athletic Department for many years. She has helped hundreds of student athletes and has, by far, the best patient feedback reviews of all her peers."

Cort makes a whistling sound while he claps, obnoxiously. I give him a death glare, and he stops, looks around, and realizes he is the only one clapping. Mandy was just about to start clapping, I could tell. She probably didn't want Cort to feel awkward being the only one clapping. That girl is so gone.

Peter continues, "As you may not know, we haven't had a designated Lead Trainer position in our department for quite some time. A few years before I came to the team, that position was cut from the budget and deemed unnecessary at the time. Well, I disagree with that assessment, and Mr. Marsh agreed with my reasoning. In addition, our department is growing and expanding. We foresee a large number of new hires coming through our unit over the next few months. So, we are pleased to announce that Ms. Amos will become the new Lead Trainer for the rehabilitation and physical therapy team."

This time, others in the room clap for me in a show of appreciation, and Cort is able to do so without sticking out like a big fat sore thumb.

My cheeks feel warm, and I must be blushing something fierce. This is so awesome but also a tad bit uncomfortable. I don't really want to be standing up here in front of the whole department. But more importantly, I'm probably missing out on several words on my bingo sheet.

I guess I should be proud of myself. I have been doing this job for a long time, and aside from my occasional tardiness, I'm the model employee. However, this assumes you don't count playing buzzword bingo as a strike against me.

Although I applied for the management position that Peter got a year ago, I never really wanted that position. Too much paperwork and not enough time with the patients. I really just wanted the extra money that would have come with the position. Plus, I knew I could do the job. Maybe that is why I didn't get it. Perhaps they could tell that it wasn't really the right fit for me. This is a much better opportunity, and I'm sure I'll be very happy in this role. Now, I can still work with the patients and help them heal, while also getting recognized for my efforts. I'm pretty much the designated trainer anyway, so I might as well get a title and pay raise to go with it.

After Peter continues on about this new position, he taps me on the back a few times. His hand stays there just long enough to be uncomfortable before he gives my arm a slight squeeze and then points toward my seat as if he is dismissing me to sit down. I can't get away from him fast enough.

He took what should have been a great moment for me and made it creepy. Just like always. And yet again, he didn't really cross any line. He is too sly for that. Nasty ass creeper.

I sit back down, try to push those feelings aside, and get back to my bingo game. I mean, get back to listening to the meeting.

A few hours later, the workday is finished. I'm walking out to the car, and I decide to text Brody and my family the good news. We always like to celebrate the victories in our family. So, I open up our group text chain and send out a message.

Me: Guess what everyone, I have big news!

Millie: You're pregnant again?

CJ: You finally recorded an album and will be going on tour to sing your heart out?

Chloe: You finally kicked your perverted boss in the junk?

G'ma Ellie: Did you get my hemorrhoid cream?

Cara: No, No, Not yet, and gross, Gram — don't remind me. No, guys — listen up. I got a promotion at work today. I'm going to be the new Lead Trainer!!!

Brody: <gif of a monkey wearing a party hat and blowing on a noise maker>

Cort: <pic of hemorrhoid cream tube>

G'ma Ellie: That's wonderful news, darling. I'm so proud of you. I'll make you a special dinner tonight to celebrate.

Cort: <gif of SpongeBob and Patrick running around waving their hands in the air in panic>

Chloe: What a nice treat, Grammy. That sounds perfect, Cara will love that.

Cara: I know where you live, Chloe.

CJ: You are all talk, no action, Cara. Grammy, you should make her your special pizza.

Cort: NO!

Chloe: No, even I know that's going too far, CJ.

Millie: Yes. Do it, Grams!

Cara: NO! Please. Gram, that is not necessary. I already have plans tonight, anyway.

Brody: That's right, she does. I'm taking her out to dinner. It's been planned for a while.

It has? Well, that's news to me. When did we decide that? I flip over from the text chain to my calendar, and nope, nothing there with Brody. I guess maybe he is trying to save me from the killer pizza. How sweet. I can play along. Whatever gets me out of Grammy's cooking. My phone chimes again with another text.

G'ma Ellie: Ok, then. I can cook for you another time, dear. Your grandfather and I will watch Miles tonight so you can go have some fun. Enjoy your Friday evening for a change instead of hanging around here. Just don't forget to stop at the store for that cream on the way home.

Cara: Got it. Thanks so much, Grammy.

CJ: Good job, Cara. Proud of you little sis!

Millie: Yeah, me too. Congrats!!

Chloe: <gif of Will Ferrell from Elf yelling: *Congratulations! You did it!*>

Brody: See you tonight, Carina. Can't wait to celebrate with you.

As I approach my car, I'm trying to figure out what I will do with my free night. I haven't had time to myself in so long, I don't know what to do with myself. I have a change of clothes in the car, so technically I don't have to go home to change. Helen is out of town for a few more days, so I can't go hang out with her. Brody was probably just saying that for the benefit of the text chain. My hero! Ha. I wish. I'm sure he has other plans.

I decide to change before I leave campus, and then I'll head to the beach and walk around for a little while before it gets dark. After, I'll grab a slice of pizza and a drink before heading home. That will be nice. I have my kindle with me, so I can do some reading and enjoy the peace and quiet of a nice evening. And then I'll get the hemorrhoid cream. Yeah, sounds like a great night to me.

I rush back inside and change into jean shorts and one of my favorite T-shirts. This one is bright purple and it says: *This Mamacita Needs a Margarita!*

Mmm... margaritas. Yeah, that sounds better than pizza and beer. Well, I'll decide when I get there.

I'm brushing my hair out after taking the ponytail out, and all of a sudden, my phone rings. *What? Why is someone calling me? What year is it? Why would they call when they can text? What is this madness?*

I look down at my watch and see that it is Brody. Well, maybe he is calling to let me down gently about the joke of our going out tonight. Instead of sending him to voicemail, I figure I owe him one since he saved me from intestinal distress, and I answer.

"So, where do you want to go to celebrate your promotion, beautiful?"

Beautiful? Well, that's nice. And unusual. Brody is always sweet, but he usually speaks like a big brother and doesn't get too mushy. I definitely could get used to being called beautiful by him. *Le sigh.*

"Oh, you were serious about that?"

"Hell yes, I was serious. It started out as an idea to save you from death by salsa pizza, but then I started to think it was actually a great idea. We should celebrate your big news."

"Oh, that's really sweet Brody. I appreciate that. I guess we can go somewhere. I was figuring that since I have a free night, I would just go to the beach, take a walk, and then grab something to eat by the pier."

"That sounds like a hell of an idea. It's a beautiful night, so I'll join you. I'm almost done at the gym and can be home to get showered and be ready in about a half-hour. Will that work for you?"

"Yes, that works. I am still on campus, but I brought a change of clothes so I can head in that direction now. I won't need to stop by my house. Should we meet at your place?"

"Sounds perfect. See you soon. Drive safe, Carina."

"You too. Bye."

Swoon. I love it when he calls me Carina. I usually hate it when people use my full name, but when he says it in his deep voice, my toes start to curl. *Oy vey!*

Chapter Five

Is this a date?

Cara

The traffic was a bit terrible tonight, so it took me about forty-five minutes to get to Brody's instead of the usual half-hour. The backup to get off the Courtney Campbell Causeway was atrocious. That's what happens at rush hour on a Friday night, though. It could have been much worse.

I pull up to his place, park, and head up to the door. My belly has butterflies the size of elephants banging around in there. *Why am I nervous? It's just Brody.* Sure, he is the hottest man on planet Earth, but I've been around him a lot. Just not usually alone. Usually, Miles is with us when we are together, come to think of it. Or he comes by the house for something, and the whole family is there. He has joined us for our bimonthly family dinners a few times. But alone? Just the two of us? This feels a lot like a date. I better not make this weird.

Stay cool, Cara. You've got this. Just Brody. Your friend. No big deal.

I ring the doorbell and wait patiently.

Brody opens the door, and my heart plummets to the floor and then springs back up again at full speed like it is on the Tower of Terror ride at Disney or something.

Wow. He looks amazing. And I can smell him from here, and oh my! *Yummy.* What is that scent he is wearing? Fresh from the shower, all clean, manly, and sexy. From here on out, this smell shall be known as *eau de sex on a stick*.

"Heh hah... hey, hey, Brody," I stutter.

That was very smooth.

"Are you always this articulate?" he teases me. I've used that dig on him before, so I guess turnabout is fair play.

"It's just been a long day, sorry. And the traffic was insane."

"Yeah, that's why I live so close to where I work." He points to his temple with his index finger and taps it twice.

"Well, I would do that too, but the last time I checked, the Academy you work at doesn't have a dire need for a sports rehabilitation therapist. So, I have to trudge across the bridge into Tampa each day. It's my cross to bear."

He motions me inside. "Do you want to come in for a minute? I'm almost ready."

"Sure." I head in, and he closes the door behind me. Now, I'm standing awkwardly in his entryway, looking around, and it dawns on me that something is different than the last time I was here.

"Did you change something? It seems different."

"Yeah, actually. My mother came over and thought it was too much of a bachelor pad, so she brought in the lamps and hung the pictures on the wall. It helps, don't you think?"

"It sure does. It feels more homey now. Except, it doesn't feel like home to me because there aren't loud old people, dozens of cats running around, and no one is having a meltdown about getting killed by a creeper in Minecraft."

He chuckles, and there are those dimples. *Damn*. One on each cheek. I want to stick my tongue in them.

He offers me something to drink, but I decline. He excuses himself and runs to his bedroom. A minute later, he comes back with his shoes on, jiggling his keys, and announces that he is ready to roll.

We get outside, and I suddenly realize that we probably need to ride together. Now I am wondering if I should bring that up or not. Maybe he wants to ride by himself so he can split when he gets bored of me. He probably has a date or something lined up for later.

That thought sours my stomach. I'm saved from having to broach the topic when he says, "I'll drive us, if that is okay?"

"Yeah, that works, assuming you don't have to rush off anywhere."

"Why would I have to do that?" he asks as he raises his handsome eyebrow and looks at me like I've lost my marbles.

"Oh, I don't know. I just figured it is a Friday night, and you might have a date or something later."

I'm one hundred percent sure he can tell I'm hunting for information, but he plays it off well so as not to make me feel bad.

"Absolutely I have a date. With you. Now, get in." He smiles and opens the passenger door for me. *Such a gentleman.*

"Oh, yeah sure. Someone like you would have a date with little old me. That's believable." I chuckle, and he just shakes his head at me as he closes the door.

I'm not trying to fish for a compliment, but I genuinely don't see how someone as stunning as him would ever go out with someone as plain as me. I might have fiery hair, which men have told me before they like, but I'm no model. I have some curves, and I'm a mom. I work out, but my body is less than perfect. Why would he waste his time with me?

Plus, I also made that comment because I kind of want to make sure he doesn't think this is a real date. So, his response might give me an idea of where his head is.

He walks around the front of the car and slides into the driver's seat. I try not to stare at his thighs as his cargo shorts ride up a tiny bit when he gets comfortable. *Fuck, that's hot.* He has the best legs. And arms. And shoulders. And neck. Well, every last inch of him is perfect. Let's just assume that unless I say otherwise, everything about him is complete male perfection.

Because I want him to respond about the date thing, he doesn't. Because that is just my luck. Instead, he puts on the radio and asks if the station is okay with me.

"Sure, I love all types of music — you know that."

"That's just one of the things I adore about you, Carina."

My thighs are now clenching together on their own volition. Now that I'm in this tiny space with him, I can feel the heat coming off his arms. He is so close, he might as well be inside me. *Wait, that came out wrong. Actually... no, that's what I meant. I'm going to stick with it. Brody might as well get inside me.*

The smell of him is everywhere, and it's intoxicating. I probably won't need any margaritas tonight at this rate, and I'll still be tipsy as hell.

We make our way through the streets of Clearwater, and I start humming along to the radio. It's Billie Eilish's *Everything I Wanted*, and man, that is a bop. It's a bit slow for my happy mood, but I still love it. In fact, I loved Billie's music before she even made it big. I feel like I was one of her first fans. I love finding new music that has a unique sound. I knew from the moment I heard her that she would be huge, and damn if I wasn't right. I give myself a figurative pat on the back.

"You know, you've really got an amazing voice," Brody rumbles from my left, and I realize that I am singing out loud now and not humming.

Normally, I don't sing in the car when others are with me. Alone in the car? Oh, hell yeah, it's like Showtime at the Apollo. I'll go full bore, and I don't care what people in the passing cars think about it. But I try not to force my voice on others when they don't have a path to escape. However, I just feel the need to sing tonight. I can't help it! I'm super happy right now.

"Oh, thanks. Sorry, I didn't realize I was singing," I say shyly, wringing my hands in my lap.

"Did you ever record anything? If so, I'd gladly accept a copy as a gift. That way, I can listen to you whenever I want, at least when you can't give me a live performance. I could listen to you sing all day long."

"What? No. No way. I'm not that good." My head shakes furiously back and forth like that's the most ludicrous idea I've ever heard.

"Well, if I recall, one of your sisters said something about it in a text today, and I've heard them mention other things like that before. Why do you think you're not good enough? Apparently, everyone else thinks you are."

"I don't know. I guess my focus has always been elsewhere. I love music and absolutely adore singing. But a recording career or being a star isn't the life path for me. I like my privacy, time with Miles, and my simple little life. And even if I didn't become a star, being a single mom and caretaker for the gray hairs doesn't lend itself to singing gigs late at night in bars and clubs."

"Fair enough. You could still do music recreationally, though. Maybe join a chorus or something? Like one of those glee clubs?"

"Glee clubs? Are you serious? You are showing your age, Brody. Glee clubs aren't a thing anymore."

"Okay, okay. I'm an old man. I get it," he laughs along with me.

I like the sound of his laugh. His voice is deep but not super deep. It's the perfect tenor voice, and when he laughs, it gets a little deeper. Such a sexy laugh. I never thought laughs could be considered sexy before. But this is Brody we are talking about, aka: "Mr. Hottie." So, yeah... he has a sexy AF laugh.

"I'm an old lady too, now. So, don't feel so bad."

"Remind me how old you are; I know you're a few years younger than me."

"I just turned thirty-eight this summer."

"Why didn't we celebrate your birthday?"

At this, I start chuckling, and it suddenly turns into a full out laugh.

"Hell, no. Are you crazy? Women do not want to celebrate birthdays past the age of thirty-five. No way, Jose. Thanks, but no thanks."

"Maybe we can celebrate an unbirthday then?"

"An unbirthday?" I ask and turn my head to see if he is serious.

"Yeah, I mean it worked for Alice in Wonderland. Maybe we can celebrate unbirthdays in the real world. We can still celebrate you without you having to get older. Seems perfect to me."

"That's sweet, White Rabbit, but I don't need to be celebrated. I'm not anyone important. It's not like I have the cure for cancer."

"Balderdash, Cara. What are you going on about? You are definitely someone to be celebrated. Don't you dare put yourself down like that." He is speaking really passionately all of a sudden, and he is getting further fired up the more he speaks.

"You help people heal every day. You make it your mission to ease their pain and get them back to the point where they can do something they love again. That is no easy task and not everyone can do it. Plus, if you got a promotion, you are obviously doing it really well. And don't get me started on everything you do for your family. You're a damn hero, woman. Shit, people should throw you a parade each year."

I sit there, speechless. I really don't have any words.

After a few seconds, I break the tension by asking him, "Did you just say balderdash?"

We both start laughing until I have to wipe tears from my eyes, and before I know it, we arrive at the beach. I hold special memories of this place. I like to think of it as *our place*. It's where he held me for the first time when he comforted me when Jimmy ripped out my heart and stomped on it. *Asshole*.

He looks over at me, boops me on the nose with his finger, and tells me, "Wait right there."

He gets out and runs around the car to my side to open the door for me. I get out and shake my head at him, pull back a little, and look at him funny. "Are you okay tonight?" I ask him, my eyebrows raised up to my hairline.

He smiles, and his stupid adorable dimples pop again, and he says, "Yeah, I'm great. Why do you ask?"

"Well, you are being all gentlemanly with the door opening and stuff. It's not like this is a real date. You were just kidding, right?"

I can't help but ask. Part of me is hoping he says something to indicate that it can be a date if we want it to be. The other part of me is terrified that if he wants that it could ruin everything we have.

He looks at my face, and I can see him thinking through his response. After a moment, he shakes his head as if to clear his thoughts and just says, "Sorry if I'm making you uncomfortable. It's just my mom taught me to always treat a lady with respect and kindness. I know you are all about equality and women's rights, so if you want me to stop, just say so."

I can't help it, but I raise my hand and place my palm on his chest firmly and… damn, what a chest it is. Does he have a bulletproof vest under that button-down shirt? Is he smuggling stone in there or what? Jesus, Joseph, and Mary. My hand has officially touched a bit of heaven. I'll never wash it again.

I look up at him and genuinely reply, "No. I'm not uncomfortable with it at all. It just seems different than how we normally are, that's all. I like it when you're a gentleman. It's sweet."

He smiles, looking a bit bashful and heads over to the trunk to pull out a beach blanket. Together, we start walking toward the beach.

This feels so perfect and so right. I wish I knew if he felt the same way I did. And I wish I had the guts to ask him. I just don't want to lose this perfect friendship. If I ask him and he doesn't feel the same, things will get really awkward. Or worse, if he does feel the same — then what? We try to date, or maybe he would just want to be friends with benefits? I could never do that with him, no way in hell. I'd fall for him so quickly my heart would be smashed. And then when it ends, we won't have our friendship anymore. I can't let that happen. He is too important to Miles... and to me.

After walking on the beach for a while, he asks me to tell him about my promotion, and we chat some more. After a while, he unfolds the blanket, we sit down, and watch the sun start to set. The perks of living on the west coast of Florida.

He is such a good listener. Why does he have to be so perfect? When I'm done telling him how it all went down at the meeting, he faces me, puts his hand on my arm, and gently turns me toward him. He suddenly looks concerned, and I'm wondering if I said something that upset him. I don't think I did.

"I'm going to ask you something, Cara, and I want you to be honest with me."

"Okay, of course. What?" I'm really starting to be alarmed by how serious he is now.

"I've noticed that when you mention your boss, your demeanor changes. And today, Chloe said something in the text about you kicking your perverted boss in the nads. Is something going on with him?"

Wow. Okay. I didn't expect that.

"First of all, she said, *'junk'* not nads. Chloe would never say nads, she doesn't know what that means. I'm pretty sure she is training to be a nun. I'm going to start calling her Sister Mary Annoying," I clarify and try to inject a bit of humor. Because serious talks make me uncomfortable, and humor cures all that ails you.

"Fine. Junk. What is going on with this guy?" he asks again, pressing me back to the topic.

I squirm a little, and my eyes can't seem to meet his. I don't like confrontation, and I don't like how my boss makes me feel. I'm not sure why, but I don't want Brody to see me like this... like a victim or someone who is too weak to stand up to her shithead boss.

"It's not a big deal, Brody. He just makes me feel a little uncomfortable at times. It's nothing to worry about."

"Uncomfortable, like how?" he asks.

I rage sigh for a moment before I speak. Yes, rage sighing is a thing, and I've mastered it.

"I just don't like the looks he gives me, and some of the things he says could be interpreted a bit... slimily."

"Cara, I don't think that is a word. Do you mean he is slimy, like a reptile?"

"Brody, you are a teacher for God's sake, you should know that reptiles are scaly, not slimy. Amphibians are slimy. And my boss. He is also slimy," I say with a smile because I find myself hilarious, even in uncomfortable situations. Hell, especially in uncomfortable situations.

He laughs because apparently, he also finds me hilarious.

He puts his arm around my shoulder, and we turn back toward the sunset before he continues, "Slimy, scaly, or otherwise — do you want me to do anything? I feel like going there and breaking his face or ripping off his nads and shoving them down his throat."

"Wow. That escalated quickly, *Mr. Hale*. Teachers should not be breaking faces, and I won't even address the other thing you said." I stress his last name to remind him that he is a teacher, and they do not behave like that. Even super mega buff ones like him. "Violence is wrong, my good man."

"Well, I just don't like the idea of some creep making you feel uncomfortable at work. Or anywhere, actually."

"Don't worry about it. Cort is there with me almost all the time, he only works a slightly earlier shift. Plus, I try not to be alone with Peter Peters Pumpkin-Eater. Such a stupid name." I shake my head with a subject change attempt. "Speaking of uncomfortable at work, how is it working with Cindy?"

"Oh, don't remind me. I try not to go in the office at all unless it's absolutely necessary. I don't know why I thought it was a good idea to date someone I work with."

"Yeah, that was pretty stupid. At least Jimmy and Miles's dad, Chaz, don't work at UT. That would be terrible. I can't imagine having to see my ex all the time."

"I don't see her all the time. And it's been a while now, and I'm pretty sure she has moved on. I sure have." He looks over at me and smiles.

Hmm. Okaaaaaay. Was that smile supposed to mean something to me? I feel like we are back in the awkward date or no-date territory again. Shit. Getting whiplash here. I can't help but prod him a little though. *I'm a shit disturber, what can I say?*

"Have you moved on, Brody? Really? I haven't seen you date anyone in a while?"

"I'm saving myself for the right girl. And speak for yourself, red. Are you still man-fasting?"

"Of course, I am. Nothing has changed. I'm still a mom to a special boy and caregiver for aging grandparents, so why would I date? It is not the most appetizing of offerings."

"Maybe you just were dating the wrong guys."

"Clearly, I was dating the wrong guys. That is the most truthful thing I've ever heard anyone say, ever."

He laughs, and we get up, fold up the blanket together, and make our way back to the car where we drop off the blanket. Taking my hand, he leads me across the street to where the bars and restaurants are.

At first, I thought it was just a gentlemanly thing like helping an old lady cross the road. But when we get to the other side of the road, he doesn't drop my hand. And now, we are walking down the sidewalk, and he is still holding my hand.

And I think I've died and gone to heaven.

Right here in Clearwater Beach. Well, they do say this is one of the best beaches in the country. That's because of Brody Hale, I guess.

Mr. Hottie. The guy holding my hand.

Chapter Six

I blame the tequila

Brody

"Is this okay?" I ask her.

"No, it's a terrible choice. I hate it. What's wrong with you?" she responds with a big grin on her face.

This woman right here. She is so cute.

She points to her shirt and then to the sign on the window that reads, "2 for 1 margaritas every Friday night 7 p.m. until close."

"I should have known. Come on in then, *Mamacita*." I open the door for her and follow her inside.

After the hostess seats us, we stare at the menu for a moment, and I wonder for the hundredth time just what the hell am I doing tonight. This is not a date. Is it? Why am I acting like it is a date? It's just friends going out for a celebratory dinner. I need to stop making it weird before I screw up the best friendship I've ever had — sorry, Hudson.

Why did I hold her hand? And why did I love it so much? And damn she smells so amazing.

When we were in the car together, I thought my heart was gonna pound right out of my chest. And then she sang. Fuck. That was beautiful. Like an angel. She is so perfect. By the time we got to the beach, I just felt like it was a date and sort of went with it.

Then, when she called me out on it when I opened her car door, I thought I really fucked up. My heart sank. It was enough to cool me off for a while and remember that I'm her friend, and that's all I'll ever be. But when she brought up that fuckwad at work, I sort of snapped. I can't stand the thought of some jerk face trying to put the moves on her. I make a mental note to talk to Cort about that the next time I see him.

We place our orders with the waitress, and after she goes away, I try to think about how to play it from here on out tonight. I just hope I can get through this night and still have my friend. I don't want to lose her. With this in mind, I bring up a safer topic.

"So, how is Miles liking his teachers this year? He doesn't tell me much about them."

"Oh, no? Really, my Miles?" She puts her palm on her chest right where I wish my hand was. "He doesn't talk about stuff like that with you? Shocking! I never would have guessed. He is usually so verbose about his feelings," she answers sarcastically, and I can't help but laugh at her.

"I know, I know. He doesn't open up very easily. I just thought maybe you've gotten more out of him about it than I have."

"No chance, man. Every time I ask about school or bring it up in any way, he gets that look on his face. It breaks my heart, so I don't push him to answer me. I just can't keep pushing him to like school. It's just not going to happen. He hasn't had a single good day since he was in your class."

That both breaks my heart and makes it swell with pride. I love that little guy. He is so sweet but so misunderstood.

"That can't be true. It's been a few years. He should have had at least five good days since then. Maybe even six."

She laughs at my attempt at humor, and we talk about Miles for a little bit longer before our food arrives. The rest of the meal goes by pleasantly, and I can't remember having this much fun. It was never this way with Cindy or anyone else I've dated. I just feel so comfortable with her. I love her sarcasm, and when she smiles, it's like an arrow straight to my heart. *Pow!*

After we eat, she has another margarita, and I pass since I'm driving. We sit and talk some more, and after a while, she starts yawning. I look down at my watch and shit, it's already 10:30 p.m. It's true that time flies when you are having fun. And this was a really fun night. And painful. Definitely going to have a serious case of blue balls. Totally worth it though.

She fights me over the bill, but I remind her that it was a celebration of her promotion, and I wouldn't feel right letting her pay. She acquiesces but says she'll pay next time, and I really like the sound of that. I'd like to make this a regular thing. Shit, really regular. Like every night regular. And bring Miles too, sometimes. And then I'd like to end the night in between her creamy thighs.

I drive her home since she doesn't feel like she should drive tonight. She ended up having four margaritas, but she got funnier and louder the more she drank. It was kind of adorable. Her laugh is captivating.

I drop her off, and as she gets out, I hand her a small bag from CVS. She looks at it questioningly but doesn't open it up and sarcastically says, "But I didn't get you anything."

Laughing, I tell her it was something I knew she needed. She shrugs and gets out, taking the bag with her. I tell her I'll come get her in the morning and bring her to get her car. I love that we live so close where that isn't a big problem. I couldn't stand it if something happened to her.

I really dig how responsible she is. She never takes her safety for granted, that's for sure. Except with this asshole at work. For some reason, she doesn't think he will escalate his behaviors. I hope she is right. He better not lay a finger on her. I meant it when I said I'd break his face. I'm not one for fighting since I'm usually pretty even-keeled. But nobody better mess with my girl. Yeah, my girl — that's right. Whether it's romantic or not, she is still my Carina.

As I drive home, I reflect on how amazing this night was. It makes me want more, so much more. I have to remember to keep my heart in check, though. She is my friend. Just a friend. Maybe the more I say it, the more I'll believe it.

I can't help but smile because since she left her car at my place, I'll get to see her in the morning, even if it is just for a few minutes. When it comes to Carina, I'll take anything I can get. I'm like a dog looking for scraps. And I don't even feel bad about it.

No hangover, no problems

Saturday morning arrives, and I head to the gym bright and early with an extra pep in my step. I woke up at the crack-ass of dawn after a very refreshing sleep, which was nice for a change. I'm fairly certain it's because I get to see a certain redhead today.

I rush through my workout without running into Hudson. No surprise there since this is his big beach weekend. I'm sure he is having a hell of a time, but I just think back on how awesome my weekend is going, and it makes me chuckle. Can you imagine if I had said yes to his invitation? I would have missed the most amazing night with the prettiest girl in the County, if not the entire Sunshine State.

While I'm working out, I get a text, and I stop in the middle of my deadlifts to check it. *It's her.* A huge smile crosses my face. I couldn't have stopped it if I tried.

Cara: Hey there, stranger. What time do you need me to get my car? If you are too busy, I can have Cort drop me off.

Brody: Good morning, sunshine. How did you sleep?

Cara: Good. No hangover, surprisingly. Got lucky, I guess.

Cara: No, wait. I didn't get lucky. Pretend I didn't say that.

Cara: <gif of Homer Simpson backing slowly into the shrubs>

Brody: I was about to ask how you got lucky if I didn't since I was with you all night. I was wondering if you roofied me and then took advantage of me.

Cara: LOL. Nope, just me putting my foot in my mouth, like always.

Brody: That's classic Cara.

Brody: I'll come get you. I'm at the gym now but should be done in about a half-hour. Any time after that works for me. Don't bother Cort.

Cara: Are you sure? I don't want to put you out.

Brody: Will you stop already? It's like 7 miles away. It's not a big deal. Just tell me when you want me there.

Cara: Okay, I'll talk to Miles and make our plan for the day and get back to you. Thanks again. <smile emoji>

Brody: <gif of Maui from Moana singing *You're Welcome*>

Cara: Dork.

Cara: Oh, I don't know how to say this and still sound cool, so I'll just go for it and put it right out there. Thanks for the hemorrhoid cream. That's the nicest gift I've ever received.

Brody: <gif of Alice in Wonderland curtsying>

Cara: Again, you are a dork. But thanks. You're a cool dork.

Brody: I had to run into the drug store anyway, and I saw on the texts that Grammy Ellie really needed that stuff. So, since you got drunk and neglected your granddaughterly duties, I figured I'd save the day. It's nothing. Just what I do. Local, neighborhood hero stuff.

Cara: <gif of Cameron saying, *Ferris Bueller, you're my hero.*>

Cara: I was NOT drunk. Just intoxicated. There is a difference.

Cara: Wait a minute. You didn't stop at CVS on the way home from the Cantina, so how did you know I was gonna get drunk and forget the cream?

Brody: Umm. This is awkward. I didn't want to tell you this, but I'm psychic. It's time you knew.

Cara: Hysterical. Seriously, how did you know?

Brody: I didn't know you were gonna get drunk. I just figured you might not have time and since I was there, I grabbed it for you.

Cara: That is really sweet, Brody. You are very thoughtful. Thank you.

Brody: My pleasure, Carina. I've got your six.

Cara: Oh, I didn't know you were in the military. When did this happen?

Brody: LOL. Actually, I did four years right after high-school in the Army. Did I never mention that?

Cara: NO! How did I not know this?

Brody: What can I say, I'm a man of many secrets.

Cara: Ha ha. All right, I gotta run. Back with you once I have a plan.

Back at home, I get out of the shower, get dressed, and make myself breakfast. I sit down to eat, and my phone rings. There is only one person who actually calls me, so I answer without looking, "Hello, Mother."

"Hi Brody. How is my baby boy today?"

"I don't know, I haven't seen him. No baby here, just a grown-ass man."

"Very funny. How are you?"

"I'm great actually. Had a nice dinner with a friend last night and got in an early workout this morning. Got some reading to do today for work, but I'm in a great mood. How about you? What are you up to?"

I love my mom sincerely. She has the biggest heart of anyone. But sometimes, these calls can be exhausting. She never remarried after Dad split, and I'm all she has. So, she still calls more than she should, and her unexpected visits can be too frequent at times.

She lives in Orlando, and that ninety-minute drive isn't enough to stop her from coming by whenever she feels like it. But I love her and would never turn her away. I know she is lonely and needs me. After all she has done for me, it's the least I can do. Plus, I'm in such a great mood, I couldn't be frustrated with her no matter how hard I tried.

"I'm doing well. I am going with Maggie today to go shopping at the outlets. But I want to hear more about this dinner you went on last night. Who is your friend? Anyone I know?"

Oh boy, here we go. She could probably sense that it wasn't Hudson or a work colleague from the tone of my voice or something. I won't be able to lie to her, so I'll just come out with it. No sense in trying to dodge her questions, she knows me too well.

"It was Cara. You remember her? I taught her son a few years ago. The boy that ended up having autism."

"Oh yes, Cara. I remember you telling me about her and her son, Murphy was it?"

"No, it's Miles. He is in seventh grade now. But I still get to see him at the Academy a few times each week. He's my little buddy."

"That's right, Miles. You're very fond of him, aren't you? You've talked about him before quite often."

"Yeah, of course, I'm fond of him. He's a great kid. He just had a hard time in school for a while, and he needed some extra attention from me when he was my student. So, I ended up bonding with him a bit."

"And remind me... his mother didn't know he was autistic, right?"

"Yeah, she had no idea. She knew he was different, and she was struggling with him big time. But she never thought it was autism. She just didn't know anyone on the spectrum before. So, when I asked her about it, it was a big deal for her. But now he is getting the therapy he needs, and things are better at home for them, thankfully. He just still struggles at school, though. I wish I could do something to help, but that is a hard age."

"And this Cara, what kind of *friend* is she now?" She stresses the word friend implying exactly what I knew was coming. Here we go.

"She is just a friend, Mom. I respect her and like her a lot and like her son too. I wouldn't do anything to mess that up."

"Maybe she needs a little messing up. If I remember correctly from the one time I saw her at your fortieth birthday party, she was quite beautiful."

"I guess, yeah, she is pretty."

"You aren't fooling me, Brody. Who do you think you are talking to? I saw how you looked at her that day. It was only a few minutes, but it doesn't take long for a mother to figure things out. I know my baby, and you had heart eyes for her."

"Mom, she is just a friend. I promise you. And I'm a tough guy so I don't get heart eyes. Now, tell me about the outlet shopping. Which one are you going to?"

I couldn't care less about which outlet mall she is going to. But I have to get her on a new topic, or I'll end up spilling it all and gushing about how I'm practically in love with the woman and have been since I first laid eyes on her. She'll just encourage me to go for it, and that's the opposite of what I need. If anything, I need someone to remind me not to go for it. I need someone to hold me back.

Thankfully, she takes the bait and tells me about her plans for the day. Soon enough, we say our goodbyes, and I load my dishes in the dishwasher and check the phone. Still no response from Cara. Now, I'm getting antsy. She said she would let me know when she needs me to come get her. I need to chill.

With nothing else to do, I decide to take this free time to do some reading of those new textbooks. So far, I'm not all that impressed. I like the ones we are using now better. But I'm still trying to keep an open mind.

Before I know it, two hours have passed, and my eyes are crossed and burning. My phone chimes, alerting me to a new text message, so I slam the book closed like I'm killing a fly in it.

Cara: Ok, Miles wants to go to the zoo. So, we are ready whenever you are.

Brody: I can come now.

Cara: Cool. Fair warning, though. The whole crew is here.

Brody: Consider me warned.

Walking up the sidewalk to Cara's front door, I can hear loud voices coming from inside. She did say the whole crew was here, are they having a party or something? I ring the bell and wait.

A moment later, Miles opens the door and gets a huge smile on his face when he sees me. "Hi, Mr. Hale. You're here!" He turns back to the room behind him while he reaches forward to open the screen door for me. "Mom, he's here!" he bellows. But it's so loud in there I'd be surprised if anyone heard him.

I walk in and try to take in the scene before me, but it's like too much is happening at once, and I'm not sure where to look first. Miles grabs my hand and pulls me farther in the house, toward the living room. He is totally chill about this chaos — like it happens all the time.

It's a nice house, good neighborhood, and classic Florida style. Lots of big windows overlooking the huge trees all around the house. It's a mix of palm trees and oak trees. Maybe a magnolia or two. The house is a bit older, but it's really spacious and has a killer backyard with a huge pool and screened in patio. It's such a great place for weekend BBQs and family gatherings. Every time I'm here, I get a bit of a strange feeling inside that I can't pinpoint. I know it has something to do with a longing... longing for something. Maybe family. I'm not sure.

I am an only child, and growing up, it was just me and my mom after Dad peaced out. The asshole. If I ever see him again, it will be too soon.

But I digress. I was sometimes lonely as a kid. I always wanted a big family. Some of our neighbors and kids at school came from big families like this, and it always was so appealing. That's probably why I've always wanted a big family of my own. We always want what others have.

Miles gets my attention again when he points across the room. There's Cara. She looks beautiful. And she is flipping out a little bit.

Awww, that's cute. She is even pretty when she is losing her shit.

"All right, fine! He can stay, but I mean it, Grammy, this is the last stray cat to come into this house. *The last!*" she raises her voice at the end of her rant.

"Cara, don't talk to your grandmother like that," rattles off the old curmudgeon in the corner. That's Richard, but they call him Dickie.

"Oh, I'm sorry," Cara retorts sarcastically. "Did I say something to offend her? It's not like I brought in yet another mouth to feed or anything. That would be a problem. Oh wait, no — that's what *she* did. So, since I'm the one that feeds the cats, takes them to the vet, and cleans up everything, I figure I've earned the right to raise my voice when she brings in another one!"

Cara is pissed. And it's kind of hot. I feel a twitch in my trousers and shuffle my feet to adjust myself without anyone noticing.

Grammy Ellie chimes in, trying to defuse the situation. "I will help feed him and take care of them. You don't have to do everything."

"That's sweet, but the last time you fed the cats, you gave them a bowl full of Temptations treats instead of kibble. I was cleaning up vomit for three days after that."

"Well, maybe I can do something else to help make things easier. Let me think on that some."

"No, Grammy, it's fine. I was just shocked to see yet another cat here that I didn't recognize. How many is this now? Eight? Nine?"

"Oh, no. Don't be silly, honey. It's twelve," Grammy Ellie responds in as completely serious a voice as possible. Like she didn't just say there are twelve cats in this house now. That's like ten more than two. Where does she find them all anyway?

"I get to name it!" Miles yells.

"Fine, Miles. You can name it. But later... when we get back home from the zoo." She pivots her head to look at the crazy old cat lady before continuing, "And you... this better be the last life you bring in this house, or you will be forced to give up another life in exchange. Yours or Grandpa's — you pick."

Grammy Ellie rolls her eyes so hard I'm pretty sure she can see what is happening out in the backyard.

With this issue seemingly settled, my attention shifts to the other side of the room where the living area blends into the kitchen. There, a sea of redheads are screaming at each other but don't look the least bit upset. It's an odd situation. Why are they yelling and smiling at the same time? Is it a genetic condition?

Well, one isn't smiling. The tall one, whom I recognize as Chloe, is talking... err... yelling now and she looks terrified. "Because if God wanted us to fly, he'd have given us wings!"

She just said that. Like it was a totally normal argument to make. What in the hell are they even arguing about?

CJ yells back, "It's just a short flight, Chloe. Calm the hell down!"

Chloe rears back up, "No. I will drive. You will just have to plan it at a later time so I can get there."

Cort is now involved and steps in between the ladies, who look like they are about to tear each other's red hair out. Speaking of which, how did Cort manage to not have red hair? His is more brownish-blond. Interesting. *Maybe he is the mailman's baby.*

"Chloe, think for a second. Do you really think they are going to push back their wedding by half a day or more, so you can drive? Plus, CJ isn't even in charge of that, so stop yelling at her. She's not even the one getting married!"

"I know that, but I really don't want to fly, and now I feel like I'm going crazy over it! Forget it. I'm not going!!"

Millie seems to have had enough at this point and joins the fray while waving around what appears to be a wedding invitation, apparently the impetus for this particular... err... discussion. "Listen, bitch, it's not about you. It's our cousin's wedding, and we are all gonna go. Calm your tits. Soothe your boobs. It's happening, so deal with it. And for the love of Pete, stop yelling at CJ, she is just the messenger. Don't shoot her! If you really need to drive so badly, then you'll need to take the day prior off so you can leave early enough to make it on time. But personally, I think that is really dumb. You should just suck it up and fly to Virginia with the rest of us on the evening before the wedding. You'd only need to get out of work like maybe a half-day early, and that will be a Friday, so what's the big deal?"

"I can't get the day off or leave early. My team has a huge project that will be ready for implementation that week. I can't just rearrange an entire product launch to please our cousin."

"I'm just going to pretend you didn't say that and tell you this one more time. It's not about *you*! It's not your wedding, and we don't have control over when and where it is held. We have to go. It's going to be held mid-morning on a Saturday in February, and that is that!"

"It's like a twelve or thirteen-hour drive. I can't make it in time after working all week on that product launch. I won't be able to drive all night long, and even if I did, I would look terrible for all the pictures the next day."

Millie looks around and shakes her head, jabs Cort on the shoulder with her index finger, and says, "This is all you, man. I'm out. Calm that twat down before I throw her out the window." She walks away.

Cort smiles and replies over his shoulder to his departing sister, "You could never pick her up. You're half her size."

He reminds me so much of Cara. He's the king of sarcasm to her queen.

Behind me, I can still hear the grandparents trying to convince Cara that twelve cats is not too many, and I see Miles is setting up dozens of green army men in various positions all around the living room, on practically every flat surface, and now he is yelling something about Kit Kats. What the hell? Does he want chocolate? It's not even lunchtime. What is going on in this madhouse? No wonder Cara has an unhealthy obsession with margaritas.

Shouting resumes in the kitchen, and I can't help but listen. This is better than TV, by far. These people are insane, and it's so entertaining. But I can tell they love each other. It's a weird phenomenon to witness. I'd never believe it if I didn't see it. It's like they communicate their love through sarcasm, yelling, and busting each other's balls. I wonder what "love language" that is? Must be the sixth one they haven't studied yet.

"I understand that you are scared to fly, Chloe. Believe me, I get it. I have my own irrational fears."

"It's not irrational. It's a perfectly rational fear," Chloe defends herself.

CJ continues, "Okay... I have my own rational fears. Is that better? Good." She nods and continues, "Maybe we can just give you a sleeping pill once we get onboard, and you'll knock right out, then we'll wake you up when we get there."

"No, I've seen that movie and read that book. It never ends well."

"Well, I don't know what else to tell you. I'm out of ideas. I'm willing to knock you out and drag you through the airport in my carry-on, but you'll never fit. You're too damn tall."

Chloe can't take it anymore, leaves the kitchen, and runs upstairs. CJ and Cort look at each other, shrug their shoulders, and burst out laughing. They tried. I'll give them that much.

Cara sneaks up behind me, touches me on the shoulder, and I jump a little. But I play it off because I'm cool like that.

She giggles at my reaction and says, "Hey, welcome to hell! Did you take a number on your way in so you are sure to get a ride on the Carousel of Chaos?"

"No, I didn't see the number dispenser." I chuckle, and she grins. Dammit, there goes my heart thumping like a flipping bass drum again.

"I'm sorry you had to witness our pandemonium, but I can't hide it anymore. I surrender. This is the real me, Brody. It's time you find out where I come from. I completely understand if you don't want to be my friend anymore," she jokes.

Friends? Ugh.

Thanks for the reminder, gorgeous.

Inwardly cringing, I tell her, "Well, I was going to bounce when she said there were twelve cats here, but then I thought about it, and it's kind of nice that she wants to save them all."

"Okay, get out! We don't need your crazy here. We're all full up on that!" She playfully tries to shove me toward the door. Of course, she can't get me to move. What is she, like 130 pounds soaking wet, if that?

Just then Miles barges over, interrupts our flirting, and says, "Mr. Hale, are you coming to the zoo with us?" with such a big smile on his face, my chest tightens a bit.

I look up to Cara, and her beautiful brown eyes are wide in surprise, and she seems to be just waiting for my reply. I can't quite tell if she wants me to say yes or no, so I just answer truthfully.

"Miles, I would love to go with you guys to the zoo, but I don't want to take you away from spending time with your mom."

"I don't want to just be with her, anyways," he answers with zero remorse and in complete seriousness.

"His brutal honesty is pretty heartwarming, isn't it?" Cara looks at me with a smile hidden behind her eyes. Then she says, "We'd love to have you join us, if you don't have plans. But if you are busy, we totally understand. Right, Miles?" She looks pointedly at him and widens her eyes, trying to encourage him to use some manners. It's pointless, but it's cute that she thinks he is gonna understand her nonverbal cues.

"It's just the zoo, Mom. It's not that far away. He can come with us, and then go do whatever he wants after that."

Like I said, no understanding of social cues whatsoever. I just love the honesty that spews from his mouth and can't help but chuckle. I try to hide it but fail miserably.

Cara raises one perfectly sculpted eyebrow at me and tilts her head to the side like a puppy does when you speak to them in a high-pitched voice. "Find something funny, big guy?" she asks coyly.

"No, ma'am. Nothing funny at all. This is the most normal and non-funny place I've ever been," I answer while nodding my head up and down trying to sell my bullshit.

"All right, Miles, put your shoes on, let's get out of this insane asylum."

"What's an asylum?"

"It's an institution that houses crazy people, bud," she deadpans.

"Well, that fits this place, that's for sure," Miles says as he heads up to get his shoes, I presume.

Cara looks back at me, and we both laugh.

It takes all my strength not to grab her and press my lips to hers. She is so beautiful and perfect.

"Aliza, put donuts on the list." I hear shouted over my shoulder. I turn to see the old man is up and moving around and shouting at the counter. Oh, it's an Amazon Alexa. Did he just call it Aliza?

"Oh, please — let's get out of here right away before he starts flirting with her. It's so awkward. I don't want to have nightmares."

"What are you talking about?" I ask, genuinely curious.

"He thinks it's a real lady in that little device, I think. He talks to her like she is human, and I have caught him flirting more than once. I overheard him ask if she was single. Another time, he said he would like to take her out on the town and asked if she could swing dance."

"I can't tell if you are joking or not, but it's hilarious either way."

"Totally serious this time, buddy. That man is a perve. He makes Peter Peters look like a saint." She looks up at me again, raises both shoulders up towards her ears, and says, "Kidding. No one could do that."

She giggles as she goes off to grab her purse and say goodbye to the family. While she does that, I pull Cort aside for a minute.

"Hey, man, how are you doing? Haven't seen you in a while. You must be hitting the weights pretty hard. You are getting really buff. Well, buff*er*."

"Thanks, dude. Yeah, I love working out," I lie. I don't love it. I need it and can't live without it. There's a difference, but I'd rather not explain. "Listen, before Cara comes back, I want to ask you something."

"What's up?" Cort asks.

"What is going on with your boss at work? Cara implied that he makes her uncomfortable. He doesn't touch her, does he? How bad is it?"

Cort chuckles a minute with a knowing look in his eye, then grows serious. "Oh, it's not awful, but I don't like it, that's for sure. He doesn't really touch her — nothing that is outright inappropriate. He just toes the line. He is a habitual line stepper."

"I'm sure you've got her covered there, but could you maybe let me know if you need any backup or if there is anything I can do to get him to back off without wrecking her career?"

"That's the million-dollar question right there. What can we do to get him to cut the shit without it backfiring on Cara? I don't have the answer to that question. For my part, I keep a close eye on her whenever he is around and try not to let him get her alone. For now, that's all I think we can do."

"Okay. Keep me posted if anything changes. I've seen this stuff before, and it always tends to escalate. She doesn't need that shit. She has enough to deal with."

"Oh, look at you all concerned and shit. One might think that she is more than a friend to you, the way you seem to be so worried about this."

"Cort, you know it's not like that. She is like a sister to me," I lie through my teeth. "I just care about her and wouldn't want to see her in trouble."

"Sure, sure. Totally believable, man." He taps me on my shoulder and starts to walk away. As he goes, he turns around and throws over his shoulder, "I'll let you know if anything changes. And you let me know if you need any help making things change for *your* situation."

Help? He wants to help me get with his sister? That's an interesting development if I'm understanding him correctly. Nah, I'm probably just imagining that. I turn to find Cara and Miles and say my goodbyes to the Amos crew.

After we are loaded up in the car, I ask her if she wants to get her car first or after. We decide to just get it later and head to Lowry Park to go see some animals.

As we pull out of the driveway, Miles yells, "I finally have a cat that I can name Kit Kat!" He laughs at his joke like it's the funniest thing since Abbott and Costello did *Who's on First*.

So, that explains what I overheard earlier. Glad to know he isn't having candy at all hours of the day. Not sure why I care so much about that, but I do.

This is turning out to be the best weekend I can remember.

Chapter Seven

From the texts of Cara and Mr. Hottie

Mr. Hottie: Good morning, beautiful.

Mr. Hottie: <gif of the Lion King sunrise>

Mr. Hottie: Also, Miles left Harry in the back seat of my car.

Cara: He did? Sorry! I'm surprised he isn't freaking out about it already. Dodged a bullet there.

Mr. Hottie: I can bring it by after school today, or you can come and get it whenever. I figured he wouldn't want me to bring him a stuffed animal at school. Probably not cool. Dare I say it might be too cool for school? #teacherhumor <emoji with sunglasses>

Cara: Please no, don't bring it to school! You know him so well, it's scary. If other seventh graders knew he still slept with stuffies, I don't think I could handle the nuclear fallout.

Cara: <gif of atomic bomb dropping>

Cara: BTW, he told me it's spelled "Hairy" not Harry. Please make note of this. It was super important, so he told me about 78 times since you bought it for him. That was really sweet, by the way.

Mr. Hottie: Sweet? Are you sure? I think it was more gallant than sweet.

Cara: My eyes are rolling so hard right now. Oops, they just popped out of my head.

Mr. Hottie: That must hurt. You should watch that. Oh, wait... you can't WATCH anything without your eyes!! #IGotJokes

Mr. Hottie: <gif of Simon Cowell giving a thumbs up>

Cara: <pic of a stop sign>

Cara: I allowed the first hashtag. The second one is immediate grounds for homicide. Any last words?

Mr. Hottie: Is this an execution, or can I defend myself?

Cara: Interesting choice of last words. <shrugging emoji>

Mr. Hottie: All right, I need to work soon. The early kids are arriving in class. Do you want me to bring "HAIRY" over tonight or what?

Cara: Yes, please, kind sir. I shall be forever grateful for your sacrifice.

Cara: We will all be home any time after 6:30 p.m. If you want to stay for dinner, let me know. I think Millie and Cort are coming over tonight. So, we'll have dinner and a show!

Mr. Hottie: It's a date. And since we will have entertainment, I'll bring the stuffie and the popcorn.

Cara: Thanks again, see you tonight. P.S. There are kids that come to school early? WHY? I don't understand this concept.

Mr. Hottie: LOL. I'm not surprised by that. Not one bit.

Mr. Hottie: Looking forward to seeing you later for our date. Have a good day.

Cara: ...

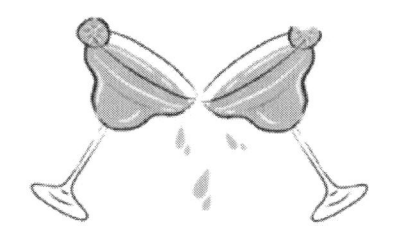

Chapter Eight

Do you carry Neal's sperm?

Cara

"Hey, Grammy Ellie, Brody is probably going to be here for dinner tonight. He has to bring something over for Miles, so I told him he could stay if he wants to. Just a heads-up."

So, I guess this is happening. Yet again. Is it a date? Is he just kidding with all the date jokes? And more importantly, can I stick my tongue down his throat at the end of the evening, or would that be weird?

I'm not sure what has changed with Brody lately, but I'm not hating it. In fact, I'm pretty much here for it. I just wish he would be a bit more clear so I could get rid of all this uncertainty. Maybe he is waiting for me to give him a signal? But do I really want to take a chance and risk losing him? And would I have the balls to pull off?

Hmm... now there is an idea. Pulling... balls. Yeah, there is something there that might make my feelings for him pretty clear. Or... no, that's not an appropriate dinner time activity. Shit, what am I going to do?

Where's the Tylenol?

"That's great, Cara darling. I'm so glad to hear that you are seeing him so much. Miles just adores him."

"I know he does. Speaking of which," I pivot my head towards the staircase and bellow, "Miles, school starts in like seven minutes. If we leave now, you might make it before the late bell."

"Perhaps if you woke him up earlier, dear?"

"It's funny that you think that A. that might work. And B. that I haven't tried it already."

"Maybe your grandfather could help motivate him in the morning?"

"How would he do that? By misunderstanding him into compliance? By annoying him until he *Naruto runs* out the door? Actually, wait... that might work."

"He isn't that bad, Cara. I don't know why you are always saying such things."

"Have you met your husband?" I ask her incredulously, with my eyes wide and eyebrows at my hairline.

"I have more thoughts about this topic, but here comes your son. So, off you go. We'll talk more about this later."

"Can't wait." Said with a heaping spoonful of sarcasm and a pointed look at this crazy coot.

Miles and I hustle out to the car, load up, and take off like a bat out of hell. A *cautious* and *safe* bat, of course. And said bat is maybe not leaving hell, per se. Just the outer realm of hell.

All things considered, this was a pretty great morning. No voices were raised in anger. We had time to eat breakfast and get dressed fully, including shoes. And we only had to go through three pairs of socks before Miles found ones that weren't bothering his toes too much. All in all, a complete success.

Plus, texting here and there with Mr. Hottie while I was getting ready really helped my mood exponentially. I didn't even get frustrated when I had to ask Grandpa Dickhead, I mean Dickie, what he meant when he put *Evita's Cheese* on the Alexa shopping list. Apparently, it was Velveeta Cheese for those of you keeping score at home.

That's almost as funny as that time he put *Neal's sperm* on the list. I looked everywhere around Target, but they were fresh out of that shit. It actually turned out to be *Neosporin*. Never saw that one coming.

"Mommy, why are you laughing? I didn't say anything funny."

"Sorry, buddy. I'll go back to frowning and scowling if that would please you."

"Mom!"

"Lighten up, I was just thinking about some of the crazy stuff your great-grandfather puts on the shopping list. His hearing is so bad that now his speech is starting to be unintelligible. Apparently, he can't hear the words he spews into existence."

Miles laughs, and he says, "That reminds me of when he told me that Tony Shark was on TV. He meant Ironman, Tony Stark."

Together we laugh, and it feels so good to have a pleasant morning with my son and my family. What is this madness? Surely I haven't woken up, and this is a dream.

We pull up to the school, and I see other cars and kids for a change. Hooray! We made it *basically* on time. Victory!

I wish Miles well and head off to work, hoping my Monday continues to improve. This should be a great week. Dinner tonight with a plus one, and my best friend Helen comes home this week. Well, best *female* friend, I suppose. *Super psyched!*

• ♥ • ♥ • ♥ • ♥ • ♥ •

Pumpkin-eaters are the worst!

It's another gorgeous fall day at the UT Campus. I arrive at work perfectly on time, and Mandy's jaw drops to the floor when I walk in carrying a latte for her. She looks at her watch, looks at me, looks back at her watch. Then, she scrubs her eyes, leans her head closer to me, and pokes my arm to make sure I'm real.

"Oh, stop. I'm not always late! Calm down, Meryl Streep. Don't get all overdramatic on me."

"Okay, let's just go with your version of the truth then." She winks as she smiles and tells me quietly, "Did you see who is on your schedule today?"

"I may have taken a peek, but why don't you tell me just to make sure we are having the same thought."

Truth time. I haven't seen my schedule yet. My morning is going well, but I'm not automatically super organized and on top of my shit. I'm still three fries short of a happy meal.

"It happens to be the one and only Mark Beckett."

"No way! And he is on my schedule?"

"Well, of course. The coach called and said to give him to our best rehab specialist and of course, that is you, Ms. Lead Trainer."

"I didn't know that I was getting bonus perks like this in addition to the new title and raise?" I add, "I don't care how young he is; that man is super fine. My ovaries are probably going to spontaneously ovulate out all my remaining eggs. Good thing I've already had a child. I'll be eggless by the end of the day."

"You know you aren't right, *right*?" We laugh, and I head off to the back to drop my stuff and grab my laptop.

In checking my schedule, it does appear that Mr. Beckett, superstar pitcher for the Tampa Spartans, will be my last patient of the day. It would seem his ridiculously buff pitching arm is causing some trouble, and they want some help with his elbow. He will probably need lots of massage time on those corded muscles. *What a shame.*

I guess I can do it, if I must. It's for the good of the college and the team. The sacrifices I have to make in the name of dedication to health and wellness. I sigh dramatically and shake my head as I chuckle at my internal antics.

If my boss knew what was going on inside my head most of the time, I'm pretty sure I'd be thrown out of here faster than a hooker approaching a Lamborghini to see if the driver is looking for a good time.

The day goes by in a blur, but I'm not complaining one bit. I've got my earbuds in a good portion of the day, and I'm singing along to my favorite upbeat playlist between patients while I update my charts and plot out my care plans.

Things are going great, so I really should have known that it was too good to be true. Time to take a bite out of the shit sandwich of life.

I'm in the ice room, which is currently empty of patients, sitting atop one of the therapy tables working away with my laptop on my lap, where it should be.

Since my earbuds are in, I don't hear him approach until I smell him, and then I feel him. My stomach sours, and I suddenly feel a deep-rooted sense of panic. I turn and jump off the table, and my laptop spills off my lap onto the floor.

Right behind me is Peter Peters, the head creep around these parts. And the look on his face is positively disgusting. He looks like a predator, and clearly, I'm his prey at the moment. I'm not sure what part of his body was pressed up against my backside, and I really don't want to know.

"Sorry if I frightened you," he says in a voice that can only be described as a mix between a weasel and snake.

He is full-on leering at me. His eyes shift down to my chest, and I take a look down to see what he is looking at. Just my breasts, apparently. I'm a full C cup, so it's not like I can hide them. I'm in the standard Athletic Department polo shirt. It's not like I'm in a corset, hoisting the girls up for his viewing pleasure.

I cross my arms across my chest defensively and ask him, "Yeah, you did scare me. Did you need something?"

He makes a sound from deep in his chest that resembles a chuckle, but it comes across as threatening. "Oh yes, Ms. Amos, I do need something from you."

He stares straight at my eyes as if challenging me to break eye contact first. No problem, buddy. I can't stand looking at him. He gives me the worst case of the willies ever.

"Well, are you going to tell me what you need or stand here staring at me somewhat inappropriately?"

He takes two steps toward me, working his way around the table. I realize that he is between me and the door, and I don't like it one bit. At this point, I'm wishing that Cort was my twin, so that I could send him some kind of freaky psychic twin message to come and save me. But he's just my regular brother, and that is probably not a real thing, anyway.

The ice room is in the back of the building, past the offices, but it's not *that* far away from the main training room. So, I know if I scream, someone will hear me. Plus, I'm 5'7" and have done a shitload of cardio kickboxing over the years, so I'm not helpless. I know where the weak spots are on his body — eyes, throat, and groin. And I know the hardest part on my body is my elbow. So, a quick jab to the eye, an elbow to the throat, and a knee to the groin, and I can get past him.

Right now, though, he isn't outright threatening me, so I just wait and try to think about what I can say as an excuse for a quick departure from this room. That way, I won't end up with an arrest for assault and battery.

Can I fake getting my period all of a sudden? Do creepy guys buy that shit?

The pumpkin-eater pervert continues leering at me as he takes yet another step in my direction. I take one step backward and bump against the table behind me. Shit. I'm stuck now.

"I was just wondering if you have spent any time thinking about how you can thank me for recommending you for that promotion? That was all my doing."

"How about I say, 'thank you for promoting me based on my merits and qualifications?' I can do that right now, if you like. Thanks for promoting me based on my merits and qualifications." My first method of self-defense has always been sarcasm and humor, so doing it now comes naturally. It's always worked to defuse situations before, and if it ain't broke, don't fix it, right?

"Let me see, that certainly is a nice start, but I've got some other ideas how you can show your *appreciation*." He takes another step closer, and I see out of my peripheral vision that his right hand is approaching his belt buckle and sliding a bit lower.

Oh. My. God. Is he going to start touching himself or expose himself? Right here in the ice room in the middle of the damn day, for Heaven's sake. Is he crazy? No way. That is enough, I don't have to take this crap. This ends now.

"Well, the heartfelt thank you is all I'm willing to offer. So, if you'll excuse me, I have a patient to see now." I quickly grab my laptop and try to brush past him. I make a little bit of progress since I don't think he expected me to bolt so quickly. Unfortunately, though, he recovers in time to grab my arm as I start moving past him.

He pulls me back firmly and leans his face toward my right ear and whispers menacingly, "I don't like being teased, Ms. Amos. Please consider your next moves carefully. I'm not a man you want as your enemy."

I yank my arm back, give him a death glare, and then storm out.

He doesn't follow from what I can tell. Although, I can't really hear much of anything because of the blood rushing through my ears. I make my way around the corner and slam right into a solid wall of muscle. It's Cort. Thank God.

I bury my head in his chest, let out a huge gush of breath, and feel relieved I've made it to a safe place. He grabs both my upper arms and bends down in an attempt to see my face. "Hey, are you okay? What's wrong?"

After looking at my face, Cort's disposition has gone from *happy-go-lucky* to *who do I need to kill* in 2.5 seconds. Got to love the protective alpha-types in situations like these.

"Pumpkin-Eater... Gross... ice room... belt buckle... touched me." I start rambling in what I think is a whisper, but I've never been the quiet type. So, Cort cuts me off once he hears what I'm implying and yanks me down the hall toward an empty treatment room where he closes the door.

"I've got you. Take a breath. You are safe. Just breathe for a minute. Don't try to talk until your heart rate slows down a bit," he says in a voice so calm it's actually a little scary.

Who knew my little brother could be the calm one under pressure? I sure didn't see that coming. I expected him to be more like Lucille Ball, freaking out, yelling, and laughing hysterically when shit hits the fan.

After an unknown amount of time with Cort hugging me and guiding me through deep breaths, I am about to start talking when we hear a soft knock on the door. He looks at me and pushes me behind the door, so he can see who it is without anyone seeing me. Smart thinking, little bro.

"Hey Cort, have you seen Cara? Her next appointment is here, and I can't find her."

It's Mandy. Sweet, kind, friendly, and innocent Mandy. Thank goodness. I don't know why I thought it might be Peter coming back after me for another lesson in *How to Sexually Harass your Employees,* as taught by the Creepiest Creep in Creepsville.

Cort looks over at me, and his eyes ask me how he should respond.

"It's fine, Cort. I can go out in a second." I stick my head around the door and look at Mandy. Her face pales when she sees me as if she can tell something was very wrong. But I continue, "Tell him or her, I'll be out in about five minutes and apologize on my behalf. Just tell them I had something urgent come up I had to take care of. I don't care. Make something up if needed."

"Sure, Cara. No problem — I'll do that. But are you okay? Can I do anything else for you?"

Bless her sweet little heart. And I mean that genuinely, not in that catty southern way where they really mean they hate you and want you to self-combust on the spot lest they have to spend another moment in your pathetic presence.

"I'll be fine sweetie. No worries." I put on what I hope is a comforting smile. Mandy nods and turns to go. Cort closes the door and faces me. "Are you sure you don't want to go home?"

"*No!*" I yell suddenly. "I can't do that. He'll know that he upset me and think he won."

"Shit, Cara, this isn't a competition. Now, quickly tell me what happened before you put on your brave face and go rush back to work. Do I need to go kick his ass? What did that fucker do?"

I give Cort a quick rundown, and the more I talk, the redder his face gets and tighter his jaw clenches. When I'm done talking, I take his right hand in mine and tell him calmly, "I'm fine. I'll handle it once I figure out what to do. Now, please unclench your fist before you break your hand."

He realizes he was about to cause himself permanent damage due to the force of the fist he was making and stops. He nods his head about seven or eight times in quick succession before he says, "Okay, sis. I'll take a chill pill for now. But I don't want you on your own at all in this place until we get it handled."

"Fine. I guess I'll just ask you to come hold my hand while I go to the bathroom or to refill my water bottle in the break room. Oh, and are you gonna work the extra hour and a half between our shift ending times each day?"

"Take this seriously, please. I don't trust this guy one bit."

"Okay, I need to go now. I promise I'm okay and will certainly be extra careful. We can talk later. You're still coming to dinner, right?"

"Absolutely. We will talk. I have to leave in a little bit to get Miles, though. I'd rather stay with you and follow you home. Maybe I can call Millie or CJ to pick him up for me today."

"No, don't worry about it."

"Well, sorry. I love you, you're my sister and closest friend, Cara. And I'm really frucking worried about it."

"Did you just say frucking?"

He sighs and smiles a little bit. "Yes, Miles has been on my ass about swearing lately, and so I've been testing out new curses. It just sort of slipped out."

That breaks the tension for us. We laugh, and I tell him to head on out. Before we get to the main training area, we see Peter walking across the room, thankfully in the other direction. A chill creeps up my spine. Now that I realize Cort is leaving, I sort of want him to stay.

I grab him by the arm really quick to hold him back and say, "Cort, I just thought of something. Brody is coming over for dinner tonight. Maybe I can ask him to grab Miles at school and bring him home with him so you could stay with me. Just for today, until the end of my shift. This doesn't need to be an everyday thing. I'm sure I'll feel better about the pumpkin-eater by tomorrow."

I'm not sure what is going on right now, but Cort gets the biggest damn smile I've ever seen on his face. Now he is nodding his head slowly and says, "Brody is coming over, huh? Didn't you spend an awful lot of time with him this weekend already? Can't get enough of each other, huh?"

Taken back by the fact that he noticed, and he seems to have some thoughts on this new development, I try to play it off and fail miserably. "No. Yes. No. I mean, yes, I guess I did spend a lot of time with him, but it's no big deal.

He's just a friend, and we happened to have a few more opportunities to see each other this weekend than normal. That's all."

"Uh huh," Cort says and keeps staring at me, expecting me to continue. Since awkward silence and I are not on speaking terms, I add, "Well, the only reason he is even coming over is because Miles left his stuffed hippo in his car after the zoo on Saturday, and he is bringing it over. Since he was coming at dinnertime, I figured I'd ask him to stay. Like I said, totally not a big deal. Wipe that grin off your face, asshole, before I do it for you."

He chuckles and shrugs and says, "Okay, go text your *just-a-friend* and ask him. If he can get Miles so I don't have to, then I'll stay. I'll hang out with Mandy and keep an eye on you."

"Oh, the hardship!"

We go our separate ways, but the rest of the afternoon, I can always feel Cort watching me. It's comforting, but I wish it wasn't necessary. Such a sad commentary on the state of sexism in this day and age that a woman can't hold a job without being fearful of sexual predators around every corner.

Of course, Brody responds to my SOS text that he would be happy to grab Miles. He also says he will send Miles a note before his last class period so he knows what's up. *Bless him and his fine ass for helping me out all the time.*

I wish I could thank him the way I really want to. With my hands and my mouth on his cock. But alas, that is not meant to be.

The rest of the day goes by without any more sightings or incidents with Douche McGee. Unfortunately, I'm so frazzled I can't even enjoy my special massage time with Mark Beckett, his amazing baseball body, and ridiculous bulgy arm muscles. On the bright side, though, he needs to come back a few more times this week and probably next. So, I'm sure I'll enjoy those other visits more. His range of motion is shit right now, and he really needs some work if he is going to be ready for the spring season.

As Cort walks me to my car at the end of the day, I check my phone and see Brody texted earlier saying that he and Miles were hanging out at his apartment complex doing homework by the fire pit. He included a selfie of the two of them, and they are so stinking cute together.

My heart swells at the sweetness of the scene, yet a wave of guilt comes over me because Miles deserves to have a dad who cares for him like that instead of the sperm donor jackass that he has instead. I don't understand how his father could have just abandoned him. He practically never calls or tries to connect with Miles at all. How could I have actually been in a relationship with someone that horrible and had no idea? I glance back down at the photo once more and feel a pinch in my chest.

Brody's apartment complex has so many beautiful outdoor areas, with the fire pit being one of my favorite comfortable places to lounge, have a chat, read a steamy novel or even just sit and think. Brody seems to go to that spot a lot too, he must like it as much as I do. The fire pit area has big comfy reclining outdoor lounge chairs and padded upright chairs situated all around the stone fire pit. Plus, there are tables and chairs along the perimeter, closer to the sidewalk. The entire area sits up against a small lake with a huge water fountain in the middle providing a gorgeous view. Over the last year, Miles and I have been going over to Brody's more and more, and we love it. It's a nice escape from the chaos of La Casa Amos.

I make my way carefully through the streets of downtown Tampa and eventually get on the Causeway heading toward my two favorite guys, singing along to Ariana Grande's new song. This one's a banger. The tension of the day leaves my body in waves the closer I get to my destination and the loved ones waiting for me.

Chapter Nine

The politics of superheroes

Brody

"Can I see what you've done so far?" I ask Miles as we sit together at the table near the fire pit. It's one of those perfect fall days with the temperature in the mid-seventies and a nice breeze coming from the Gulf.

He looks up at me and studies me carefully before he replies, "Not yet. I want to finish it first."

"Fine, but it doesn't have to be perfect. You know that, right? I'm not going to judge it. I just want to see what you are writing so far."

"You're most definitely going to judge it. You're a teacher, and I'm pretty sure you can't read an essay without judging it with your red pen ready to fly across the page."

"Hey now, mister. I am perfectly capable of checking my need to grade it, thank you very much," I say only a tad indignant. "I just want to see how you are incorporating Marvel Superheroes into an assignment regarding honesty in politics. I am struggling to see the connection."

Miles gets a shit-eating grin on his face and says, "It's too bad you aren't autistic. We have amazing ideas like this all the time. Sucks to be you."

That gets a big gut laugh out of me which causes Miles to crack up.

This kid. He is something else. I'm so dang proud of him and how far he has come since getting diagnosed with autism. It's not even been three years, and he is able to joke about it and focus on all the great aspects of his situation instead of the negative. His mom is really doing a great job with him, not that it surprises me one bit. I knew she would be great once she figured out what it was all about.

As Miles goes back to making superheroes relevant to politics in some way that my poor basic brain can't comprehend, I start to think about how his autism diagnosis came about...

♥ • ♥ • ♥ • ♥ • ♥

November, three years ago

"All right parents, good morning and thanks for volunteering to be a chaperone for our first field trip of the school year. I'm sure your child has been sharing their excitement with you leading up to today's trip because they sure have been sharing the excitement here in the classroom. It's all they have been talking about for weeks now."

The five parent chaperones look back at me with smiles on their faces, probably almost as excited for the trip to the Tampa Aquarium as the kids are. Either that or they are just happy they got to take a day off from their day job to do something decidedly more fun than a typical nine-to-five.

One smile among the group catches my eye more than the others, though. Whenever I saw that Miles's mom wanted to be a chaperone, I both rejoiced and cringed. Happy as hell to be able to see her again and for an entire day, no less. But terrified that it will only make my attraction to her even more troubling than it is already.

Ever since the Open House the week before school started a few months ago, she has been on my mind quite a bit. The image of her big brown eyes looking up at me in embarrassment when she barged in late has been burned into my brain and never fails to bring a grin to my face. And my memory of watching her lips move when she spoke has a bad habit of coming to the front of my mind at the most inopportune times. Like when I lay down to sleep at night or take a shower after a grueling workout or even when I'm grocery shopping for God's sake.

Damn, what is wrong with me? I'm not usually hung up on women like this, and I'm starting to doubt my ability to keep it professional until the end of the school year. I'm dying to ask her out and get to know her better. Sure, I could try to make it like I wanted to meet for a drink and just talk to her about Miles, which I really do need to do. But truthfully, it's because I'm dying to crash my lips to hers and make her mine, inside and out.

I'm ashamed to say that I haven't been able to stop myself from fantasizing about her and envisioning all the ways I could make her scream my name. I wonder if she has any dirty teacher fantasies that I can bring to life for her. I'd be more than happy to oblige. I wonder if she thinks of me when she touches herself like I think of her.

One such fantasy of mine which keeps recurring during my *happy hand time* is of her dressed up in a short plaid skirt, hair in pigtails, and the button shirt that's pulled a little bit too tight across her voluptuous breasts, so much so that they look like they are about to burst out and send buttons flying. I'd grab her by the pigtails and bend her over my desk. Get my ruler out and redden that gorgeous posterior before pulling her panties down and plunging inside her.

The teacher fantasy might be a little played out and cliché, but there is nothing cliché about Carina Amos. That's for damn sure. She is a hundred percent original, and I get a little more obsessed with her after each interaction we have, which happens more often than I interact with other parents. In this case, I haven't orchestrated it that way. I'm starting to wish I didn't have to see her or talk to her so much, but Miles is not doing well, and I think I've figured out why.

It's still early in the school year, and Carina had to come in and talk about Miles's behavior twice already. And we've shared many emails and phone calls in between those meetings. She is extremely concerned about him, and rightly so.

It's touching to see how much she loves him and wants him to succeed but is also willing to put in the effort to help make it happen. You'd think that would be a common thing for all parents. But after being a teacher for a decade and a half, I can tell you that it is not. Some parents blame the school for everything and refuse to take part in their child's education. They think that making sure they get the child to school each day is enough and that we'll just handle everything else. I wish it were that easy, but with the amount of homework we have to send home to meet the rigorous state guidelines and insane standardized testing requirements, it's simply not possible for the school to fully handle everything that is needed. The parent has to be a partner in the process, or the student will suffer.

Excuse me for a moment while I step down off this box of Irish Spring. Sorry for the rant, I tend to get fired up about education.

And I also get fired up about the woman walking up to me right now as we start to load up into the bus along with the other fourth-grade classes.

"Mr. Hale, is there a reason why you put only girls with Miles in our little group?" Carina asks shyly as she approaches. "I was hoping Miles might have a little boy to spend some time with today, so he can work on making friends without the pressure of being in the classroom."

Each chaperone was assigned four kids to be responsible for throughout the day, their child included. Breaking them up into small groups like that helps make sure no one wanders off on their own. And shit. She noticed what I'd done. I was hoping she wouldn't catch it, but nothing gets past those gorgeous eyes.

"Yeah, actually there is a reason." I nod and put on what I hope is a comforting smile.

This conversation is going to be awkward, and I'm not looking forward to it. But after conferring with the school psychologist, it needs to happen soon. I guess she is gonna force my hand, and today will be that day.

I look around. "I need to talk to you about that, actually. But right now isn't the best time with all the kids around. Perhaps you can sit with me on the ride, and we can quietly chat about it?"

"Sure, as long as I'm still close to Miles. He wanted to sit with me too. I guess I'm pretty popular around here." She grins like she is bragging, but I'm pretty sure she is just messing with me.

"Well, it would be best if we talked without Miles around at first. Come to think of it, the bus isn't going to give us enough privacy. I'll find some time today to pull you aside… or worst case scenario, we can talk when we get to school today after the field trip, okay?"

"I guess so. You've got me a little worried, though. Did he do something wrong, something inappropriate?" She whispers that last part, and it occurs to me she probably thinks the gender separation has something to do with sexually inappropriate behavior. Oh shit, I don't want her to be worrying about that all day.

"Gosh, no. Not at all. I don't mean to alarm you. It's nothing bad or inappropriate... in fact, nothing that you need to be worried about now. Just something I've been meaning to bring up to you. When I explain, it will all make sense. Sorry to worry you." I touch her on the arm as I trail off and give a light squeeze, then quickly drop her arm before I end up leaving it there and turning it into an inappropriate caress.

This is the first time we've touched, and I think she realizes it too. Her expression hints at a little shock, and she innocently glances at her arm where my hand just was as if she could still feel my hand there. To be honest, I can still feel her skin on my hand. So soft and silky. Just like I knew it would be. Dammit. That isn't going to help with my unhealthy obsession. Pretty sure that is what this is becoming at this point.

"Okay then. I'll just try not to worry, and we will talk later. Thanks." She nods and walks back to where her son and the three girls are waiting to load up.

Soon enough, we arrive at the aquarium, and I finish going over the rules and explaining a bit more about our plan of attack for the day. We break up into our groups and head off to the first exhibit — which is the wetlands trail, where we will see otters, gators, snakes, and birds.

The fact that the other day after school, Miles quietly asked me if there were otters at the aquarium because those are his favorite has absolutely nothing to do with why I've decided we are going there first. Nope. None whatsoever. I do not have favorites. I love all my students equally. Except Bobby. Bobby is a shit disturber and is causing me to seriously consider making drinking before class a part of my daily routine.

I'd never do that, so quit judging me. I was just kidding. Except the part about Bobby being a shit disturber. That part was totally true.

Once Miles realizes where the class is heading, he grabs his mother's arm and drags her as fast as his little legs can carry him over to the otter habitat.

That kid is really passionate about things he likes. However, the flip side of that coin is that he is equally dispassionate about things he doesn't like. Mainly writing assignments and doing his practice math problems. Anything beyond one or two problems, and he completely shuts down. This is a common behavior with kids like him.

Additionally, his handwriting is really bad, and he doesn't seem to be able to grasp the pencil correctly, no matter how many times I show him. Pretty sure he is struggling with his fine motor skills. This is also common with kids like him. I'm surprised no other teacher has picked up on this before now. He has all the classic symptoms. Especially the way he flaps his hands when we are playing games in class, like Jeopardy and Heads Up Seven Up.

After leaving the otters, we take a walk through the rest of the wetland trails taking in the lush swamp-like scenery while reading the little plaques that explain about each animal. I pause the group here and there and ask them questions to see if they are paying attention. Correct answers are rewarded by me tossing them either a little green army man or a small rubber bouncy ball.

In retrospect, the bouncy balls probably were a bad call since now a third of the class is bouncing them as high as they can. I'm pretty sure that the fish tank housing the snook has about four balls in it. Quickly recovering, I tell the chaperones to hold the balls for the kids, and they can get them back at the end of the day and take them home. There, that's better.

That was a rookie mistake. I blame the cute redhead for distracting me. I was so pumped up to see her today that I made a stupid decision when I hit the dollar store last night for giveaways.

As we leave the wetlands trail, I tell one of the employees about the ball mishaps and apologize. She runs off to have them removed. Now I feel like shit. Oh well. Not going to feel much better when I drop the truth bomb on Carina later.

Two hours later, we have all the kids seated safely inside a dark theater where they are going to be watching a film about conservation. I figure this is as good a time as any to get Carina alone, and so I ask another chaperone to watch her four kids while they are seated and contained in one area. She agrees, and then I ask Carina to join me outside so I can get this over with.

Dread settles like a knot in my stomach. I am not looking forward to this. I only want to make this woman smile, and this will certainly not make her happy.

"I hope you aren't heartbroken about missing the film," I joke with her as we make our way outside to find a picnic table to sit at. We have about twenty-five minutes to talk, and I'm hoping that is enough. It should be.

"Are you kidding me? Did I ever tell you what my sister does for a living?"

"No, I didn't even know you had a sister," I answer honestly.

"Three sisters, actually. And one brother."

My eyes widen. That seems like a pretty large family. But as an only child, anything more than two kids seems huge to me.

"Yeah," she starts and stretches that out before continuing, "My parents were apparently pretty frisky."

I bust out laughing because I was not expecting her to say that. She is always laughing and smiling, that's one thing I've noticed about her. She takes our talks about Miles seriously, of course, but she somehow manages to handle serious topics with a lighthearted nature that I find really attractive.

Of course, she can't just be physically attractive, she has to have a desirable personality too. Just my fucking luck.

"Okay, wasn't expecting that response. But what does your sister do for a living?"

"My sister CJ, she's the one closest to my age, is a marine biologist. So, we've all been thoroughly indoctrinated into the world of conservation and know all about sea life. It's a requirement when you are in her presence to acknowledge verbally at least once per conversation that you understand we all must do better in order to save the planet."

"Wow. First, that might be a tad bit extreme. But second, that might explain why Miles is so into all things aquatic."

"Yeah, she certainly has taught him quite a bit. And he is a sponge and just absorbs it all. It's fascinating how many little details he can remember."

"It's interesting that you mentioned it because that is part of what I want to talk to you about," I say, bringing a more serious tone to the conversation.

"You've noticed how crazy his memory is and think he should join the circus?" she kids, trying to hide her nervousness with a joke.

I smile but keep on topic. Best to just rip the band-aid. Here I go.

"Have you ever had Miles tested to see if he is on the Autism Spectrum?" I blurt out.

She is visually taken aback, her mouth opens slightly while her eyes widen in shock. She did not see this coming at all.

After an uncomfortably long pause, she asks me, "Are you serious?"

"Yes, I think he has high-functioning autism — which used to be called Asperger's Syndrome. He displays a lot of the classic symptoms. No one has ever suggested this to you before?"

"No. No, not at all," she states, and for the first time since I've met her, she is uncharacteristically quiet and completely calm. I can see the wheels turning in her mind, and she is starting to breathe more deeply, her eyes are getting red, and I can see tears pooling. If she starts crying, I'm going to lose my shit, and I won't be able to stop myself from dragging her onto my lap and comforting her. So, I try to ease her concern by adding some of my reasoning and explain what she can do about this. If I inject enough logic, maybe her emotions can settle a bit.

"Carina, it's not necessarily a bad thing. There are many resources out there to help you and Miles through getting diagnosed, and if he is, in fact, on the spectrum, getting the therapy and treatment he will need to have a functioning and happy life, just like everyone else. I know this is shocking to hear, but it's not the end of the world."

Clearly, I've just said the wrong thing.

"The end of the world?" she says, a bit loudly, with a slight quiver in her voice. "Of course, it's not the end of the world. It's just great. It's perfect. Best news I've had all year. Thanks for telling me this. And of course, you have a medical license or perhaps are a psychiatrist or whatever you need to be to diagnose conditions like this, right? Do you do this often? Why are you teaching the fourth grade when you are clearly a medical professional?"

I tell myself that this is just a defense mechanism, and I'm not going to let it bother me. She is trying to find someone to blame. I guess I'm gonna be her target because I'm here and the bearer of bad news.

"Carina, I am not a medical doctor, and no, I don't go around making diagnoses like this all willy-nilly. I'm not even saying for certain that he has autism. I know I'm not qualified to make a diagnosis — you don't need to tell me that. I just suspect he does and think you should have him tested. That's all I'm saying."

I pause for a second and see that her face is softening. My words are clearly sinking in, and she knows I'm not doing this to be mean or mess with her.

I continue, "Look, I've seen dozens of kids come through my classroom through the years that have the same tendencies and struggle the same way that Miles does and 99% of the time, they are on the spectrum or have some other type of sensory disorder or related issues. Although no two kids are the same, there are some consistent symptoms, and Miles definitely seems to exhibit quite a few of them. And I also talked about Miles with the school psychologist, and she agrees."

"I'm sorry for snapping like that. I don't know what came over me." She bows her head down and takes a deep breath, gathering her composure before continuing, "What types of behaviors or symptoms are you seeing that make you think this?"

"Well, for one thing, he doesn't make friends easily, if at all. Autism is a social disorder first and foremost. He doesn't make much eye contact, and he flaps his hands around when he gets excited about something — like he can't contain the excitement, and it has to come out through his hands." She nods as if she has observed this too. "He tugs at his clothing a lot and wrings his hands often. I've caught him sucking his thumb when he thinks no one is looking. Now he is hiding it behind his arm, but I know he is doing it. Oh, and he also has a tendency to get very frustrated with repetitive practice exercises, like a worksheet of addition and subtraction, for example. He will do one or two problems and then just stop — zone out completely and refuse to continue, no matter the consequence or incentive. When I talk to him about it, he doesn't see the point in continuing to do more problems because he feels like he already knows the answers."

"Yes, I know what you mean. We've had so many arguments and issues about homework because of how repetitive it can be. Homework time at the house is the worst part of the day for us. It's full of tears for both of us. Anything else?"

"When he finds things frustrating or challenging, and if he can't get it perfect right away, he breaks down and completely gives up. I can tell that inside he is about ready to burst. Somehow though, he is managing to keep it inside. If I had to guess, I'd say it is because he doesn't want the other kids to see him totally lose it. I bet if he were at home, or somewhere he felt more comfortable, he would probably have a full meltdown in a similar situation. Does he ever completely flip out and become very loud, aggressive, possibly even violent, and you can't seem to get him to calm down, no matter what you try?"

"Yes, quite often, actually. And sometimes I have no idea what even sets him off. I feel like I'm walking on eggshells around him. It's like a toddler tantrum, but he is way too old for that. And I've seen him sucking his thumb too. We've tried everything to get him to stop. I'm surprised he does it at school, though. He told me he doesn't do it there because the kids would tease him."

"He probably does it for comfort and doesn't realize he is even doing it all the time. It's a self-soothing behavior. It's not a behavior exclusive to autism, but when coupled with everything else..."

"So, what do I do now?" She looks at me, and for a moment, I can tell she feels a little bit lost and hopeless.

She is wringing her hands on the table, and it reminds me of how Miles acts when we talk about tests.

I can't resist anymore, so I take her hands in mine and look into her breathtaking eyes and quietly say, "I know this is overwhelming and shocking, but it's going to be fine. I'll help you through this."

At this she almost looks confused, "You will? Why?"

"I am not totally sure, but I feel like you need me to help guide you through this, and I want to help. I like Miles a lot. He is a terrific kid. Autism is not all bad. There are so many positives about it, like his incredible memory, and he grasps concepts that are really way ahead of his time. I bet he has an insanely high IQ. He has a beautiful mind. And he is really sweet and funny too. I think he gets that from you." I smile at her, and she seems to be pleased with my answer.

"Thank you. I don't know what to say."

"You don't have to say anything right now. The first thing we'll do is have a sit-down with the school psychologist. I'll e-mail you some options when she can meet with us next week, if that works for you?"

"Yeah, that would be fine. I'll get out of work and do whatever I need to do."

"I know you will." I can't help but smile at her, she is already gathering her strength, and I can see her mind working through it and going into fight mode — she is going to conquer whatever is thrown at her. It's clear she is tough.

"What will happen then? Should I tell Miles? What do I say to him? Have you told him?"

"No, I haven't said anything to him, and I don't think you should either, not yet. There isn't much to tell. We'll meet with the psychologist, and she'll go over some options for testing. There are ways for the school to help get him tested. Or you can get a private psychiatrist to refer him for testing. After that, we can regroup and do what we need to do to get an IEP together for him."

"A what?"

"IEP - Individualized Education Plan. It's a really formal process involving the parent, teachers, administration, and more, but in short, it would be a plan for us to make sure Miles has everything he needs to excel in school. It will help a lot. For now, I'll start trying a few things here and there to see what he responds to. I already give him a little extra time and a quiet place when we are doing timed activities and that seems to help him stay calm and focused. Sometimes, I wonder if he has ADHD as well. The testing will tell us that too. Nothing to worry about, though. Just go on like you have been, and we will meet to talk more next week."

"Mr. Hale, I can't thank you enough for helping me through this and for caring for Miles. He doesn't have a father around to take care of him like..." she trails off, and I think she was about to say something that she didn't want to.

Easing the awkwardness of her pause, I say, "It's no problem. I'm happy to help, and I want to do what is best for Miles... and you. And please, call me Brody."

Not sure why I went there. No reason for her to call me by my first name other than I want to hear her say it. I think she realizes this is a bit odd too, but she humors me.

"Okay, Brody. Well, thank you again. You can call me Cara if you want to. Carina is fine too. I normally don't like it when people use my full name, but it hasn't bothered me when you have said it."

I just nod at her, not sure how to respond to that revelation. But she looks down at where I'm still holding her hands, and I realize it's probably getting weird. So, I release her. Instantly, I miss the feel of her skin against mine. It really felt good to be able to touch her, and I want more, so much more.

I check my watch and see that we are almost out of time. "Well, let's head back inside, and I'll e-mail you about next week after I speak with the school psychologist."

"Sounds good. Thanks. Oh, and one more thing."

"Yes?"

"Why didn't you put boys in our group today?"

Shit. I was hoping she would have let that go. This might upset her.

"Well, some of the boys have been starting to pick on him a little bit, and I didn't want him to be uncomfortable today. This is supposed to be a fun day, and I wanted him to have good memories of it. The girls seem to be more forgiving of his eccentricities and quirkiness. He has a better chance of making friends with the girls than the boys at this age."

"Picking on him?" Her entire demeanor has changed, and she is going into full Mama Bear mode. It's insanely hot.

My hands go up in front of my chest, palms out, in a placating posture. "Nothing that bad, you know how kids can be. Anytime I see it, I nip it in the bud right away. But at PE and lunchtime, he is struggling a bit. It's those times when they are left to socialize that he really struggles the most. But I've asked the PE teachers to keep a closer eye on him too. Nothing to worry about at this point, and I'm confident it is lessening given some of the chats I've had with the other boys. I'm on the case."

"Wow. Okay, thanks again. Are you a superhero too? I don't see any glasses, so not a very good superhero disguise if that is the case."

"Glasses are not necessary because my costume has a full face mask. Like Batman."

"Makes sense, I suppose," she says back playfully.

We laugh a little as we head back to the theater. She seems to be in much better spirits, and I'm more determined than ever to get Miles all the help he needs. She and I will be a great team for the kid. His dad isn't around? Well, fine. I'll step up and watch her back, making sure she has the support she needs.

·❤·❤·❤·❤·❤·

Bang, Bang, Bang

Present Day

As we head over to Cara's house, Miles is singing along to the radio. Just like his mom did the other night on our non-date. He has a pretty good voice too, it would seem.

"You like AJR, Miles?"

"Yeah, they're great. I dig their vibe. This is a really good song. I also really loved that song they had with the SpongeBob bit at the beginning. Remember that one?"

"Wasn't it called 'I'm ready' or something like that?"

"Yes. Good job, Mr. Hale. I guess you aren't too old to know good music after all." From the rearview mirror, I can see that he is smirking at me. An actual smirk.

"Watch it, kiddo. You don't know who you're messing with," I say as I reach over the seat and ruffle the brown hair on his head and give him a slight noogie.

He swats my hand away and gets back to singing "BANG!" I like this song too, so I sing along with him.

Let's go out with a bang. Bang, bang, bang.

That tightness in my chest returns. I recognize it as happiness. Complete and total happiness.

A few hours later, I have a full belly and am thankful that Grammy Ellie didn't do the cooking. Cara can cook a mean pot roast.

Another five points to House Gryffindor. That woman checks all the damn boxes.

Dinner was actually really calm, especially when compared with how insane this house was the last time I was here. Cort and Cara were in a very reserved mood today and didn't seem nearly as boisterous as they usually are. I get the feeling that something is wrong.

We all help clear the table, and while I'm doing so, Cort catches my eye and motions his head towards the hallway. Surmising that he wants to talk and doesn't want Cara to know, I quietly make my way over there to see what is going on.

"So, you may have noticed Cara isn't very cheery tonight."

"Yeah, you either. Did something happen?"

"I'm pretty sure she won't tell you about it, so I'll give you the short version, and maybe you can try to talk some sense into her because she sure as hell isn't listening to me."

"Okay, what is it?" Now I'm getting worried, and my hackles are up.

"That asshole Peter Peters said some very inappropriate things to her today, implying that she should be very thankful that he got her the promotion, and he may have pressed himself up against her back and possibly touched himself in front of her." He rushes it all out so fast that my head is spinning.

And I'm seeing red.

Pure. Red.

Rage. I'm raging inside.

That fucker is going down. I'll kill him with my bare hands.

"How did he do that with everyone around, man? What the fuck! I thought you weren't leaving her alone with him?"

"Calm down. I'm as pissed off as you are. And she was in the back doing some work on her laptop, and he snuck up behind her. She had only been gone a few minutes, and I was just about to come looking for her. In fact, she ran smack-dab into my chest when she came flying out of there."

"Jesus. This is crazy. What happened next? What is she thinking of doing? Tell me she went to management or HR or something."

"She was pretty upset, and I pulled her aside to calm her down. For now, she doesn't think she can do anything because there were no witnesses. It will be his word against hers. There aren't cameras in that room because sometimes people have to strip down a bit to get massaged. That's probably why he picked that room to make his move. Fucking asshole."

"She has to report it. He must face the consequences or else it will just continue."

"She knows that too. I'm just not sure how she is going to play it, and it is her call as much as it pisses me off. She just got that promotion, and she isn't interested in making waves or being seen as a troublemaker."

"This is so fucked up. I'll talk to her later and see if I can help her see reason."

"Good. That's why I told you." He looks around the corner to see where Cara is before continuing, "Thanks for helping me talk to her. She can be a handful. She is too much of a people pleaser to stand up for herself sometimes. But I think she did tell him that he was being inappropriate, and to hear her tell it, she gave him a real bitch face." He laughs a little, then shakes his head. "But anyway... thanks, man."

I slap the back of his shoulder and tell him thanks for keeping me in the loop, and we make our way back to the family room.

Whether she wants to talk about it or not, she and I are going to have words later. I really want her to report this douchebag. If she doesn't, I might just need to take matters into my own hands and have a word with this pumpkin-eater son of a bitch. Cara is right. That is the dumbest fucking name.

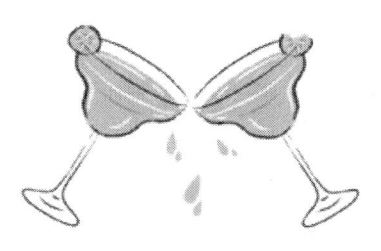

Chapter Ten

Oh, Popeye!

Cara

"You are dripping all over the place!" I yell as I see Miles standing in a towel after getting out of the shower with a blank expression on his face as if nothing is wrong.

And now I'm rage sighing again. That's just great. This day has been a roller coaster of emotions.

"Son, do you see that you are getting the floor wet? I know you love sea animals, but we are humans and can't live underwater so stop trying to bring the water world into our home. Most people dry off before they leave the bathroom. You should try it sometime."

"I prefer to air-dry," he retorts as he continues dripping and slowly walks away, heading toward his room, leaving a trail of water across the deep mahogany hardwood floors as he goes.

"Whatever, Aquaman, just wipe the floor when you are done soaking it, please. I'm going to walk Brody... I mean, Mr. Hale, out, and I'll be back to tuck you in shortly."

I still feel a little weird calling him Brody in front of Miles because he always refers to him as Mr. Hale. I should ask Brody about that. I wonder if it feels awkward for him or what he prefers. Something tells me that he doesn't care either way when it comes to Miles. That child has that man wrapped around his finger.

I slip on my flip-flops and walk Brody out. He said he wanted to talk to me in private before leaving tonight. Ever since he told me that, I've been nervous as hell. Well, fifty percent nervous and fifty percent excited that maybe he will make an actual move on me tonight.

A girl can dream. Even this girl who has a crazy demanding family, zero time for relationships, and a perverted boss harassing her. Yeah, maybe I should play it a bit cold and push him away so I don't suck him any further into my drama-filled existence.

"So, I noticed that you weren't as upbeat as usual this evening. Anything you want to talk about?" Brody asks as we sit down on the swing on the front porch overlooking the tropical front yard already darkened by the early setting sun.

I take a moment to think through how to respond and give us a shove with one foot so we start rocking slowly.

"I know something happened. It will feel better to get it off your chest, Cara." He continues, "And judging by how loudly you just sighed, it must be something that makes you uncomfortable. I know you well enough to know that you're trying to hide something. Please don't. Just come out with it already."

"Fine. Something happened at work today. It was uncomfortable, and I can't stop thinking about it. That's all. But it's not a problem. I'll handle it."

"That's not gonna be enough, Carina. Talk to me."

Damn, this man. I can't lie to him, and whenever he asks for something, I'm compelled to give it to him. He does so much for me, and he is such a comforting presence in my otherwise insane life. He doesn't deserve a bullshit answer. I just don't want to worry him, and I know this is going to upset him just like it upset Cort. It's like I have two brothers.

Except I don't want to climb Cort like a tree and ride him off into the sunset like I do Brody. So, maybe brother isn't the best way to describe my relationship with this gorgeous brown-haired Adonis on my right.

"I know. I am just not thrilled to talk about it, and I don't want you to worry because it's going to be fine." I offer with honesty and hope that it is enough.

Of course, it's not enough.

"Don't worry about me. Tell me, I want to know."

"You already heard from Cort before he left, didn't you?" I look at him from my peripheral vision, not brave enough to look at him full on. If he does know, does he think I'm weak? Stupid for not reporting it already? Or maybe he won't believe me and thinks I'm just trying to be overdramatic and get attention.

I have no idea where that last thought came from. That's something my sisters might think of me but not Brody. He would never think badly of me. He is too kind for that.

"Yeah, Cort told me his version, but I want to hear it from you."

"Well, that's just great," I say while shaking my head. Not mad, really. I just wish Cort would trust me to handle this. But I guess I can't have it both ways, where I demand Cort stay with me and comfort me, but then tell him to back off and stay out of it. That would be pretty hypocritical of me.

Brody just waits in silence, patient as an oak tree.

"All right, so the short story is that Peter snuck up behind me while I was in the ice room alone, working on my laptop. He pushed up behind me and startled me. He was looking at me with some serious psycho vibes and said some shit that basically came off as that I should be grateful for his help getting the promotion, and he wants me to show him some *appreciation*. Yuck! I feel like ten thousand showers couldn't rinse off the slime."

Brody exhales audibly, drawing my attention to his handsome face. I can see he is gritting his teeth by the force in his clean-shaven jaw line. *Serious Brody* is even hotter than normal Brody.

"What did you do or say to him?"

"Well, once the shock receded, I pointed out that he didn't get me the job. I earned it, and I am more than qualified."

"That's good. What else?"

"I also told him that he was acting inappropriately, and I also stormed out after giving him the bitch face to end all bitch faces. Or at least I hope that's what my face looked like."

"What are you going to do about this?"

Now I'm starting to get agitated. I know it's not Brody's fault, but I'm not a child or an idiot.

"For now, there isn't really anything else I can do except try to steer clear of him. There were no cameras in that room and no witnesses. No one will believe me, especially when I technically have an ax to grind with him since I also applied for the position he got. I need to get some evidence if I'm going to take this asshole down. I'm thinking of setting him up, but that feels a little too double-oh-seven for me."

"That's not a bad idea, actually. And Cort can't be the only witness because they might not consider him credible since he is related to you."

"I'll keep the wheels turning on that one. For now, I just want to forget about it. It wasn't pleasant."

"I can imagine. Were you scared?"

"So, the badass bitch side of me wants to deny any feelings of inadequacy, but I can't lie to you. Yes. I was scared."

He sighs again and takes my hand. Just the feel of his skin on mine sends a million tiny bolts of lightning up my arm and throughout my whole body. He electrifies me with his very presence.

He also makes me feel safe and calm. I wish things were different. That I was different, and I could have him without the potential to lose so much for both me and Miles.

"I want you to know that you are not alone, and I will do anything to help you. He doesn't know me, and I'm told I can be pretty intimidating when I want to be. I could approach him to let him know that his behavior won't be tolerated and that he needs to cut the shit if he knows what is good for him. Do you think that would help?"

I chuckle a bit at the image in my mind. A fourth-grade teacher threatening my boss. Then again — Brody must be over two hundred pounds of solid muscle. He would tower over Peter if they were face-to-face. If I had to guess,

I'd say Brody is about six foot two, and Peter can't be more than five foot nine.

"Oh, Popeye, you're my heroooooo," I say dreamily in my Olive Oyl voice in an attempt to lighten the mood. I need to change the subject here. That was way too much seriousness for one day.

Plus, I don't want Brody to risk his career. If he went off half-cocked and did something to Peter, he could get arrested. The Academy would be forced to let him go. Can't have a criminal record when you are molding the country's youth.

"Ahhh... gah, gah, gah, gah," Brody busts out with a spot-on Popeye impression, and we both crack up. He lets go of my hand, and instantly, I long to have it back.

"I know you think you are Wonder Woman and all, and hell I think you are too. But sometimes, even Wonder Woman can use help from the rest of the Avengers."

"Wow. That is so wrong. Wonder Woman is *not* an Avenger. She is part of the Justice League. Even I know that. If Miles heard you say that, you'd be banned from ever stepping foot in his presence again. How dare you dishonor the superhero fandom like that?"

"I knew that. I was just testing you and trying to make you smile again. I love your smile, Carina." He reaches up and touches a lock of my hair and holds it for a moment while staring into my eyes. Instinctively, I bite my lower lip, and it draws his attention to my lips. He starts to lean in and... *oh mylanta*, this is happening. Brody Hale, "Mr. Hottie," is about to kiss me.

Internally, I think about my breath and wish I sucked on some mints after dinner. But I banish that thought because it is decidedly unsexy, and this moment calls for confidence. Brody could have any woman he wants, and he is looking at me like I'm an ice cream cone in the heat of July.

"Mom! Can you tell Grandpa Dickie that I'm not being weird? He is being really mean!" A yell comes out of the front door and breaks the moment.

I always knew Miles would be a beaver blocker.

Nervously, I look around, shake the fog from my brain, and jump up. "Okay, Mr. Hale was just leaving. I'll be right there and will handle it."

I give Brody an awkward salute, like I'm a Naval Cadet and back away towards the door.

"Well, it's late. Thanks for bringing Miles's hippo over, and I guess I'll see you later."

Brody rises, puts his hands in his pockets, and takes a deep breath. "Of course, you are welcome. Thanks for dinner, it was delicious, and I really enjoyed myself. Have a good night, *Carina*."

I turn to go inside and shut the door behind me. I lean up against it and take a deep breath before I put the *children* in time-out.

"Miles, Grandpa, can I see both of you in the living room?" Time to referee.

You'd think being in his eighties, I wouldn't have to moderate arguments between him and a twelve-year-old. But you'd be completely wrong. Secretly, I think they argue because Miles is far more mature than Grandpa Dickie.

I turn to the old man, "Grandpa, Miles says you were calling him names and said he was weird. What's your side of the story?"

"I did not call him weird."

"Yes, you did! Mom, he did. He was very mean, and he said I was weird."

"No, I said you were *acting* weird and you were. When I was a kid, my parents would have hauled me around by my ears for doing what you were doing and forced me to pick up everything or it would have been thrown away!"

"Wait, what were you doing, Miles?"

"I was arranging my army men, and he came over and set his stupid newspaper down and knocked some of them down! Who even reads the newspaper anymore? *That* is acting weird. Hey, Grandpa, there is a new invention called the internet, perhaps you should check it out and stop killing trees with your *archaic* and pointless habits."

Miles is not wrong here.

"Hold on, please remember you are talking to a grown-up, and be respectful. Nice word choice by the way, *archaic*." You have to remain positive as a parent, and whenever I chastise Miles, I always like to include a compliment too. Over the last few years, I've learned that he is less likely to flip out if I soften it a bit.

"Grandpa, I've told you many times that Miles is very particular about the army men and action figures when he is setting them up. If they get moved, he feels a lot of anxiety. We are working on that issue, aren't we Miles?"

He puts his head down and concedes the point with a curt nod.

"For now, can you tell me what you did when grandpa knocked them down?" I ask Miles, but Grandpa rushes to answer first.

"He flipped out. That's what he did! He was shaking his hands, pacing back and forth, mumbling something, then yelling, and then whispering. That was weird!"

"Grandpa, please stop. He is not weird. He just handles things differently than we do. Please don't call him weird again!"

Mama Bear, reporting for duty. Don't call my kid weird. He gets enough of that shit at school. He needs to be in a safe space at home.

Grandpa simply doesn't understand his autism, and no matter how many times I try to explain, he just can't seem to grasp the concept. He still thinks this can be disciplined out of him or even that we could bully him into submission. It's frustrating as hell, and I hate that I have to police the family when it comes to their own great-grandchild. Here, at Miles's home, we should all be on the same team with him. But sometimes, I feel like I'm the coach, Miles is playing every position, and Grandpa is the mean ass umpire who couldn't see the strike zone to save his life.

"Grandpa, we've talked about how to handle it when Miles starts to stim and gets agitated. He needs to feel like he has some control over the situation and needs to be reminded to use his self-soothing strategies. Don't you remember? Calling him weird is only going to make it worse."

Shit, speaking of which, I can see Miles is sucking his thumb and rocking his legs back and forth. He is trying to hide it behind his arm again, just like Brody said he used to do at school. Dammit. I thought we were so close to breaking that habit.

"Miles, honey, go upstairs, get your sensory kit, and try to calm down, okay?"

He nods and heads upstairs, and I turn to the old man, who now seems apologetic at least.

"Cara, honey, I'm sorry. I'm just not used to seeing behavior like that. It's really strange. I was just thinking that if he knew he was acting strange that he would stop. Imagine if he started acting like that at school. He'd be the laughingstock of the entire school."

"I know that Grandpa, and I understand where you are coming from. I'm working on that with him in therapy. Please don't make it worse by calling him names. He takes what you say so seriously. He doesn't understand that the words we say aren't meant to upset him or that you are coming from a place of concern. He takes things very literally. That is part of his autism. Just please respect my rules, and when he starts to backslide, come and get me if you think you need backup responding to him in a loving way."

There. I said my peace. That's enough drama for tonight.

"Fine. I love you, my beautiful granddaughter. I'm sorry I upset Miles. I love him too."

"I know you do. I love you too. Most of the time," I tease and get a slight smile out of him. "Well, I'm off to get Miles ready for bed. I'll see you tomorrow. Good night."

"Good night."

As I make my way up the stairs, I think about how quickly my day changed back and forth from happy to sad to happy to freaked out to calm to horny and then angry. I think I've processed every single emotion possible all in one day. And I'm exhausted.

After getting Miles settled, my head hits the pillow, and I'm out like a light.

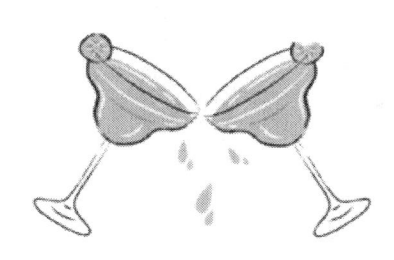

Chapter Eleven

Like Tom Petty, I won't back down

Cara

"Cheers, bitch!" We raise our glasses and clink before downing a shot of Patron and then sucking on the lime wedge.

"Damn, I can't believe I let you talk me into a tequila shot. You know I'm too old for this, Helen. I'm going to be hating life tomorrow."

My best friend sits on the barstool next to me, looking like a little Asian pixie goddess complete with a shit-eating grin on her face. It's so good to see her. Damn, I've missed the crazy tramp.

Friday night couldn't come soon enough this week. It's been such a crazy week, and this girls' night out is just what the doctor ordered.

First, Monday was the day from hell, and I was afraid that the rest of the week would go downhill from there. But thankfully, the rest of the week went by in a blur. We were slammed at work since so many of the university's sports teams are hitting their stride, and mid-season muscle burnout is in full swing. Little things are causing their tired bodies to give out, and injuries are increasing. Same thing this time every year. Job security, I guess.

Fortunately, Peter has been hands-off and stayed clear of me this week. The only interaction I had with him was when he needed to talk to me about expectations for the new position. I suggested he e-mail me because I was busy, and luckily, he obliged. Later, I found out it was because Cort was standing behind me with a menacing look on his face. Regardless of the reason, I was happy that I escaped an awkward conversation with him where it would have been hard to get someone else in the room.

The only bad thing the rest of the week was that I didn't see Brody, and he hasn't sent many texts this week. Maybe he is regretting that almost kiss and wants to make sure he doesn't lead me on or something. That's for the best.

"Girl, you should have seen the men in Bali. I have never seen so much cocoa brown buff flesh in my life!" she squeals and continues to talk about her vacation.

I don't have independent funds like she does. I'm no heiress, so my Bali adventures will have to be experienced vicariously through her.

"I'm sure you took lots of pictures and will share them all with me. I'll just be over here waiting patiently to feast my eyes upon all that flesh," I tease her and poke her in the arm.

"Didn't you catch my TikTok videos? You should have seen plenty of hot men on those videos already!"

Helen is pretty big on TikTok at the moment and is considered an influencer on social media. Her username always makes me chuckle. Her online persona is *Helen on Wheels*, which suits her to a tee. This woman is hell on wheels, and a party follows her everywhere she goes. When she arrives, just cue up the debauchery.

I'm so envious of her life, it's pathetic.

"Actually, I haven't been online much lately and haven't seen any of your TikTok posts or your Instagram stories. Sorry. Don't hate me for being a shitty friend."

"I could never hate you, you know this. Girl, you are the *she* to my *nanigans*. I adore you and your simple life," she jokes.

"It's been anything but simple this week."

"Yes, you are going to have to tell me all about your new promotion and whatever the shit went down at work with your boss. From what you mentioned, I feel the need to go to campus, get a stool, and slap that asshole in the face for you. Or skip the stool and junk punch him. Either way, something needs to get hit."

Helen is very petite, and she embraces it. Just like me, she is always willing to joke about herself. That's one of the things that first connected us back in school.

We met in elementary school and just "clicked." We have been best friends ever since, despite how very different our backgrounds and lives are. It was the one-year that she went to a public school. Her family is extremely wealthy. Her dad is an executive at one of the top US defense contractors, working with high-level clearance at MacDill Air Force Base in Tampa. Apparently, outfitting the military with weapons is very lucrative.

She kept getting in trouble at her exclusive private school, and daddy threatened boarding school. Instead, she convinced him to let her try public school. She lasted for one year. Eventually, her dad decided getting a private tutor was easier than dealing with her antics. He wasn't wrong. *This bitch is now and always has been a handful.*

Helen doesn't work, aside from her social media presence. And you just can't call that work. I'm sorry, but I don't buy it when she complains about how hard it is to always come up with new and fresh content for her adoring fans.

Suck it little lady. I'll show you what's hard — just try one day in my life. It's like herding cats trying to keep the old gray hairs at home and Miles in line. Throw in my work, plus my insane siblings, and clearly, my life is not for the weak of heart.

"Well, let's have another round of margaritas, and then we can discuss my shithead boss, Peter Peters Pumpkin-Eater. I think I want a watermelon one this time." I motion to the bartender and order our next round of drinks.

Helen has now pulled out her phone and is bringing up her TikTok account.

Together, we look at some of her posts, and she is right. That is a lot of grade-A top choice man meat. Damn!

"And did you sleep with all these guys or did you pick a favorite to have repeat performances during your stay?"

"You know I don't bang and tell, darling."

We look at each other and bust out laughing. Because that is exactly what she does. She tells me all the torrid details about her sex life. Since I'm going through a man-fast in the interest of protecting my wounded heart, I have to get the goods from her or else I'd have zero sexual knowledge.

Before she starts spilling the beans about her sexy times in Bali, a new TikTok video pops up, and it catches my attention because I love the song that is playing, something about *coffee for your head*.

One of the things that I love about the cantina bar is that it is quiet enough to hear each other talk but lively enough that you don't feel like you are in a funeral home. It's the perfect place to hang out and catch up. And I have really good memories of this place since Brody and I had our non-date night here last week.

Something about this video is catching our eyes and drawing us in. After it ends, Helen and I sigh and swoon. She taps a few times and another video with the same song comes on — this time a different couple. There are words on the screen explaining what is happening.

After that one finishes, another one comes up. Then another and another. She and I are both so wrapped up in the emotions of what we just witnessed. It seems this is a TikTok challenge or something that is catching on. I guess you could say it is a surprise sneak-attack best friend kiss.

The videos follow the basic premise of two friends, a male and a female, being shown in various playful scenes. Playing video games together, or basketball or watching TV, playing cards — whatever normal friend stuff they do. Then, the narrative continues that the girl has a secret crush on her best friend, and she is going to surprise kiss him to see what happens.

The responses that come from these sneak-attack kisses are varied. Sometimes, the guy is so shocked, and they just freeze, eyes wide as if to say, *what the hell is happening right now*? Sometimes, he laughs and pushes the girl off him jokingly, and you can tell he isn't interested in her like that but plays it off well. And then there is the third type of reaction.

That's my favorite. And it is the reason for all the sighing, swooning, and *awwww-ing* that Helen and I are doing.

In these videos, the guy is shocked slightly at first, but then his mind catches up, he takes over the kiss, and gives the girl the smooch to end all smooches. That manly, possessive kiss that basically says, oh hell yes! We are doing this, and I've been waiting forever to kiss you like you deserve to be kissed.

Le sigh.

Of course, my mind immediately goes to Brody, and I wonder what he would do if I just kissed him out of nowhere. That brings a giggle to my tipsy brain, and I start laughing.

Helen looks over at me and says, "What is so funny? These are so sweet! I've never seen anything so cute before!"

"I know. They are super cute. I was just thinking it would be funny to see what Brody would do if I just pulled a sneak-attack kiss on him."

Giggle, giggle, hiccup, giggle, hiccup.

"That's it! You are a genius!" Helen shouts victoriously.

"What's it?" I ask, genuinely confused. I've had a lot to drink, so it is entirely possible there is another conversation that has been going on that I've missed.

Damn, these chips are so good. Do they put lime on them with all that salt? Fuck. That's delicious. And I'm totally going to *hiccup* drink that salsa. I need a straw.

"You just gave me the perfect idea for my next TikTok video," she proudly proclaims.

"Oh, okay. Glad I could help." Still not sure what she is going on about.

"When are we going to do it? Can you set something up for this weekend? When do you see him next?"

"I don't know what you are talking about. Are you ready for another round? I'm going to try mango next."

"Shut up about the margaritas for a second and focus. TikTok sneak-attack kiss video. You. Brody. This is happening."

"First off, I don't ever shut up about margaritas, you know that. Check out the shirt." I point to my chest that proudly states: *Some girls drink too many margaritas. It's me. I'm some girls.*

"Second of all, I am not going to surprise kiss Brody." *Hiccup.* "He is just a friend. That crosses a line we can't uncross."

"That's the way the videos work, Cara. That's kind of the point. You surprise a kiss on your male best friend. That's Brody. Plus, I know you secretly love him anyway."

"Ha ha ha. Very funny. I don't know what you are talking about."

"You like him. I know it, and you know it. He probably knows it too."

"What? No, he doesn't know it!"

"Ha! Gotcha. You just admitted it. You like him. You want to kiss him. You want to bang him. You want to ride his face to the promised land," she singsongs at me like a little girl on the playground.

I put my hands over her mouth to shush her. "Shhhh! Shut up. What is wrong with you? We are in public. Keep it down. And that's gross. Don't talk like that. It's not true."

It's totally true. I want to ride every part of him anywhere he will take me.

I'm looking around to see if anyone heard her totally inappropriate, albeit true, outburst. Looks like we got lucky and were saved by the mariachi band that showed up and is now playing… wait, are they playing, "Hey Ya!" by Outkast? Really? What happened to the Mexican Hat Dance?

I give her my best evil eye and slowly remove my hand. She licks it just before I get it away from her.

"Gross! What is wrong with you, Helen? You don't lick your friends."

"You can if you are friends with a super buff and gorgeous fourth-grade teacher. You can, and you should lick him. Everywhere. All over."

My thighs are clenching, and my panties are dampening just at the thought of that.

"Come on, Cara! You have to do this. It will get me so many views. If he doesn't like the kiss, we can tell him I made you do it for my views and play it off. It will be fine. He doesn't have to know that you secretly lust after him."

She has a point. If she were there, which I guess she would be in order to record it, she could always take the fall for me if it doesn't work out. *What's the harm in a little kiss?*

More than likely, nothing would come of it, except for just once, I'd finally know what he tastes like. And how his lips would feel pressed up against mine. I've been dreaming of that mouth for more than three years now. It's starred front and center in so many of my X-rated dreams.

"No. That's not something I could do. I'd chicken out."

"Well, I didn't want to do this, but you leave me no choice. *I dare you!*"

My jaw drops to the bar, and I pick it back up again. "You did *not* just go there! You bitch. You promised me no more dares after the last time when I almost got arrested for streaking through your neighborhood."

She tosses her head back and laughs like the evil villain she is.

"It's just one kiss. I bet you can't do it. In fact, I'm sure you aren't going to be able to woman-up and kiss that hunk. Maybe I'll do it instead. What's his number?"

Wow. Just wow. She is pulling out all the stops and hitting me with a three-course meal of manipulation. She starts with an appetizer — the dare. Main course is hot and spicy reverse psychology. And she ends with a dessert of jealousy. *Fuuuuuccccck. I'm going to end up doing this, aren't I?*

What's one little kiss? It would help Helen out with her online following, and I'd get a chance to kiss Brody. If it doesn't work out, she takes the blame, and we play it off like it meant nothing. I can reason this one out.

Honestly, I'm not sure I can see the downside. Of course, I have had a tequila shot and am currently on margarita number three. Probably not the best time to make a decision like this.

But fuck it. I've had a shitty week, and I want to kiss him. There, I said it.

I want to press up against his firm body, grab him by his ripped shoulder with one hand and the back of his head with the other, and yank his face to mine with all my might. Just like all those cute videos. I want to know how he will respond. Part of me thinks he would laugh and push me away. But a bigger part thinks he might take over the kiss and blow my socks clear off my feet.

I look down but see I'm not wearing socks. Just my strappy sandals. I'm so buzzed I don't even understand that my own internal monologue is simply making a metaphor.

I look back to Helen and eye her cautiously.

"Helen, damn you. You know I can't back down from a challenge like that." I shake my head but continue, "For the sake of argument, if we were to do this... how do you see it going down and capturing it on camera?"

The look on her face is one of pure victory and mischievousness. She rubs her hands together like the Klumps about to hit an all-you-can-eat buffet in Las Vegas. She's practically salivating over this opportunity.

Shit. What have I just done?

Chapter Twelve

What just happened?

Brody

"Courtesy. Integrity. Perseverance. Self-Control. Indomitable Spirit."

A sea of white uniforms with thick corded belts in all colors is spread out before me. Each child lined up facing the flags at the front of the Dojang. They are all standing ram-rod straight with their legs tightly together and hands straight down at their sides. After reciting the five tenets of Tae Kwon Do, the instructor changes his stance and brings his right fist over his heart. The children then do the same move before reciting an oath of some sort.

The instructor then loudly yells something that sounds like *herrow*. The students go back to their first stance before the instructor shouts out a few other phrases that lead the kids through various other poses and formalities. Before I know it, there are a series of bows, and it seems that things are wrapping up.

I see Miles towards the middle of the pack, sporting a big frown. I'm pretty sure that is his concentration face. I've seen it a few times before when he was in my class. He did so great during the ceremony, demonstrating his moves. I'm so stinking proud of him, even though I probably have no right to be. I'm just thrilled he invited me to come see him today at the Belt Ceremony.

A glance to my left, and I see the entire Amos clan, most of them snapping pictures on their phones like they have been doing the entire hour we've been here. It's basically a sea of red and auburn hair, and at the end is Cara's friend, Helen, who just arrived back in town this week. She is sticking out like a sore thumb with her short black hair and dark skin in sharp contrast to Cara's family.

I have to admit, I was a little bit shocked to get a text asking me to join them today. Things like this are typically reserved for family members, and it nearly brings a tear to my eyes that Miles and Cara felt like I should join them. I'm turning into a damn softy around those two, I swear.

I was having a few drinks with Hudson last night in Ybor City and getting ready to call it a night. I just can't keep up with him. I don't know where he gets all that energy. When I glanced at my phone to see what time it was so I could make my excuses to Hudson, I saw that I had an unread text from Cara.

Cara: Any chance you are free tomorrow around 11 a.m.?

Brody: I can probably make myself available for the right motivation.

Cara: How about watching a 12-year-old test for the next level belt in Tae Kwon Do class?

Brody: Is he going to get his red belt tomorrow?

Cara: I hope so. Otherwise, there will be a lot of disappointed family members that the sensei will have to deal with. Miles has been working hard practicing his little butt off. There isn't a patch of air at the house that he hasn't kicked or punched into submission.

Brody: <gif of the karate kid doing the crane>

Brody: Are you sure it is OK for me to come? Isn't that something for family?

Cara: You're practically family at this point, plus he asked for you. You wouldn't want to turn him down, would you?

Cara: <gif of Puss in Boots with the big begging eyes>

Brody: There is nowhere else I'd rather be at 11 a.m. tomorrow. It's at the one near the school, right?

Cara: Yep. I'll save you a seat. See you then.

I remember how my heart leaped into my throat when she said I was practically family. Man, don't I wish. I'm sure she doesn't mean it the same way I do, though.

Regardless of my role in the Amos family, I woke up early, hit the gym, came back for a quick breakfast, got showered, shaved, dressed, and then rushed to get here a few minutes before 11 a.m. Just as promised, Cara had a seat saved for me. I was shocked she wasn't sitting next to Helen since those two are usually joined at the hip when she is in town. But Helen was in deep conversation with CJ about something having to do with black sand beaches and expensive coffee. Probably has something to do with her most recent trip. That girl is always on vacation.

When I sat down, Cara reached over, squeezed my thigh, and leaned over to whisper a greeting in my ear. I have no idea what she said because once I got a whiff of her sweet coconut scent, my only thought was how fast could I get her naked. Of course, then I immediately had to mentally recite baseball stats and picture old men sitting in a sauna in order to keep my hard-on from popping my jean's zipper.

The audience stands and suddenly breaks out in applause. I see that while I've been daydreaming, they have wrapped up the ceremony. After a while, Miles is heading over to show us his new belt. The smile on his face is fucking priceless. For all the bad shit he has dealt with from being abandoned by his deadbeat dad to dealing with bullies in school, he has managed to keep the same tough spirit as Cara.

"Hey Mr. Hale. You came! You came!" he says once he sees me. "Did you see me do my Poomsae?"

"Is that what it was called?"

"Yeah, it's like a routine that we have to learn. Each belt level adds more moves. It's getting really hard to remember, even for me." He smiles, and I can tell he is so proud of himself, as he should be.

"I'm so proud of you, buddy. You did great!" Cara chimes in and swoops down for a big hug.

"Mom! Stop. I'm all sweaty, and the other kids will see you hugging me," he says in a very stern whisper, and I can't help but chuckle.

"The other boys will just be jealous that they don't have such a beautiful lady hugging them." I'm not sure why I said that, but I had to cheer Cara up because I could see in her face that she was sad that he brushed off her affection. She looks over at me, and I give her a wink.

"Eww. Gross. She's my mom. She's not a beautiful lady."

"Oh yes, she most certainly is. Have you seen your mom?" I ask.

Miles cocks his head to the side and looks at me before asking, "Do you have a crush on my mom or something?"

My eyes go wide, and Cara jumps in to save me before I honestly answer him. "Miles, that's not nice. Hush up. Go say hi to Aunt Helen along with the rest of the family. They all came to see you test."

"Fine." He walks off like that is the most horrible idea he has ever heard. Next thing I know, there is a loud squealing sound as Helen picks him up and spins him around. I have no idea how she did that; he's almost as big as she is.

"I guess she missed him," Cara says to me shyly. She is probably trying to not address what Miles just said, and I'm damn glad that is the case.

"I'm not sure he feels the same. Just look at his face."

We both laugh at the horrified expression on Miles's face, and she adds, "He's not a hugger."

"I'll remember that."

"So, I was wondering if you want to come out to lunch with the family? Since we are all together, we are going to count this as one of our biweekly required family meals."

"Required meals?"

"Yes. Grammy Ellie has a rule that as long as we all live in the same state, we must come together every two weeks for a full family meal. Or else. It's been such a huge incentive for me to find a job out of state, but I've been too busy to apply for jobs in Alaska."

I can tell she is just playing. She loves her family so much, and although they frustrate her, I know there is no chance she'd ever leave them.

We gather up everyone and head to lunch at Crabby's Bar and Grill over on Gulfview Blvd. Crabby's is the perfect choice for this large and rowdy group. It's right on the beach with a casual vibe and an upstairs balcony with outdoor seating. The view of Clearwater Beach from up there is quintessential Florida living at its finest.

And it's a damn good thing I worked out this morning because nothing is going to keep me away from their homemade kettle chips covered in chorizo queso sauce.

During lunch, Cara seems a bit nervous, and I'm wondering what she and Helen are conspiring about over there. They have been very secretive about something, but I haven't a clue what it could be. Every now and then, I look over at them, and when I meet their eyes, they get quiet, smile awkwardly, and start drinking out of their shared Rum Runner bucket. Then again, nothing is normal when Helen is involved. I should know this by now.

After the meal, I excuse myself to the washroom, and I see Helen nudging Cara on the arm and making big eyes at her. What the hell is going on with that woman? She is certifiable. To make things even more strange, she grabs my hand as I attempt to walk by her and places an Altoids mint in my palm. Well, that certainly qualifies as super bizarre.

But still... a free mint.

I pop it in my mouth as I walk through the restaurant and head to the hallway that leads to the restrooms. After taking care of business, I wash my hands and walk out the men's room door. And Cara is standing there in the hallway with a strange look on her gorgeous face.

It's not a smile, but it's not a frown either. If I had to call it something, I'd say it looks like she has indigestion.

"Hey, are you okay?" I ask her, concerned that she is going to be sick.

"Uh-huh. Nope. Yep. All good. I just... I mean... I was gonna... and you were... and now..." she is rambling and not getting a single complete sentence out.

She's adorable when she is like this. But I'm starting to get worried about her. We're in this hallway all alone, and there are no benches nearby if she starts to faint. I have no clue what's wrong with her.

I can't be sure exactly what happens next because one moment I'm wondering if she had too much rum, and the next minute I hear her say, "Oh, fuck it!" as she charges right at me in one big stride before pressing up against me, grabbing the top of my collared shirt, and yanking my face down to hers.

Her lips crash against mine, and our teeth clank slightly from the force of the surprise attack. My eyes are still wide open, and my hands are at my side. What the fuck is happening right now? I'm in shock.

My body figures out what is happening before my brain because instinct takes over, and I grab her hips and pull her toward me. My mouth takes control of the kiss, if you could even call it a kiss. It seems like so much more than just a kiss. My tongue darts out to swipe at her full luscious lips, and she opens for me as I get my first taste of Carina. Of heaven.

Bliss.

Rapture.

Elation.

Fire.

Passion.

And home.

I'm home. This right here is what I've been missing out on all my life. This woman is fire and ice. She is heaven and hell. She is happiness and sadness. She is everything, and I'm lost to her completely.

There is a reason why no other woman could ever compare to the lithe redhead that is plastering herself against me like she can't get close enough. It's because there is only one Carina. And I want more. I need more, and it seems like she does too.

My cock surges to life, hard enough to break bricks, and I press her into the wall as I grind up against her, my hands now roaming her hair as she gasps, moans a little, and then reaches up to the back of my neck. My hands move down to her lush ass and give it a squeeze. She runs her hands from my neck down to my chest and then back up again before squeezing my shoulders, and somehow pulling me even closer.

She tastes like mint, rum, fruit juice, and fire. She is so perfect, and I'll never forget this feeling of holding perfection in my arms as our mouths explore and taste each other for the first time. She bites my lower lip, and I break for a quick breath before I dive back in for more.

I don't know how long we've been like this. Everything else has faded away except Carina and me and this perfect fucking moment.

"Okay, I think that's enough. We got it!"

Cara and I break apart, our eyes still searching one another with both shock and awe. Then, that other voice pierces through the fog again.

"Guys, break it up! You're in a public place, and clothes are not optional here. I can only keep this hallway blocked off for so long. If this were to continue, I'm pretty sure your clothes would burst into flames. I'm also thinking my own panties just melted right off my body. I'm going to get a waitress to ask for a mop to clean up this wet spot where I'm standing. *Fuuuuuuuck,* you two are insanely hot. That was way better than porn."

At this point, Cara and I are still pressed up against the wall, but we are both looking at Helen. I notice she is pointing a phone at us. Did she just fucking record that kiss? What the absolute fuck is wrong with her?

I take a step back from Cara to gather my wits. Helen turns tail and heads back to the table. I reluctantly pull my hands off Cara and turn to meet her eyes, both of us gasping for breath. She looks like a deer in the headlights. Frozen.

Guess I haven't lost my touch if I can leave her speechless. And Helen was right. That was fucking hot. The hottest kiss of my life. And I can't wait to do it again. And again. And then do it again but without clothes on.

"I'm sorry. I have to go." Cara pushes me back farther and runs... literally fucking runs... out the hallway and through the restaurant. I start to follow after her but then freeze because if I go out there now, everyone in the restaurant will see what I'm packing. So, I take a few deep breaths, count to ten, and then say... *fuck it* and run after her regardless of the tent I'm pitching.

By the time I get to the parking lot, I can see she is already inside Helen's car, and they are pulling away onto Gulfview.

What just happened?

Chapter Thirteen

From the texts of Cara and Mr. Hottie

Saturday

Mr. Hottie: What happened? Why did you leave? We need to talk.

Mr. Hottie: Cara, please answer the phone. I need to talk to you.

Mr. Hottie: Please, don't leave it like this. Talk to me.

Cara: I'm so sorry.

Mr. Hottie: Why are you apologizing? You have nothing to be sorry for. If anything, I should apologize to you for attacking you. Well, after you attacked me. But it was a mutual attacking. So, no apology needed.

Mr. Hottie: I'm not mad at you. And honestly, I'm not sorry.

Mr. Hottie: Please, answer the phone and talk to me.

Mr. Hottie: <gif of Sheldon hyperventilating into a paper bag>

Mr. Hottie: I'm coming over.

Cara: No, please. I just need some time.

Sunday

Mr. Hottie: Are you ready to talk yet, or are you going to continue ignoring me?

Mr. Hottie: Fine. I can take a hint, and I'll leave you alone for now, but we need to talk about this. I don't want to lose your friendship. You mean too much to me.

Wednesday

Mr. Hottie: <gif of Lionel Richie singing *Hello*>

Friday

Mr. Hottie: Are we ever going to talk?

Mr. Hottie: I went by your place the other night, and no one answered. I'm pretty sure you were home. Your car was there. You know where to find me if you want to talk. Fuck this.

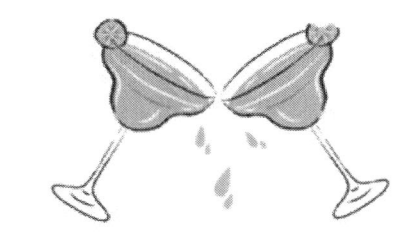

Chapter Fourteen

Hey guilt, nice to see you again

Cara

"Okay, I'm going to do it. Wait. No, I'm not. I just can't. I'm scared. He's gonna be mad. He should be mad. I was an awful bitch. Are you sure this is the right thing to do? It doesn't feel right."

Helen exhales loudly on the other end of the call, and I brace myself for another lecture. It's only going to be the seventy-fifth one this week.

"For fuck's sake, yes. I'm sure. Pull up your big-girl panties, go up there, knock on the door, tell him that you are sorry, and see if he will forgive you. You don't have to kiss him again if you don't want to — although we all know you want to — but you have to talk to him. He didn't do anything wrong and doesn't deserve the cold shoulder from you. In fact, from where I was standing, it looked like he did everything right. *Everything*!" She stresses the last word out, and I know exactly what she is implying.

And she isn't wrong. That was the most transcendent moment of my entire life. That kiss was everything I always hoped a kiss could be and so much more. I'm thirty-eight years old and have had my share of kisses in my life. Not a ton, but enough. And *that* was one for the record books.

I knew I liked Brody, and I always thought kissing him would be amazing. I just didn't expect that level of wonderful. It scared me. In that kiss, I saw my entire life with him unfold before me. I saw us in bed on a rainy morning. I saw us sitting by a bonfire on the beach. I saw us holding hands and walking down the street. I saw him standing down at the end of an aisle waiting for me to say I do. I saw us holding a newborn baby.

That last one was the one that made me totally freak out. I already have a son, and one is most definitely enough. Especially one that has been as challenging as Miles. Plus, I'm way too old to have fantasies like that.

Then, the fact that I realized I probably don't want another baby meant that if I were with Brody, I'd be robbing him of a chance to have his own kids. He needs to find someone else who can give him the life he deserves. I'm too big of a mess and come with way too much baggage for someone like him.

I can make all the excuses in the world, but when it came down to it, I just panicked. I freaked out and ran to hide like a scared little girl. Then, all his texts and phone calls this week broke my heart. It took all my strength not to call him or text him back. I just knew that if I responded, I would tell him how crazy I am about him, and how much I want to be with him. And dammit! He deserves better than me, and that led me right back to my fears and why I ran in the first place.

"Girl, are you still there? I can hear you breathing. Bitch, answer me!"

"Do you need me to send you some sunshine, Helen? 'Cause you are being shady as fuck right now. I need some support, please. Don't badger me. I'm terrified of what is going to happen."

"Here is what's gonna happen. I'm going to drive over there, grab you by your big ass Mr. Spock ear, drag you up to his front door, and I'm going to knock three times very loudly. Then, I'm going to sit you down, park myself on your shoulders, and make sure you don't run away like a coward."

"Hey! That is not supportive. Didn't I just say I need support?"

"Okay, how about this then? Cara, you can do this. He likes you and wants to save this friendship and maybe see about taking it to the next level. I've never seen anyone get kissed like that, and you owe it to yourself to go and see his penis. Plus, that video is totally going viral, and you need to thank him for me."

"I don't even know why I called you. And I still can't believe you posted it. I told you not to."

"You called me because I'm like your conscience, and you know I'm right."

"You are not my conscience; that implies you are giving good advice. You're more like the little devil sitting on my shoulder."

"Whatever you want to call it, you know I'm right. Plus, I had to post it. That was a solid gold money shot. Besides, you can't really see his face all that well, so no one at his school will recognize him. I'm not an amateur. Now, call me when you get done sucking his tongue down your throat again. I gotta go. Time to get my nails done. Ta Ta, bitch. I love you. You got this. Go make that man's dreams come true."

"Bye, babe. Thank you."

After another five minutes of deep breathing exercises in my car and another four minutes of singing along to Adele at the top of my lungs, I finally suck it up and get out of the car.

And then I immediately get back in the car and turn it back on. I'm just about to pull out of the parking lot when I change my mind. Again. For the two-hundredth time today.

I turn off the car, get out, and run up to his apartment before I have a chance to chicken out again.

I'm tapping my toe frantically while I wait for him to answer the door. Then, the door opens, and I'm momentarily speechless. This isn't what I was expecting.

An older woman who looks slightly familiar answers the door, wearing work clothes splattered with paint and holding a paint roller.

"Hello there. Cara, right? I was expecting you to show up. Eventually." She had a bit of a snark to her voice at the end of her greeting. Like she is a little mad at me. I guess I deserve it. I'm pretty sure this is Brody's mom. I think I met her a few years ago.

She steps outside onto the front porch area with me and closes the door behind her as if she wants to keep me out.

"Yes, I'm Cara. You're his mom, right?"

"I am. My name is Linda. Nice to see you again."

"You too. Is Brody here?"

"Of course, he is, dear. I'll get him in a moment. But first... why don't you tell me what you intend to say to my son to make up for this little incident that happened at Crabby's last week?"

"Oh, he told you about that, huh?" My cheeks get so hot so fast I'm afraid I have no blood left anywhere else in my body. Just thinking about that kiss. And now his mom knows? Kill me now.

"Well, he didn't tell me so much as I dragged it out of him. He wasn't acting like himself lately, and I finally came over with my special no-bake cookies and got him to spill it. Those were always his favorites and his only weakness. I never let him have the recipe, so I'd always have a secret weapon. Maybe one day I'll give you the recipe, if you are worthy."

I can't help but chuckle. She is just so funny, and I like her spunk. She looks at me expectantly. I realize that I didn't answer her question.

"Well, ma'am, I guess I'm here to apologize and see if I can mend our friendship. I don't really have a plan beyond that."

"Friendship? Is that what they call it these days?"

"Well, we've been friends for a few years now, and that was the first time anything crossed the line. And it just ruined everything, so I'm really sorry."

"I am not one to stick my nose in where it isn't needed, but... oh, who am I kidding? That's exactly what I'm going to do. Listen, honey, I don't think your little incident at Crabby's ruined everything. In fact, I think it changed things big time for the better. What had the potential to ruin everything was you ghosting him afterward without so much as an explanation."

"Ghosted him? You know what that means?" I can't help but smile at this firecracker of a woman.

"Yes, I might be on Tinder and OkCupid. It's crazy out there, though. Don't tell Brody." She winks at me conspiratorially.

"Your secret is safe with me." I make the sign of a cross with my index finger over my heart. I want to be her when I grow up. I can see myself fighting for Miles's honor if any girl causes him any pain. And judging by the way she is coming at me, I'm pretty sure I hurt Brody with my silence this week. *Shit*.

And here comes *Guilt* to kick me while I'm down.

Long time, no see, Guilt. How have you been?

Oh, you know. Just waiting for the perfect moment to make you feel even worse about your tragic life. Seems like now is that moment.

"I know you're right, but I didn't mean to ghost him or hurt him. I was just so overcome with emotions that I didn't know what to say to him. I was so scared that I ruined everything by kissing him. Or if we spoke, I would say the wrong thing, and *that* would ruin everything. He means a lot to me, and I don't want to lose him. He means a lot to my son, too, and I can't screw this up."

"Perfect. I think that's exactly what you need to tell him. Now, come on in and see him. He's in his room."

She opens the door, ushers me in, and I take in the apartment. She's painting his kitchen walls.

I can't help but ask, "Are you allowed to paint in here? I mean, he is just renting, right?"

"Yes, I am. I asked the front office manager. He said as long as we paint it back to white when he moves out, it's no problem. So, since I was over here taking care of Brody, I figured I might as well continue making his place less of a bachelor pad."

"Taking care of him?" This catches my attention. Was he that broken up that his mom needed to come care for him? Brody never seemed like the cry-to-mama type. This shocks me a little bit.

"Yes, after he hurt himself the other night, he called to ask for a little help around here."

"He hurt himself? What happened?"

"Why don't you ask him yourself? And while you are at it, bring him his painkillers and this glass of water, so I don't have to see his grumpy ass again for a little while. Make yourself useful, toots." She hands me the glass of water and pills, then slaps me on the ass, and shoves me toward the hallway that leads to Brody's bedroom.

Yep. I'm totally going to be her when I grow up.

Shit. I've never been to Brody's bedroom. And I've always wanted to. Looks like my wish is coming true in the worst way possible.

I approach the door and knock gently.

"Come in, Ma."

"Surprise!" I jump in the room with a big over-the-top smile and one jazz hand (the other is holding the water) and try to set the stage for a happy visit when I know this will be anything but happy.

"What are you doing here? Where's Ma?"

He looks pissed. I figured he would be. I deserve it. I've been an ass to someone who has never said one cross word to me, and someone that I really care about. And for no good reason at all.

I'm slime. I suck. I don't even need my friend Guilt to tell me that.

I take him in and notice that he has his left knee elevated and wrapped up in an Ace bandage with ice on it. What happened to his beautiful strong knee? I thought he was half-god. Half-gods don't get injuries like us mortals.

Before I answer him, I take a look at the room around me and am pleasantly surprised. It's clean and well decorated. Big king bed with a delicious-looking injured man sitting atop a crisp white comforter.

"Umm... your mom is in the other room, painting up a storm, and she asked me to bring you these pain relievers. So, here you go." I walk up to him on the bed and set the pills and water on his bedside table and take a big step back then awkwardly put my hands behind my back. Not sure what to do next.

"So, my mom called you to come over and bring me the painkillers instead of walking down the hall herself? Is that the story you are going with, Cara?"

"Well, it doesn't sound like you are going to believe it, so I guess I'll have to tell you the truth instead."

"Yes, let's go with the truth."

"I stopped by to apologize. I'm so sorry, Brody. I was wrong to do that to you."

"To do what, exactly? I want to be sure I know what you are apologizing for."

"For all of it. For kissing you out of nowhere, running out like a chicken shit, and then avoiding you all week like a teenager. And... for hurting you. You've never done anything even the slightest bit mean to me, and I was horrible to you. I suck. I'm the worst. I'm pond scum. I don't deserve to live. I should be made to walk through the city while a mean old nun rings a hand-bell behind me while yelling *Shame! Shame! Shame! Shame!*"

"Stop. Stop. Just stop already. Damn you, Cara." He's smiling at me. "How do you make me laugh when you are apologizing? Who does that?"

"I guess me. I mean, I'm pretty amazing." I roll my eyes dramatically, toss my hair over my shoulder, and buff my nails on my T-shirt.

Incidentally, said T-shirt is another favorite of mine and says: *Margaritas count as my juice cleanse, right?*

"So, do you accept my apology, and can we be friends again?"

"Yes, of course, we can be friends again, but only if you tell me why you did it."

"Which part?"

"Any of it. All of it."

"Okay, I'll tell you, but first tell me what happened to your leg? Why are you laid up?"

He sighs and rubs his big hand down the front of his scruffy face, and it makes a slight scratchy sound. Looks like he hasn't shaved in a day or two, and it certainly suits him. I mean, I love him when he is freshly shaved too, but the barely there scruffy beard is not hard to look at, that's for damn sure. And even though he probably hasn't showered yet today, judging by the small amount of grease in his hair, he fucking smells delicious. All man. Mmmmm.

"It's been hurting for a while, and I think I overdid it at the gym the other night. I guess my mind wasn't on what I was doing, and my form must have slipped a bit. After doing the last set of squats, I felt something pop, and it really started hurting."

"Oh shit. Did you go to the ER? Did you get an X-ray yet? It could be your meniscus or an ACL tear. Popping isn't a good sign. Where does it hurt? Show me where the pain is, and how would you describe it? What position was your knee in when it popped?"

"Easy, Florence Nightingale. Yes, I went to the urgent care the next day — which was yesterday — and they did an X-ray. They are sending me for an MRI next week, but the doc doesn't think anything is torn. He thinks—"

"Wait a second," I interrupt him. "You said your mind wasn't on your workout. Why wasn't it?" I think I know the answer, but I really need to hear him say it. Guilt requires that I hear this answer.

Brody just stares at me, his gorgeous brown eyes looking at mine. He doesn't want to tell me. I can see it.

"It was me, right? You were upset because of me, and it's my fault you hurt yourself. Fuck. I'm so sorry, Brody."

"As I was saying, the doctor suspects it is some IT band thing. IT syndrome or something. I forget what he said exactly, I just heard that he doesn't think I'll need surgery. He said until I get the MRI, just to elevate it and ice it for a few days. I'm sure I'll be fine. It just sucks ass that I can't go to the gym. Mom won't let me leave the house unless she goes with me, and I use these stupid crutches. All of a sudden, I'm ten years old again, living with her rules."

I take a big sigh. He's not going to blame me. He's too sweet for that. But I know it was my fault.

"Sounds like Mom is right. Tell me about the pain. Maybe I can help. I do have some experience with this type of thing, you know. So, the doctor thinks it is Iliotibial Band Syndrome? Does that sound like what he said, ITBS? Or IT band syndrome?" I rattle off, talking so fast I'm going to be surprised if he can follow the conversation... especially if he is on pain medication.

"Yeah, I think that is what he said."

"Does your hip area ever hurt or feel tight?"

"My hip? Cara, it's my knee."

"Which one of us is a sports physical therapist here?" I shake my head at him.

"Fine. What do you mean my hip area?" He gestures to his hip and groin area. "I guess I get stiff around here sometimes. But I work out really hard, so I get tight all over."

Well, now my mind is firmly in the gutter thinking about how tight and stiff his entire body is. And I want to run my hands all over it. Fuck.

Hey, bitch, you did this to him. You hurt him, so you don't get to enjoy him.

Fuck you, Guilt. Who asked you anyway?

"All right, I'm going to put this out there, and I want you to say yes. Since it's clearly my fault you were distracted, and I know you are too nice to admit it. So, let's just move past that part. Let's just agree that I owe you. I will help you, free of charge, and get you feeling better in no time. I can't let you hurt any longer than you already have. Will you please trust me to help you heal?"

I'm looking at him with complete honesty and as serious as I've ever been. I hope he lets me work with him. It's the only way I can make this right. I can help him get better faster than any urgent care doctor who probably barely passed med school. Fuck, I can't believe they didn't get him an MRI already.

"Cara, I know you are really busy all the time and have too much on your plate. It's fine. It's not that bad, really. I'm sure the painkillers, anti-inflammatory drugs, and icing will be fine, and I'll be back at the gym by Monday or Tuesday."

"Fuck no, you won't! This can be a serious issue. It's probably been brewing a long time and just got exasperated when you overdid it with the squats. Did you run that day too? Or use the bikes?"

"Yes and yes. Why?"

"Because I know how these injuries happen, and I've seen them take people down and out. Please, let me help you. I'll get Cort and CJ to pick up the slack with the elders and Miles for a little while so I can work with you every evening. Please. I want to do this. You need to say yes. Just say yes."

Say yes, say yes. Please, say yes. The guilt is going to eat me alive if he doesn't let me help him.

"If I say yes, will you promise not to talk about being to blame for anything anymore? I know how you love to feel guilty for shit that isn't your fault. This wasn't your fault."

"Sure, fine, whatever you want. Just say yes." I look at him and turn my head to the side, shrug up my shoulders toward my ears, bring both my palms up into prayer position, and widen my eyes in what I hope is an adorable begging spectacle.

"Okay. Yes. Now, quit looking at me like that. I can't take the puppy dog eyes."

"Yes! Thank you. You won't regret this. I promise to help you feel better in no time. Can we start tomorrow? You should probably keep icing on and off for another half day or more before we get started. Try to move it a little bit though, you don't want it to lock up. Just be easy on it."

"Fine. Tomorrow. What time, and where do I need to meet you?"

I look around his room to assess how much space we have. "I think it will be fine to start here. We won't need much equipment to begin with, so I can start working you over here. This should work. Tomorrow is Sunday, so we are both off. How about 10 a.m.? Is that too early?"

"That will be fine. Thank you."

I hop up, pleased that I've managed to accomplish all my goals with this visit. I apologized, he forgave me, and he agreed to let me help him get better. Plus, I didn't have to tell him the super embarrassing reasons why I acted like a chump this week. Score one for me!

"All right, I'll see you tomorrow around ten. Get some rest, and take it easy. Thanks for agreeing to this. Have a good night."

I back out of the room, and he just watches me then slowly shakes his head. I turn tail and book it out of there. On the way out, I tell Linda that all is well and that I'm coming back tomorrow to help him with his rehab for his knee. She looks at me strangely, but I just hustle out before something happens to screw up this forward progress.

As I head home, I feel about a million times better than I have all week. I'm feeling optimistic.

Until I'm not.

I'm pulling in the driveway when it dawns on me just what I've agreed to. It's not just that I'll be seeing him every evening, most of which time will be in his room. It's that some of the things I'm going to have to do *to him* and *with him* to help him heal involve my hands going in places where they have only dreamed of going before.

Oh shit.

I will have to massage him in some pretty intimate areas and get him into some very provocative positions.

Shit. Shit. Fuck. Damn. Shit.

I really did not think this through. I'm getting totally turned on just by imagining what he is going to look like gliding back and forth on the foam roller. I can already feel how wet I'm going to be by the time I massage his... nope, not gonna think about it.

There is no way I'm going to be able to do this and not attack him again with another surprise kiss or more than likely, a surprise dry hump or two.

Fuck. I'm going to be right back where I started.

Hot, bothered, and freaked out about relationship drama.

Chapter Fifteen

Hurts so good

Brody

"Ouch. Ouch. Hey, stop it. You do know I'm injured, right?" I holler dramatically, but it doesn't seem to faze her.

"I haven't even started yet. Are you kidding me right now?"

I'm not totally serious, but it's fun to get her worked up. And it's a bit of payback since she's had me worked up for the last hour since she got here in her little black athletic shorts and purple tank top. Her ass is incredible in those shorts, and they show off her toned thighs which I can't seem to stop picturing wrapped around my waist or my head — either one would be fine at this point.

I get a nice view of her cleavage each time she leans over to force my body into another awkward position thanks to that top, which surprisingly doesn't have any reference to margaritas on it. This one just says: *I like coffee and maybe two people.*

Everything about this woman makes me smile, even her clothes.

Except for last week.

I was most certainly not smiling when she kissed the life out of me and then ran off, refusing to talk about it. Right now, we are pretty much avoiding the topic and pretending it didn't happen, but I know I'll never be able to shake that memory from my mind. And I don't want to. It was perfection.

I just have to find out what scared her away, so I can fix it, and we can move on and get back to the good stuff. I just need to be patient since apparently she is a little skittish about her feelings. *Maybe the cats that roam her house are rubbing off on her.*

"Well, maybe I'm being a little dramatic, I suppose." I give her a cheeky grin, and it brings a smile to her sweet face. I live for that smile.

She moves me into another position, this one much less painful on my knee and hips. Apparently, she was right, and my hips are really tight. How that relates to my knee pain is not quite clear yet, but she said I should trust her, and I will.

At this point, I'd do just about anything for her to stay with me and keep putting her hands on me. Even if a little pain is involved. Totally worth it, especially since she smells so amazing and looks so mouthwatering. Now that I've had a taste of her, it is even harder to keep my feelings for her in check.

"All right, just a little bit more stretching, and then we move to the good stuff!" she taunts, but I'm not so sure I believe her because she has a positively evil glint in her eye. I suspect good stuff is code for painful stuff.

"Why don't I think you and I have the same understanding of what good stuff is?"

"Ten more seconds, then rest," she tells me. I'm currently on my back on the floor, one leg bent and crossed over the other leg. Both legs have been pulled up to my chest in a stretch that is targeting my glutes, hamstrings, and piriformis muscles. We've already stretched my quads, hips, hamstrings, and pretty much every single body part you can think of. I had no idea there were this many ways to stretch your muscles.

"All right, are you ready to really work?"

"Okay, woman. Let me have it!"

"Careful what you ask for. Here, hold this. I have one too. I'll demonstrate on the mat, and then it's your turn." She hands me a ball that is slightly firmer than a tennis ball, but not as hard as a baseball. It's covered in a rubbery blue coating.

She moves onto the mat and adjusts her position, so she is face down, slightly to the side, facing me. She raises her hips, slides the ball under her hip, and begins a rolling motion, back and forth. She is working the ball into the front of her hip, and then she twists her body so that the ball is now pushing into the side of her hip.

Her mouth is moving, and she is explaining something. It's probably important but beats the shit out of me what it is. I can't keep my eyes off her hips moving back and forth, round and round. My dick is most definitely noticing it too. How am I supposed to do this with a semi?

"Your turn." She moves out of the way so I can take her space, and I'm so sad the show is over.

"No, I don't think I understand. Can you show me again?" I give her a naughty smile.

She swats at my chest and points at the mat, looking a bit like a drill sergeant.

"Yes ma'am. I like it when you are bossy."

I can't help but flirt with her. It's like a built-in response when she is around, and it's one hundred percent automatic after watching her move the way she just did. I could practically see her moving like that on top of me, and fuck, I need to have her.

I'm trying to get in the same position she was in, and I can't help but wonder if it will have the same effect on her that it did on me. I sure hope so.

After some awkward maneuvering, I think I'm in the position and begin to move around on the ball. Fuck, that hurts. No wonder she hinted that it was about to get worse.

"Jesus, Cara. Is it supposed to hurt that bad?"

"Engage your core and your upper body more to take some of your body weight off the ball. That feel better?"

"Yeah, a little."

"Good, keep it up then. If it gets to be too much, keep adjusting the pitch of your hips to come at the area from a different angle. So, to answer your earlier question, yes. It is going to hurt, and the tighter those muscles are, the worse the pain. Clearly, you are really tight since you're hurting that bad. In fact, this area right here," she jabs her finger toward the side of my hip area, "is where the entire problem is. From what I've seen today, your knee is fine — aside from maybe some arthritis. It's the muscles up here, where the IT band attaches to your hips and pelvic area that are too tight. It causes the band to pull really tight throughout your leg, especially at the spot where it connects to the knee. So, it keeps popping over the side of your knee joint, and it's all inflamed. That's the popping you've heard most likely. Make sense?"

"Yeah, it does. So, are you telling me if I would have kept this area better stretched out, I wouldn't have had to stop working out?"

She probably has no idea, but I simply must get back in the gym and be able to keep working out every day. I can't let myself slip-up, or I might fall back into old comfort routines. Then the next thing you know, I'll be back to my old miserable fat self. Not that there's anything wrong with people who are on the larger side, if that makes them happy. But for me — I was miserable. I couldn't stand being in my own skin. Now that I know what being in shape feels like, I don't ever want to go back.

"Well, yes and no. This is actually really common with athletes. Running and cycling make it worse, and it's basically due to overuse of the muscles without enough rest between workouts and well, old age." She shrugs her shoulders and squishes up her nose as if she is afraid of how I will react to the old age comment.

"When you get back to working out, you'll need to keep this area rolled out regularly. Supplement with some massages and keep with the stretches that I show you. And take more time off in between workouts. Your body will continue to break down if you don't give it time to heal."

Shit, now she is starting to sound like Hudson.

She swaps out the ball for a foam roller, and I start working out my hips and legs as she instructs.

"Did you say massage? Now you have my attention," I ask to take the topic off working out too much. Not going there with her.

"Yes, actually I'm going to try some after we get done with the foam roller to see if I can break up the fascia around your knee and on both sides of your IT band. You should feel some immediate relief today after all this stretching, rolling, and the massage."

"You're giving me a massage?" I ask. I wonder if she can hear the hesitation in my voice.

There is absolutely no way I'll be able to keep my erection under control if she is rubbing lotion all over me. As much as I want her hands on me, I don't want to embarrass myself like a fourteen-year-old who just found his dad's porno magazine stash. I don't want to make her uncomfortable. Ever.

"Yeah, it's part of your treatment plan. It's not gonna hurt, don't worry. I'll be very, very gentle." She lowers her voice, and fuck, she is flirting back. Maybe the massage is a good idea after all.

"I'm not worried about it hurting; I was just curious. I didn't think physical therapists did that."

"Yes, we do all kinds of things to help speed up healing. Athletes are very hard on their bodies and need their muscles to recover quickly to prevent further injury. Massage is a large part of recovery for some injuries. And your pain in particular will benefit from regular massage."

I have no idea how to respond, so I'm going to just shut up. The thought of her regularly massaging me is more than I can handle right now. I swallow the lump in my throat, and I notice her watching my throat move. She is also breathing a little bit more erratically, and she just licked her lips. Clearly, she is affected by me too.

Glad to know I'm not the only one. Not that she could have hid her attraction to me after that kiss.

"All right, this feels good and loose now. What's next?"

"Well, I think we can move to your massage now. You don't really need much strengthening, so I'm not going to try out any exercises with you just yet. I don't think strength is your problem. I mean, look at yourself. It's all about reducing the inflammation and loosening up the muscles that surround the IT band."

"Okay, how are we gonna do this then?"

"I'm not entirely sure. I can do it on the floor, but I think you'll be more comfortable on the bed. I brought some towels, and I have my oil. So, let's try it there and see how it goes. Yeah?"

"Sure, sure, sure." My head is nodding up and down, and I'm sure she can see I'm nervous. She seems to be as well because she isn't making eye contact, and she is looking around the room as if looking for a place to hide. It's endearing how shy she has suddenly become.

"Okay, I'm going to wash my hands while you get on the bed. Maybe lie toward the center of the bed so I have some room to kneel beside you and can move to either side. Next time, maybe I'll see about bringing a folding table. How much do you weigh? You're like a beefcake. I might need an industrial strength one that can hold all those muscles," she jokes, getting her groove back.

There's my girl. Humor always makes her more comfortable. When she jokes, it always makes me feel better too.

I make my move to the bed as she heads to the bathroom to wash up. I holler, "How do you want me? On my front or back?"

Sounds like she just dropped something in the bathroom — maybe the bottle of liquid soap hit the sink.

"Uhhh…" she trails off.

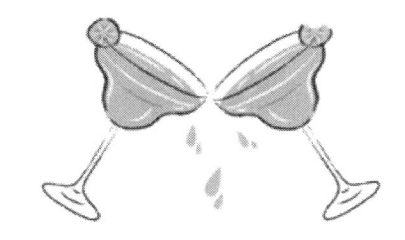

Chapter Sixteen

What's a butt rub among friends?

Cara

I pick up the soap bottle I dropped when he asked that question and try to formulate a response.

How do I want him? Well, let's see. Probably the easiest question I could ever answer.

Up against the wall. On the floor. In the bed. Hanging from the ceiling. On the couch — specifically me bent over the couch and then me riding him on the couch. The kitchen counter. The back seat of my car. Front seat of my car. The roof of my car. Ditto all that but this time in and on *his* car. In the sleet. In the snow. In the ocean. On the beach. In a pool. In the rain. In a plane. On a train. In a house. With a mouse. Here, there, anywhere! Fuck, I just want him.

I really, *really* tried to tell myself to just be professional and pretend this was any other athlete at the clinic. But who was I kidding? This is Brody. He is the perfect male specimen, and I've been lusting after him for more than three damn years.

Plus, that kiss is still so fresh in my mind. It's like I can still feel him on my lips if I think about it hard enough.

Hard. Just like my nipples are right now.

How am I going to massage him and *not* strip and rub my breasts all over him? *How*? I don't think I have enough self-control. I haven't had sex in a few years, and I'm so lit up inside when I'm around him. It's like the Fourth of July in my pants.

"Uhhh."

There. Perfectly stated. Attagirl.

I hear him chuckling. Great, the beautiful asshole thinks I'm funny when I'm speechless.

"It doesn't matter; I'm going to need to do both sides, more than likely, so maybe start face down."

Girding my loins, I head out of the bathroom and try not to trip over my tongue, which is probably wagging out of my mouth. It's likely hanging down to the floor excreting mass quantities of drool at the mere sight of this man on the bed, his immaculate ass, back, and shoulders on display. Fortunately, he is still clothed. Which reminds me...

Really, Cara? You must figure out how to do this massage without him needing to take his pants off. Please, girl.

Or don't.

Fuck it. Maybe I'll take my pants off too. Wouldn't want him to be the only one pantless.

I grab the oil out of my bag and approach the bed, picking up the towels as I drag my feet toward my doom. Or to ecstasy. Not sure which.

"Okay, let's get started then. Are you comfortable enough, or do you need a pillow under your hips? Sometimes that takes the pressure off your low back."

Just keep it clinical, and you'll be fine, Cara. You got this.

"I think I'm okay without it, but I'll let you know if I get uncomfortable."

"Perfect. So, just relax then, and let me know if the pressure is too hard or not hard enough. This will feel good for the most part, especially in the beginning. There will be a point though when it gets a little painful. I'll talk you through it. Have you had many massages before?"

I situate myself next to him on the bed with his left leg closest to me. I place the oil and towels at the bedside table and glance at his impressive ass and realize I'm going to have to adjust his shorts to get at the target area. "Gotta move your shorts up a little. Sorry."

"Do what you gotta do. I'm never going to complain about you touching me, Carina."

No, don't call me that right now, Brody. I am only so strong.

I pull a little bit, and oh shit. They aren't exactly the most flexible material.

"Shift your butt up a little, so I can try to shimmy them up, Brody."

He does, and I try again. And fail. I try a different technique and almost get it, but it doesn't look comfortable. It looks like they are going to end up cutting off his circulation.

"Umm… do you want to maybe try to put on some looser shorts that I can roll up? To be blunt, I have to get right up there to where your, um, back of your leg hits your, um, glutes." My voice softens to a near whisper, and I continue, "In fact, I'm going to have to get the glutes too. This is awkward."

He chuckles, sits up, and gets off the bed. He strips his shorts down and leaves himself in just his boxers. "This better? Should I lose the shirt too?"

"Yeah, might as well." He tosses the shirt off and gets back down on the bed, now just in his boxers.

Okay, so real talk. There was absolutely no reason why he needed to take his shirt off. That was just a gut reaction. When a man that hot asks if he should take his shirt off, you say abso-fucking-lutely. And you say it without regret. And right now, I have no regrets.

I had no idea, but my Brody has a gorgeous tattoo on his back. It looks like some type of tribal symbol that I don't recognize. As if he needed to be even hotter.

"Oh, you have some ink. It's… nice. Really nice."

"Glad you approve. I would have had it removed if you didn't like it," he says with a smile in his voice.

He is taunting me a little bit, and I like it.

Not taking the bait. "So, I'm going to drape the towel over your tush for modesty purposes and work your boxers up a little bit."

I proceed to cover him with the towel and then reach under, feeling my way to roll up his boxers to just where his ass meets his legs. I hear him exhale, and I do the same.

I reach over and pump some oil onto my hands and rub them together briskly to heat it up. I begin the massage a bit lower down his leg with light and broad strokes — just starting to warm up the area and get the blood flowing.

I'm telling myself that the heat coming from his body is all in my mind. I'm also telling myself that his skin is not absolutely perfect. I'm telling myself that I do not want to replace my hands with my tongue. In short, I am telling myself lies. Big. Fat. Lies.

After a while, my training takes over, and I get into the zone. My touch gets firmer, and I incorporate my elbows, forearms, and knuckles. The massage gets deeper and deeper, and holy shit, his legs are incredible.

As the massage proceeds, I have to inch up closer to his buttocks, or ass of steel to be more specific. I can't help the hitch in my breath as my hands begin to caress it. I have to start out softly to wake up the area, just like I did the lower area. But it feels very intimate.

His breathing is picking up too, and he suddenly starts rambling. His voice is a little shaky, and it's kind of nice to know that I'm not the only one suffering here. Clearly, we are both very attracted to each other. I just am not sure if I can do anything about it.

We kissed once, and it ruined everything for a solid week. Imagine if we went further. I don't want Miles to lose him.

I will myself to stay professional while he starts babbling about his mom, her antics, and the crazy stories she has been telling him. He also mentions that she told him she thought I was a very pretty and lovely young lady after I left yesterday. This makes me chuckle.

"You know your mom busted my chops when I got here yesterday, right?"

At this, he lifts his head off the pillow and looks over his shoulder at me. When our eyes meet, there is fire in them. Pure fire.

"Really? What did she say?" he asks me.

"Oh, she wanted to know what I did to make her little boy cry. And she said something about me taking your virtue. I can't remember exactly, but she was very protective of your delicate emotions. Something along those lines," I joke. I can't even deliver it with anything close to a straight face.

He picks up a pillow off the bed and throws it back at me. I swat it away, and we laugh.

I get back to business and start working his glutes even more. He is very tight in here, and I can't resist poking the bear a little bit.

"So, do you do like fifteen hundred squats a day, or is that every other day?"

"Is that admiration I detect in your tone?"

"Oh, there is plenty about this to admire, I'm not gonna lie."

"Any time you want to touch, let me know. I can get you an all access pass to the front of the line."

"The line? Excuse me, how did you fit your ego into this apartment? Surely it doesn't fit in a one-bedroom unit."

"My ego, like everything else, is sized just right. And don't call me Shirley," he jokes, and I can't resist, but I swat him on his ass.

"All right funny man, roll over for me. Time to do the quads, and then I can get at that hip a little bit better."

"Just give me a minute, please."

"Mmm kay..." Interesting. "Any reason in particular you need time to roll over? Did it feel so good you've become like jello and can't move?"

"Actually, the opposite of jello. At least in one area in particular."

"Oh. My."

If he could see my face right now. I'm biting my lip, and my eyes are huge. I can feel my eyebrows raised so high, they are fighting my hairline to be the top hair on my head.

"Well. Umm. Do you want me to step out for a few minutes, so you can, umm, handle it?"

He laughs. "No, just shut up for a minute. Hearing your voice isn't helping the, uh, situation resolve itself."

I can't help but chuckle at that.

"This actually happens to lots of guys when getting a massage. It isn't anything to be ashamed of," I try to offer something to make him feel less uncomfortable.

"Oh, I'm not ashamed. I'm proud as hell of it. In fact, maybe I should show you the effect you have on me." He starts to roll over, and I stop him.

"No, that's not necessary. Thank you for the offer. I have an adequate memory of it from last weekend."

Why did I say that? Now we are probably both thinking of that sizzling kiss when he pressed his firm and impressive length up against me.

"I guess that is true. Well, you know what — fuck it. You already have an idea of what I'm dealing with here, so might as well see it for yourself."

"Brody, stop. Don't say that."

"Why not? We never did talk about it. Now is as good a time as any." He turns on his side and is looking up at me with a sense of longing on his absolutely perfect face.

Please note that I said his *face*. I'm forcing my eyes to stay on his face and upper body, but it is extremely hard — pun intended — to not let my eyes drift lower.

"What did you want to talk about? We don't have to talk about it. We can just pretend it didn't happen."

"Maybe I don't want to pretend it didn't happen."

"Maybe I don't either. But maybe I'm also very scared and think maybe it shouldn't happen again," I respond truthfully, my eyes dropping down to the comforter.

"Maybe you should tell me why that might be the case, and then maybe I can tell you why I think it *should* happen again."

"Fair enough." I exhale deeply and look at him right in the eyes, mustering all my courage. "I'm scared that I like you too much, and if we take this further, it will ruin our amazing friendship, and you'll end up leaving Miles and me, just like everyone else has."

Well. I guess there is no reason to hold back. I just laid that shit right out there, didn't I?

He sits up, moves closer to me, and puts his hand on the side of my cheek, cupping it gently.

"Carina, I would never leave you and Miles. You know I'm crazy about that kid and would never abandon him."

"You can't know that. When it ends, you won't want to see me, and I won't be able to see you again. I wouldn't be able to handle that." Tears are starting to prick at my eyes, but I try with all my might to suck them back into my eye sockets as if that is a skill that is humanly possible to possess.

"Why do you think it would end? I don't think it will."

I can feel my forehead wrinkle, and my hands are grasping at the hem of my tank top like it is a lifeline.

"That's very sweet of you to say, but Miles is *a lot* to handle, and most people can't do it. I know you are usually great with him, but you only see him in small doses. And when you add my crazy grandparents, and my overbearing siblings — it's just too much to ask anyone to put up with. If you remember, my last relationship ended because of how hard it is to deal with Miles. And he has to be my number one focus."

He slowly starts to move his strong hand away from my cheek and down my jaw and to my neck. He now is pulling me slightly closer into him, and he is leaning in toward me. I'm feeling breathless as he grasps his hand more firmly now behind my neck.

His voice is a low rumble — just on this side of angry — as he says slowly and carefully, "First of all, that guy was an ass-clown. Second of all, how about you let me decide what I'm willing to put up with? I know what I'm getting into with you, and I think you are worth it."

My heart is thumping along like the elephants on parade from the *Jungle Book*. It's going to burst from my chest if he doesn't stop this.

"Are you sure? My life is no picnic. It's all fun and games until Miles starts slapping everything off all flat surfaces and screaming at the top of his lungs, Grandpa Dickhead is yelling at him to keep it down so he can hear his *programs,* and Grammy Ellie thinks it will all be better if she can just give him some cookies. Even though that would be far worse since she probably used salt instead of sugar 'cause she can't see for shit."

He just grins and says, "I've never been more sure of anything in my life. This isn't something that just popped up out of the blue, Carina. I don't know what on earth possessed you to kiss me, but I am grateful that you did. I was too much of a chickenshit to do it myself, even though I've wanted to since you burst into my class late for Open House."

"Really? You have?" He nods in response, which leads me to admit, "I have wanted to kiss you since then too. But the timing never seemed to be right."

"Feels pretty fucking right now, doesn't it?"

"Yeah, yes. Yes, it does." I'm nodding while my head and heart are getting on board with the idea that this is gonna happen. Me and Brody. I can't believe how lucky I am to be in his presence, let alone the object of all that heat and passion that he is projecting onto me.

"Good. So, we are on the same page then? We are gonna do this, you and me?" he asks cautiously.

"Okay. Let's do this. Should we seal the deal with a kiss?" I ask cheekily.

"Come here, you little minx."

With that, he lunges for me and pulls me on top of him as he leans back on the bed and crashes his lips to mine. I press my hands to his bulging pecs and brace myself on him, giving my all into this kiss.

Once again, I see stars and fireworks, hearts and sparkles, pixie dust and moonbeams, and every other celestial thing you can name. I see them all. Kissing him is like Christmas, New Year's, Valentine's Day, and fucking President's Day all rolled into one. And I'm not even sure what that all means — but I'm going with it cause this kiss is all the happy feelings.

This man kisses like he means it. His large hands move from my head where he was holding me captive and slide gently down my back, rubbing and caressing me as he shifts them lower and lower. Once he gets down to the bottom of my tank top, he moves his hands under the fabric of my shirt, rubbing the bare skin of my back. The feeling of his warm flesh pressed up against mine is nothing short of magical.

My legs come up involuntarily so I'm straddling him. He turns his head to angle the kiss even deeper. This is sheer ecstasy. I can't help but rub my center over his straining cock, trying to ease that ache that is burning from deep within me.

He groans at the contact, and I gasp into his mouth in return. My hands wander all over his bare chest, and I could swear his shoulders were carved from stone. He is not human — he can't be. He feels so perfect against me, and I'm desperate to feel more of my bare skin against his.

I break the kiss suddenly and sit up, reaching to the bottom of my shirt to pull it off. Before I can do it, he sits up and grabs my hand, stopping me.

I eye him skeptically, "What's wrong? I want to keep going."

"Me too. But my mom is in the next room, remember?"

Splash! It's like a huge bucket of ice water to the libido.

Shhhhhhhhhiiiiitttt.

"I forgot about her. Oh my gosh, I'm so sorry."

He smiles, begins stroking my hair, and says, "Don't apologize. That was fucking amazing. But you need to go now and get out of here before I say fuck it and take you regardless if she can hear you scream or not."

"Good call. I'd probably prefer she starts to like me as a person before she hears me coming."

His eyes widen when I say that, and he leans back and slams his pillow over his face.

"Go, you temptress. Take your seductive ass with you. I can't resist you when you say shit like that." He groans loudly into the pillow, and I can't help but chuckle. "Fuck, the idea of you talking dirty is enough to make me come in my boxers like a teenager, devil woman."

As I get off the bed, I can't help but notice the head of his cock peeking out of the top of his boxers. Damn, that looks good enough to eat. Maybe just a little taste before I go?

"Don't even think about it." I hear him say, firmly shaking me out of my blow job fantasy.

I meet his eyes and see he's removed the pillow and is giving me a look that telegraphs: *I know what you are thinking.*

"How do you know what I was thinking?"

"Carina, you were staring at my cock and licking your lips. It doesn't take a rocket scientist to figure it out." He laughs, and I can't help but smile.

"All right, fine, you party pooper. I'll get my stuff and go, then you can hang out with your mom. I'll come over tomorrow night and stretch you out again, and maybe we can even finish the massage." I wink and giggle.

What has come over me? Who is this harlot impersonating me?

I, Carina Skyler Amos, do not giggle and wink at mostly naked hot men!

"I'm going to try to get my mother to leave in the morning to head back to Orlando. I can already tell my knee feels much better, so I'll be able to get around better. No need for her to be here hovering over me."

"Yeah, she's a real beaver blocker."

He tilts his head to one side and just shakes his head with a big shit-eating grin on his face. "I've never heard that one before, but it's pretty clear what you mean. And you're not wrong in this case."

I love that he doesn't get offended by my sense of humor. I realize I'm a lot to handle and not everyone's cup of tea. Being the court jester can grate at times. My sisters have told me before that my lack of seriousness is a real turn-off. Aside from Brody, the only one that gets me is Cort.

It's not that I don't take things seriously, it's just that I process things through a comedic lens. I can be serious when the situation calls for it, but I think life is too short to not laugh at anything and everything you can.

Laughter burns a lot of calories, and margaritas are a high-calorie drink. So, I'm just doing my best to not gain a ton of weight.

"Okay, bye then. I'm out of here, hot stuff." I lean over and give him a quick chaste kiss and run off before he pulls me back on top of him. If that were to happen, wild horses wouldn't be able to tear me away from him until we were both spent and satisfied.

I wave to Linda on the way out and tell her that I'll see her later. She smiles and waves at me as if she knows what we were up to. Maybe she does.

As I head home, I sing my heart out at the top of my lungs to Bebe Rexha's "*In the Name of Love.*" This song is an older banger from 2016, but it fits my mood perfectly. I'm not going to worry about things going wrong for once in my life. I'm going to trust Brody when he says that he wants this, and he knows the mess he is getting into. He is right after all, why should I be the judge of what is best for him? He's a big boy and can make his own decisions.

A very big boy indeed.

Chapter Seventeen

Alone at last

Brody

"Brocephus, my dude! Where ya been?" Hudson asks as we FaceTime with his typical easy-go-lucky attitude.

I haven't seen him in almost two weeks since that night we went out in Ybor City for bro's night.

The following week, I was licking my wounds over my falling out with Cara and the kiss that rocked both our worlds, and I didn't want him to see me like that. He is too perceptive; I wasn't ready to deal with his opinion on the matter. So, I intentionally hit the gym when I knew he wouldn't be there. And then this week I haven't been at the gym at all because Cara made me promise to restrict my activity to what is required to get to work and back home.

To make sure I don't backslide too much, each morning when I wake up, I do a shitload of sit-ups, push-ups, and other body weight exercises that my knee tolerates fairly well.

Each evening this week, Cara has come over after work for more physical therapy, also known as torture. We don't spend all our time working on my injury though, we usually spend at least twenty minutes or so making out and driving each other crazy with need. It's a lot like being in high school again, making out with your crush while trying to avoid the parents in the next room.

The sexual tension between us is killing me since Mom flat-out refuses to go back to Orlando. She has been cockblocking… or beaver blocking us all week long. I don't know how much more I can take before I snap. It started out with her helping me around the house and then she started redecorating and can't seem to stop herself.

As far as the rehab goes, I'm improving, and the pain is lessening. Unfortunately, it seems to return when I do too much or too little. It's hard to find the balance Cara keeps talking about, but I try.

As we've progressed through the week, she has added some strengthening exercises too. Surprisingly, she has found some muscle groups that I can enhance. She's actually a tough cookie when it comes to challenging my body physically — and I mean that in more ways than one.

At least we have the massage time at the end of each torture session to look forward to. It's like a reward for the frustration we are both experiencing. Having her hands on me is like having a taste of heaven.

I've even managed to let her work on my hip and quads while I'm lying on my back, instead of face down trying to suppress my raging hard-on like usual. Last night was phenomenal since she finally convinced me to let her give me a happy ending. She made me be completely quiet so Mom wouldn't hear. It was hot as hell.

She wanted to use her mouth, but I wouldn't let her because I want to be able to repay that favor immediately. She said she tends to be a little loud and doesn't trust herself with Mom in the next room. And her saying that made it that much harder for me to resist.

I can't wait to hear her come for me and scream my name.

"I've been around, Huds, but I had a little injury pop up and I haven't been able to hit the gym this week." I don't want to tell him this because he warned me this would happen. But I'm not going to bullshit my friend.

"What the hell happened? Are you okay? What do you need?" he asks, like the true friend he is.

"It's my knee — well, Cara says it's actually the *tensor fascia latae* muscles that are the problem, but it's causing pain in my knee." I'm super proud I remembered that really complicated word. I might be a teacher, but anatomy is not my specialty.

"Cara, huh? Haven't seen her for a while. How did she happen to diagnose you, man?" He has a glint in his eye, and I have a feeling I know where this is heading.

"Well, as you know she is a sports therapist at UT and when she found out I was laid up, she came over and has been helping me... recover." I can't hide the cheesy ass smile and I don't want to hide it. I'm not sure I've ever been this happy.

"Really, do go on," he prods.

"Dude, she is so amazing and her massages at the end of each session could inspire poetry."

"Did you finally make a move? That smile on your face says you did."

I nod, and he yelps, then pumps his fist. "That's my boy. Hell yeah! You are the Sultan of Stoke right now, man! Finally! Fuck, I'm so happy for you."

"Yeah, she actually made the first move, but I was more than happy to take it from there."

"Yes! Man, I'm so stoked for you. That's dank!"

"Is that a good thing?"

"Dank? Fuck yeah it is. Like, you could say, 'That is some dank ass weed.' Just as an example."

I chuckle. "It doesn't sound good, but I guess you would know better than me. I don't usually have the opportunity to rate weed quality."

He grins. "So, are you two like official? Did you propose yet? I know you've been sweet on her for a while, no matter how much you tried to hide it."

"How did you know?"

"You always get this dopey ass look on your face when you talk about her. And I saw how you looked at her when we all went out for your fortieth birthday party."

I remember that night. She showed up with Jimmy, and it ruined the rest of the night. Fuck that guy.

"Shit, man. That was like two years ago. I'm surprised you have enough brain cells left to remember that," I joke.

"I'm not just a pretty face, sweetheart." He winks at me, the shithead.

"We haven't talked labels yet, but I can see this lasting for sure. I'm already halfway in love with her and we haven't even screwed yet."

"What are you waiting for? Get in there, man!"

"Mom won't fucking leave us alone long enough for anything to happen."

"That's what you get for being a mama's boy."

"Yeah, yeah. She should be leaving soon since I'm doing much better now, and I think she is running out of corners in my apartment to decorate or *de-bachelorize* as she calls it."

"Well, I am psyched for you, man. Listen, I gotta run, but I'm glad to see your smiling face. You deserve to be happy. Let's catch up later in the week. I'll come by and keep you company next weekend, okay?"

We say our goodbyes and I check my watch, excited that Cara should be here any minute. It's time for our evening routine, and tonight is going to be special. I light the candles and dim the dining room lights, putting the final touches to the table setting. *I'm such a romantic bastard.*

I may have bribed Mom's friend Maggie to invite her out to dinner and a movie tonight. So, I've got a few hours alone with Cara and I'm going to make the most of it.

I've got a chicken pot pie in the oven and made a salad to accompany it. I don't have many meals that I would consider my specialty, but I've been told my pot pie is phenomenal. It's not traditional date food, but Cara isn't someone who needs surf and turf to be impressed. I know she'd appreciate a peanut butter and jelly sandwich, just as much as filet mignon. Just another of the things I love about her.

I turn when I hear a soft knock at the door, and I eat up the space between the dining room and the front door in record time.

When I open up the door and see her gorgeous brown eyes looking at me and the shy smile on her face, my heart tries to break out of my chest. She's a knockout and takes my breath away just with one look.

"Please come in." I open the door and beckon her in with a sweeping gesture.

"Why thank you, my good man. Are you ready for your daily dose of pain and torture? How are you feeling?" She leans in and gives me a peck on the lips, then pulls back, looking around — probably searching for my mom.

"Actually, I feel amazing today — thanks to you. I was thinking we could do something else for a little while before you beat me up." I'm still in some pain, but I'm not letting that stop me. "As a thank you for helping me, I made dinner and have cheesecake for dessert."

"Oh, that's so sweet Brody, but you didn't have to go to any trouble. Where's Linda, she is usually waiting to tell me something embarrassing about you as soon as I get here. And I so look forward to hearing more about when you used to shove dirt down your pants as a young lad. What was up with that anyway? It's a little strange," she jokes, still looking around.

"Well, it just so happens that you and I are going to have a few hours alone this evening because she and her friend went out to dinner and a movie and just left a few minutes ago."

"So, we are alone?" she asks, not missing a beat.

"Yes, we sure are. Just the two of us." I take a step closer with the intention to give her a proper welcome kiss now that she knows we don't have an audience.

"Huh. Well..." she trails off and climbs me like a tree, acting like a possessed woman on a mission.

Grabbing my shoulders, she hoists herself up, and I reflexively grab her ass, helping her wrap her legs around me. And then she kisses me fiercely, with three years of pent-up lust and emotion.

With her arms wrapped around my neck and shoulders, I back her up toward the living room wall, press her against it to brace her, and allow my hands to roam. I capture her sexy moans and gasps in my mouth. She is all heat and sweetness and tastes like sin, and I need more. *Must have more.*

Now.

I had every intention of treating her to a special meal tonight. I was hopeful things would escalate, but I would never assume anything. But with the way she is attacking me, she is showing me that she wants me just as much as I want her.

And I don't think I can wait any longer to be inside her.

I pull away from her lips and trail kisses, nips, and licks down her jaw and neck, while my right hand gently squeezes one breast and then the other, ending with a slight tweak to her nipple.

She whimpers, and in-between panting breaths, she purrs, "Bedroom. Now. Want you."

"As the lady wishes."

I keep her wrapped around me like a spider monkey and pull away from the wall, making our way to the room while still kissing and worshiping her with each step.

Just as we pass the bedroom threshold, I hear a buzzer from the kitchen, and we both freeze.

"Is that the fire alarm? Cause you are hot as fuck." Always with the jokes, this girl. Fuck, she makes me so happy.

"No, it's the oven. I need to turn it off unless you want me to burn dinner. Get in bed, and I'll be right back."

"Hurry up, hotness, or I'll get started without you." She slides down my body, rubbing my bulge softly with her hand just one time before shoving me out the door with a giggle.

I race into the kitchen, peek inside the oven, noticing dinner isn't burned, and turn it off. I'll leave it inside so it stays warm for a while. Because we are going to need more than few minutes for what I've got planned.

When I rush back into the bedroom, my jaw nearly hits the ground at the sight before me. Cara looks like Aphrodite laying on my bed in nothing but a teal blue lacy bra and matching panties.

I immediately remove my shirt and toss it on the ground, then yank down my jeans and kick them off as I move toward the bed with a speed that I didn't know was humanly possible.

Knee pain? What knee pain?

"Thanks for hurrying. You're right on time," she says playfully as I climb on the bed and make my way up her gorgeous body, one delicious inch at a time.

My gaze tracks my hands as they roam up her legs, over her hips, and then caress her stomach before I place a soft kiss on her tummy, just below her belly button. I inch up farther, placing teasing kisses across her skin as I go, before pausing to admire her luscious breasts while wedging my lower body between her soft, strong thighs.

She is beauty personified.

I don't hide my appreciation for the artistry that is her smooth skin and curvy figure. I even look to the heavens and whisper, "Thank you, sweet Jesus for sending me your most gorgeous angel."

She laughs boisterously, just like I knew she would. As I look into her eyes, she inhales sharply. I know she feels this as strongly as I do. This pull to be near each other.

This need to touch, caress, and hold… and to love.

She reaches up, grabs my face, and pulls me in for a sweet kiss that grows and grows in intensity until we are both nothing but a wash of writhing bodies. We press against each other so firmly and completely that our skin seems to be trying to fuse together.

Kissing her, lying with her like this, is like a gift that I won't ever be able to repay no matter how long I live. I don't know what I did to deserve her, but I will spend every day for the rest of my life showing her how grateful I am that she chose me to grace with her affection and body.

As our kisses become more frantic and the groping becomes more desperate, I break my lips and make my way back down her body. "As much as I love the taste of your sweet kisses, Carina, there is something else that I need to taste right now."

"Brody…" she sighs my name as she moves her hands through my soft brown hair and bites her lower lip.

Her eyes meet mine as I rub my nose, lips, and chin over her warm center, over the dampening fabric of her panties.

"Fuck, baby, you smell like heaven." I nip and tug gently at her most tender spot, causing her to gasp in shock.

Her hips press up instinctively, and that's the last straw. I'm done waiting. No more dragging this out.

I need to taste her.

Now.

I quickly grab the top of her panties, pulling them down her silky legs, then toss them over my shoulder.

A second later, I'm back between her legs, and she is spread out before me like a buffet of all my favorite food. I lick my lips and then start kissing her on the inside of her thighs, one side and then the other, until both of our breathing becomes erratic.

Finally, my mouth is where we both want it to be.

Her essence explodes on my tongue, and I almost come in my pants from the sound of her reactionary moans. She tastes so damn good, just like I knew she would.

Without preamble, I go to work like a man possessed, drawing the flat of my tongue up and down her silky pink flesh in long, languid strokes, before gently sucking her clit into my mouth.

She bucks off the mattress, but I hold her down by the hips. She has a firm grasp on my head, and I can tell by how hard she's gripping me that she's in ecstasy. I love getting to know what she likes, what makes her grind harder into my face, what makes her gasp, and what makes her moan.

And damn, she was not lying. She *is* loud when she's enjoying herself.

She warned me, but fuck if it's not the hottest thing I've ever heard. She's rambling in that adorable way she does when she gets flustered, but the words coming out of her mouth are sexy-as-fuck.

"Yes, Brody."

"Oh my freaking hell. Yes. Just like that."

"More of that."

"Right there, oh my God."

"I love your tongue. It's fucking perfect."

It's like having my own personal cheering section, and I'm totally here for it.

I press one finger inside her to see how tight she is, and *holy hell*, I'm going to die when I finally get inside her.

My mouth continues to work her clit, swirling around as she builds and builds while I move my middle finger in and out, faster and faster. Slowly, I add a second finger, and I feel her quivering around me.

When I crick my finger, she yells, "Shit, yes, oh, that feels amazing, baby."

A few seconds later, she's rambling again. "Oh, I can't wait to suck your cock. I can't wait to taste you and make you feel just as amazing as you are making me. Fuck… you are so good at that. Don't stop. I'm so close."

When she grabs her breasts and tweaks her nipples through her bra, I swear it's the hottest thing I think I've ever seen.

I look up her body as I work her into a frenzy, and although she's trying to hold eye contact, eventually, her eyes roll back into her head as her orgasm takes over. She arches her back, and her thighs squeeze my head like a vise.

Witnessing her let go in complete ecstasy, and knowing I was the one to bring her this pleasure, is something I'll never forget as long as I live.

Gently, I remove my fingers and slow down the rhythm with my mouth, letting her ride it out. As she comes down, I pull my mouth away and catch her eyes as I lick my fingers, sucking them off one at a time. She whimpers as she tries to catch her breath.

After discarding my boxers, I work my way back up to her perfect face that's glowing with unfiltered joy. Pulling her close, I kiss her deeply while sneaking one hand around her back to find her bra clasp. Sensing I'm struggling a bit, she takes pity on me, moving her hands behind her to make quick work of it.

Once she shrugs out of the lacey bra, I'm faced with immaculate, milky white breasts that fit in my big palms perfectly. Shit, it's like she was made for me.

I roll my tongue around one pale pink nipple, then the other before sucking it deep in my mouth. While moaning and panting, she moves under me, trying to get herself lined up with my cock, which is proudly jutting out between her legs, poking around like a heat-seeking missile.

"Hang on, baby. Let me get a condom."

I reach over into the bedside table, where I had the foresight to put a new box of condoms after our first make-out session. It's been a while, and the old ones were expired. As much as I'd love to put a baby in her, we haven't talked about that, and I am not going to do anything to risk upsetting this goddess.

And yeah... I know I'm getting way ahead of myself with thoughts like that. But I've never felt a connection like this before.

I know she's meant to be my forever.

She grabs the condom out of my hand, tears it open frantically, and slides it down my length, giving me a few good hard strokes in the process.

"There. All set, now get inside me before I explode."

And that's all the encouragement I need. Moving swiftly, I line up and slowly make my way inside, one delicious inch at a time. In a little and then back out, going a bit further each time. She is so tight, wet, warm, and perfect.

Once I'm inside her to the hilt, we both pause our movements and simply take in the rapturous sensation of being joined. Connected. *Finally*.

Our gazes lock, and for a moment, we simply exist — together.

Three years.

Three damn excruciatingly long years I've waited for this moment. To feel every inch of her skin pressed against mine. To be connected to her. To be wrapped up in her. To make her mine, inside and out.

Three damn years, and it was worth the fucking wait.

I claim her with a passionate kiss, and she growls like a feral cat. She pulses her walls around me, bucking up her hips. Without a word, she's telling me she's ready.

And fuck, so am I.

"Are you ready for me, baby?"

"Hell yes," she replies with a cheeky smile which quickly sobers as she notices the heat in my eyes.

"I've wanted this for so long, my sweet Carina," I whisper across her lips.

Starting slowly, I began sliding in and out of her warm, wet silk. "You feel so amazing. Better than in my dreams."

"So good," she gasps. "So perfect, Brody. My God, this feels like a dream."

Through her smile, she kisses me. Her expression mirrors my own happiness. As we move together, our slow and passionate lovemaking gradually becomes fast, hard, and intense. She stays wrapped around me tight, always pulling me towards her, like she can't get close enough to me. I feel the same way.

I break our kiss to tell her, "It's like I've died and gone to heaven."

It's the last thing I can say because there's no longer a need for words.

In fact, no mere words of man could ever do this moment justice or summarize the poetry that is our bodies moving in perfect synchronization. No language — ancient or modern — has the characters, sounds, or meaning to translate what we are saying to each other with each thrust, each kiss, and each breath.

Feeling the stirrings of my release approaching, I'm determined for her to join me over the edge. Twisting and grinding against her clit with each thrust, I feel her inner walls flutter and quiver.

Her nails pierce the skin of my back when she starts chanting my name, like a mantra, until her climax overtakes her. I follow right behind her, gasping out her name.

After the flashing lights have cleared from my line of vision, I know I've finally found everything I'll ever need in this one, chaotic, and amazing woman.

I'm home.

And I'm completely head over heels in love with her.

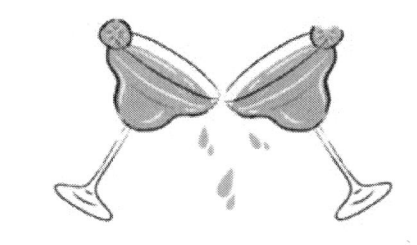

Chapter Eighteen

Worth the wait

Cara

"Hey, hooker! Happy Saturday! How have you been?" Helen chirps through the phone, bringing a smile to my face. As if I needed another reason to smile.

"Oh, I have no complaints. In fact, I have the opposite of complaints. I have many accolades that I should be handing out. Many, many accolades."

"Now you have my attention. Talk to me, Goose."

I snort laugh before continuing, "So you see, Maverick, it all started with a butt rub. No, scratch that. It all started when my crazy-ass friend dared me to kiss this dreamboat I know and recorded it for a stupid internet video."

"Yeah, yeah, I already know that part. And I already know you apologized and weaseled your way into rehabbing his injury. Why do you sound like you've been sniffing glue? I thought I told you to stop it with the glue sniffing." I laugh and she takes that as a sign to continue.

"Also, it's not a stupid internet video. It's a stupid TikTok video, you need to be more specific. By the way, I've cross-posted it to my Instagram and Facebook, and the comments are insane. People are really invested in your relationship. There is a relationship, right? I need to give my fans what they crave! What's the latest?"

"Well, let's see. After several days of hot and heavy petting and getting cockblocked by his mother, he finally got rid of her last night and cooked the most delicious chicken pot pie. But we didn't eat it until it was super cold, because I jumped his bones as soon as he told me his mom was out with a friend for the evening."

"You banged him? Please tell me that is what you mean by *jumped his bones*?"

"Oh, we certainly banged. He banged me first. Then, I guess I banged him the next round. And he banged me again a little while later in the shower. That man is insatiable. He has the stamina of a twenty year old. Blows Jimmy and Chaz away, there is no contest. Brody wins all day, every day, hands down. As in, hands down his pants. That's where my hands shall be from here on out. It is the official happy place for my hands."

"Girl, I am so turned on right now. How big is he? Did he do anything extra or was this straight banging? Is he freaky? I need to know all the details, please. I've waited so long for you to get a good dicking, you can't leave out anything. Go!"

"I think I've shared just about all I'm willing to share. But I guess I can say Brody is a big guy as you know. And he is very well proportioned if you catch my drift. And it was indeed a good dicking, as you so eloquently put it. You are such a lady. My gosh." I roll my eyes, and an extra-sharp cheddar cheese grin is still ridiculously overtaking my face.

"All right. Keep your secrets, you greedy hussy. I'll remember that the next time I run into a rugby team as I go about my travels."

"A team? You wouldn't! Wait... would you? You probably would."

"Oh, now you want details? No way, Miss Priss. You'll never know about my rugby adventures, nor any other athletes that may or may not cross my path."

"Fine. I can live with that. I have enough sexual energy around me now, I don't need your vicarious escapades to fuel me anymore."

"So, are you calling to thank me for daring you to kiss him? And also for forcing you to apologize? I accept thanks in the form of baked goods, alcohol, and Gucci or Prada — oh, or Gucci *and* Prada."

"Sure, just go ahead and wait for those gifts to arrive. Checks in the mail. But actually, yes, the reason I'm calling — aside from bragging about the aforementioned good dicking — is to thank you for encouraging me to go for it with Brody. I don't think I've ever been this happy. I am sincerely grateful that you're my friend and encouraged me. I love you, tramp."

"Oh my gosh, I'm going to cry. Why don't you send me a text restating all of that so I can screen capture it and post it to my Insta? Include a bit about the dicking too. That would get lots of hearts."

"I think you've already used up your quota of allowable posts on social media referencing your friendship with yours truly. I don't want to saturate the market. I need to leave them wanting more," I joke, loving that we have this easy banter. She is like the sister I never had. Oh wait... she is the *fun* sister I never had. That's better.

"Fine, you really suck, hooker. But you're *my* hooker, and I love you too. I am glad I pushed you out of your comfort zone. So, when are we going out again? I'm only in town for a few more weeks. My next trip is going to be Greece at the end of next month. I've never been and am hoping to find a young John Stamos to show me around."

"Not sure, I'm still helping Brody with his physical therapy. Cort, CJ, and even Millie have been helping with the old folks and Miles. So, I don't think I can ask them to watch Miles any more than they already do. But I'll figure out something before you leave."

I can hear Grammy Ellie yelling from the other room, so I make my excuses and say goodbye to Helen before running downstairs to see what is going on.

"Shit, what happened down here?" I look around and see that there is glass splattered all over the kitchen floor.

"Cara, honey, I'm so sorry. I was trying to unload the dishwasher to help you out. I guess I couldn't see the shelf in the cupboard as well as I thought I could, and I accidentally broke a few glasses," she says as she looks at me with tears in her eyes.

Boy, she has even more guilt than I do by the looks of it.

"A few glasses, Grammy? It looks like a few dozen. But that's okay. I'm just glad no one is hurt."

"I tried to sweep it up, but I can't see where the glass is, it blends right in with the wood floors. I'm afraid that Mittens or Marshmallow or one of the other cats is going to get glass in their little paws. Can you please help me clean it up? I already told Miles to stay out of the kitchen for now, and your grandfather is taking a nap. I just can't let anything happen to the poor kitties. I'm a wreck about it."

"Well, that's the thing with glass, Grammy. It tends to blend in, being clear and all. Don't move! Stay right there. I can see some glass by your feet. Last thing we need is for you to step on it. With your blood thinners, you'll be bleeding out in no time."

And I can see that was the wrong thing to say. Sometimes I wish I would shut up while I'm ahead... or less behind actually.

"Oh no. You are right. This is so horrible! I'll try to not move. I'm so sorry, dear. I know we burden you so much."

"Stop it right now. You took care of me and the rest of the family when our folks died. I don't want to hear another thing about being a burden. I might bust your chops at times, but I'm always going to be here to help you when you need me."

Tears leak from her eyes earnestly now, and I just wish I could get over to her for a big hug. She tries so hard to help me out around the house, but she just can't do what she used to. I hate it for her, and I'm sure I'd be the same way if I were her. It must suck going from the caretaker to needing someone to take care of you.

"Just wait right there. I'm going to slide on my thick sneakers, and I'll be right back."

I rush upstairs, throw on my sneakers and come back down. After I clean up the mess and help Grammy sit down in the living room, the doorbell rings. Great, what now?

I open the front door and am dumbstruck as I see it's a delivery person holding a huge bouquet of red roses. It must be three dozen. It looks so heavy for the poor kid holding it.

"Delivery for Ms. Carina Amos."

"Yes, I'm Carina," I say with a smile as wide as the Grand Canyon.

"These are for you, then. You must have a big admirer; this is a huge bouquet."

I take it from him and nearly drop it. "Would you like me to set them down for you, inside? We normally aren't supposed to go inside — but it's really heavy. I don't mind." His cheeks blush. Isn't he sweet?

"No, I work out, man. I can handle it," I joke. "Thanks so much for delivering them."

I kick the door closed as I carefully move the roses into the dining room before placing them down on the table and grabbing the card as fast as my grubby hands can.

"*One dozen for each year that I watched and waited for you. And I'd wait a million more for another night like last night. Love, B.*"

And. I'm. Dead.

Tears prick my eyes because that is the sweetest thing anyone has ever said or done for me. I am going to fall for this man so hard, if I haven't already.

Yes, roses can be considered cliché, but I don't care. No one has ever sent me red roses before.

I once got white roses when I was a kid, after our parents died, but those were from Helen... of course, the only seven-year-old with enough money to send roses. I'd only known her for a few months at that point, I think. But it did make me feel special during an otherwise horrific time in my life.

But these roses... they are making me feel special at a time when I already feel precious, desired, and cared for. I'm so lit up inside that the butterflies in my stomach seem to be more like a bunch of canaries taking flight.

"Wow!" I hear from over my shoulder.

"Yeah, I know, buddy. Have you ever seen anything so beautiful?" I ask Miles.

"No, not really. Who are they for? Who sent them? Why?"

"One question at a time, silly. They are for me. And what do you mean why? Don't you think I deserve something beautiful like this?"

I'm still staring at the flowers in awe, wiping a few tears which have escaped down my cheeks.

"Who is B? And what happened last night?"

Wait. What?

I turn and see that Miles is holding the card that I had set down on the table in front of the roses. *Oh shit.* What do I say to him? How do I explain the morning-after-amazing-sex flowers to a twelve-year-old? Fuck me with a spoon.

"Um... well, they are from a friend who I did a favor for last night," I try.

"What friend?"

Of course, he isn't going to accept an answer like that. He is too smart for me, and I'm too spent with emotions to come up with anything, so I attempt a little honesty, while softening it with a white lie.

"The friend is Brody. And I have been helping him heal from an injury to his knee. You know that."

"Well, what was so special about last night? You've been helping him for a while now."

Oh, son, I love you, but you are being a real shit right now. Please just take my half-ass explanation and go away before you figure out that I banged your favorite teacher.

I'm not ready to explain it and I haven't had time to talk to Brody about what we will tell Miles and when we will tell him.

"Miles, did you clean up your room yet? Didn't I tell you to clean up your room earlier? Quit trying to get out of it or you won't get video game time tonight."

Take that, kid. I just pulled the mom card.

"Ugh, fine but I can tell you are hiding something. I might have trouble understanding non-verbal signals, but you are sending some really weird ones right now," he says under his breath as he walks upstairs.

I exhale. Fuck, he isn't going to let this go.

I need to call Brody. First, to thank him for the amazing flowers and second, to tell him that we need to talk about Miles. I'll also try to not tell him that I love him. Because I don't want to freak him out.

I'm starting to be freaked out enough for the both of us.

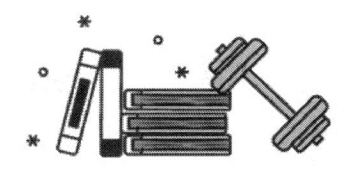

Chapter Nineteen

Name that tune

Brody

"Hello, good morning, beautiful," I answer on the first ring when Cara calls.

Has she ever called me before? By using the phone as an actual calling device and not just a text machine? I don't think so. Another first in our relationship! Three points to House Gryffindor.

"Well, hi there, handsome. Good morning to you too."

"It's nice to hear your voice on the phone. You know, I don't think you've ever called me before."

"Really? I don't think that is right."

"It's totally right. And I know this because I've never heard the ringtone I assigned you before. I forgot I even assigned it."

Shit. Now she is going to ask what the song is. Should I tell her?

"Well, now you have to tell me what my song is, Brody."

I knew it. *Think. Think. Think.*

"That's confidential information, ma'am. I set that song when I was your son's primary educator, and there are laws protecting my privacy."

"I'll tell you what yours is, if you tell me mine."

Well, that certainly sweetens the deal. "Hmm, before I decide if I want to play this dangerous game, when did you set that ringtone up for me?"

"After our first parent and *hot* teacher conference. Same question for you."

"*Before* our first *hot* parent and teacher conference."

"Yeah, I can't let you off the hook here. I really have to know what song you picked before we really even had a chance to start talking or get to know each other. I'm willing to do many things to find out this information. Name your price."

I'm going to do it. I'm going to tell her. I can't say no to her.

"Before I agree, how about you take a guess so I can see how embarrassed I stand to be? Let me know how far off the mark I might be."

"You drive a hard bargain. I accept these terms. Let me think…"

"I haven't agreed to reveal this information yet, I just want to hear your guess first before I decide."

"Fair enough. Let's see you said you wanted me since we first met, so if that were true… maybe it is 'Let's Get it On' by Marvin Gaye."

"Really? You think I went straight to Marvin Gaye? Well, maybe my answer won't be so bad then," I tease her because I can.

"No? I really thought I had it. If not Marvin Gaye, then maybe it was 'You Sexy Thing' by Hot Chocolate?"

"That would have been an amazing choice, and you are a sexy thing, and I do believe in miracles now. But no. Wrong again, beautiful."

"All right, I need a hint. What decade are we talking about? How old is this song, Father Time?"

"It is from the eighties, and you are almost the same age as me, so I'm rubber and you're glue, whatever you say bounces off me and sticks to you."

She chortles and then says, "Ooohhh. Okay, I got it then. George Michael, 'I want your sex.' Boom! Mic Drop. Nailed it."

"Wow, you have a very dirty mind, and I think I like it. In fact, I know I like it. But you are once again wrong. Three strikes and you're out."

"I give up. Spill it!"

"Well, since I really want to know what you picked, I'll tell you. Drum roll please." I pause for dramatic effect, because she brings out the playful side of me, and I'm enjoying taunting her.

"Oh, come on already!"

"Okay, it's 'Heaven' by Bryan Adams."

"Well, now I'm going to feel like a pervert, since you picked something that's actually romantic and sweet. I admittedly did not."

"That's okay. No one expects you to reach my level of romance, Cara. Now, what's my ringtone on your phone?"

"It's 'Hot for Teacher' by Van Halen, of course. What did you think it would be?"

"I was hoping for something like Roberta Flack's 'First Time Ever I Saw Your Face' or maybe 'In Your Eyes' by Peter Gabriel."

"No, I'm very superficial and it's all about the hot-teacher sexy vibe. Sorry to disappoint you."

"You could never disappoint me. I just think it's hilarious that we both assigned ringtones for each other back then. I think only about two other people in my entire Rolodex have their own ringtones. You are in very exclusive company."

"Well, I'm flattered, and I think your song is very special, and that reminds me. I received a delivery today that may or may not have made me tear up a little bit. It was incredibly sweet, and I thank you. No one has ever sent me roses before."

I can't believe none of her douchebag exes sent her roses. What the fuck is wrong with them? "I was thinking that might be the reason you called me instead of texting."

"Well, that and I wanted to hear your voice." She lowers her volume as if she is leaning in to whisper a secret through the phone as she continues, "I really liked when you said naughty things in my ear last night, and I wanted to hear your deep sexy voice again."

"In that case, why don't you come over and I'll kick Mom out? She can wait outside while I do it again."

"You are so bad. We can't do that to your mom. Linda is too sweet to be treated like steerage."

We continue bantering back and forth. Before I know it, an hour has gone by. I feel like I could talk to her forever. In fact, it scares me how much I actually want to do just that.

"Oh, shoot! I almost forgot about the second reason for my call. We need to talk about Miles."

I sit up and stiffen a little at the more serious edge her voice has taken. "What's the matter? What does he need?" I've instantly gone into protective mode.

"Aww, listen to you. So sweet. No, it's not a problem, really. And I know we haven't put a label on whatever we are doing, but he saw the roses and read the card before I could snatch it away. He started asking a lot of questions. You know how persistent he can be, and I sort of panicked a little bit. I don't want to pressure you into anything. But I figured since you see him at school, he might ask you the same question to try to bust me in a lie. I thought we should have our story straight."

"Oh, I see. Now, I'm really glad I didn't go with my first draft on the card."

"You aren't going to make me guess again, are you?"

I chuckle. "Not this time. The first card read something like, 'I can't wait to taste you again and I can't stop thinking about how tight your pussy felt on my cock.' But I thought that might be a little bit awkward to tell the florist over the phone. So, I went with my second draft."

"Yeah, that would have made my conversation with my twelve-year-old much more awkward. Thanks for changing your mind," she says in between deep breaths.

I am thinking I may have gotten her a little worked up, which is good since I don't want to be the only one on the flight to Lust Land. And that is most definitely where this woman is sending me.

"Carina, are you panting? Or are you impersonating an obscene caller?"

"Shut up or I'll kick Linda out myself. Maybe she can take Miles for a walk."

"Actually, that's not a bad idea. Come on over, right now."

"Very funny."

"I'm completely serious. She has heard me talk about him before, so I'm sure she'd want to meet him."

"First, that's really adorable that you've talked to your mom about him. Roman numeral deux: I couldn't do that to her. He'd break her in less than two minutes, flat. And C: I can't just show up without telling him something. Remember, that's why I brought this up. I don't know what to tell him."

"What did you tell him so far?"

"Something like, you were thanking me for helping with your knee. He totally didn't buy it. Even the twelve-year-old socially awkward boy knows that three dozen red roses is *not* a thank you. Well, not for physical therapy."

"I'm sure he didn't believe that one bit. You want me to talk to him? I don't mind telling him that I'm absolutely crazy about his mother and one day I'm going to marry her. In fact, I'll get his permission."

I'm met with dead silence, so I check my phone to see if the line is dead.

Shit. I think I went too far.

"We can't tell him that, Brody," she says with a shake in her voice.

Did I upset her? I have to fix this.

Shit, now she's sniffling.

"You aren't crying are you, Cara? Relax. I'm sorry. I'm just kidding."

Actually, I'm not kidding, but she's clearly not ready for the breadth and depth of my feelings.

"No, I'm not crying," she lies. "I just have a tickle in my throat is all."

Not buying that, but no reason to push her, so I go for a new approach.

"How about this, instead? We can tell him that we really like each other and are thinking about becoming more than friends? Do you think that is enough to pacify him? Or we could tell him we are dating. Or that we are boyfriend and girlfriend or whatever terminology you think is best. I don't see a reason to hide it from him, unless you do."

"Is that what we are going to be, then? Are you my boyfriend, Brody?" She is back to her old self and injects a little bit of sass in her voice. "I guess since we are already having this awkward conversation, we might as well rip the bandage all the way off."

"Cara, I'm not going to be seeing anyone else, and I sure as hell hope you aren't either. I don't care what we call it, but for me at least, I have very strong feelings for you, and I think maybe, you feel the same. I want a committed relationship with you."

She exhales. "Same here. I guess I just feel like it's moving a bit fast, and he might not understand it."

"Damn, I wish this was face-to-face, but no sense in not saying it while we are on this topic. It's taken three years, baby. If it were any slower, we'd be moving backwards. Because I already know you so well, I can say with certainty this is serious for me, and I don't feel like we are rushing at all. We are getting to skip the getting to know you phase, simply because we have spent more than thirty-six months getting to know and like each other."

"Amazing body and good at math too? My panties can't take much more."

"I adore your humor, but before you change the subject on me, I need to know… are you with me on this, Carina?"

I hear her take another deep breath and inside, I'm freaking out a bit. I'm putting her on the spot a little, and I'm terrified that this might be too much. I know she has been burned before and has trouble trusting men. But I think she knows me better than that.

"Brody, I'm totally on the same page with you. I don't want to be with anyone else, and I want to be serious with you. And if I find out you are with anyone else, I'll cut a bitch."

Chapter Twenty

Turd nuggets

Cara

"Why are you so smiley today? Did you sneak some tequila in your coffee again?" Cort asks me.

"Eww, Cort, gosh. No! Is that what you think of me? No person in their right mind would spike coffee with tequila. They'd use Baileys or Kahlua, like a decent person with a sophisticated palette."

"Fair enough. But dude, you look really happy. What's going on? Don't tell me you are *that* happy to be at work on a Monday morning."

"As a matter of fact, I am happy to be here. I love my job and I take it very seriously. You could learn something from me, young man."

As fun as it is to mess with Cort, I can't help but recall details of the amazing weekend I had with Brody. Friday night was everything I imagined it would be and more. The only thing that would have made it even better is if I could have spent the night. But I have responsibilities, and he had a mom who came back to his apartment to sleep on his couch. Then on Saturday, we met at a ball field and played soccer with Miles. Then went out for dinner at this little mom and pop Italian place. We told Miles we were officially dating, and the kid was so happy, I thought he was going to explode with joy. I have never seen him that excited about anything before.

Miles's emotional range is either flat and you wonder if he is even engaged in the conversation or full on emotional meltdown. Very few stages in between the two.

Of course, there are times when he thinks he is hilarious and might bust a gut laughing at his own jokes and sometimes at Cort's jokes — but almost never at mine. For the most part though, he usually is very even-keeled. So, to see him that happy about the idea of me and his former teacher, was very touching. He *never* smiled like that around Jimmy. I guess that should have been a sign about that doomed relationship.

I still haven't told the rest of the family about my new boyfriend, *giggle*, but no doubt Miles is going to spill it the next time Cort picks him up. Then it will be breaking news for the entire family within minutes. But I really like messing with Cort, so I'm going to drag this out a bit more. He'd do the same to me, so it's only fair.

"Are you going to keep avoiding the question?"

"What question?"

"See! You just did it again. Why are you glowing and shit? Did you get a facial this weekend or something?"

I try to hide my chuckle at the image that just jumped into my mind. And yes! It's exactly what you're thinking. But just in case you have only pure thoughts, allow me to corrupt you and bring your mind into the gutter with mine. In this image, I'm on my knees, and Brody is giving me a facial with his special sauce. I've never let a guy do that to me before, but with Brody, I'd try just about anything once.

"I did not get a facial, unfortunately. No spa trips for me."

"Cara, are you kidding me right now? I know something is going on with you. I'm going to start guessing soon."

"All right, fine. Gosh, you are so annoying. Did you major in crawling up asses in college because you really are good at trying to get on up there. Or, if it was more like an extracurricular for you, then you are at least a second-degree black belt of ass crawling."

"I'm not going to pick-up Miles this week unless you tell me. Last chance."

"I can't believe you would abandon your only nephew. Shame, shame, we know your name, Cortland Michael Amos."

"As amusing as this conversation is, I'm going to go out on a limb and say that you are so happy because someone got into your tight pants this weekend. Am I close?"

My eyes snap up to his, and I can't hide my expression. It's a mix between shock, smug, and the Cheshire cat.

"I knew it. It was Brody, right? Please tell me you and Brody are finally together. If so, I can collect my money from CJ next time I see her. I've been waiting for years to collect from her."

"You made a bet with CJ about my love life? Are you kidding me? I'm insulted by that. And if you won the bet, then does that mean CJ bet against me landing Brody? Why? She doesn't think I'm good enough. That bitch is off the Christmas card list."

"You haven't sent out Christmas cards since I've known you. And that's been my whole life."

"That may be so, but if I sent them, she would *not* be getting one this year. So, tell me about this bet. How did you know, and why doesn't she have faith in her little sister?"

I need these details. He better spill it and quickly, before I give him a lesson on crawling up someone's ass to fish out information.

"Calm down. She didn't say you couldn't land Brody. She simply said that he would try, and you would turn him down because she didn't think you'd be willing to date again until Miles was in college or at least upper high school."

"Really? Did she say why she thought that?"

I don't like to think that my own sister thought that about me. And CJ is only two years older than me and typically is the kinder and gentler of the elder Amos gals. She doesn't like to make waves, and she tends to have nothing but support to give for everyone. She's the peacemaker of the family.

The more I think about this, the worse I'm feeling. I'm now more than a little concerned if she thinks I'm making a mistake by dating before Miles is older. Does she think it's going to be bad for him? Is it me or Miles she is worried about? Or both?

"From what I gathered, she just thought you were done with trusting men around Miles after how things with Jimmy ended."

"Well, she does have a point. I didn't think I was going to go down this road again, that's for sure. The way Jimmy left, blaming it on Miles, that really fricking hurt. But I really don't think Brody would do that. Do you?"

"Hell no. Brody is absolutely the opposite of Jimmy in every way. Plus, he already knows Miles, and I think he likes the kid. Plus, I've seen Miles around you and Brody together, and the feeling is mutual. You don't have to worry about Brody doing what Jimmy did. You believe that right?"

I think he can tell this topic is bothering me a bit, because he is angling his head closer to me, trying to catch my eyes as we fold towels fresh out of the industrial size dryer in the back of the rehab clinic.

Side note: We go through a shitload of towels here each day. But I love the feeling of towels fresh from the dryer. Pausing for a moment, I eye Cort back and take a big sniff of the fabric softener, leaving me warm and cuddly all over.

"I do believe you, Cort. I'm just afraid to make a mistake and screw things up. Miles really likes Brody and looks up to him. And Brody has been a great friend to me. I am terrified that if things don't work out, then my heart and my son's heart will both be broken. That's why I have never pursued Brody before."

"So, what changed? Not saying that I agree with your logic, I'm just wondering why now if you still have those concerns?"

"I guess Brody and I just couldn't fight it anymore. You've probably figured out that I have had a huge crush on him since we met and apparently, he felt the same. All this working together on his ITBS rehab just pushed us over the edge."

"Makes sense, but I think you really are worrying too much. I mean, I know I'm not a parent, but don't hold back from what could be, because of what might go wrong. Make sense?"

"Yes, it does make sense. And your vote of confidence in Brody and me is comforting. Now, are you going to take your own advice one day and let someone get close to you or are you going to keep holding back because you fear losing them?"

"Woah. Hey, no. Don't go there. We are not talking about me. This is all about you. Don't try to turn this around on me."

"Whatever. But seriously, Cort, thanks." I give him a real smile, no sarcasm at all.

He just nods his head and looks back at his stack of towels. And because we are the way we are, he takes a swing at my stack of towels and knocks them down to the floor, so I have to refold them.

"Hey, asshole!" I yell as Cort hustles out with his stack of towels before I can knock his over. But my volume control lever is busted, and I pretty much just yelled a cuss word at my job. Shit. I'm too loud. Always have been. People say they can hear me coming from a mile away, especially when I'm laughing. Cort brings that side out in me. So does Helen, honestly. And of course, Brody. Sigh.

"What is wrong with you, Cara? Do you mind keeping it professional, please? I could hear you all the way in my office."

I turn around abruptly and oh shit. There goes my good mood.

"Sorry, Peter. I just got frustrated because my towels fell. It won't happen again."

He takes three big steps into the room, coming straight at me as his eyes shift from the disciplinarian to creepy perve. Fuck, not again. He's blocking the exit, and Cort just left me alone. I don't know if there are cameras in here, but I hope so.

He closes the door behind him. And shit — did he just lock it?

Fight or flight mode launching in 5, 4, 3...

"Apology accepted, Cara. We all get stressed out around here from time to time. Maybe I can help you feel more relaxed?" He leans in as he whispers the last word, and he is totally invading my personal space. *Jesus, what is with this guy?*

I backup as he advances, meeting me step for step. The towels that I was in the process of picking up are now bunched up in my arms and they are serving as a coat of armor between us.

"No, thank you. I'm perfectly relaxed and don't need anything from you. At all!" I stress the last two words and lift my chin defiantly. "Now, if you'll excuse me, I think I left something in the other room."

I realize I don't have my phone on me, and this room is far too secluded from the rest of the facility. If I yell, I don't really know who will hear me with the washer and dryers running and the door closed. Fuck, is Cort coming back? This is bad. I'm going to have to kick his ass if he doesn't let me pass. Shit, shit, fuck, damn, shit. Or as my son would say, *turd nuggets*!

I try to move around him, but it seems he is done playing nice guy. He shoves me up against the dryer and presses his erection into my lower belly while he puts one hand across my throat, the other on my right breast. He is not quite choking me, it's more like the threat of choking.

"Get your fucking hands off me, asshole. Stop it! Let go of me now!" I shout, my voice raised to even louder than my usual volume ten.

"What does a guy have to do to get your attention? I see the way you look at me, Cara. Why are you playing hard to get? No one has to know what we do. We are both adults and are free to express our mutual attraction."

I am swatting at the hand on my breast and manage to knock it loose, right as his hold starts to tighten on my neck. My knee is about half a second from meeting his groin when the door handle jiggles and I hear my savior, Cort, knocking loudly and calling my name.

"Cara, you still in there? Open the door, now!"

Peter takes a step back and removes himself from my space before menacingly saying "If you value your brother's job here, you won't say anything to anyone about our little tryst. I've got plenty of young female athletes willing to say how inappropriate he has been with them. Are we clear?"

He said that so fast and with so little forethought, he clearly had that little threatening speech practiced and prepared to drop when he needed it. And did he really just call this a tryst? For fuck's sake, he is certifiably insane.

Cort continues to bang the door yelling my name, prompting both me and Peter to respond.

I yell, "Yes, I'm here, Cort. Help me open the door." We really should have worked out a code word.

At the same time Peter says, "Cort, this door appears to be sticking. I'll have it open in a second."

Rather than yelling rape or help like I want to, I'm afraid to say anything to Cort. I certainly can't do it right in front of Peter. I don't know if I believe him that he has girls willing to lie about Cort. But I can't risk my brother being accused of what this creep is implying. He won't be able to get hired anywhere if accusations like that started flying — bullshit or not. That stuff can't just be brushed away.

Peter makes a big show of wiggling the door and shaking it before quietly twisting the knob, so Cort doesn't hear the lock catch. Then he grandly yanks it open, as if he just saved the day. The delusional psychopath. I've never wanted to commit murder so badly in my life.

"Catch you later, Cara. Good job today. Keep it up," Peter says in a fake-ass kind voice before he brushes past Cort and leaves me alone with my brother.

Said brother is fuming. His head is about to blow as he visibly seems to be holding himself back from charging after Peter. Instead, he storms over to me, "What the fuck just happened? Was the door really stuck?"

I don't look him in the eyes. I just shake my head, barely perceptible and tell him quietly, "Can't talk in here. Leaving. I'll call you tonight."

His eyes go wide, but he nods. I guess he is satisfied that I'm not physically in any pain and thankfully accepts my blow off.

I leave the towels on the floor where they fell when Peter assaulted me — and yes, it was fucking assault — and leave the room without looking back. I go get my purse and tell Mandy that she needs to reschedule the rest of my appointments because an emergency has come up, and I buzz past her without waiting for her reply.

I'm not leaving the campus just yet. I have a stop to make first.

A few minutes later, I'm walking into the campus administration building and hustle right up to the University President's office like I belong there, even though I totally don't.

I approach Jane's desk, meet her eyes, and say, "Hey, I'm cashing in on that favor now. I need you to check something out for me."

Chapter Twenty-One

Huddle up

Brody

"Hey, get in. We're gonna be late," I say after rolling down the window and motioning Hudson to join me in my Camry.

"There he is, the freshly laid stud of the fourth grade and his substantially lighter balls" he says as he gets in and we pull out, heading to Cara's house.

"That sounds wrong on so many levels, Hudson. How are you doing, buddy?" I say, lightly clapping him on the shoulder in an approximation of a bro-hug.

"Just kicking ass and taking names, same as every day. You?"

"Oh, I'm freaking awesome, man. Can't wait to see my girl tonight. Speaking of which, thanks for coming on such short notice. She didn't say what it was about, but regardless I'm stoked to see her and see you at the same time. Oh, and you'll get to meet some of her sisters and her brother, Cort. Miles too most likely."

"Shit, dawg. I think I'm finally rubbing off on you. Did you just say you were stoked? That's dank."

"Shut up, ass."

We bust each other's chops the entire way to Cara's house, and I catch him up on the decision for Cara and me to be an official couple and that we told Miles about it too.

"I don't know if she told the rest of the family yet, but maybe she is going to tell everyone tonight and that's why she wanted me to come over. They are a really close and large family, so I can see stuff like this as being big news. Honestly, I'm not sure how you fit into that thought process though."

"Maybe she is gonna propose, dude, and she knew you'd want your best bro to be there to give you a shoulder to cry on, 'cause I'm sure you are going to bawl all over the place like a baby when she gets down on one knee."

I punch him in the arm. We laugh and proceed to bullshit each other the rest of the way.

I can't help envisioning various proposal scenarios involving Cara. No way in hell am I going to let her propose to me, though. I know she is a feminist, and I'm sure she'd have no problem doing that. But I want to do it, and it'll need to be epic when that time comes. She deserves all the romance and big gestures in the world, and I intend to give them to her.

And true to my word with that, I even stopped by the store on the way and grabbed a bottle of white wine. It's a Moscato — one of Cara's favorite drinks if she isn't having a margarita. I'm going to spoil her every day that I can.

When we pull up outside Cara's house, I can see that it is going to be a full house tonight. We have to park on the street since the driveway is full. But before we even walk halfway up to the front porch, Cort comes charging out straight at us, and he looks as pissed as I've ever seen.

He rushes up and nods his head at me then Hudson. "What's up, Brody? Thanks for coming," he says briskly in a very un-Cort-like manner.

He's usually the fun guy, the life of the party. A lot like Hudson in that way.

"And you must be Hudson, right? I'm Cort. Nice to meet you."

"Yeah dude, the pleasure is all mine," Hudson says and they shake hands amicably. But the tension pouring off Cort is so thick you can practically see it permeating the air around us.

"All right, listen up. I probably have about fifteen seconds to give you a heads up. Something fucking happened today at work between Cara and our asshole boss, and she's acting strange. I haven't seen her react to anything like this before."

I interrupt him. "What do you mean something happened? Specifically…"

"Somehow Peter the Asshole got locked in the laundry room with her. I was only gone for like sixty seconds, two minutes tops, and he weaseled in there and must have locked the door. But he pretended like the door was stuck when I came back banging on the door. Cara wouldn't tell me what happened, but I can sense it was something bad. She left work immediately without saying a word to anyone, and then she sent that cryptic ass message to the group text, asking for all of us to be here for dinner now. That's all I know."

"Thanks for the heads up. Does she seem very upset? You said she was acting strange."

Inside, I'm screaming and ready to run through the door. I want to see Cara with my own eyes and make sure she is okay, but I can't pass up the chance to get the info from Cort since I know he won't try to sugarcoat it, like Cara might.

"No, that's just the thing. She is so unusually calm. I can't get her to talk at all, and she is almost acting like a robot, like nothing is happening. It's fucking weird. Dude, you know how she is — you can always see exactly how she is feeling, she never hides her emotions at all; she wears them on her sleeve. But she has some shit bottled up tight right now."

"Okay, let's go inside now. I want to see her."

He nods and leads us in. When I get inside, the scene is pretty much exactly as he described. It's just a normal day at the Amos house. Miles is messing with his action figures. Grammy Ellie and Grandpa Dickie are watching TV, with it turned up too loud. The kitchen is teaming with red-haired beauties, all cooking and chatting as if nothing is amiss.

I stride over to Cara, kiss her on her cheek, and hand her the bottle of wine. She gives me a placating smile, but it's fake as shit. She's *not* happy. I'm about twenty seconds away from driving to the campus to find that asshole and hang him up by his toenails until he tells me what he did to my precious Cara.

Hudson is here for the first time. He's only seen Cara a few times and that was mostly in passing like that one time at my birthday party a few years back. He's never seen the chaos that is the Amos family in action. And so, I'm not surprised to see him standing in the kitchen entryway with a terrified and yet fascinated look on his face as his eyes bob from CJ to Millie to Chloe and on to Cara, Cort, and myself before starting back at CJ again.

I wish I wasn't so upset about Cara, because otherwise it would be funny to watch how Hudson interacts with the sisters.

"Hudson, this is everyone. You remember Cara and you met Cort. This is CJ, Millie, and Chloe. Everyone, this is my best friend Hudson."

"What's up everyone? I'm fired up to meet you, especially all you lovely ladies — no offense Cort, dude."

He is now making eyes at each of the sisters, and I can't help but shake my head at him. He can flirt with the best of them, but they would eat him alive if given the chance. Those women are all very intense.

He starts chatting up the ladies as they finish plating up dinner, while I pull Cara aside. She resists at first, but she finally concedes and follows me to the hallway.

She immediately tries to distract me with an intense kiss. As much as I love having her lips on mine, I stop her... well, after enjoying a few moments of feeling her pressed up against me.

"Hey, babe. How are you doing?" I ask, waiting to see how she is going to play this. She must have something in mind if she called everyone here.

"I'm fine. Thanks for coming over. I missed you. Is that weird? I just saw you this weekend, like a lot. And every day last week. But I missed you anyway. Hope that doesn't freak you out."

"No baby, it's not weird at all. I missed you too. I miss you as soon as you leave my place." I smile and kiss her nose.

"Two things: One, does your family know about us yet, and two, what the hell happened at work today? I know something went down with that asshole."

Her face freezes. Yep, she's holding it all in. Knowing Cara, she's gonna blow soon. She was simply not made to hold in her feelings. I just want to be there to help her avoid a nuclear meltdown when she finally does explode.

"Well, let's see. I told Cort, and of course, Miles knows. Cort was not surprised at all and so likely, the entire family knows. So, I'm not going to say anything specific, but if they ask, I'll answer them. Is that okay with you?"

"Yes, whatever you want. That's fine with me. I guess I can cancel the singing telegram and the marching band. They were supposed to be here in fifteen minutes to make a big spectacle of our new relationship status. And please notice that I said new *status*, not new *relationship*. Just in case you start to think we are moving too fast again. Because that is not the case, right?"

She smiles at me, and this time it's genuine. I can't resist going in for another kiss, and she responds exactly like I hoped she would. Passionately.

I pull back again. "Okay, now the other thing. What happened?"

"Honestly, Brody, I wanted to talk to everyone about it at the same time so I don't have to go through it more than once. My plan was to have a nice dinner, then ask the grandparents to take Miles for a stroll outside or otherwise excuse themselves. Then the rest of us can sit outside on the back porch and discuss. But I don't want you to worry throughout the meal... and I know you will."

She takes a deep breath, and I just continue watching and waiting patiently for her to continue. "So, I'll just tell you now, and only you..."

I love that she's trusting me and respecting my feelings for her enough to tell me first.

Glancing over her shoulder, she makes sure no one is eavesdropping. "He attempted to assault me in the laundry room today. I'm not going to sugar coat it."

I grit my teeth, and a growl reverberates up from deep inside my chest.

She gives me a firm look. "Fortunately, he was stopped before it got severe. But don't worry. I have a plan to take that fucker down, and that's why I asked you guys over here. I need a bit of help executing the plan and also need thinking partners to help me spot any holes in my strategy and shore them up. I don't have all the answers yet, but I'm sure with a team consisting of an incredibly intelligent and sexy teacher, a marine biologist, a marketing executive, an IT project manager, a social media goddess — who should be here any moment by the way — and whatever the hell Hudson is doing for work these days... between all of us, we will figure it out. Okay?"

I nod in understanding. Despite my desire to take control and protect her, I'm going to show her that I trust her judgment and will follow her lead in this. Unless she needs me to step in. She's been alone a long time and doesn't need me to come in like a bull in a china shop and take the reins.

I wrap her up in a firm embrace to silently express my support for her, and for a minute, I can feel her mask drop. She takes in all the comfort she can soak up from me. After a minute or so has passed of us just standing there, holding each other, she releases me, and gives me a sweet but short kiss before heading back out to the kitchen.

I trail behind her and think about what I just heard. I'm so conflicted right now. For starters, I'm proud of her for being so damn strong, but also enraged that he tried that shit again. I'm also worried that he will get away with this and she'll have to quit her dream job. And I'm anxious to hear her plan and figure out what she needs me to do.

Even if she needs me to drive the getaway car or pull the trigger, I'm there for her. Whatever she needs.

Chapter Twenty-Two

The brain trust in action

Cara

I will *not* drink this entire bottle of wine, even though it is my favorite. Nor will I drink the box of wine in the back of the fridge. I will also not guzzle the huge bottle of pre-made Jose Cuervo Watermelon Margaritas I have hidden in the bottom of the cupboard. Despite what my shirt says, I do have work to do tomorrow.

For those of you at home tracking my t-shirts, tonight's shirt says: *This margarita tastes like I'm calling in sick to work tomorrow.*

I just need to get through this dinner, and then I can dump all this shit off my chest to my little *Circle of Trust*. Vent it out. Yell a little bit if I feel like it and then me and the brain trust will figure out how to end this shit.

I'll be damned if I'm going to let that sick sack of shit make me leave my happy place at UT, and Cort isn't going anywhere either, unless he wants to.

I feel like I'm taking a stand for women all over who have been marginalized and treated like decorative scenery by misogynistic assholes who think we live to please them. I'm still fuming over that word, "tryst" and it was like six hours ago. And then to threaten my baby-brother?

Not on my watch, pumpkin-eater.

Despite the shit swirling through my mind, dinner is actually pleasant. Miles is in a great mood, sitting right next to Brody and looking at him like he hung the moon. That brings a smile to my heart, regardless of what else transpired today.

Also, Hudson is really hilarious and charming too. Each of my sisters and even Helen all practically have heart eyes for him, and I honestly can't blame them one bit. Hudson has this inner light and peace that he brings with him. But he doesn't seem to be looking at any of them the same way, except maybe Chloe. I've caught him staring at her a few times when he thinks I'm not looking. Very interesting indeed. But that's a project for another day. I've got enough on my plate for now to play matchmaker.

"Thanks for helping clear the table everyone. Miles, can you head upstairs, get showered, and ready for bed, please? If you do everything without a fuss, you can have an hour of video game time, okay buddy?"

"Yes! Yes! Yes!" He goes running up the stairs. Well, I guess I said the magic words.

"That was easier than I thought," I say to Brody with a smile. A real one, not the fake one I've been wearing the second half of the day.

"Grammy and Gramps, I'm taking the rest of the crew outside for a talk. Please listen out for Miles, okay?"

"Yes, darling. I'll listen out for him because you know he won't hear anything." She motions at Grandpa Dickie, a warm smile on her teasing face.

"And I'll watch out for Miles since she is blind as a bat," he fires right back.

For all the trouble they give me, I still love them.

Millie breaks the silence. "Cara, are you pulling us all together to tell us you and Brody are finally a couple? Because we're not gonna lie, we already know. Cort texted us all earlier. And can I just say — finally!"

Hudson chimes in, "I hear ya sister, preach on! Finally, indeed!"

Everyone, including Brody, is laughing and I can't resist a chuckle too. Apparently, everyone but Brody and I realized we were destined to be together. Whatever. *Thanks for letting a sister know, ass-hats.*

"Well, glad that is out in the open now. Therefore, I reserve the right to sit in his lap as needed."

"And Chloe, I don't want you to feel left out, so I gladly offer up my lap as tribute if you need a cuddle," Hudson says to Chloe with a wink, and the rest of us can't help but *ooohhh* and *ahhhh* at that offer.

Judging by the cold ass look on her face, I don't think she will be taking him up on that offer. If she doesn't though, I can almost guarantee Helen will be sitting on his lap by the end of the night.

"I have called you here tonight for a different reason. And thanks for turning out though. Mad Respect." I tap my fist over my heart twice, as if I have some smidgen of swag.

Of course, I don't, and Millie immediately calls me out. "Please stop trying to impersonate someone with street cred. I implore you."

"I don't think I will be taking critiques on street cred from someone who just used the word, *implore*, thank you very much."

"You are plenty street, baby. You tell her," Brody encourages, and I love that he is playing along and fitting in with my family.

"Thanks honey," I respond.

I'm met with a chorus of: *Gross. Gag me. Stop. Ugh, so sweet I just got diabetes,* and other choice phrases from the peanut gallery. For good measure, I lean in and give Brody a big wet kiss. He immediately does me one better and yanks me on top of his lap, where I happily remain for the rest of the conversation.

"All right, let's focus. I actually have some serious shit to talk about."

I explain, in detail, what happened today at work. I also remind them of a few recent occurrences involving the pumpkin-eater and by the end of my little story, everyone is dead serious, and they look like they are ready to head off to battle on my behalf.

"So, here is what I've come up with so far, in terms of a plan. It's rough, and I am asking for everyone's help to flesh the plan out further."

I begin listing out my high-level thoughts, one by one.

"Number one. I have to take him down. He can't be allowed to continue behaving like this. If he has done this shit to me, he has probably done it to others, and will do it again. I'm not going to be part of that fucked-up cycle."

I feel Brody give my shoulder a squeeze, and I soak in his support.

"Number two. The only way I can protect Cort's career and reputation is to catch Peter red-handed. It needs to be big and out there in real time, for everyone to see live, thus eliminating his chance to turn the tables on me or Cort."

Cort nods in a show of appreciation and agreement.

I continue, "Three. Unfortunately, there were no cameras recording in the laundry room — I checked with my friend Jane in the administration office today. I have to wonder if he planned that and had them turned off somehow. That's where you come in, Chloe." I turn to my eldest sister. "Can you use your super-IT skills to figure out how he hacked into the school security cameras and managed to either stop the filming in that room or to immediately erase the recording afterward? He had to do one or the other. We need to know what we're dealing with in terms of his tech skills."

Chloe nods and says, "I'll get my best nerds on the case, little sis."

I smile at her, then march on with my list. "Number four. In addition to checking the security feeds for me earlier today on the lowdown, Jane is willing to do whatever else she needs to do to catch this asshole with his hand in the cookie jar. I'm thinking something big that is broadcast in the middle of a Trustee meeting or something equally splashy. She said she'd help us do it, and there is a Trustee meeting coming up in the next week or so. Chloe, you might need your geeks to help her if she asks. But I suspect Jane has some secrets because she didn't hesitate to come up with that suggestion — as if she has done something similar before."

"You are legit like superwoman right now," CJ says with a smile.

"Excuse me, CJ. Clearly, I'm Wonder Woman — get your shit straight. That or maybe Captain Marvel. She's a badass too."

Everyone laughs, breaking the tension a bit before I continue.

"Number five. Hudson, you were once a journalist, right?" I turn to the stoke lord with a very colorful past that Brody has regaled me with a few times before.

He nods, so I continue, "Do you still have contacts in the news media? Anyone come to mind that you could maybe tap to help get something out there? Tip someone off maybe if we can figure out how to make something happen? I don't want this fucker to work anywhere else where he has influence over others, ever again. To make that happen, we either need to involve the police or the media. I'm game for either, but figured we could start with the media."

Hudson smiles. "Absolutely, Cara. I'd be happy to do that. In fact, a few people are coming to mind already. Once we have a firm plan laid out, I'll get some attention from local print and TV media, as appropriate. Whatever and wherever we decide it is most beneficial and offers the biggest payoff."

Wow. That was surprisingly intelligent and articulate. He didn't come across like a pothead surfer at all. Huh. Is the whole Spicolli thing just an act? Question for another time...

"And six. Helen, I am thinking that we can tap into your sphere of influence on social media at some point to either apply pressure or give us exposure. I'm not entirely sure what makes the most sense — whether it is a live stream of however we set him up — or if you get the video out there after the fact and drum up lots of noise, forcing the University to take a hardline against him. Or maybe just the threat of putting something out to your followers would be enough."

While nodding, Helen says, "Whatever you need, bitch. You know I'm your ride or die. And by the way, this take-no-prisoner's attitude you have is hot as fuck, and if Brody over there doesn't mind, I'm getting super hot right now and want to bang you."

Brody is speechless while everyone else laughs their asses off, until we are crying. I turn around to face him, trying to be serious. "What do you think, honey? Can you share me for a night?"

I feel his cock harden a little under my ass, and he stutters. He fucking stutters and it is the most adorable thing I've ever seen. I take pity on him because I'm honestly not sure how he would answer and tell him, "Just kidding, baby. You are more than enough for me. I like dicks, not chicks."

His face turns beet red. All he can do is shake his head. We've left him completely speechless.

"CJ, Millie, Cort, and Brody — I don't have specific roles for you yet, but you are in my *Circle of Trust*, so I need your brain power to help figure this shit out." I take a breath and fall back deeper into Brody's lap. "Okay, that's all I have so far. What do you guys think? And no — Helen, no more discussing how hot you find me. It's making Brody uncomfortable." I laugh, while he shrugs it off.

Helen just pouts. She's so damn funny. I never know what is going to come out of her mouth, and it's the best thing ever.

I lean back into Brody's chest and exhale. I'm simply relieved to have gotten all that shit off my chest, while everyone around us breaks out into discussions.

Brody leans into me, kisses the side of my neck and says softly, "I'm so fucking proud of you. Can I please get inside you, like immediately after this meeting ends?"

"I think we can arrange something. Thanks for letting me handle this my way. You're really something else, Mr. Hale."

"No need for me to takeover, baby. I'm here for whatever you need, but you're the strongest woman I've met. You're more than capable of handling anything life hits you with. Honestly, I don't know what you see in me."

I lean in and whisper, "That's simple, Brody. It's your hot body and enormous cock. And that tongue, *Oh My God* that tongue. Ten out of ten… would die to experience it again."

"And I think I can arrange that." He kisses the side of my head, squeezes my shoulders, and we get down to business with the group.

After the plan is decided, everyone starts to head home. Cort ends up giving Hudson a ride, since they just figured out they are practically neighbors. I foresee that Brody is going to have some competition with my brother, in his longtime bromance with Hudson. He and Cort really hit it off tonight. That isn't surprising since they are both so upbeat and fun to be around.

I check on Miles who is almost asleep in his bed. I kiss him goodnight and tell him I'm going to run out really quick and the grandparents are downstairs if he should need anything. Then, I head with Brody back to his place so we can make good on our promises.

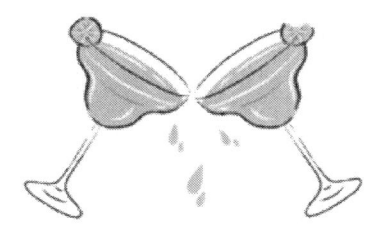

Chapter Twenty-Three

What is going on upstairs?

Cara

Cara

I'm beginning to notice a trend about myself, and it honestly surprises me it's taken this long for me to figure out this part of my life. Weird and chaotic stuff tends to follow me around. That's the trend. And it has taken thirty-eight years to realize this. Shocking, I know.

Here's how it works.

I appear somewhere, literally anywhere, and then chaos bursts into the room all dramatic and loud to shake shit up like a dirty martini for James Bond. Or if that metaphor isn't good enough, here's another one to try out. Chaos in my life is a lot like your gay best friend bursting through the door saying, "Hey, girlfriend! Oh my gosh, what has happened to your hair and that outfit? Dreadful! Thank God I came when I did to straighten you out. I don't know how you ever survive without me. Leave it to me, and I'll take care of everything."

And then chaos proceeds to make itself at home and takes absolutely everything normal about my life and makes it an insane sandwich. In the end, I'm left standing there scratching my head and wondering what the hell just happened.

Case in point, the last few days. It's not that things have been bad, necessarily, but things have certainly not been normal.

Exhibit one: It's been a few days since the nightmare incident with my ass-hat boss and the subsequent dinner with the brain trust. That was certainly full of chaos.

Later that night, I snuck out to head to Brody's house so we could get lost in each other, but his mom was still there. We found a quiet, somewhat secluded spot by the firepit at his complex and proceeded to get freaky as quietly as possible — which was a challenge for me — and thankfully did not get busted by the apartment complex security. Whether or not there is security footage of our late-night antics remains to be seen.

After unleashing my inner public exhibitionist, I had to sneak back inside my house only to be caught by my grandparents, who could probably smell the sex and satisfaction wafting off me.

And did I mention my age and the age of my, *giggle*, boyfriend? We aren't exactly kids, and yet here we are sneaking around his mom and my grandparents. Nothing about that day was basic and normal, right?

Full of chaos!

Exhibit two: Each of the nights since then, after putting Miles to bed, I've left at my grandparents' insistence to go see Brody. Yes, finally, he was able to get his mother to head back to Orlando. I thank the merciful gods of middle-aged sex addicts. Ding dong, the beaver blocker is gone. It's not normal for my grandparents to encourage me to get lucky and help make it happen. I repeat. That is not normal, it's chaos!

Exhibit three: Tonight, Grammy Ellie said she was setting her alarm and would make sure that Miles was up and ready in the morning when I get back to pick him up to take him to school. Then she handed me an overnight bag she packed for me. She insisted that I actually sleep over at Brody's because she hates the thought of me driving back in the middle of the night. Now, considering he lives only about five minutes away, it's more likely she can tell how happy Brody makes me, and they just want me to bitch at them less. Since Brody's cock is functioning as my new anti-depressant, my grandmother is helping me get laid on the regular. That is definitely not normal, right?

Additional exhibits too exhausting to explain in detail include things like:

A) Having to plot to take down your perverted boss and somehow incorporating a marine biologist into the mix. CJ is determined to somehow make sure a dolphin is filming the set-up and take down of the pumpkin-eater, I just know it. We still have a few more days until we can put our plan into action though.

B) Having robotic litter boxes at my house because we have so many stray cats running in and out at all hours of the day and night that human litter box scooping would be a full-time job. The blind old crazy cat lady can't scoop worth a damn since vision is a talent one needs to accomplish said task.

C) Not being able to use any available table or desktop space in the living room or hallways of your home without being verbally chastised by a very particular twelve-year-old who has worked way too hard setting up action figures into various battle poses.

D) Listening to your grandfather trying to get your Amazon Alexa to talk dirty to him.

I could go on, but let's just accept that pretty much nothing about my life is normal. It's all chaos, pure and simple chaos, surrounding me like a winter coat, which I don't know anything about since this is Florida, and at most, I wear a hoodie like twice a year.

I don't wonder why Jimmy split when he had the chance and I'm terrified that when Brody figures out how nuts my life is, he will be gone. Poof! He'll just disappear, and all that will be left of my heart will be a shattered, empty shell.

But I can't think about that anymore because as I slide in bed with Brody, he manages to make all other thoughts disappear except him and our mutual pleasure. Chaos can be good sometimes, I guess.

"I'm so glad you don't have to leave in the middle of the night tonight," Brody whispers huskily in between licks and nips to my neck and nipples.

"Me too. I just hope Miles doesn't flip out in the morning when Grammy wakes him up instead of me."

"He won't. Have some faith in the kid. He's not as bad as you make him out to be, you know."

"Oooh, baby, that feels good." I gasp as he slides his hand down my belly and into my panties, teasing my clit.

But I need to finish making my point. "You don't know him like I do. You haven't seen his head spin around three times and his eyes shoot out firebolts when something suddenly changes his routine."

Brody slowly slides two fingers in and out of me. Oh, he's so good at that.

I lose my train of thought completely when his tongue swirls around my right nipple. An orgasm builds inside me like a tsunami. Suddenly, he stops and looks up at me over my breasts.

What the hell?

I protest, letting out a whimper. "I was so close."

He gets a very naughty grin and says, "Have I ever left you hanging before?"

"No, but that was gonna be a good one," I pout.

"They're all good ones." He winks and starts moving his hand again, and I exhale. Then he says, "Why are you always warning me about Miles?"

"Enough talk; ask me later."

"I've asked you this before, and you always manage to change the subject or distract me with jokes, and so now I'm going to use guerrilla warfare tactics to get an answer out of you."

He stills his hand again and looks at me expectantly with his gorgeous brown eyes. The lamp in the corner reflects the coppery specks, making him look even hotter than he usually does — which is a fuck ton.

I don't answer. I just stare at him with a sad, puppy dog expression on my face until he goes back to working my breast. He leaves his fingers inside me, perfectly still. Despite that, he manages to bring me back to the brink before stopping again.

"Dammit, Brody!"

"Tell me," he says gently, but firmly. "Do you think I don't understand what Miles is really like? Why do you feel the need to scare me away?"

I sigh loudly and throw my arm over my face, shielding my eyes from his probing ones. Technically, it's more of a rage sigh. Orgasm deprivation will do that to a person.

"I'm not trying to scare you away," I say quietly, trying to process my thoughts through a fog of arousal.

"It sure seems like that, gorgeous. Why are you always reminding me how bad it can be with him then, if not to scare me away?"

Damn him for being so insightful and for knowing me so well.

"I guess I didn't think about it that way. I really just want you to realize things with him are touch-and-go, and maybe it will always be that way. He might be okay one week, and the next, he could totally freak-out; one nightmare turns into the next. I don't even know what's going to set him off, and although I try to keep things routine, predictable, and easy for him, I can't always protect him. He is going to show you his other side at some point. I guess I'm afraid that you'll realize this isn't the place you want to be. Just like..."

I bite my tongue, holding back the rest of my thought.

"Like... Jimmy," he finishes my sentence for me.

"And Chaz," I answer, surprised by my honesty.

He cocks his head sideways, silently asking me to continue.

"I think they both left for the same reason. When Chaz was around, Miles was completely out of control, and neither of us knew how to handle him. We had no clue why he didn't respond like the other kids. Everyone seemed to blame us for having an out-of-control kid, even though I know now it wasn't our fault. The looks we got in restaurants or stores were terrible. I don't think Chaz could take it, and he just left one day, never to return."

"Good riddance then," Brody says, and it brings a sad smile to my face.

"But the fact that they both gave up and left me to deal with the fallout really fucking hurts — even still. Not because I still have feelings for either of them because I don't. I don't feel anything for them except disgust. What hurts now is the fact that my child was blamed, and I wasn't worth the trouble. And maybe he really was to blame, who knows? At least Jimmy had the balls to say what he felt, unlike Chaz... and... unlike me."

I feel the tears filling my eyes so fast until they start to spill down both cheeks.

Brody slides up and pulls me into his arms. We're on our sides, chest to chest. I snuggle into his big strong chest, tucked under his chin and let the tears fall in earnest. I'm not sobbing, but the tears flow freely one after another.

I've never said it out loud before... that sometimes I do blame Miles.

Hell, I hardly ever let myself feel it or think it; I banish the thought as soon as it creeps in there. Some jackass guy telling you he can't be with you because of your son is one thing. But believing him to be right and even agreeing with him is a whole other ball of wax. An awful ball of disgusting earwax.

The hatred and disgust I feel with myself for ever thinking that I was single because I have a son with special needs is significant. It burns deep in me and makes me nauseous.

Brody just holds me. And I feel *so* loved, despite my many, many flaws.

"What kind of mother blames her kid for her own failures in relationships?" I mutter.

And here come the sobs, deep shoulder shaking ones. Brody tightens his hold around me and makes a shushing sound, soothing me. His hand rubs up and down my back in calming strokes.

After a minute or so, something dawns on me, and I sit up and pull away from Brody. Suddenly I'm so angry with myself that I can't stand for him to comfort me.

I don't deserve his comfort.

"Maybe I'm not feeling guilt about occasionally having the passing thought that Miles is to blame. I'm starting to think that is not quite right. No..." I drift off, deep in thought before continuing, "I think I feel guilt and hatred toward myself because it *is* my fault, not Miles's. I caused it because I couldn't handle my child, and I've messed him up so bad that everyone has to walk on eggshells around him. I'm not a good mother. It's all my fault."

Brody sits up beside me, turning me toward him. He cups both my cheeks, pulls my face toward his, and says, "No. Stop it right now. Lots of marriages and relationships fail when a child has special needs. It's hard to deal with and not everyone is cut out to make it work. Don't ever say that you are not a good mother. You are a fucking great mother," he says emphatically.

He believes it so much that I almost believe him too.

But I interrupt him, shaking my head adamantly, "No, a good mother would have realized something wasn't quite right with her son and pushed the school or counselors or the doctor to get it figured out sooner. His fourth-grade teacher shouldn't have had to tell me what was wrong with him.

It's my fault he didn't get help sooner. It's my fault he has no friends. And it's my fault he doesn't have a father."

The tears pour out, and even Brody looks like he is getting choked up. Saying all this feels like a thousand pounds has been ripped off my shoulders. I don't feel better, really, but I feel… lighter. I take a deep breath, deeper than I've been able to take since Jimmy left and maybe even since Chaz walked away from me and his son.

Brody looks into my eyes. "Listen to me right now because I'm only going to say this once. You are the most incredible person I've ever known. You love your son and are heavily involved in his education. You take him to tons of extra-curricular activities, trying to get him to better his social skills. I've seen him do musical theater, Tae Kwon Do, soccer, and he even talks about being in debate club next year."

"He is?" This is news to me.

"Yes, he told me about it the other day. But that's not the point. Listen, you take him to therapy, behavior specialists, psychiatrists, and occupational therapists. You make sure he is surrounded by people who love him, and you fight for him like a Mama Bear. Remember that time I told you some kids were starting to pick on him when he was in my class?"

"Yes, I think so."

"Despite me telling you that I had it under control, you sent your brother and sisters to school a few times over the next few weeks for surprise lunch visits and to volunteer to help the coaches out at PE — and that's when you weren't there doing it yourself. Don't think I didn't notice that lunch and PE were the two places I told you where he was most vulnerable, because I noticed. No other parent has ever sent an army in to protect their child before."

That makes me laugh, because, yeah, the Amos family is a lot like an army.

"So, please don't beat yourself up, Carina. You are doing the best you can with what life handed you. Not everyone could handle all the shit you have. It's not your fault you used to pick guys who didn't appreciate how perfectly imperfect you are, how amazing you are, how big your heart is, and how funny you are, and strong. And it's not your fault that those same assholes didn't realize that Miles is the same way. I don't ever want to hear you blame yourself again. Please don't ever talk that way about the woman... the woman I love."

Gulp. Did I just hear that?

"Brody, I'm in a swirling vortex of emotion right now, so I want to make sure I heard you correctly. Did you just say you love me?"

He grins, and it's the most perfect grin I've ever seen. "Yes, Carina, you heard me just fine. I am one hundred and fifty percent head over heels in love with you. I think I have loved you for a long time. I just can't hold it in anymore. And I love Miles too."

He leans in, gives me a chaste kiss on the lips, and pulls back before saying, "Don't feel like you need to say it back."

I shake my head vehemently. "I do feel like I need to say it back. I've wanted to say it for so long, so let me say it. I love you too, Brody. I love you so much. Sometimes I think I can't breathe without you, and I'm so afraid to lose you too."

I sniffle a little, and he smiles. His white teeth are shining bright in the darkness of the room, in sharp contrast to his tan Florida-sun-kissed skin and dark hair.

He cups my cheeks and uses the pad of his thumbs to wipe away my remaining tears, then kisses me again, full and deep this time.

We don't talk any more. There aren't further words needed, not now.

He pulls me back down on the bed and then rolls on top of me. And with his body, he shows me exactly how he feels about me. It's impossible not to believe him. The truth of his feelings comes through loud and clear with each touch, caress, kiss, lick, and whispered breath dancing across my skin.

After sliding into me and filling me deeper than I've ever been filled, he laces our fingers together and places a kiss on my knuckles before moving them over my head. He keeps them pinned above me as he moves slowly inside me, grinding against my clit with each forward thrust. He keeps his gaze locked on mine the entire time. I've never felt more exposed and vulnerable but also so safe.

Our chests press flush against each other. I can feel him everywhere, all over my skin and in my heart and soul.

My hips rise to meet his until his pace increases so fast I can't keep up with the rhythm.

All I can do is lay there and take it. And I do.

I take everything he's giving me.

All his love. All his kindness. All his calm. All his heart.

I love this man so much.

He makes me feel so special, so cherished. With him, I'm not a chaotic mess waiting for her padded room to be ready.

No. With Brody, I'm whole. I'm happy.

And I'm loved – I'm finally worth the effort. Worth the struggle.

I'm awed by the way his soft groans mix with my gasps, pants, and moans – an erotic chorus singing just for us. At some point, he must have unlaced one of our hands because he's flicking my clit, driving me right up and over the edge of the cliff as he pistons in and out of my slick center.

Screaming his name, I climax, feeling him jerk and twitch a moment later with his own release.

The only sounds are our ragged breaths and soft kisses.

"I love you so much," he says, his voice thick with emotion and reverence.

"I love you too."

He places the most gentle and loving kisses across my lips, cheeks, nose, and forehead. I never thought I'd find someone who could love me the way he does.

Later, as we are cuddling with him as the big spoon, I can't help but ask him something that has been at the back of my mind for a while. Since I spilled my deepest darkest fears, maybe he will finally do the same.

"Why don't you ever talk about your dad?"

"Where did that come from?" he asks, clearly shocked by this sudden out-of-the-blue question.

I place my arm over his where it sets across my breast, as if I'm helping him pull me tighter into his chest. Now that he's no longer inside me, I can't seem to get close enough to him.

"I know that came out of nowhere, but I was just wondering because your mom is so awesome, and you talk about her so much. She is around all the time, even though she lives almost two hours away. But you never mention your dad. You are such an amazing man. I can't imagine that your father wasn't in your life. It doesn't make sense. How did your mom do it? And can she teach me to make Miles like you?" I raise my voice a little at the end, in an almost humorous lilt.

I started out serious but can't help but add a tiny punch of humor. Like Popeye, *I am who I am*. That was Popeye, right?

The vibrations of his laugh shoot up my spine and his warm breath tickles against the hair at the nape of my neck. A chill washes over me, and I squeeze his arm around me even tighter still.

"I will be happy to help Miles become a good man, Carina. I'll teach him everything my mom taught me, but you are already doing an impeccable job on your own."

"Now, who is dodging questions?" I tease. "Do I need to use guerrilla warfare tactics on you?" I start to move around and make a show of reaching towards his half-hard cock.

Laughing, he brushes me off. "No, you don't need to use sexual torture practices on me. I'll tell you. Just give me a minute."

He leans forward into my hair and takes a deep breath in, almost as if he can absorb some strength from the scent of my coconut shampoo. The thought that he is gaining superpowers from my shampoo causes me to chuckle.

"I'm not going to ask what is so funny, because who knows what you are thinking about now. That mind of yours is a crazy place."

"It's a crazy and chaotic place, yes. Tell me about your dad whenever you are ready. I'll be here. At least for tonight since Grammy said I can stay out with my boyfriend."

Together, we laugh, and he strokes my hair with his free hand as he moves me around to face him. I lay my head across his broad chest and tuck my leg over his, breathing in his masculine scent.

"My dad is a first-class asshole. I don't talk about him because I try not to think about him. None of my memories of him are any good. When he was around, he was a subpar dad. I don't think he ever wanted to have kids and so, he wasn't affectionate with me, and he didn't help me with homework, coach little league or do much of anything with me. He was mostly there for my mom. I was an afterthought."

His deep sigh ruffles my hair. "It was almost like living with a distant relative, or at least that's what I would assume it would be. Then one day, when I was about eight or nine years old, he just told my mother that he didn't want to be married anymore, and he left. Said goodbye to me with a pat on my head and left, without even looking over his shoulder. Can you believe that? What an asshole."

"Sounds like it. Who could do that to their son? Did you have visitation with him afterward?"

"No, not at all. It was always just me and my mom after that, and she never dated either. I guess that is why I have always wanted a large family. I didn't like how lonely we both were, Mom and me. They were divorced not too long after he left. He paid child support from what I recall and sent an occasional birthday and Christmas card. That was all. A card and a check. Never came around to see me. He just vanished from my life. I guess a lot like Miles's dad, huh?"

"Yes, except Chaz rarely sends child support."

"You got to be fucking kidding me. Really, Cara?"

"The state goes after his wages when they find him, but I think he must work cash under the table jobs or leave each job after they find him. I'll get a few deposits occasionally and then it will just stop suddenly. Not a big deal though, I've managed to do well with my career and can provide enough for Miles. Plus, living in the family home with the grandparents has its perks. I save a lot on rent that way."

"I admire your attitude about that. You don't even seem that sad when you talk about him, excluding tonight of course. Mom cried a lot at night in her room — it went on for a few years after he left. I could hear her, but she would never let it show in front of me. It hurt so bad to know she was hurting and there was nothing I could do about it. Now, on the rare occasion someone mentions him to her, I can see the pain on her face, but at least she doesn't cry. We just change the subject. Her pain became my pain, and I think I just channeled it into a deep-seated need to do better, *be* better than my father. To never hurt her or hurt the woman I love. That's another reason I know I'll never leave you. I couldn't live with myself if I made you cry. You mean so much to me."

"Thank you for telling me about him. It means a lot that you can talk to me like this."

"Same, babe. Same."

"I love y... wait, what is *that*?" I stop suddenly and look at Brody.

He closes his eyes and shakes his head in frustration and says, "Oh no. Not again!"

"Is that what I think it is? Brody, are your neighbors fucking super loudly?"

"Super loudly?" he asks, laughing. "I'd have to give your grammar a big fat F, honey. But yes, that is my upstairs neighbor. This happens from time to time. I'm pretty sure she has the squeakiest bed in the free world. And the men she brings in are not all that quiet either."

"Wow, will you listen to them go? Maybe you should give her some WD-40. Just put it on her doorstep one day, as a hint. Do you think that's more than one couple going at it?" I ask, with mirth in my voice.

It's like a herd of buffalo stampeding through the room above us. In all the time I've been here over the last few weeks, his neighbors have been very quiet and respectful. There seems to be very good soundproofing in this place, it's not a cheap complex. But damn... they are really getting freaky up there.

"Maybe, I'm not sure. My gosh, this is insane. And listen to him cheering her on. Wow."

"Do you think we sound like that? I mean, I know I'm not quiet."

"You are perfect. I love it when you get loud." He cuddles into me and kisses my neck. "Do I need to cheer you on like he is doing?"

"No, please don't." I laugh and swat at his chest. "I like you the way you are. His cheering is a bit over the top."

We listen and chuckle for a little while longer and then I say, "This is actually starting to make me a little hot. How creepy is that?"

"Well, when I'm here alone and this happens, I just put the pillow over my head and turn on the TV to drown it out. So, I can't say that I've ever gotten hot to it. But now that you mention it, it does have a certain pornographic vibe to it, doesn't it? Maybe we can give them a run for their money."

I can't help but reach down and start to stroke him, because the squeaking and moaning coming from upstairs is seriously making my blood boil.

"Who knew I was such a freak, Brody? First, I let you take me by the firepit, and now I'm getting horny because of your bangin' neighbors. Ha ha. Get it? Bangin' neighbors? Like, they are bangin' as in hot and also bangin' as in fucking?"

"Yes, I got it, Cara. I was able to follow the breadcrumbs of your amazing witty humor, despite all the blood rushing from my brain to my dick."

"Smart ass." I give him an extra firm stroke, maybe even a little punishing.

"Oooh!" he gasps and then his hands are roaming over me with more passion.

Suddenly, we both freeze and cock our ears up like dogs listening to a dog whistle.

"Is that coming from down here or upstairs?" I ask, referring to a very loud banging sound. It is so loud it could be someone banging on our front door.

"I think it's someone banging on her door upstairs. Listen. And the squeaking has stopped too."

"I know you are in there, Tammy! Open the fucking door now!" a very angry, very loud male voice shouts.

Brody and I look at each other with our mouths open wide enough to catch flies.

"If he is in there with you, I swear to God, I'll break his fucking legs!" the voice yells again and the door banging continues.

"Holy shit, Brody. Your upstairs neighbor is a nasty whore who is apparently cheating on her boyfriend! This is better than TV!" I shout, with way too much excitement.

I can hear feet shuffling above us, the floor creaking here and there. Clearly the fuck fest is over now that the angry boyfriend has arrived.

"Do you think we should call the cops? Will he really hurt the other guy? What if he has a gun? This could end up as a murder-suicide. A crime of passion. Where's my phone? I need to record this in case the police need it for evidence. Does your neighbor have a gun? If she does, it could be like a shoot-out. Should we leave while we still can? Do you have a safe room?" I ask, rambling questions and thoughts off faster than Brody can possibly follow, let alone respond to them.

"Look! What was that? Did you see that?" Brody shouts and points out his window, where a shadow shaped like a man has just come falling from the balcony or window above us. Brody gets up, goes to the window, and pulls the blinds aside to peek. I follow and we see a naked man, grabbing his shoes off the ground and shuffling into his jeans before running off.

"Where is he? God dammit! I know he's in there! Where is he at?" the angry male voice yells, still coming from upstairs. He must not realize the lover has already escaped.

Since we are so close to the window now, we can hear it all even better. It's clear that the lady upstairs, Tammy, must have had her windows open, which helps explain why the banging was so damn loud. Either that, or the bang buddy must have jumped out the window, instead of the balcony to escape the angry boyfriend in an effort to save his legs from certain breakage.

"Listen to that, now. I think someone running down the steps. I bet it's the boyfriend," Brody says, referencing what sounds like someone rage hustling down the stairs.

"Come back here, coward. Fight like a man!" he yells into the darkness.

Brody and I are glued to the window now, riveted by the scene unfolding. After a few moments, the boyfriend yells again, "Fuck it, you can have her. I'm done with this shit." And he storms off. Good for him. No one deserves to be cheated on.

"I guess the show is over. Bummer. He had a really white, flabby ass, huh? But I'm glad no one got hurt in this kerfuffle," I say to Brody.

"At least we didn't have to hide in the safe room." Brody starts laughing at me. "What the fuck, Cara? Did you really ask if I had a safe room, in my one-bedroom apartment? I'm a fourth-grade teacher, not a member of the mafia. And kerfuffle? What the fuck does that even mean?"

And now we are both cracking up. I put my head on his chest, and we laugh until tears pour out of my eyes. It's the second time I've cried tonight, but these are the type of tears I prefer. And these are the tears that a lifetime with Brody will surely provide.

I love this man.

And wasn't I just talking about chaos? Apparently, my presence in this apartment has caused my chaos to rub off on poor Tammy upstairs.

Chapter Twenty-Four

A cup of coffee for your head

Brody

It's happening today. It should have started already if it is going according to plan and I'm jumping out of my skin with nerves. I keep checking my phone for updates, but nothing yet. I text Cort again for an update, but I'm not expecting a response.

I glance at the clock on the back of my classroom wall and it's only ten to three. This day is dragging so slow. Still ten minutes until the end of school day and even longer until I'll find out what's happening. When school ends, I'm supposed to grab Miles, head to her place, and just wait until they get home or someone calls me to let me know the status. This waiting is agonizing. They are taking that asshole down today and my job is to be the babysitter. Watch the kid and make sure the grandparents don't do crazy shit since the entire family is otherwise involved in various parts of the plan. How is that my role? Surely I have more value than this.

My inside voice says, "Of course you do and don't call me Shirley."

Shit, my inside voice is starting to sound like Cara's outside voice. At least that thought brings a smile to my face.

Maybe after school, I'll head to the University so I can be there for Cara firsthand. But damn... I can't do that. I can't bring Miles there and drag him into whatever chaos might be underway at the University. Shitass. I feel impotent.

My phone buzzes on the desk and I scramble to grab it, setting a horrible example for my students. Fortunately, they don't seem to notice since I've got them working on a creative writing assignment. I check the phone and see it is Hudson.

Hudson: Dude, you there? I got some interesting news.

Me: Yes. I'm here, I can't talk for another 20 mins or so, but I can text. What is happening?

Hudson: You are going to owe me. Are you gonna pay up?

Me: Yes, fine. I'll pay up, whatever you want. Just tell me. I'm dying over here.

Hudson: We are still waiting for them to come outside, but I got the info we needed about Peter's past. It took all my investigative journalism skills, but it seems this asswipe has a pattern of shitty behavior towards his female subordinates. And he keeps getting away with it. UT probably had no idea about his past.

Me: That's great. How does that fit into the plan?

Hudson: I'm not totally sure, but let's see how today goes and we can figure out how to use it if we need to.

Me: Can you send it to me? I'd like to take a look.

Hudson: Sure, thing. I'll forward you the e-mail I just got from my contact right now. And try not to worry. Just watch the little dude and trust that everything's gonna work out just fine. <peace sign emoji>

Me: Gee, thanks. Wish I shared your optimism. But that's my girl putting herself in the path of a sexual predator, and I'm just the fucking babysitter.

Hudson: That's your job every day, bro.

Me: You know what I mean! <middle finger emoji> Just go and do what you have to do to get this fucker off my girl's ass.

Hudson: You got it. Later! <thumbs up emoji>

I help a few students with questions about their assignments and that helps me take my mind off things for a while. Next thing I know, it's the end of the day. The class exits, I say my goodbyes and wait for Miles to join me in the classroom. He knows he is supposed to meet me here, so I have nothing else to do but wait.

Great. More waiting.

While I'm waiting, I check my e-mail and see that Hudson just sent me a shitload of details about this prick's past. What a sick fuck. I quickly print out the e-mail, roll it up and slide it in my back pocket. I'll read it through later.

Still no sign of Miles. He must have gotten held up talking to a teacher or something.

So, I check to see if Helen had to blast anything on her social media or if there is anything showing on any of the news channels yet. It's probably too soon for that, but I'm desperate for information.

I click through Helen's various Instagram, Facebook and TikTok pages and nothing yet. As I'm scrolling through, I see something that catches my eye. What the fuck? Is that... no, it can't be.

But it is. Holy shit.

That's a thumbnail pic of the kiss the changed my life. Right there on social media. That's why Helen recorded Cara attacking me at Crabby's? For her social media shit? In the fallout those few days after the kiss, I had completely forgotten that Helen was recording us. Damn, that's a lot of comments and likes. Looks like this is one of her more popular posts.

I turn up the volume on my PC and watch the video from the start.

It starts out with what looks like random video footage thrown together with some words on the screen that sort of narrate what is happening. There's Cara and I sitting together at Miles's Tae Kwon Do Belt Ceremony, and then she whispers something in my ear making me break out with a big smile. I can't remember what she said, because I was focused on the feeling of her being so close to me. And now, here we are, walking up to the restaurant together. I didn't know Helen was recording any of this. It's not really super obvious that it is me in the majority of the shots, Helen was clearly trying to protect my identity. But I know it is me.

The video is really well put together and it tells the story of two friends, secretly crushing on each other unbeknownst to the other person. There are also a few still photos of Cara and I together, taken over the years, like a collage of our friendship. And one of me with Miles while we are at the firepit. A sweet little song about *"A cup of coffee for your head"* is playing and this whole thing is set up like a love story. It's touching as hell.

How did I not know about this? My heart is pounding along with the rhythm of the song as the video continues.

The audio of the song turns down to mere background noise, and now Cara is talking to Helen about how she has always had a crush on me, she really wants to be more than just friends, but she has been scared that it could ruin our friendship, which she treasures. She ends that little clip by saying, "I'm just going to kiss him and see what happens" with an adorable smile on her angelic face.

That's my girl. She looked so nervous, beautiful of course, but nervous.

Now the video shows Cara waiting in the hallway for me to come out of the bathroom with the words, *Moment of Truth*, on the bottom of the screen. She is rocking on her heels and wringing her hands in the way she does when she is nervous. The door opens and we stand there looking at each other for a moment. The song reaches crescendo as she attacks my shoulders and pulls me toward her.

I chuckle at the memory of how unbelievable it was and how shocked I felt. And then the passion took over. *Shit, Helen is right, we are hot together.* The memory of this is causing my cock to stir. *Nope, down boy. Not at school.*

The video ends with a phrase on screen that says, *And they lived happily ever after.*

I'm not a crier, but shit, I kind of want to cry right now.

I know I should be mad that all that was done without my permission and uploaded online for the world to see, but I can't watch that video and feel anything but joy and love. That was probably the most meaningful three minutes of my life, captured right there on a video, and filmed by a crazy woman. But it was… amazing. She kissed me and changed my life. Forever.

I am a little curious why Cara never spilled the beans about this. Obviously, she couldn't tell me about it before it happened, but she could have after the kiss. I wouldn't have been mad, I don't think. But she did run out and ghosted me for a week afterward. I guess once we got back together, it wasn't important anymore.

Regardless, I'm so touched and full of emotion right now. I couldn't be mad at the insane foul-mouthed Asian pixie who probably cooked up the whole plan or the gorgeous woman who owns my heart as a result. In the grand scheme of things, it doesn't matter that I was trending online and was clueless to it. *All that matters is Cara is mine. And I am hers.*

And that reminds me, I still don't know what the hell is happening at the University. So much for keeping my mind off things.

Oh, and fuck! Where is Miles? He should be here by now.

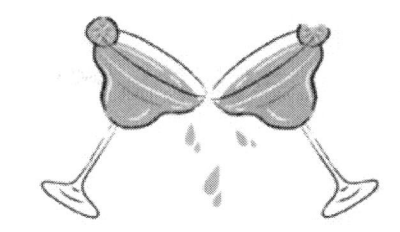

Chapter Twenty-Five

Let's smash that pumpkin eater

Cara

I walk past Mandy and make eyes at her, silently inquiring if everything on her end is still a go. She looks from side to side ensuring the coast is clear before giving me a wink and a thumbs-up. Sweet; she's ready. Next, I text the others to see if there are any last-minute questions or anything that might prevent us from moving in the next five minutes.

Mandy purposely kept my schedule clear for the next hour so that we could pull this off. And Cort's next appointment is fake. His *patient* is Mandy's friend, who is coming in with a terrible case of tennis elbow. She doesn't even play tennis, and her elbow is just fine. She's merely a decoy.

The last few days have been insane with planning, plotting, strategizing, and checking items off the to-do list. Everyone has done an amazing job pulling this together. I just hope nothing goes wrong. It's such a tight timeline with so many moving pieces.

Something shocking was uncovered the other day by Chloe's hackers, who found out that Peter has been using a backdoor computing channel to sneak into the security camera server. Apparently, he goes in there to adjust camera feeds hiding his creepy perverted antics. We could see by the times and dates he has done it before, most of them correlate to times he came after me.

What a piece of shit. He actually hacked into the school's security cameras to hide his behaviors so he could target me. Sadly, it looks like I'm not the only one though because there were a few other times that he messed with feeds that we can't correlate with his encounters with me. It seems he might be harassing someone else. This makes me even more compelled to stop this asshole today.

Jane replies to my text right away. I love that little lady.

Jane: <thumbs up emoji> I just sent the e-mail about the "outage" to Mandy, so she can print it to show to Peter. I also called and gave my friend in Security a heads up about the upcoming blips he may experience in the security camera feeds for your building. He also knows that I will tell his wife about his recent lunchtime antics if he ever mentions my phone call. <winking emoji> <high heel emoji> <Graduation cap emoji>

Cara: Thanks, you rock! <emoji of a rock>

Who knew the head of security had a penchant for dressing up in high heels and a graduation cap and gown on his breaks? Jane did. And who is using that information to make him shut up about what is going to go down today? Jane is. And who is my new favorite person? Jane is.

It's not like she is asking him to do anything bad, and no one is in danger, except technically me. We just need security to look the other way and not ask any questions during two brief periods where the camera footage in the Athletic Training building will get a bit wonky on their end. That's all. No big deal.

The first "blip" security might notice will occur in a few minutes and kicks off our plan. That blip will happen when Chloe's hackers go in to make it look like the cameras are going down in our building, which they will for about four or five minutes. As soon as they go down, Mandy will immediately show Peter the e-mail Jane sent her, which was sent by the *school president*, aka: from Jane. That e-mail will explain there is a planned outage today and as of right now our building will be without security footage for exactly one hour, but there is nothing to worry about.

During those four or five minutes when it is actually down, we expect Peter to use his backdoor access to verify the cameras are in fact down. We are certain someone as crafty as him won't believe it with just an e-mail — even if it comes from the University President. So, when Peter goes in, it will truly look like they are down. He will think he has a golden opportunity to make another move on me. And I'm going to put myself in his path right around that time to entice him a bit more.

The second "blip" will occur after Peter has verified the cameras are down when Chloe's hackers will actually bring the cameras back online so they are truly recording again and will thus, capture whatever Peter attempts with me. He'll have no idea he is being recorded.

My phone buzzes in my hand. I check it.

Chloe: My geeks are waiting for my signal. Everything looks good. Are we ready to take the cameras down? Can they go into Jane and Mandy's e-mail yet to delete the paper trail?

I ask Mandy quietly and she holds up the paper showing me that she printed the e-mail, like a good girl. So, I text Chloe back.

Cara: They can delete the emails now from Jane and Mandy's PCs. But wait on taking the cameras down until I hear from the rest of the team. I need everyone to be in place. We are only going to get one shot at this.

Chloe: 10-4. Wiping emails now. Holding on cameras until your signal.

My phone buzzes again, and I take a deep breath before reading it.

CJ: Millie and I are both here, outside the meeting room. We are supposed to be called in about ten minutes to start our presentation to the trustees. I have my laptop all set to show the feed. We are good to go! Jane just texted me that they are running on time with their agenda so she doesn't anticipate any delays in getting us in there.

Cara: Awesome. Knock em' dead!

It seems like everything is coming together. So far, so good. *Oh, shit! Let me find some wood and knock on it. There, that's better.*

Hudson hasn't texted back yet. Nor has Helen. Shit. Damn. Fuck. They are critical pieces to the puzzle. If they are somewhere screwing off, I'm going to blow a gasket.

I look up and see that Cort's fake tennis elbow girl is heading in, and she is grinning like the cat that got the canary. Cort has that effect on young girls. He is pretty hot, even if he is my brother. He has the vibe of that actor who played "Four" in the Divergent series, Theo something. He's got the same seductive grin and come-hither eyes. I can see why women swoon when he looks at them that way. But I still wish he would turn it down once in a while. He's probably breaking hearts all over town.

The last few days, Cort has been my shadow here at work and that has been by design. We wanted to get Peter worked up with Cort constantly blocking him. That way, the first time Cort is away, the mouse will play.

As Cort walks by, he leans over and says he just got off the phone with Hudson. Thank God. Hudson says he and his guys are in position outside the building. It also seems Hudson found some additional incriminating evidence about Peter's past incidents and is talking to his reporter friend about what to do with the intel. That's great news I wasn't expecting, which makes me start to think this might work.

Shit, where is that wood again? Knock, knock.

"Any word from Helen though?" I whisper back to Cort.

"Not yet, but don't worry. She isn't going to let you down. She is probably just waiting to make a big entrance so she can look like a hero. You know her style is to be really flashy," he jokes, clearly trying to calm me down. But I am anything but calm.

Cort takes his gal over to his area to conduct a bogus evaluation about her pesky elbow.

Thirty or so agonizing seconds later, my phone buzzes with my last puzzle piece. *Yesssss!* Mentally, I'm running around the room fist-pumping and giving high-fives. In actuality, I'm biting my nails and squeezing my phone really tight as I read her text.

Helen: Okay, calm down, bitch. I'm here to save the day. I just posted a teaser on FB live and cross-posted to my Insta. I'm sure we will have thousands of people tuning in to watch IF I need to go live. I'm moving into position now.

Helen: By the way, what fabric softener do you guys use on these towels? It smells amazing in here.

Cara: I know, right? It always smells so good.

Cara: But back to the point at hand. Thank you. I'll be back in there shortly. Cort will be down the hall, listening in and waiting for the signal as to when to barge in. I'm counting on you to save me if I need it, okay? Make sure your phone is on silent and no vibration. We can't have Peter hearing it. Don't forget that he is likely to lock the door so you have to unlock it quietly for Cort to be able to get in.

Helen: I got it, girl. Don't worry. I might be little, but I will choke that fucker out if he gets too fresh and Cort can't get in fast enough. Let's do this. I'm in position and ready when you get in here.

Cara: Ok, here I come in about 2 minutes. Deep breath.

Cara: Chloe, take down the cameras now.

Chloe: 10-4. Going down in 20 seconds and will turn them back on when Mandy calls me to let me know Peter took the bait.

Cara: Thank you.

Chloe: Get em' sis. Be careful though! Make me proud. Do it for all of womankind!

Cara: Oh, so no pressure then? <eye roll emoji>

I glance to Cort and give him the signal. He's ready.

As planned, about ten seconds later, Mandy comes barging through the therapy room floor and heads right towards Peter's office holding that e-mail printout. Perfect!

About thirty seconds later, she comes out and whispers to me as she walks by that he was practically salivating over the e-mail, and he grabbed his mouse as soon as she went to leave the room. Excellent! The bait is in place. Now, to make sure he takes it.

Next up, Cort and I are on the move. We walk to the hallway, and I peek to make sure Peter's door is still open, and it is. Excellent. Going in for the kill.

"I'm going to head to the tennis courts with my patient to check her backhand swing form. Do you need anything, Cara?" Cort asks me, just loud enough that Peter will overhear, but not so loud that it is obvious we are putting on a show.

"Nope, I'm good. Thanks. Just going to get some towels since my next hour is free. See you when you get back," I say and walk toward the laundry room, breathing deeply and trying to control my racing heart.

Now that Peter knows I'm moving to the laundry room, which has a lock on the door, and he thinks that Cort is outside, I'll seem like easy prey. Add to the fact that he also thinks all the cameras are down, this should work. I just don't want his slimy hands on me. *Ugh. Yuck. Gag me with a spoon.* But it has to happen to get the proof we need of his dastardly deeds.

I make my way into the laundry room, I peek behind the large stack of boxes that are filled with therapy supplies like wrap tapes, bandages, Therabands, cords, stretchy straps, and other gadgets. Hidden behind the box is a five-foot-two Asian pixie who is holding her phone and ready to record when the pumpkin-eater comes in to try to get me to touch his squash. *Icky*! I kick the box closest to her, and she giggles. I shush her and we wait to see if he took the bait.

I grab some towels from the dryer and proceed to fold and stack them on the table, just like I was the last time the creep caught me in here. A chill goes up my spine as the memory surfaces of him pressing me against the dryer, but I shake it off. I have to stay focused.

A few moments later, I hear the telltale footsteps approach. I hum to myself acting as if I don't hear him. I have my earbuds in, but nothing is playing, so I can hear everything.

He closes the door gently, and I hear the ping of the lock. The sick fuck is so predictable. And now I can smell him as he approaches. I have to swallow the lump in my throat to stop myself from gagging. Even his smell is unsettling. And this room smells amazing with the fresh laundry. So, you know his aroma is pungent if I can smell it over all the Downy freshness.

"Hello, my darling, we meet again. I'm beginning to think of this as our special place," he says in his quiet voice, which he probably thinks is sexy, but is truly disgusting.

He presses up against me from behind, shoving me into the table. Ugh, this is so uncomfortable. I remember to act like I normally would and get him to talking like last time.

"Eww, stop. Get back. What is wrong with you?" I shove back toward him as I turn around and face him. He only took one step back, since he was obviously expecting me to rebuke him and was braced for my attack.

"Are you really going to keep playing hard to get, Cara? It's getting tiresome. I know you want me. And I want you. So, let's do something about our attraction already." As he speaks, he moves closer and once again is blocking me. I move toward the dryer, shuffling to the side so I can get his back to Helen and she can get out and unlock the door without him seeing.

He stops me from shuffling to that side and shoves me back into the table instead. I try again, and again he blocks me, shoving me back.

"Knock it off. Let me go." I stare him down and make it clear that this is unwanted behavior.

"I'll let you go, if you give me what I want, Cara."

"What do you want?" I ask, even though I really don't want to know.

"I want you. On your knees, preferably. Or you could bend over the table and take it from behind. I'll let you choose this first time." He smiles like he actually thinks this sounds like an offer I'd accept.

"No! I don't want you anywhere near me. Now, get away. You are my boss, and this is not acceptable behavior. Stop it right…" He stops my rant by wrapping one hand around my mouth and keeps his other right beside me, resting on the table blocking my exit to that side — which is the side that I need to move to. If I don't move us both to that side, he will see Helen move to the door out of his peripheral vision. Shit, I have to get him to move or else the door will stay locked.

"Cara, I got you that promotion, and you need to be grateful. I'm tired of you teasing me and wasting time. I want my reward. Now!" he growls.

"No!" I spew from under his hand. And start to really raise my voice while pushing at his chest, trying to get him to move backwards.

"Do you really want to do this the hard way? Fine. You are leaving me no choice."

He grabs a towel from the pile and balls it up with the hand that was blocking my path. He makes a move to shove it in my mouth, presumably to gag me. While he is doing that, I seize my opportunity and take two giant steps to the side and towards the dryer.

He responds immediately, shoving me up against the dryer. Now, I've got him right where I want him.

I try to nod so that Helen will see it. I can't let my eyes follow her to the door, because I don't want Peter to see me watching her and then turn around to catch her. So, I just look at him right in the ugly face.

"You are making this harder on yourself, but I like it rough," he says as he presses himself up against me.

"No means no, asshole! You aren't going to get away with this. What are you going to do if I tell people?" I yell, and he shoves the towel in my mouth, knocking my head back into the dryer. That's gonna leave a lump.

"Simple, just like I told you before. If you tell anyone about our affair, I will make it so your brother never works again. I've been gaining favors around campus. I've got plenty of girls who will say whatever I tell them to. I will gladly use that power to make them say that Cort has been assaulting them. I know you love your brother and don't want to see that happen. So, just shut up and give me what I want."

Okay, we definitely should have everything we need. It's time to end this shit. I've had enough.

I kick my foot into the bottom of the dryer two times creating a loud rumbling sound, the signal to send in the cavalry. Within seconds, Cort is charging in, with Mandy and her fake-elbow friend behind him. He grabs Peter by the back of his shirt, yanking him off me. I take a deep breath and look at Helen, who is still filming and nods at me as if to say, "we got him!"

Cort drags Peter out of the room, and we follow them. He drags his feet, trying to make it hard for Cort to move him, but Cort is way bigger and stronger. He just keeps dragging Peter along, looking like something out of *Weekend at Bernie's*. Mandy opens the front door, and Cort shoves him out and onto the sidewalk right in front of the building.

Surprise, fucker! Guess what?

Hudson is standing by the building entrance along with his reporter friend and a cameraman, where they were shooting some B-roll footage for an upcoming "news story" they were working on. Well, that's what it looks like they were doing, but they were really here to catch this shit show.

They catch the whole scene as it unfolds. But best of all, Peter still has no idea he is being filmed. He is indignant as he turns to Cort and starts cussing him out, further incriminating himself.

"You are done, asshole! Do you hear me? You'll never work again. Neither of you. Consider yourselves both fucking fired!" he yells at Cort and then at me once he sees I've joined them outside.

"I don't think so. You can't assault your employee, blackmail her into being quiet about it, and think you can get away with it!" Cort declares with fire in his voice and daggers in his eyes. I've never seen him so angry.

"I can do what I want. You can't stop me. She wanted me, anyway. I'll take you both down for this. By this afternoon, I'll have a line of women here talking about how you assaulted them!" Peter yells, basically confessing to what Cort just accused him of, and making it even worse by saying specifically how he was going to blackmail me.

The idiot. He really made it too easy.

Helen marches out and smiles, "You might want to calm down there, buddy. I caught the whole disgusting thing on my phone. Unless you want me to post the video right now to my two million plus followers, I suggest you shut up and go give notice that you're resigning effective immediately."

Bam!

The look on his face is priceless. And when he turns around and sees the news camera has also captured this entire scene, he nearly falls down. I can see his knees buckle as the realization dawns on him.

Justice, much like revenge, is a dish best served cold.

I cross my arms over my chest and stare him down.

"What's taking so long, asshole? Get marching upstairs to the administration office and resign. Now! Or I'll hit the post button, and life as you know it will be gone faster than an intern's virtue at a Clinton Cigar Club meeting." She is waving the phone around but is smart enough to stay behind Cort so Peter can't grab it and smash it. Not that it would even matter given the scene he is causing has drawn witnesses, and the media is still recording the entire thing.

I look over to Helen and just shake my head. "I know it's a little dated, but it's still damn funny," she says back to me, as if reading my mind. I just shrug.

"Excuse me, miss. Did you say you have camera footage of him assaulting this woman?" the reporter asks Helen, and she nods her head in reply, still shaking the phone.

"Would you be willing to show us?" he asks, prompting Peter to take action.

"No, I'll go resign. Just delete it, and I'll be gone."

"I'm not deleting shit until you've resigned. I'll follow you. Let's go, needle dick. You resign, and I'll even let you hit delete."

And this caravan of chaos starts moving toward the administration building. Hopefully, that part of the plan is in place, just in case he tries any funny business. He still might have an ace up his sleeve for all we know.

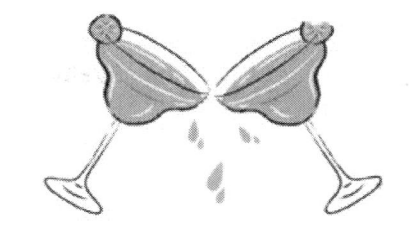

Chapter Twenty-Six

Drama everywhere I look

Cara

We march upstairs into the administration building, one by one in a line like soldiers. Peter is first, then Cort, acting as his prison guard. Then, it's me, Helen, Hudson, and the news crew who are happily still recording. As we walk through the lobby, all the heads turn, and I'm not surprised. We must look like a freak show. Honestly, I don't give a shit what we look like — not after what just transpired.

My phone buzzes. I glance down and see a text from Brody. I can't read it now though, so I let it wait. I have to trust that he can handle Miles and my grandparents. I need to count on him; I can't be distracted right now, but I'm sure he has my back. Probably just texting good luck or checking to see how it went.

As we approach the President's office, Jane comes from around her desk with a look on her face that makes me chuckle. As if she didn't know we were coming.

"Excuse me, you can't bring a film crew in here without permission from our media relations team. And Mr. Peters, what are you and your staff doing here? You don't have an appointment. What's going on?"

Bravo, Jane. Academy Award winning shit right there.

"I need to see Mr. Davenport, right now please. It is urgent."

"Well, he is in a meeting with the Board of Trustees. There was some big situation in there a few minutes ago — lots of commotion — and I don't know if I can get him to come out. Hold on."

She walks toward the conference room, slides in the door discretely, and I smile internally thinking about what that big situation must have been.

A few minutes later, the University President Mr. Davenport comes out, followed by a few board members and then my two sisters — CJ and Millie. CJ gives me a thumbs up on the sly. *Yes*!

With that little thumbs up, she is telling me they witnessed the whole thing via the video feed we sent to the conference room. He isn't going to be able to talk himself out of this.

Exhale.

My phone buzzes again. I glance at my watch and see Brody is *calling* me now. My gut twists as I send him to voice mail. I hate doing that.

"Get that camera out of here right now," Mr. Davenport says to the news crew. I give a nod to Hudson, and he gets them to move out of the room, so it doesn't halt progress on what is about to be an epic firing.

"Hit delete, now," Peter turns to Helen and instructs her to delete the video. She just rolls her eyes and continues to stand there watching — making no move to hit delete.

"We had a deal," Peter says to her again.

"You haven't done your part yet, so get cracking," she says back at him with her trademark sass. Fuck, this feels good.

Peter exhales and says, "Sir, it is with great regret that I tender my resignation. I'm very sorry to leave you with such short notice, but I must be leaving at the end of the pay period."

"You'll do no such thing, Mr. Peters," Mr. Davenport says firmly, causing me to look at Cort and Helen in concern.

"Sir?"

"You'll leave immediately. Jane, please have Security report here this instant to escort Mr. Peters off the campus now. We'll ship his personal items to him."

"Sir, I don't understand."

"We saw your little *encounter* in the laundry room with Ms. Amos, due to some mix-up with the security footage while these ladies were making a presentation a few minutes ago..."

He gestures to CJ and Millie, who were attempting to put on a presentation to the Board. It's about a marketing campaign aimed at getting more students involved in and funding set aside for a new marine biology education program, which doesn't really exist by the way.

The presentation was a ploy to get them in front of the Board and allow them to connect our special laptop to the conference room's Smart Board interactive projector system. The laptop then conveniently malfunctioned when Chloe's geek team fed in the security camera live feed from the laundry room. Instead of showing their presentation, the screen was showing Peter coming after me again. CJ and Millie played dumb about what was happening and asked Jane to come in and help.

Jane was supposed to say something like, "IT was in here earlier doing some upgrades. They must have gotten the Smart Board's wires incorrectly routed with the Campus Security feed's wires."

Now, if these were normal people, they probably would realize that to be highly unlikely and probably impossible. But these are millionaires and figureheads who have no idea how all the machines and little wires make things appear on the big screens. So, she was able to pull it off. She can be very convincing.

Mr. Davenport continues reaming Peter a new one. "Leave immediately without causing a further scene, and we won't call the police. But you are done here. I don't want to hear that you have put so much as one foot on university property ever again."

He turns and storms back into the conference room, the board members following behind him. Before he shuts the doors, he turns to CJ and Millie and says, "I'm very sorry, but you'll need to reschedule your presentation for another time. Sorry you've had to see this, but I trust you can keep what happened here confidential."

"Of course, sir. Thank you for your time," Millie says in her best marketing professional voice, while CJ nods beside her.

They aren't rescheduling shit.

Security is here now, and Peter is being escorted away with his head down and mumbling under his breath.

After the meeting room is closed, Security and Peter have left the building, and only my crew is alone in the room, we all jump up and down celebrating. I hug Cort first, give him a big kiss on the cheek, and call him my hero! Then, I give Jane a huge hug and promise to give her and her daughter all the free massages and PT they may ever need for the rest of their lives.

We leave in a cloud of euphoria. I can't believe we pulled it all off.

The only thing that would make it better is if we were able to get Peter brought up on assault charges — but I know Mr. Davenport doesn't want the bad publicity associated with an arrest. At this rate, he will be able to get another job. The cycle will repeat eventually, once he gets comfortable again. But I'm not going to think about that right now. This moment is for celebrating!

Chapter Twenty-Seven

Prove you can handle it

Brody

Miles never made it to my classroom. After a few more minutes, I leave a note for him in my classroom on the door in case he shows up, and I head out to find him. I have never felt this type of panic before.

None of his teachers know where he is. It's seventh grade, so it's not like they hold the kids' hands and make sure everyone is always in their right place. But this is really unlike Miles. He knows not to run off. He has never been a runner.

And why is this happening today, of all fucking days?

After checking each of his six classes individually, I look in the office, lunchroom, library, computer lab, art room, and counselor's office. I am running around like a mad man, thinking to myself, "You had one job, asshole!"

I pass a janitor on the way to the PE fields and ask if he's seen a brown-haired boy and describe Miles to him.

He says, "There is one crying in the seventh-grade area bathroom right now, actually. I was just coming out to tell someone, 'cause he sure as hell wouldn't listen to me when I told him it was time to go home."

I run off full speed to the bathroom and drop to my knees in front of Miles when I see him... finally. He sits huddled up in the corner of the boy's bathroom. His head is resting on his knees and his arms are wrapped around his legs, as if he is trying to hold his body together. It fucking guts me. He's breathing deeply and sobbing softly.

Fuck, what happened to him?

"Miles, buddy, it's me," I say to him quietly. "It's okay, bud. I'm here. Everything is going to be fine. What's the matter?"

No response.

"Are you hurt, Miles? Is something hurting you physically? Are you in any pain? Can you talk to me, buddy, so I know how to help you?"

Nothing.

I sit next to him, holding him to my side as he sobs. He leans on me and wraps his arms around my waist, clinging to me like a lifeline. But he still won't speak. I don't know what is happening or what to do.

Feeling the panic rising, I text Cara asking her to call me ASAP. I hate doing it, knowing what is going on at UT, but this is her kid. She needs to know something is very wrong here.

"I need to call an ambulance if you are hurt or in pain." I am about three seconds from calling 911 when he finally speaks.

"I'm not in pain." That's all he says.

"Can I pick you up and carry you out of here? Is that okay?"

He nods. *Thank God. At least we can get off this disgusting floor.*

"We can go to my classroom or to the car and I can take you home. Which do you want?"

He doesn't answer. Just shrugs his shoulders as I pick him up and he clings around my front, like a spider monkey. I hug him to my chest and tell him I've got him and he is going to be okay. Tears prick at my eyes.

I have no idea what happened to set him off, but I've never seen him like this. It's terrifying. No wonder Cara is always saying I haven't seen him at his worst. Fuck, I feel bad for not believing her. I was so cocky to think I knew him as well as she did.

But that doesn't mean I'm going anywhere. I'm here for this kid, one hundred percent. And for his mother too.

"Nod if you want to go to the classroom."

Nothing.

"Nod if you want to go straight to the car and go home."

He nods.

I carry him out of the bathroom without worry about where his backpack might be or the state that I left my classroom in. We head straight to my car, and I put him in the backseat and buckle him up. He has finally stopped crying, but is just sitting there, basically nonresponsive.

"Do you want me to sit in the back with you for a little bit or just drive?"

"Drive," he says in a barely audible whisper.

"Okay, buddy. I'm going to drive you home now. It's all going to be okay. I'm going to stay with you the whole time."

I run around to get in the car. I try to call Cara before I drive off, but she doesn't answer. Shit. I am not sure what to do next. I'll just keep speaking calmly to him and hopefully, she will call me back soon to tell me what he needs. Or maybe his grandparents will know what to do.

I decide to play some music on the way home, yet I have no idea what it is. Just whatever radio station was on, but I don't play it too loud. I know he can be sensitive to noises when he is overwhelmed.

Wracking my brain to come up with something helpful, I remember that he used to have some earbuds that he could use to block out some noise.

"Do you have your earbuds? Would that help?"

"My backpack," he says with a big exhale, and I can hear the quiver in his voice, like he is winding up again or something. His breathing is starting to get more rapid.

Well, fuck. The damn backpack.

I reach over into the console praying that I have some earbuds in there. *Yes*! I do. Thank goodness I put them in there after my last trip to the gym.

"I don't have your backpack, buddy. But I have my own earbuds that you can use." I hand them back to him. He takes them and puts them in his ears. He starts rocking a bit. I think he is trying to soothe himself. I guess that is a good thing.

"Almost there, buddy."

We finally pull up his driveway, and I go around to get him out of the car. He's sucking his thumb. Haven't seen that in a long time. Whatever happened must have really upset him. I wish he would talk to me and tell me what happened. I hate this feeling.

He lets me carry him out of the car and into the house, while he keeps the earbuds in his ears. I knock and Grammy Ellie comes and answers the door. Her expression goes from pleasant to concerned in one second when she sees the way I'm holding Miles and the look on my face.

"My goodness, what has happened?" she asks gently as she reaches up to pat Miles on the back. I feel him stiffen and cling tighter to me.

"I'm not sure what happened, but he isn't really talking, and he seems overwhelmed or scared. What would Cara do in this situation? He isn't really talking to me, but he is letting me hold him."

"Then that is what you need to do. Here, come sit down. I'll get some of his soothing items that he uses sometimes."

She moves me over to the couch, and I sit down with Miles on my lap. He rocks back and forth on my lap and keeps sucking his thumb.

I just keep rubbing his back and whispering comforting things to him. I don't know if he can even hear me with those earbuds in his ears, but I don't care.

Grammy comes down and hands me a shoebox-sized clear plastic bin filled with various items. Things like fidget spinners, pieces of silk cloth, beads on rope, blocks, balls of different shapes, sizes, and textures, and little discs with different types of patterns and textures on them.

"Here you go, baby. Take your box."

Miles grabs the box from her, takes his thumb out of his mouth, and grabs the silk fabric piece and one of the discs. I set the bin down next to us on the couch and watch him. He rubs the silk in between two fingers and then against his lips, like in a pattern. His other hand is squeezing and rubbing the disc and he taps it against his leg occasionally.

Grammy Ellie comes back over and puts a dark blue blanket on us, and it's heavy as fuck. A weighted blanket, I guess. He likes it; I can feel how he is relaxing his body even more.

After a few minutes, he has calmed his breathing and stopped rocking. A few minutes later, he looks up at me and says, "I'm sorry." And then he starts crying.

"No, buddy. Don't be sorry. You didn't do anything wrong. Why are you crying now?"

"This is probably him letting out all the emotions he was holding in while he was in that zone earlier," Grammy tells me and that makes sense. So, I hug him and tell him to just let it all out.

He only cries for about two minutes and then he stops, almost as suddenly as he started. He looks at me again and says in a perfectly calm voice, "Can I go play video games in my room?"

What?

I look at Grammy and raise my shoulders, asking her for guidance here. She shrugs like she has no clue. Well, fuck. I don't want to risk upsetting him again, but I'm also not sure that is the best idea if he was that overstimulated.

"Is that a good idea, Miles? What do you normally do after you calm down? Won't that work you back up again?" I ask him, hoping he is talking enough to guide me here.

"I will only play Minecraft. It helps me calm down. Only building, no fighting."

"Okay, that seems fine. Do you want me to come with you?"

"No. I'm okay now."

"Are you going to tell me what happened at school?"

"No. I'll tell Mom later. When is she coming home?" he asks me with no hint of worry or alarm in his voice anymore. Thank fuck.

"Not sure, buddy. But I'll wait here until she gets home. It shouldn't be much longer."

"All right. Can I go upstairs?"

"Sure, Miles. Just holler if you need anything, okay?"

He nods, shrugs the blanket off, and climbs off my lap before putting his items back into the bin. He grabs the bin and takes it upstairs with him.

I look at Grammy Ellie, who has a huge smile on her face. I just exhale and rub my hand down my face and across my afternoon stubble.

"You are great with him, you know," she tells me.

I don't even have a response; I'm so damn drained emotionally.

"I think you might be better with him than Cara, but don't tell her I said so." She chuckles and it brings a smile to my face. We both laugh a little, and it's a nice tension killer.

I sit with Grammy and tell her about what happened at school today. She listens quietly, asking a few questions now and then. And finally, she says, "Don't be surprised if you never find out exactly what happened at school to set him off like that. It's happened before. Cara and the therapist aren't always able to get him to fully explain. I suspect that even Miles doesn't know what causes it sometimes."

"How often does that happen? I've never seen him like that," I ask.

She scrunches her forehead up and eyes me carefully, as if trying to find out what is driving my question. I wonder if Jimmy ever asked something like that before.

"Not that often. Sometimes he might have a short meltdown, maybe five minutes of screaming and crying. It could be a few times a week. Or he might go an entire week without making so much as a peep. Typically, when he feels one coming, he shuts himself in his room and gets stuff out of that box. After an hour or so, he will come out like nothing ever happened. But a big one like today is pretty rare. Used to be all the time, but he has really gotten better."

Her reply felt like it was laced with disappointment... in me. She expected better of me.

I shake my head and feel the need to defend my question. "I wasn't asking because I'm afraid it is too much for me to handle or that my relationship with Cara will suffer because of it. I want you to know that. I'm just asking because I want to be prepared for how often he and Cara will need extra help from me. I want to be there for them, and I will be... whatever they need. No matter how often it happens."

She nods and wipes a tear out of one eye. "Thank you, Brody Hale. You are a good man. Thank you for loving them."

With that she gets up, pats me on my shoulder and walks away toward her bedroom, the only room on the first floor. She shuts the door behind her.

I just sit there and think through how my life has changed in the last few weeks. It suddenly dawns on me that although my knee has felt better for the last few days, I haven't had the compulsive need to go to the gym. I'm still doing my morning calisthenics and the rehab routine that Cara taught me. However, I don't feel that nagging feeling that if I don't go to the gym, I will slip back into my old habits of finding comfort in food.

And what is even more interesting is I don't feel like I'm getting out of shape, and I certainly don't feel like a failure. In fact, it's just the opposite — I feel like I'm finally comfortable in my own skin. Loving Cara and Miles and being part of this crazy family feels so fulfilling, I finally feel complete for the first time in my life. There are no holes left inside of me that either need to be filled with junk food or with excessive fitness.

It's not been all that long that we have officially been together as a couple, but I've never felt so *right* before.

As I sit and begin to count my lucky stars, I take a look around and realize I've been sitting here alone for at least thirty minutes. Until I notice that I'm actually not alone.

A giant black and orange cat that must be at least twenty pounds with huge green eyes is staring at me from across the room. He appears to be judging the shit out of me and is clearly not impressed by what he sees. And for some reason, it makes me bust out in laughter. I laugh and laugh and fall over sideways onto the couch letting the stress of the afternoon roll off me.

A few minutes later, my phone rings, and it's Hudson. *Finally!*

I answer and he quickly tells me how things went down. He says that Cara and Cort just headed back into the PT building to wrap up some things. Apparently, now that Peter is gone, she is now the most senior person and therefore, in charge by default. Cort is helping her get a few things in order. They should be out of there within an hour or two. He tells me not to expect to hear from them until then, but not to worry.

What a relief. I'd like to hear it from Cara, but at least that panic has ebbed.

Before hanging up, Hudson also mentions that there won't be any consequences for that son of a bitch, other than he had to quit his job.

Shit. That's not gonna be enough for me. Looks like it's time for me to get a bit more involved.

My teeth grind and a sour feeling permeates my body, originating from my gut. I didn't want it to come to this, but I can't let him get away with this unscathed. Cara needs me to fight for her, and she is worth it.

I run upstairs quickly checking on Miles, who is perfectly fine in his own little Minecraft world. I ask him if he minds if I run out for a bit. He doesn't care either way. Now I know how Cara feels when she says she sometimes regrets asking him how he feels about her. The brutal honesty can sometimes sting a bit. But at least I can feel confident that the issues he had from earlier are temporarily resolved.

Before leaving, I knock on Grammy's door and let her and Grandpa Dickie know that I'm heading out, asking her to keep an ear out for Miles.

I head out the front door. I know what I have to do, and I hate that it had to come to this.

Chapter Twenty-Eight

When the going gets tough

Cara

It's well after six when Cort and I finally head out to the parking lot, and I'm absolutely exhausted — mentally and physically. But I also feel good. *Damn good.*

Cort pulls away, and before I do the same, I grab my phone when it hits me that in the commotion of this afternoon, I never got back to Brody. Shit. I hope everything is okay. It must be fine because Grammy Ellie hasn't tried to call. If there were a big problem, she would have called me or Cort.

I call Brody, and it goes to voicemail. That's odd.

I decide to call Grammy Ellie to make sure everything is okay. Maybe Brody didn't hear his phone.

"Did you take that sucker down?" she asks, as soon as she picks up, with no greeting.

I smile as I respond, "We sure as hell did. It went down perfectly. And I'm happy to report that Peter Peters Pumpkin-Eater is no longer employed by the University of Tampa. You are talking to the interim department manager, at least until they can find a replacement. The director asked me if I wanted the job permanently once he heard what happened, but I told him I would miss working with patients too much. So, he is going to search for new candidates. He probably offered it because he doesn't want me to sue the school for sexual harassment. But I wouldn't do that anyway. I got what I wanted, and that is to get rid of that pervert."

"That's wonderful news, Cara. Honey, I'm so proud of you. If your parents were here, they would be too. I'm sure they are smiling down on you and your siblings today... working together like that. It's a beautiful thing." She gets choked up.

"Oh stop it, Grammy before you make me cry."

"I'm sorry, but it's just been a very emotional day for all of us, I suppose."

"What's going on at home? Brody brought Miles home, right? I tried to call him, but he didn't answer."

"He did bring him home, but he left a little while ago. He didn't say where he was going or if he was coming back," she says and my heart drops to the floor. That doesn't sound like Brody at all.

"Why did he leave, did he say?"

"No, he didn't say, but it was a very stressful afternoon. Apparently, Miles had a really big meltdown at school and Brody had to search the entire school to find him. He was hiding in the boy's bathroom crying on the floor when Brody found him."

"What? Oh my God. Is he okay?"

Fuck, fuck, fuck. That must be why Brody was calling me at a time when he knew I was involved with taking down the ass-clown. If something happened to my baby, I won't ever forgive myself.

"Yes, yes. Miles is fine now. Brody did a wonderful job comforting him and brought him home. Cara, you should have seen how he carried Miles inside and sat on the couch, holding him. It was beautiful. I had to excuse myself to go into my room and cry. I was so touched."

"That does sound... sweet. But why did he leave then? And are you sure Miles is okay now?"

"Yes, we got him calmed down with his soothing box and then he wanted to play his building video game. After a while, Brody said he needed to leave and asked me to watch over Miles."

"Can I talk to Miles?"

She brings the phone upstairs to Miles, and he gives me the most helpful answers ever. He is so verbose when I need him to be, filling in all the missing pieces to the story. Hashtag sarcasm.

Getting the bare minimum info from Miles, with such great responses as, "Yes. No. I don't know. Yes. Maybe." And other helpful phrases.

Despite his, ahem, brevity, I was able to ascertain that he basically flipped the fuck out — like a full-blown meltdown reminiscent of the good old days, pre-diagnosis, and pre-therapy. He probably freaked Brody out. Shit, I knew it was too good to be true. One day Brody would see how bad it can be. It doesn't sound like it was a violent meltdown, thankfully. But scary and overwhelming all the same.

On the bright side, Miles is fine now — thank God — and agreed to talk to me more when I get home. But he doesn't know where Brody went or if he is coming back.

Miles did tell me that he apologized to Brody though, and I could hear the guilt in his voice. It ripped my heart out a little bit.

I don't know if Miles knows what Jimmy told me when he left. But it is entirely possible he has overheard something at some point that might make him think he was to blame. Shit. I need to talk to him about that and make sure he knows it wasn't his fault.

Right now, it almost sounds like Miles is scared that Brody is gone forever, and he feels guilty.

No, no, no. I can't let him get hurt again. I won't let another man abandon him.

Brody wouldn't do that, would he? I don't think so. I really don't. But then why did he leave so suddenly, and why isn't he answering his phone?

I try him once more after I hang up with Grammy and Miles. Still no answer.

As I head home in the evening traffic, tears stream down my cheeks. *Not again. Not Brody.*

This is all my fault. I should have trusted my gut and stayed away. Why did I let my guard down? I should have stayed true to my original plan and just stayed single until Miles was away at college. I was selfish, and now my little boy is going to be heartbroken... again. And I am too.

Shit, what have I done? I wish Brody would just answer the damn phone.

Chapter Twenty-Nine

The tough get going

Brody

"I know I haven't been the best father, but I'm glad you felt like you could come to me with this," my sperm-donor says as I stare at him across his big fancy desk.

I hate being here with him.

I hate that I had to ask him for help.

I hate that I ever had to see him again, and he sees me when I'm in a position of vulnerability.

I never wanted to need him for anything. Never again.

But Cara is fucking worth it. So, I sucked it up and presented him with the e-mail I got from Hudson earlier today. I asked dear old dad to look into prosecuting Peter, so he can't hurt other people ever again.

As an Assistant State Attorney in Florida's Thirteenth Judicial Circuit, based in Tampa, my father is in the perfect position to make a case against Cara's boss and prosecute him not just for the harassment, but also for the assault.

Hudson's research uncovered a history of Peter suddenly quitting jobs with little to no explanation and no notice. When he dug further, he found past co-workers and subordinates who were willing to talk. A pattern started to become clear. He and his reporter friend were actually able to find six other victims who had either been paid off or coerced not to report his actions to the authorities. Management at his past employers would much rather just sweep this shit under the rug, so they don't suffer the publicity fallout.

This includes hospitals, high schools, and other colleges where this asshole has worked in various physical therapy departments, all right here in the greater Tampa area. *Unbelievable.*

In each case, Peter ends up resigning suddenly and usually even gets a bullshit letter of recommendation. It's unbelievable how fucked-up this is. The victims are never *truly* believed and are bullied into shutting up.

Not my Cara, though. She was too smart and strong for that. Instead of just complaining to management, like I wanted her to do, she comes up with an amazing plan that forced the University to act and not put any blame on her. *I'm a lucky bastard.*

I tell my father that in addition to the list of witnesses and evidence I've just given him, there is also going to be video evidence of another attack that occurred today that I'll be able to get him tomorrow if he agrees to move the case forward.

My father tells me that the evidence we have is compelling and makes it a more attractive case for his office to pursue. Without the demonstrated history of repeated offenses, there would be a chance today's incident could be boiled down to a misdemeanor and plea bargained down to basically nothing; which isn't something his office would want to take on without significant external pressure. But with the history of repeated harassment and potential assaults, Peter will be looking at a felony and significant jail time.

I owe Hudson big time.

I part ways amicably with my father and shake his hand, thanking him for staying late to see me and doing so on such short notice. I guess the guilt I sent his way via a scathing text after his secretary tried to send me away since I didn't have an appointment, helped compel him to see me. Maybe the old bastard does have a soul in there somewhere.

Not sure how he can be a good guy in the world by helping take down the bad guys but was such a shitty father and husband. At least he was able to come through for me this one time.

After all these years... finally saying things I've been holding inside, getting them off my chest, and then giving him a chance to apologize by helping the woman I love, a huge burden has been lifted off my shoulders and I feel a hundred pounds lighter.

I make my way through downtown Tampa and head straight to Clearwater. I can't wait to see Cara and tell her the great news. Then, we can celebrate… right after we figure out what set Miles off today and make sure he is really okay.

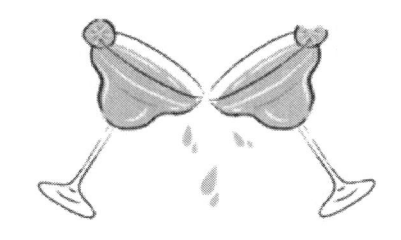

Chapter Thirty

Pizza is best served with hugs

Cara

"That's a good hug, wow," I tell Miles, after racing upstairs to see him as soon as I got home.

Still no sign of Brody or call back. But I'm trying my best not to worry about that. I have to prioritize, and Miles comes first. Always. That will never change.

Miles is really giving me a super tight hug, and I can't help but sink into the embrace. He hasn't hugged me like this in a long time, and I realize how much I've missed it. He's growing up, but moments like this remind me that he will always be my little boy.

"Want to tell me what happened today?" I ask gently, while maintaining our comforting hold and stroking his back with my hands.

"Not really. Mom, I'm just so sorry. I didn't mean to, but I couldn't help it."

"Baby, what on earth are you apologizing for? Tell me what's going through your head."

He sighs dramatically, then pulls back to look at me and says, "I couldn't hold it back, I tried so hard, but I couldn't get back in control. And... Mr. Hale, he saw me like that and had to take care of me. I tried to be brave and hold it in, but I couldn't." Tears pool in his eyes, and he puts his head back on my chest and hugs me again.

The guilt I can feel coming off him is suffocating me. I hate it.

"Baby, you didn't do anything wrong. You hear me? You didn't do anything wrong. You don't have to hide your emotions all the time. You don't have to be brave all the time. I don't know what happened to cause your panic to set in, but whatever it was, it's most likely not your fault. Sometimes your emotions are going to be too overwhelming for you to handle, and that is okay. You keep trying to get better and better at managing your feelings. You are doing so great. But you can't be perfect all the time, right?"

I pause for a moment and let that sink in, before continuing. "I'm sure Brody isn't mad at you. You know how kind he is, and he loves you. I know he does. You don't need to apologize to me or to him for being yourself. Understand?"

I need to remember to be more brief with him. His therapists have told me before to not pontificate with him so much, since he is likely to tune out after the first sentence, but dammit — I need him to hear all of this. I need him to know he didn't do anything wrong.

"What if he doesn't come back? I don't want you to be hurt again, Mommy."

"Oh baby, don't worry about me. Let me worry about me. You'd never hurt me, baby. Except that one time you did a Dutch oven in my bed. That was painful in so many ways," I joke and get a big smile in return.

"Seriously, buddy. If Brody doesn't come back, we will deal with that, and it won't be your fault. I will be okay too. But do you really think he will walk away from us? Because I really don't. He is not like... not like your father and not like Mr. Jimmy. Brody is a good man, and I don't think there is anything you could do to push him away. I truly believe that, baby. You believe me, don't you?"

"I guess so. I like him so much better than Mr. Jimmy. I know you liked him, but I never liked him at all."

"You should have told me that. I don't want you to hide your feelings from me, buddy. You and I are a team, right? Teams count on each other and tell each other everything."

"Liar, liar, pants on fire," he says, teasingly. He is just like his mama. Finding humor in a terrible situation. *I'm so proud. Sniff, sniff.*

"What? How am I a liar?" I ask with a dramatic gasp.

"I remember how you told me that Mr. Hale was just your friend when you got the roses from him. But I'm not stupid, Mom. Nobody sends that many flowers to a friend."

"Well, you may have busted me there. I just wasn't sure what to tell you yet. Everything was a bit new. But it worked out, right?"

"We'll see if he comes back, and then I can answer that question," he says. He has a lightness about him now. I can see that the guilt he was feeling is melting away, thank goodness.

"Is this a private party, or can anyone join in?" I hear a deep rumble from behind me, and my heart speeds up.

"Mr. Hale, you came back!" Miles says as he jumps up and runs over to where Brody is leaning against the door frame, a huge smile on his handsome face.

Brody stoops down, picks him up, and they embrace. It's too much. I can't take it, so I don't even try to hold back the tears of joy.

Brody peeks at me over Miles shoulder and gives me a wink. Did I just swoon? *Yeah, I think I did.*

I don't know if I want more kids. Plus, I might be too old, but my body is fully on board with Brody putting a baby in me. I'm pretty sure that wink while he was hugging Miles caused spontaneous ovulation.

My heart is so full right now.

"I'm going to set you down now, because I need to talk to your mom really quick, okay?" he whispers to Miles, who nods his head in response.

It's super hot that my man is big and strong enough to hoist up a twelve-year-old like that. I haven't been able to carry him for years. But Brody can carry me, and Miles is half my size, so I suppose it makes sense.

He puts down my offspring, and I stand and go to him. He leans in to kiss me on my forehead, takes my hand, and pulls me out of the room towards my bedroom.

I look over my shoulder to see Miles smiling up at us both. "Back to your Minecraft for a bit, and then how about we go out for pizza?" I ask him.

"Yes!" he shouts, then immediately sits down and turns his game back on.

Parenting really isn't all that hard when you can use pizza and video game bribery. I really should stop overcomplicating life and just remember these tactics at all times.

"Thank you," Brody says to me as he wraps me up in his arms.

We stand clinging to each other just past the entrance to my room — which looks like a crime scene, by the way. I didn't make my bed this morning, and clean laundry is in baskets all over the room — with underwear and bras hanging out of them, some of which has spilled onto the floor. I'm such an organized, classy bitch.

They can build a house on those home improvement shows in two weeks. Meanwhile, I can walk back and forth past the same clean laundry baskets for a month and never touch them except to dig out clean underwear.

"Why are you thanking me?" I ask him as I kiss his chest and then stare up into his eyes.

"For what you said to Miles. For trusting me to come back."

"You heard that?" I ask, gulping, and super glad I didn't let all my insecurities show when I was talking to Miles.

"I think I heard most of it. It sounded like he needed to hear it. You were doing such a good job; I didn't want to interrupt. And... maybe I was really curious to hear what you were going to say about me." He chuckles a little as he smiles. Then he gently kisses me before pulling away.

"Seriously though, you trusting me really means a lot. I panicked a little bit when I got here a few minutes ago. Grammy accosted me to tell me that you were really upset that I left. It didn't dawn on me when I left that I wasn't clear that I was coming back. I should have realized that might set off some warning bells in your mind, given how the day went and how your past relationships ended. I can imagine what you must have been thinking. I'm sorry for worrying you, but thank you for believing in me."

"Thanks for coming back. And for being someone I can trust." I reach up to kiss him, this time a bit deeper, and we start to get wrapped up in our passion for each other. But just as his hands start to roam lower down my back, I pause as a really big question pops into my mind.

"Wait. Why did you leave, though? Where did you go? And why didn't you answer my calls?"

He sighs, steps back, and leads me over to the side of the bed. He guides me to sit beside him and puts an arm around me, pulling me into his side.

Seems like this is going to be important, and I can't quite suppress the nagging worry that something is wrong. It might be leftover worries from the *almost-abandonment* that never happened.

"Hudson called and told me today's events from his point of view. He mentioned that Peter was simply allowed to resign with no other consequences."

"Yes. Well, that's true because I'm sure the school doesn't want word to get out about it. If we called the cops, the real media would show up and make a big deal about it. That wouldn't look good for the school."

"Well, true as that may be, someone needed to hold that ass-wipe accountable for his actions. It turns out he has a history of leaving jobs suddenly without notice in very suspicious circumstances."

"Hudson told Cort about what he found out. I heard something about that before. Honestly, it doesn't surprise me. Once a predator, always a predator," I say, with a resigned sigh. "But you didn't go find him and kick his ass or something, did you? Brody, please tell me you didn't go out and do something stupid. It's not worth it."

"Shhh, just listen." He boops me on the nose.

I grin and then make a zipping motion across my lips.

"I didn't go do something stupid. As much as I would love to kick his ass into next week, that is not really my style. Instead of using my hands, I used my contacts."

I stare at him in confusion, but I don't speak.

"I don't think I mentioned it, but my father is an Assistant State Attorney... a state prosecutor in downtown Tampa."

I gasp.

"So, I went to see him and gave him the evidence and witness list that Hudson dug up with his reporter buddy. I told him about what the asshole has been doing to you and that by tomorrow, we would likely have video evidence that we could share with him to help him nail the shithead to the fucking wall."

"You are kidding me. You went to see your dad? Who you haven't seen in years?" I ask, my eyes probably the size of saucers.

"Yes. I went to see him. For you. And I feel really good about it, actually. In order to get past his secretary slash pit bull guard dog, I hit him with a healthy dose of guilt in a text. He came out and let me in his office a few minutes later. And Cara… it all just came out. Everything I've bottled up for years. I let him have it for about five minutes. He let me rant and rave, and he listened to it all. He apologized and explained that he never felt like he had what it took to be a father. He wanted more for me than he thought he could provide."

He exhales deeply then continues, "I never knew why he left. It helps knowing he was trying to do what he thought was best for us, as misguided as his actions may have been."

"Wow, Brody. I'm so glad you got to hear that. I'm so proud of you." I reach up and kiss his cheek.

"Thank you, baby. So… after we cleared the air, I gave him the information we had on Peter Peters. He said once we get him the recording, he would go after him, pushing for a felony. So, I would imagine that Peter will be arrested very soon, and he is facing a criminal record and jail time."

"Fuck yes!" I jump off the bed and then turn around and tackle Brody back onto the bed.

"Easy, killer." He jokes, but still holds me close to him.

"I can't believe you did that. Brody, that is such amazing news. Wow. What a fucking day! Can you believe we pulled this off? I still can't believe this is all real."

"You did it, baby. You deserve all the credit. I'm happy for you," he says honestly, and my heart expands about thirty-two sizes.

I love this man.

"Thank you for everything you did for Miles today too. Grammy told me you were so wonderful with him." I give him a kiss again, because I want to give him all the kisses. All the time. I never want to stop kissing this man.

Eventually, though, I come up for air and confess something.

"I admit I was terrified for a little while that Miles's breakdown might have freaked you out, and you ran. But when I got over my fears and really thought about all the things you said, I knew you'd be back. And damn... you went to your dad for me? Shit. How am I ever going to top that?"

"I can think of a few things you can do to top that," he says deviously. "But no thanks are required. As long as I have you and Miles, I've got all I need. You two make me so happy. I feel so lucky. I love you, Carina."

I go in for another kiss, but my stomach starts growling and we both laugh instead. He jumps up and pulls us off the bed.

"Come on woman, there is a pizza somewhere out there that I need to share with my two favorite people."

We grab Miles and head out to dinner after I make sure that the grandparents are fed. Fortunately, the leftover meatloaf from the other night is good enough. Grammy Ellie sends us out the door, insisting she has it covered, and that she'd like a night alone with her husband for a change.

Ugh. If I ever find out that they are still having sex at their age, I might be sick. In fact, I'll definitely be sick.

A half-hour later, we sit in a booth enjoying a plain cheese pizza — Miles's choice, of course, because toppings are gross. *Cue the eye roll.*

Brody is next to me, holding my leg under the table. Together, we eat, smile, and laugh. This feels so damn good. My family has just grown. I can actually see us like this forever.

No matter what chaos surrounds me in the future, I know Brody will be there helping us get through it. As my partner and as the father that Miles deserves.

We fit so well together, the three of us. It is almost as if he were made for loving us. And I will spend the rest of my life showing him how grateful I am that he came into my chaos and showed me that I'm worth it. *We* are worth the effort. Somehow, we all ended up right where we belong.

Epilogue

Cara

Three months later

"Breathe, Chloe. Breathe," I tell my eldest sister, who is grasping my arm so hard. At this rate, I will likely need it to be in a cast by the end of this flight.

It's February and the evening before our cousin's wedding. I have no idea how we did it, but Chloe finally agreed to fly up to Virginia with the rest of the family. She finished the implementation of her big project earlier today. Perhaps she was riding so high on another big success in the flashy world of IT project management, that she decided not to make a run for it at the last minute, like she threatened to do all month long each time the subject came up.

She may have taken some Xanax right after work and had a shot or two of tequila at the airport. Clearly, that was my idea. Roll your eyes if you must, but she got on the plane. Aside from holding her breath more than what should be allowed by the laws of nature, she has been doing surprisingly well. I mean, except the way she is trying to break my arm into submission.

I peek around her and see she is doing the same thing to CJ on the other side of her. I nod my head at CJ and flash the two-finger Katniss salute of solidarity with my good hand.

As soon as I set it down, Brody grabs it and pulls it to his lips for a sweet kiss. *Le Swoon*. My man is so damn romantic, sometimes I can't take it.

Just kidding. I can totally take it.

"Are you excited to meet more of my family?" I ask him, with a look in my eyes that practically screams: *Be afraid — be very afraid!*

"You don't scare me, Carina." He winks and then adds, "Every person in your family I've met so far has been great, so I'm guessing the Virginia branch of your family tree will be equally enchanting."

"Enchanting? Have you met my family? We are talking about the Amos family, you handsome, delusional man. For God's sake, my grandfather just tapped the flight attendant on the ass. Now, I have to beg her not to press charges, and hopefully she buys the *senile defense*. That reminds me, did you bring the duct tape like I asked you? I forgot to tape his arms to the arm rest."

"Stop, he's not that bad. And he just pretended to pat her ass. He didn't actually do it."

"That does not make it better, and you know it."

He laughs, that deep rumble in his chest causing my thighs to clench and goosebumps to break out on my skin.

I lean in to whisper in his ear, "You know what that laugh does to me. Remember, you are far too big and beefy to fit in the tiny bathroom with me. So, I kindly thank you to be less sexy the rest of the flight. Otherwise, you'll be buying me new, dry panties when we arrive in Virginia."

He chokes a little on a sip of water when he can't hold in the laughter. He gets back under control and says to me, "Sorry, baby. If I have to sit here and pretend not to keep looking down your V-neck shirt, then you have to listen to my sexy laugh. Fair is fair."

Today's shirt says, *Margarita Time! The only time when rim licking is deemed appropriate public behavior.*

Shut up. It's totally acceptable travel clothing.

The rest of the flight is surprisingly uneventful. Miles is comfy in the seat next to Cort, one row behind us. They have been taking turns playing on his new Nintendo Switch. Brody got it for him as a Christmas gift, thus cementing his place as the greatest adult of all time. He is going to spoil my son rotten.

But I'm going to let him because it's nice to have someone care for Miles the same way I do. Miles is already blossoming with the extra attention Brody gives him. He even calls him Mr. Brody now, instead of Mr. Hale.

The Christmas gift I gave Brody was pretty cool too, if I do say so myself. Well, the one I can mention in public was at least. I finally stepped out of my comfort zone and had a friend in the Music Department at UT record me singing a song for Brody. He says he listens to it all the time. I was wracking my brain trying to figure out which song I should sing for him. Then one afternoon, he had me call his phone to find it when he misplaced it in his apartment, and when I heard my "Heaven" ringtone play, I knew I'd found the winner! It's our song now, which is really weird since it is a super old, cheesy, rock ballad. But oh well. It's ours.

I have a few other songs already recorded for him, which I'll give him on his birthday next month. These song choices are more reflective of my typical humor. It's a fantastic medley of such great hits as, "Let's get it on," "I want your sex," "You sexy thing," and then I threw in Roberta Flack's "First time ever I saw your face," just because I can't let him think I only love him for his body.

Brody is so much more than just an amazing, hot, rock-hard body with an enormous cock, magical tongue, and heavenly fingers. *Wait, what was my point?*

We've been talking about moving in together, but I am not sure how to make it work. CJ keeps telling me that if Miles and I get a place with Brody, we won't be abandoning the grandparents like I thought it would be. Instead, she thinks it will cause the rest of the siblings to step up to help them.

Honestly, that is probably how it should have been all along. I never minded being the full-time caregiver because I needed the extra help with Miles. Living there with the extra hands, as blind and deaf as those hands may have been, was extremely helpful. I don't mind caring for them in return. The pharmacy runs, doctor visits, shopping trips, and helping make sure everyone is fed and watered has become a habit now.

And it comes in with the bonus entertainment of trying to figure out what Grandpa Dickie put on the Alexa Shopping List. Last week, I had to figure out that *Brockwire* actually meant *Bratwurst* and *Cheesy Elbows* actually meant *Macaroni and Cheese*. So, you know there are added benefits of living with the old folks.

Despite how attractive staying with the elders is, the idea of me and Miles getting our own place with Brody is really tempting. I want to sleep with him every night and wake up in his arms every morning. The few times here and there when we've done that have been amazing. But good things come to those who wait. I waited thirty-eight years to find the perfect guy. A few more months until we can live together isn't going to kill me.

The rest of this flight, however, might just kill me. Between wanting to jump Brody's bones the longer he holds and rubs my right hand and losing all feeling in my left hand, I'm just about ready for the flight to be over.

·❤·❤·❤·❤·❤·

BRODY

This wedding has been a blast, and I'm having the time of my life. Just as I suspected, the Virginia Amos family is a hell of a lot of fun to be around.

I thought Cara was going to cry tears of joy when she saw they had a margarita fountain at the reception. The only other time I've seen her that happy is when my head was between her legs.

Cara and I have been dancing and laughing the evening away. I gave Grammy Ellie a spin around the dance floor too, just for the hell of it. At the end of our dance, Grammy kissed me on the cheek and said she can't wait until I'm officially part of the family. I guess that was a not-so-subtle hint.

Not that I need the hint. Shit, I've been carrying around the ring for three damn weeks, just waiting for the right time. I have been through sixty-two thousand, seven hundred and thirty-two different proposal scenarios — give or take a few — and none of them have felt perfect enough for this amazing woman. So, I decided I'll just do it when the moment feels right.

I asked Miles last month if he would be okay with me asking his mother to marry me. He rolled his eyes, said *Yes* with zero voice inflection whatsoever and then walked away as if I just asked him the stupidest question in the world.

That kid cracks me up. I wonder if I could actually adopt him one day.

A few minutes ago, Miles asked a blond girl in a pink dress to dance after I gave him some pointers. But that poor kid has zero rhythm. I probably should have taught him how to dance. Oh well, that gives me something else to do with him between now and when I marry Cara. I love teaching him new things. We've been trying to work on baseball. He doesn't quite have the hang of catching and throwing yet, but he's getting better. I am enjoying the shit out of being officially in his life in this role of almost-stepdad.

I look over at the pair of them dancing and smile, then give Cara a nudge as we spin near the kids. The little girl, who is probably about ten years old, has been really sweet despite Miles's lack of dancing skills. They just keep stepping back and forth from side to side with about a football field length of space between them. Their arms are straight out ahead of them like robots, bracing each other's shoulders. It's the most awkward looking dance I've ever seen. But I'm proud of the little dude regardless.

The song comes to an end. I lean in, give Cara a short kiss, and ask her if she wants to sit down for a bit. But then the next song begins. Our eyes meet, and we know we aren't leaving the dance floor. *Seriously?* They are playing "Heaven." Really? She rolls her eyes, and we both chuckle.

Is this a sign? Shit. I think it's a sign.

We start dancing again, pressed even closer together this time and everything feels so right. Her entire family is here, her son is here, our song is playing, and she looks like a goddess in that slinky teal-green dress. It's such an amazing color for her with her milky white skin and gorgeous red hair. She looks like a walking wet dream.

Rather than make a scene in the middle of the wedding reception, I spot an area off the side of the dance hall that leads to an outdoor patio area adorned with twinkling lights. It's a bit too chilly for many people to be outside, despite the large heaters. *That will be perfect.*

I lead her to the patio, glad we can still hear the song — *our* song. I pull her back into my arms, and we dance for a few more moments before I take a deep breath and slow our swaying until we are standing still — simply holding each other close. As I stare deep into her gorgeous brown eyes, I see exactly what I'm looking for.

I give her a quick, chaste kiss before I take her hands in mine and drop down to one knee in front of her.

The moment she realizes what I am about to do, I see her breath hitch, and she raises one hand to cover her mouth. Tears are already coming to her eyes.

"Carina, before you blew into my life I was a bit lost. I was always looking for something, but I had no idea what it was or how to find it. There were empty places inside of me that I could never fill. You came into my classroom, and with just one look, I felt happier and more hopeful than I'd ever felt before. In getting to know Miles that first year, I got to know you even more. Your goodness and light are reflected in him, and the love you poured into him shines through. You are the most amazing, strong, powerful, and caring person I've ever been lucky enough to know."

I take a breath, swallow the lump in my throat, and then continue, squeezing her hand gently.

"I don't know why on earth you let Helen convince you to kiss me for a damn TikTok video, but I am so glad you did. In that moment, I knew with absolute certainty that I found my other half. My crazy, hilarious, and chaotic other half. I want to spend the rest of my life making you feel as good as you make me feel. I want to be the father that Miles deserves and a partner worthy of you. I love you with my whole heart, and it would be the biggest honor of my life if you would agree to be mine. Will you marry me, Carina?"

I pull out the ring and wait for her to answer. It doesn't take long.

"Yes, oh my gosh, yes. I love you so much! I can't wait to marry you. Yes. Yes. A million times, yes!" She nods her head, tears spilling down her cheeks.

I slide the ring on her finger, with a slight tremble in my hands. Then I stand up and kiss her like my life depends on it.

She takes a break from kissing me long enough to hold her hand up to admire the ring. It's a white and rose gold roped band adorned with a smattering of small pink and white diamonds, all leading up to a 1 carat marquise-cut white diamond in the center.

"Do you like it?" I ask in between kisses.

"Are you kidding? It's amazing! I want to joke and say it's awful, because I figure that's what you'd expect from me, but I love it so much. I can't even pretend to hate it," she laughs.

I swing her around in a small circle in that cheesy way that only newly engaged couples can get away with doing and kiss her soft lips once more.

"Oh my gosh, we need to go tell Miles," she says with a blissed-out look on her face.

"I couldn't agree more. I just hope your cousin doesn't think we are trying to steal her thunder. I just couldn't wait anymore once that damn song started playing."

"Oh, please! She put a margarita fountain at her reception for heaven's sake. It's like she practically wanted the celebration to be all about me!"

Laughing and holding hands, we go back inside to tell her family the good news and to begin our happily ever after, together.

Thanks for reading!

BONUS CHAPTER: If you'd like to read a girthy bonus scene taking place a year and a half in the future, scan this QR code with your phone.

Scan QR code for Bonus Scene

Continue the series with Hudson and Chloe's story – Love & Other Mistakes – available now!

Acknowledgements

Dear Amazingly Wonderful Reader:

THANK YOU for reading my first ever full-length romance novel. Writing and self-publishing this story has been a lifelong dream come true and I'm thrilled to have shared this experience with you in some small way. A million thank yous would never be enough to express my gratitude.

I hope you enjoyed reading Cara and Brody's story as much as I enjoyed writing it. I love these characters and the entire Amos family so much; I can't wait to see what new adventures I can take them on in the future. These characters have taken root inside my psyche and are demanding I tell their stories. Who am I to deny them?

As a single-mom to a child with high-functioning autism and someone who also lives with an aging relative, there are some similarities between Cara and me. Oh, and I do love to imbibe in the occasional (okay... frequent) margarita-fueled girls night out. However, most of this story is pure fantasy and it was a blast to stretch my creative muscles and give the characters a journey in self-discovery, passion and general *badassery*.

Writing a novel is a funny thing. When I started, I thought I had it all worked out in my head and knew what would happen. In fact, when I started, I had zero intention of writing the side-plot regarding the harassment by the dastardly villain Peter Peters Pumpkin-Eater. However, once I added a few interactions between Peter and Cara, the story just flowed out of me and I had to make it so Cara and her (mostly female) badass squad gave him his comeuppance. If you are a female and have worked a day in your life, sadly, there is a real good chance you've felt exploited, marginalized, or uncomfortable simply because of your gender. It's a terrible reality that all women deal with each day and writing this aspect into the story felt right for me. In my own little way, I used Cara as a therapeutic exercise in sticking it to the man, in a way that I haven't been able to in reality. I hope you enjoyed taking this little side-journey with Cara, Helen, Jane and the Amos family. *Girl Power!*

I'd be remiss if I didn't thank a few people for helping me make this dream into a reality. The family members who supported and encouraged me along this journey: Casey, Justine, Jennifer, Connie, Dave, Josh, Jeannie, and David and my volunteer beta reader team. All my cats (you know who you are) who cozied up to me and sometimes rage meowed at me to force me to take a break from writing to pet you and feed you. Grandpa Joe who talks to our Amazon Alexa like she is a real person. Kim Bailey, at Bailey Cover Boutique for revamping my cover into the beautiful masterpiece that it is now – I adore you! Patrick Neve at 73Creativ, a huge shoutout for all hardwork with my website and other projects. My editor and cheerleader, Fatima Sibyl Ramos, who provided such great feedback on my manuscript and joined me in lusting/drooling over the pictures of extremely hot men who served as inspiration for Brody, Hudson and Cort. *Le Sigh.*

Thanks to my romance author inspirations: Pippa Grant, Lucy Score, Kathryn Nolan, Claire Kingsley, Tara Sivec, and Meghan Quinn. If you haven't read work by these ladies - you are truly missing out. Might I suggest you start with Pippa Grant's *Mr. McHottie* for the best elevator scene of all time.

Oh, and I guess I need to give some back-handed thanks to COVID-19, because without you, I wouldn't have been laid off and had time to write this story. So, I guess while you've ruined the world temporarily and taken far too many innocent lives, I guess there is a silver lining. You know what, that all just feels wrong still. Too soon. Please strike this last paragraph from your memory and pretend I ended with thanks to my author role-models.

Much love and sloppy margarita kisses!
Jackie

Please don't forget to leave a review. Reviews are so important to independent authors like me. Thank you!

Also by Jackie Walker

Dive into the rest of the series!

Love & Other Mistakes (Chloe's story)
Love & Other Lies (Cort's story)
Love & Other Trouble (CJ's story)
Love & Other Accidents (Millie's story)

Redleg Security Series

A Love and Laughs Spinoff Series
(Romantic Suspense with RomCom vibes)
Heartbreak Hero
Forbidden Hero
Comeback Hero
Rival Hero
Bossy Hero
And more to come!

About the Author

Jackie is a new face on the romance scene destined to shake things up with her signature blend of light-hearted comedy, over the top characters and romantic heartwarming moments. A voracious romance reader herself, Jackie writes stories featuring the four S's: Snark, Swoons, Steam and Sarcasm. Her heroines are badass and her heroes are easy on the eyes and heavy on the charm.

When she is not writing funny stories about swoony heroes and the women who get to play with them, she is reading all types of romance novels or taking care of her army of cats and her teenage son (who also speaks fluent sarcasm).

Connect with Jackie

Website and Newsletter Sign-up: www.authorjackiewalker.com
Facebook: @AuthorJackieWalker
Instagram: @AuthorJackieWalker
Facebook Reader Group: Jackie's Junkies
TikTok: @AuthorJackieWalker
Find me on Goodreads: Author Jackie Walker

Printed in Great Britain
by Amazon